Kat Winchfield was so beautiful, so entrancing with her long, raven-black hair and dark, dark eyes, that the people of Amoston were sure she was a witch.

They didn't know about her family legacy, about the centuries of inbred perversion before her, but they did wonder what happened to all those little children the Winchfield family took to the island, to the "school."

And when they found out, they went to the island with one thought on their minds—murder!

Fawcett Crest Books
by Doris Shannon:

☐ BEYOND THE SHINING MOUNTAINS   24306 $2.50

☐ CAIN'S DAUGHTERS   23961 $2.25

The Punishment

A Novel of Terror by

Doris Shannon

FAWCETT CREST • NEW YORK

THE PUNISHMENT

This book contains the complete text of the original hardcover edition.

Published by Fawcett Crest Books, CBS Educational and Professional Publishing, a division of CBS Inc., by arrangement with St. Martin's Press, Inc.

ISBN: 0-449-24501-2

Printed in the United States of America

First Fawcett Crest Printing: May 1982

10 9 8 7 6 5 4 3 2 1

This book is for
KIRBY McCAULEY,
my agent and my friend

Prologue

The two cars traveling west on U.S. 98 were buffeted by gusts of wind from the Gulf of Mexico. In those night hours there was little traffic in the Florida panhandle. The lead car, larger and more expensive than the one following, swung off the highway, brushed under moss trailing from a huge oak, and drew to a stop. The driver was out of the car before the second vehicle drew to a stop. Something metallic gleamed in his hand as he gestured impatiently to his passenger. She stumbled around the fender and stood crouched in front of the headlights, her colorless face and burgundy suit exposed in a pitiless glare.

From the second car another passenger was herded. His hands were lashed in front of him, a thin trickle of blood wormed a path down the warm olive of his cheek. Above the wound his dark eyes blazed with defiance and a hint of fear. The headlights caught the four figures, and threw long, wavering shadows along the sand. The driver of the second car, looking much too small for the length of his shadow, was fingering a leather wallet.

The revolver in the other driver's hand pointed at the wallet. "Back where you got it. First wipe it."

Fingers riffled through the thick wad of bills, reluctantly fell away, and the wallet was jammed into the hip pocket of

7

the bound man. Raising lashed hands, he wiped at the blood on his face. "Why?" he asked. "Who are you? Let her go. Take our money—"

"Shut up." The revolver disappeared into the man's pocket and he held out his hand. After a moment the driver of the second car handed over a short thick club. Holding it aloft as though it were a torch, the bigger man advanced on the woman in the dark red suit. She backed away from him, the eyes in her ashen face raised to the club, her lips writhing.

"Don't!" the man called and it was a plea.

The club descended, mashing the woman's hair, crushing the frail skull, spattering the burgundy suit with bits of bone, gobs of gray jelly, and gouts of blood. Without waiting to watch her body crumple to the sandy surface of the trail, the man with the club swung around. The headlights caught his face, his blazing eyes, the bloody club clenched in his fist.

The eyes in the olive face watched the club, as fascinated by it as the woman had been. His lips moved. "Tell me why. I deserve at least that!"

"Dies irae!" his killer shrieked, and brought the club down in a short arc.

To the man who in seconds would be dead, those final moments seemed to go on forever. He offered no last plea, no last prayer. His whole being reached out, in his mind urgent words formed. *Tammy, watch,* he ordered, *know. Tammy, your mother—*

Miles away from the panhandle, curled against the headboard of her bed, Tammy watched. She saw, through the doomed man's eyes, the club descend. When it reached his skull and crushed his last spark of life, the scene vanished, and she was left in her snug room with wind gusting against the windows, the familiar, soothing sounds of the old, secure, loved home around her.

Warmth was welling from her small body, warmth and a wet stickiness, a stickiness that stained her hand when she groped beneath the sheet to find its source. She lifted the hand and stared at the stain. It wasn't red like the blood that had gushed from the woman's shattered head onto wine-red wool had been, but dark, as dark as the long night that had closed around her.

Tammy opened her mouth to scream but she found even that was to be denied her.

8

One

Staring through the window at the rocky Maine coast, Dorothy Quiller became increasingly irritable. She found she resented the monotonous view sliding by, the leaden late fall sky, the two people in the car with her, and this stupid, hurried trip. Watching a trawler, nose down, heading out to sea, she found herself shivering despite the warmth of Jim's latest luxury car. Back in Florida about this hour she'd be lazing by the pool, perhaps sipping her first martini, relishing the warmth of sun on her body. This resentment was out of character. Marc used to call her my lady of serenity. Well, Marc's serene lady was feeling and acting like a bitch.

From the corner of her eye she watched Jim's hands on the wheel, hands as tanned as her own, not particularly well-formed hands but like the rest of him, much beloved. If she wanted a target for hostility, Dorothy told herself, Jim should be it. He was the one who'd dreamed up this idea, who'd insisted on her coming into this cold, forsaken country. He'd even insisted on taking Tammy, and that had involved an argument with the child's doctor as well as Tammy herself— whoa, time to stop thinking of Tammy as a child. Last week had been her nineteenth birthday, hardly a little girl any longer. Tammy was actually the focus of her hostility. Dorothy didn't even have to turn around to know the position her daughter was in. No doubt curled up like a fetus, jean-clad knees pulled up against her chest, her face obscured by wisps of blond, sun-streaked hair, round dark glasses hiding the rest of her face. Dorothy's hands clenched into fists. How she longed to rip those damn glasses off, force the child—whoops, the girl—to look at her. But Doctor Thule had cautioned her about Tammy's sunglasses. Let her have them, he'd urged. She's hiding behind them, Dorothy had protested. Of course she is, he'd agreed in that soft comfortable voice of his, but for now Tammy needs a place to hide. At least she's better than she was a few years ago. She was. Doctor Thule was the one who'd brought Tammy out of the cataleptic seizure she'd had the morning of her fourteenth birthday. Dorothy moved a hand as though to cover her own eyes and then forced it back to her lap. She took a deep breath. It was over. For a time she hadn't been in much better shape than Tammy was, but Jim had cured her. Ignoring his own loss, Jim had looked after both Tammy and her. Thank God for Jim.

As though sensing his wife's thoughts, one of Jim's hands left the wheel and moved to cover Dorothy's. Her fingers curled around the warm hardness of that hand. He slanted a smile at her. "Forgive me yet?"

She found herself smiling back, the touch of his hand transmitting a flow of joy through her body, that treacherous body. Her legs were parting at his touch. Here she was, a woman over forty, acting and feeling like a love-smitten teen-ager. It was Jim who'd really made her a woman. In all the years of her marriage to Marc Syles she'd never glimpsed what love could be. Had she ever really loved Marc? Granted he was handsome, an attractive man with that pure Grecian profile, that olive skin, those great dark eyes. Marc had given her wealth, consideration, affection...and Tammy. Dorothy wrenched her mind away from her first husband. Marc had been dead for five years. Marc and Jim's wife—adulterers, both of them.

Her fingers pressed Jim's. "Forgiven. But I still think that Tammy—"

"She's my daughter now. Time for her to meet the rest of her family." His hand gently disengaged itself from her clasp and moved back to the wheel. "A reunion," he told her softly, "a family reunion with all the members present."

Some of the resentment came seeping back. She stared

from the window at the rock-rimmed coast, waves spraying across a headland. "A great place for a reunion. Anyway, how can Tammy and I be reunited with people we've never met?"

"It's a reunion for the rest of us."

"Sorry, I'm being a bitch."

He jerked his head toward the back seat. "Don't use words like that."

"She's asleep, isn't she?"

He twisted around. "Might be. Hard to tell with those glasses. Best to be careful."

"She's not a child. Tammy's nineteen now."

"In many ways still a child. Doctor Thule told us that. Her life stopped short five years ago. The combination of her father's death and then getting her monthlies—"

His voice trailed off and Dorothy felt her lips twisting into a smile. What an old-fashioned man Jim was. In a day when television commercials bared all the most intimate parts of a life, when words like menstruation and tampons and pads were batted around indiscriminately, Jim still faltered over the words. Monthlies!

Dorothy's smile vanished. That morning at the ranch house five years before—that unlikely Florida ranch where Marc had played at breeding and raising cattle—that morning when the news had been broken to her about Marc's death and Vinnie's. A car accident, their bodies burnt beyond recognition. The motel, two rooms taken but only one room being used. Vinnie's clothes and Marc's intimately mixed in the closet, in the bureau drawers. And Jim, pushing aside his own grief, his own betrayal, to comfort her. Tammy must be told of Marc's death, Jim had insisted, forcing Dorothy to dry her eyes. Compose yourself, think of the child, she's been so close to her father. An accident, Jim said, tell her only about the accident. Dorothy dabbed at her tear-streaked face. Tammy will have to know the truth, she insisted. In time, Jim cautioned, not now, she's only fourteen.

Dorothy went to her daughter alone, to that room with its stuffed animals, its pennants, all the souvenirs of fourteen years of childhood. At first she thought Tammy was asleep but when she smoothed back the hair from the girl's face, Tammy's eyes stared into her own with no sign of comprehension.

"Your father's dead," Dorothy blurted, trying to force something from those eyes. They hadn't flickered. Then, in

11

a burst of senseless rage, Dorothy found her fingers fastened like talons to her daughter's shoulders, shaking, shaking, until the sheet fell back and she saw bloodstains on the child's thin white nightgown. Tammy came to womanhood on her fourteenth birthday, to womanhood and to the death of her father. She retreated into catalepsy—a rigid, wooden doll of a child with wide, staring, uncaring eyes and so she remained for nearly a year.

"She *knew*," Dorothy told Jim in a hoarse whisper. "She knew Marc was dead before I entered that room. She always knew before I did—"

"Easy." He jerked his head toward the rear seat again.

"When she was only five, when Marc was thrown from a stallion and broke his ankle, she knew. Daddy, she told me, daddy's hurt. Tammy clutched her right ankle with both hands as though she were in agony. Then the men brought Marc home and his ankle was broken, his *right* ankle. Tammy's queer. I'd tell Marc, she's...strange. Gifted, he said, a gifted little girl. The gifted little girl and her father had their own private world, one that closed me out. Come in, Dodie, Marc would tell me, the door is open, come in. I couldn't, Jim, it was a world for two, for Marc and Tammy, no room for me."

"It's over," he told her and his tone allowed no room for argument. "Calm yourself, Dorothy."

Jim's voice, saying her name, calmed her. What music he made of that simple, prim name. Dor-o-thy, a love song. Marc had always called her Dodie. I don't like it, she'd tell him, and those white teeth in the darkly handsome face would flash. It suits you, he'd tell her, my long, cool lady of serenity. Strange about Marc. Women were taught that the man who takes their virginity always has a special place in their memory. Marc, despite his good looks and strong compact body, had given her nothing but a fumbling, sweaty, unfulfilled sex life. His love was something to be borne, to be avoided if at all possible. Yet all through the years of their marriage she'd never been unfaithful to him. Yes, Dorothy admitted, when Marc had hired Jim as his business manager she'd felt an immediate attraction, when their hands touched or their eyes met, there had been a feeling but Marc was her husband and she'd been true to him. How long had his affair with Jim's little wife gone on? And those business trips—had they, like

12

his last one to Pensacola, been only cloaks for romantic interludes with Vinnie Quiller?

Tiring of these unrewarding thoughts, Dorothy slid sideways and examined her daughter's reclining figure. Tammy was just as she'd imagined her to be, her knees drawn up, her hair and glasses hiding her face, still in many ways a wooden, unresponsive doll of a girl. Yet, how much Tammy resembled her. We'll have a big family, Marc had told Dorothy and she'd agreed. Tammy came soon and effortlessly. Then there had been three miscarriages and finally the birth of a son, a son who had lived only hours. Never mind, Marc had comforted, I have you and Tammy. Everyone claimed that Tammy was Dorothy's double but they were exaggerating. Granted Tammy gave early promise of the same long, fine-boned body, the same spun blond hair, but Dorothy admitted to herself she had only average looks. Her eyes were small, her nose a shade too long, the set of her mouth just crooked enough to be noticeable, but Tammy! She had her father's beautifully set eyes, the finely boned nose, cheekbones, and chin...Tammy was a child of exceptional beauty. A strange, fey child who'd stood directly between Marc and her mother.

Sighing, Dorothy turned back to Jim. At least he was all hers. As though reading her mind, he smiled, detached a hand from the wheel, and caressed the inner side of her thigh. "Forgiven?" he asked.

"I said you were."

"Ah, but then you didn't mean it. Mean it now?"

Through the denim pants she fancied she could feel the heat of his hand. She slid closer to him. "If this means so much to you, darling. But Tammy—I'm nervous, afraid she may embarrass you."

"My dad understands about Tammy. In fact, he insisted that she be with us. Don't be nervous, you're going to love all of them."

"You seem to be so fond of your family and I've never met them. For five years...well, it seems odd."

His mouth set. "Vinnie didn't like them. I think she was a bit jealous of them. Phil, when he was a toddler, spent a couple of weeks with dad and my sister but Vinnie raised such a fuss about it that I never bothered her with my family again."

"But I wanted to meet them. When we were married I wanted them at the wedding."

13

"I remember, but they're busy people, Dorothy. It's only lately that dad has had time for a little relaxation. Even though I haven't seen any of them in years, we've been in touch."

Yes, Dorothy thought, you've been in touch. I've seen the stubs from the checks you've sent them, large checks, but what the hell. There's lots of money, thanks to Marc's Greek dad and that shipping line he had. And I don't care except... you could have told me, you didn't have to sneak money to them. She asked aloud, "How many will be there?"

"Dad, of course, my sister Ruth and her husband Andy Thaler. He's a doctor—"

"I know. You told Doctor Thule there'll be both a doctor and nurse there. In case—for Tammy."

"Ruth and Andy Thaler's son, Norman, married a nurse. So there're Norman and Thelma and their small son."

"You had another brother."

"Micah."

"He did marry."

"I've never met Micah's widow. He was Ruth's twin and they were close. Then, of course, there're the three of us, and—" His head jerked toward the back of the car.

Not toward Tammy this time. Peering through her window at the wing mirror, Dorothy caught a glimpse of a black van, painted in swirls of orange and yellow and red. Philip, she thought, her lips curling. Philip and his latest craze, or fad. Perhaps Jim's weird son would take some attention from her own weird daughter. At least Jim had forced his son to get out of that robe for the trip although he couldn't do much about Philip's hair, or rather, lack of hair. Thank God the boy had insisted on driving his own van, she wasn't penned up in a car with both Philip and Tammy.

Dorothy's conscience pricked her. She must stop thinking about Tammy like that. She had a habit of blaming everything that upset her on the girl. God, how she'd adored Tammy when she was a baby, when she was a toddler, before she began to turn into that odd little stranger. Doctor Thule had tried to explain Tammy's condition in what he'd termed layman's language. Tammy's overimaginative, he'd told them, she uses her mind to project drama on and then is convinced that it's reality. But, Dorothy had cried, Tammy actually *knows*. She's always known things before I have. Lucky guesses, the doctor said flatly, from watching TV, reading, going to movies. She must *not* be encouraged to believe these visions are real.

Dorothy sighed again, and her husband heard her. "Tired?"

"A bit stiff. Breakfast seems a long time ago. I'm hungry."

"We'll soon be there."

"Where?" The landscape looked the same. Maine's coast slid past, surf pounding against granite shores, the sea thrusting ruthless fingers into tiny harbors. Dorothy could smell a salt tang in the air and the car window framed a monotony of wave-washed headlands, the colors black and gray and sere brown. "We haven't even gone through a village in miles."

Jim's broad shoulders moved in a shrug. "Dad made all the arrangements but he assured me we'd be comfortable."

"Why couldn't they have come to Florida? We've lots of room." Her voice sharpened. "Where do we meet them?"

"A place called Amoston. Not even a spot on the map. Dad said it used to be a fishing village but all that's there now is a combination cafe and motel. He said those would soon be closed for the winter too."

Her voice became more shrill. "Then where in God's name will we stay?"

"I *told* you I don't *know*, but be assured it will be some place you'll like. Dad and Ruth are rather fond of the creature comforts too."

She pushed back her long hair. "Sorry, darling, I'm behaving like a bitch again."

This time he didn't complain about her language, he simply smiled warmly. "My little sun worshipper," he told her fondly. He glanced over his shoulder. "Seems the other sun worshipper is awake now too."

Dorothy swung around. Tammy had pulled herself up and was peering through the window at the stark scene. Light reflected from the large dark lenses of her sunglasses. "Have a good nap?" Dorothy asked her daughter. The girl's head inclined in answer. "What are you thinking?" her mother asked.

"I can't see any birds."

Jim waved a hand. "Sure, there're birds, honey. Gulls, right over there."

The dark glasses moved. "I see them."

"Why birds?" her mother asked.

"Words from a poem, mother, a couple of lines."

15

"That's nice," Jim said heartily. "What poem?"

"I don't remember. Just a couple of lines."

"Say them for us," Dorothy encouraged.

The dark glasses moved until they looked directly at Dorothy.

"'Pass not beneath, O Caravan, or pass not singing.'"

"That's lovely, honey," Jim said. "Any more?"

"'Have you heard the silence where the birds are dead yet something pipeth like a bird?'"

"Very nice," her mother said automatically. "Any more?"

"It isn't *nice*." Tammy jerked back to the window. "I can't remember any more."

Damn! Dorothy thought, double damn! Jim and I talk to her as though she's about three and every time we open our mouths she puts us down. Jim was only trying to draw her out, he's so fond of her, why I don't know. Jim's voice cut soothingly through the awkward silence. "Look ahead—that must be Amoston. And the sun's coming out especially for my two lovely ladies."

The sun was peeking out of the heavy cloud layer, gilding the buildings ahead of them. A few frame cottages wandered along the margin of the road. Most of them were dilapidated structures, the windows boarded up, but from one larger building a wisp of smoke curled from a lopsided brick chimney. In front of the place a shabby station wagon and a late model car were parked. Jim eased his car in next to the station wagon. Dorothy didn't wait for him to circle the car to open her door. Tugging her jacket collar around her throat, she stepped out and breathed deeply of the tangy air. God, but it was cold. The parking area had a sand surface and bits of drifted seaweed and salt ice littered its surface. Some place for a vacation. Shivering, she turned toward the cafe. Behind the bigger building she could see a forlorn huddle of cabins. They all could have used a fresh coat of paint. At least the wide window of the cafe was steamed up. Warmth.

"Come along," Jim called and headed eagerly toward the door.

Dorothy took a few steps in the same direction but was detained by a touch on her arm. Tammy's long hair was blowing back from her face and the lovely lines of that face were revealed. "I've remembered another line," she told her mother.

"Your poem, dear? What is it?"

"'Pass out beneath, O Caravan, Doom's Caravan, Death's Caravan!'"

Coming to a dead stop, Dorothy's eyes widened. "Must you always be so morbid? Please, Tammy." Her voice softened and it was an appeal. "Please don't."

"I'm sorry, mother." Tammy's fingers tightened on the older woman's arm. "I'm sorry about the trip too, how I acted to you and Jim. You should have left me in Florida."

"Perhaps it would have been best." Dorothy sighed. "But Jim insisted you come. Now you're here, try and be nice to his family. It's important to him—" Dorothy broke off and looked over her daughter's shoulder. "Here's Philip."

Philip was there. He climbed down from his psychedelic van, what remained of his hair secured in a leather thong and blowing straight out behind his head like the tail of a horse. Apparently a cap to cover that unsightly head hadn't been included in the deal with his father. Unaccountably, Dorothy felt her spirits rising. With Philip around few people would be likely to notice Tammy.

"Come along," Dorothy echoed her husband's words, and without waiting to see if the young people were following, she started briskly toward the door and the promise of welcome warmth. As she walked she noticed a hand rubbing a clear circle on the steamed-up glass of the window.

Two

Rubbing his hand against his pant leg, Rob Brome turned away from the circle he'd cleared on the steamy glass. More of the family arriving, four this time, two women and two men. It was shaping up as a large party, three in here, four more about to join them, and what was it Rayburn Quiller had said? Ah yes, two more groups to come. Rob wondered at his own interest. Tourists came and tourists went and it was seldom he cared enough to even look directly at them. The Brome Cafe and Motel had had a flourishing season, a summer studded with a glut of vacationers: bikers, fishermen, families trailing swarms of children, young people traveling either alone or in packs. They had crowded the sand dunes fringed with sun-coppered beach grass, had had their clambakes, downed enormous amounts of cold beer, eaten tons of lobster, clams, and greasy hamburgers, and gone their way. Perhaps his interest in the Quiller party was sparked because they had decided on their vacation in this bitter month when sensible beach bunnies were snugly at home where they belonged.

Rob eyed the Quillers. Most vacationers were completely forgettable, but not these three. Even in the summer rush he'd have noticed them. Rayburn Quiller, the sire of the clan and obviously a patriarch in the best sense of the word, had

19

captivated his mother. Minnie Brome, generally hardheaded despite her wide, cheerful face and motherly figure, was close to simpering and even Rob's laconic father had thawed and was hovering around Quiller. Quite a tableau the trio made. They reminded Rob of a king and a queen and a young prince, only in this case royalty perched on chrome and plastic chairs instead of golden thrones.

The woman, Ruth Thaler, was Rayburn's daughter and was, like her father, expensively dressed. A pale mink coat fell from her shoulders exposing a wool dress in a shade almost identical to the coat. Ruth was the type of woman whose age it was almost impossible to guess. The child perched on her lap was her grandson but she looked much too young to be a grandmother. She was a delicate, porcelain figurine with a drift of dark hair and huge dark eyes. She should be beautiful but somehow had missed it. Perhaps that was because of her hands and feet. They'd been inherited directly from her father and they dangled from slender wrists and ankles, too large, too square, bordering on ungainly. On her father the hands and feet were fine, in scale with his height and build. Rayburn was a symphony in gray from his thick hair to the well-tailored tweeds. Black touches were provided by thick bars of brows and a dashing black mustache.

A nice guy, Rob decided, with a quick smile and a genial expression. Good with the kid too. When they'd arrived Rob had expected that as a grandmother and a great-grandfather Ruth and Rayburn would be indulgent, let the little boy raise hell if he felt like it. They hadn't. Buddy had darted around as kids will, trotting between tables and looking at everything, but when his chubby hands started to reach toward catsup bottles and sugar containers Rayburn had simply shaken his head and the boy had darted back to Ruth's lap. She'd pulled a coloring book and a box of crayons from her tote bag and for a while Buddy amused himself with those. Right now he'd lost interest in coloring and had his head pillowed sleepily on her shoulder. Rob's mother had asked the kid's age and Ruth had told her he was nearly six. He was a handsome little boy, bearing a marked resemblance to Rayburn, even to outsized hands and feet. The kid's parents and Ruth's husband were supposed to be on their way and Rob found he was looking forward to seeing them.

Wondering if they were among the four now arriving, Rob watched the door. The older man of the new group came into the cafe first; he was tall, well built and with a vague resemblance to Rayburn. He lacked the patriarch's assurance and poise though; Rob would never have noticed this one in a crowd. He also was too old to be the lush Ruth's son. Must be her brother from Florida, the one they'd been chatting about. Jim, they'd called him. Yes, Rayburn was calling his name, reaching up to pat the younger man's arm. Jim ruffled Buddy's hair, smiled down at his sister, squeezed her hand, and turned to beckon to the woman who was following him. She came eagerly over to the group at the table. This had to be the Florida branch of the Quiller family. Both Jim and his wife had deep tans.

As Rayburn got to his feet to bend gallantly over his daughter-in-law's hand, two younger people entered the cafe. The girl was tall and slim, wearing a suede jacket and expensive jeans similar to the older woman's. No need to guess about the relationship there. They had to be mother and daughter. Same build and long, sun-streaked hair rested on suede shoulders. But the mother—they were introducing her, ah, Dorothy—Dorothy stood tall and moved with grace and poise. The girl—was it Tammy? Anyway, she moved stiffly, her shoulders slumped and hunched forward, her face hidden by huge dark glasses. Sunglasses! Was she blind? No, she skirted a table and a couple of chairs without effort. So now we had Jim and Dorothy Quiller, and daughter Tammy. Dorothy seemed to be succumbing to that warm charm of Rayburn's as quickly as Minnie Brome had. She was positively glowing.

Now it was Tammy's turn. Here was one person immune to that charm. She ignored Rayburn's extended hand and after a moment he pulled it back. If he felt slighted he didn't show it. "Tammy," he said gently, "I'm so happy to meet you. Your father has told us so much about you."

"My father is dead," the girl told him.

Rob felt a quick stab of shock. So Jim wasn't her father, only a stepfather, but Rayburn had only tried to be decent, to make her feel welcome. No reason to be so curt. However, the girl's voice intrigued him. It was out of character with the masking glasses, the slumped posture. A cool, clear, beautifully articulated voice that meant exactly what it said.

For a moment Rayburn stiffened but then he relaxed and smiled at the girl, that quick smile of warmth and charm. "Of course, thoughtless of me. Jim has told us so much about you and we're delighted we'll have a chance to know you. I...we consider you a member of our family, my dear." When the girl made no response he turned his attention to the boy behind her. "And Philip! How long it's been. You were Buddy's age, about six—"

"Seven, granddad," Philip told him, and eagerly seized the extended hand. "Too long."

"Yes, indeed." With obvious amusement his grandfather eyed the boy but all he added was, "We must talk, Philip. It would seem a talk is overdue."

Rob watched the color inching up the boy's face. He could see the reason for Rayburn's amusement. Philip's plaid jacket, T-shirt, and denims looked out of place with the shaven head, the dangling scalp lock. From the neck up he looked like a young monk, the hairless scalp lending an expression of purity and suffering to his fine features. His wide-set, pale blue eyes increased this impression but there were sensual lines around his lips. Studying Philip, Rob had a vision of saffron-robed figures with shaved heads, dancing and jiggling tambourines on street corners. His attention jerked back to the patriarch.

"Now," Rayburn was saying, "introduction time. Dorothy, who is now a Quiller, and her daughter, Tammy Syles." He pronounced the girl's last name carefully, as though attempting to atone for his earlier mistake in calling Jim her father. "Dorothy, Tammy, this is my daughter, Ruth Thaler. And this little lad is my great-grandson and namesake." He rested a hand on the little boy's brown hair. "We call him Buddy. He's nearly six and you'll be meeting his parents, Thelma and Norman." Rayburn slanted a smile at Dorothy. "Norman is Ruthie's son."

"It's going to be a little confusing," she murmured.

"Oh, you'll have us sorted out in no time. Now, Ruthie, you must remember Philip when he was a little chap and visited us that summer."

His daughter lifted dark eyes to Philip's head. "The Philip I remember had such lovely thick hair, dad."

Jim grinned at his sister. "He'll have it again. Just another stage Phil's going through." He eyed his son and his smile vanished. "And hair grows in. Believe me it does." He glanced around the cafe. "Where are Andy and Norman? And Norman's wife...I never can remember her name."

"Thelma," his sister told him. She nudged the little boy

off her lap. "You're getting heavy, darling. Play with your coloring book for a while. Andy and the other two should be along soon, Jim. Andy insisted on driving his old car down. Both dad and I argued they should come with us but Andy had to have his way."

Rayburn looked at his watch. "They should have been here a couple of hours ago. I hope they haven't had trouble. That car's a wreck."

Rob Brome peered out through the patch he'd cleared on the window. "If they drive a brown station wagon it looks like they're just pulling in."

"That's good. Finally here." Trotting over to the door, Rayburn swung it open. "Where did you get to? We were starting to worry, Andy."

At his post by the window, Rob counted the next bunch of Quillers. Three this time. Ruth's husband, her son, and her daughter-in-law. Ruth's husband was wearing a suit with a hip-length overcoat thrown around his shoulders. The young man and woman were dressed in mackinaw jackets and jeans. The woman's jacket wasn't buttoned and the wind drove it back from her body. Rob stifled a quick whistle. Thelma Thaler was short and heavyset, a bit hefty through the hips and thighs but her sweater strained over large, obviously unfettered breasts. Eye-catching and all he could see until they were in the cafe were those bobbing, swaying beauties.

The latecomers clustered around Rayburn, explaining something about a tire blowing. Rob glanced at the rest of the party and noticed that he wasn't the only one enthralled by Thelma. Philip, not looking very saintly now, was also ogling Thelma. Except for the chest, Rob admitted, the woman was hardly a beauty. Leaving that chest to Philip, he turned his eyes to the two men. They were as definitely father and son as Dorothy and Tammy were mother and daughter. Both had reddish hair, protruding eyes, colorless brows and lashes. Again, in spite of the resemblance, there were differences. Andy Thaler didn't need a black bag to proclaim he was a doctor; professional man was written all over him. He was as tall as his father-in-law but didn't have as good a build as Rayburn. He wasn't dressed as well either. His suit was well pressed but hardly the quality of the English tweeds. He had a habit of smoothing his thinning hair over a balding scalp and his face was lined, dark circles smudging protruding

23

eyes. Not enough sleep, Rob decided, a doctor's lot. Hardly a handsome man, this doctor, but imposing.

His son, Norman, was far from imposing. He was thinner and shorter than his father. He had more hair too, sporting a scraggly rust-colored beard and longish curly hair. Also he appeared to adore his grandfather. You could see it in his expression, in the pale eyes turned up to the older man. Looping one arm around Norman's shoulders, Rayburn used the other hand to draw Thelma toward the rest of the party.

"Introduction time again," he told them. "I'll just call names, you'll have plenty of time to get acquainted. Dorothy, Tammy, this is my son-in-law, Andy Thaler. As I mentioned in my letter, Andy's a doctor so we'll be in good hands. And this young lady is also in the medical profession. Little Buddy's mother and a fine nurse. Jim, I don't believe you've met either Thelma or your nephew, Norman."

"We haven't met but dad's written so much about you I feel I know you. He tells me you've been a big help with the rest home." Jim smiled at the two young people and shook the doctor's hand. "Great to see you again, Andy. You look as though you can stand a holiday. Don't you doctors ever look after yourselves?"

"Exactly what I've been telling Andy," Rayburn said.

Jim winked at his father. "You're a fine one to talk, dad. From what I've heard from Ruth you've been overdoing too. I was damn glad to hear you'd decided to retire."

"I hated to do it," Rayburn said. "So many people dependent on us. But Ruthie and Andy insisted and I guess I am getting a bit beyond it."

Rob caught his mother, standing behind the counter, nodding sagely at Rayburn's words. Minnie Brome had raved on about what she'd learned about Rayburn Quiller from his daughter Ruth. He'd got sick of listening, of hearing about Rayburn's rest home, about his dedication to the old, the sick, the homeless. Mom managed to make the man sound like a combination between Dr. Schweitzer and a contemporary Florence Nightingale. She'd talked too much and both Rob and his dad had been prepared to dislike the man, picturing him as smug and self-satisfied. Much to Rob's surprise Quiller seemed exactly as she'd described him. He appeared genuinely devoted to his family and it didn't take much imagination to picture his kindness extending to the unfortunates to whom he'd devoted his life.

24

Rob continued to watch the Quillers milling around, shaking hands, chatting. Kind of a nice family reunion. Some jarring notes though. The stiff hunched girl, Tammy, was a weird one. She stayed away from the rest, standing quietly by the table where Buddy bent over his crayons and coloring book. When anyone approached her she made no offer to shake hands or even be pleasant. If anyone was to be a party pooper, Rob decided, Tammy was the one. Ruth's bearded son, Norman, and his busty wife were odd acting too. Norman tagged along after Rayburn, and Thelma puffed on a cigarette and chatted to Dorothy. Neither of them paid the slightest attention to their little son. Such a well-behaved kid too. As parents they were shaping up as cold fish. Rob shrugged. None of his business.

Rayburn rapped sharply on the table and his relatives turned to him. "I don't know about the rest of you but I'm hungry. We waited lunch. What about it?"

Dorothy pushed back her tawny hair and beamed at him. "I'm starved."

"Our hostess, Mrs. Brome, will take care of that."

Rob's mother bustled forward. "Of course, Mr. Quiller. It's the end of the season and I can't offer a large selection but I've got a pot of fish chowder and some roast beef."

Orders were given and Rob lounged back watching tables pushed together and the Quillers—funny, he didn't even think of Thaler in connection with them—gather around them. I make a good observer, Rob thought, I've got a good memory and keen eyes and, let's face it, that's about all I've got. Let's see if I can sort this out. First we've got good old Dr. Schweitzer, alias Rayburn Quiller, and his lovely daughter Ruth and his Florida son Jim. Then there's Ruth's impressive doctor husband Andy, and her unimpressive rabbit son Norman. Mustn't forget Norman's wife with the ungainly hips and the bobbing boobs. Buddy, child of this pair, who pays no more attention to mommy and daddy than they pay to him. Don't really blame the kid, I prefer Rayburn and Ruth to them myself. Anyway, there's the other family with the tans. Jim, his blond wife Dorothy, and Jim's son Philip, with the face of a saint and the mouth of a satyr. Let's not forget Dorothy's daughter Tammy, who has made it really clear that Jim is no relative of hers. An interesting bunch and the byplays were interesting too. The way monkish young Philip allowed one hand to nudge Thelma's hefty bottom in an un-monkish way, the quick look she tossed over her shoulder at him, faintly coquettish? The sideways motion of Tammy, inching away from the chair next to Jim, finding a place at the foot of the table between the doctor and Norman. Andy was still patting his thin hair over the bald spot and Norman, fingering that scraggly beard, still had his eyes fixed on Rayburn. As befitted a patriarch, Rayburn was seated at the head of the table and to his right was his daughter, Ruth, feeding Buddy from her own plate. Dorothy was at Rayburn's left. Now, that's a good-looking woman, Rob thought, California type, with the slender body, outrageously long legs, and a tumbled mop of blond hair. Little old for the hair style though. Under the heavy tan tiny lines radiated from the corners of her eyes, bracketed her mouth. Dorothy was dividing her attention between her father-in-law and her husband. A woman in love, Rob decided, watching her eyes as they dwelt fondly on Jim Quiller's unexceptional face.

Rayburn smiled expansively at his clan and waved a large hand at Rob. "Sorry, forgot to introduce this young chap. Meet Rob Brome, who is in charge of the boat that will ferry us to and from the island. In fact, Rob has already done a great deal of work on our behalf, taking out supplies and so on. Will you join us for lunch, Rob?"

"Not hungry, sir, I'll get coffee." Moving behind the counter, he picked up a cup.

Dropping her fork, Dorothy stared at Rayburn. "Island?"

Rayburn beamed at her. "Surprise, isn't it? Yes, my dear, I was fortunate enough to rent an entire island for our visit together."

"Where?"

Putting the chowder pot down, Minnie Brome pointed at the steamed-up window. "Offshore, in fact quite a distance, ma'am. Can hardly spot it from here even if you could see through those dratted windows. Called Winchfield, after the people who built the house."

"I don't like the sea," Dorothy wailed. "I'm afraid of boats."

"You'll enjoy this, my dear," Rayburn assured her. "As for boats, there'll only be the trip out and another one back. Rob, I promise you, is a fine sailor."

"He is indeed," Minnie chimed in proudly. "Better even than his dad, and that's saying something. Wilfred and me, we're leaving in a couple of days, but Rob, he'll be here all winter and he'll see to anything you need."

The doctor was staring at Rob. "What keeps a young fellow like you here in the winter months?"

Some of the rest were swinging around, staring at the young man by the coffee urn. Mind your own business, Rob told them under his breath. His mother rested a plump hand on his shoulder. "Rob was in Nam. He's...well, he's getting better." Go on, mom, Rob thought wrathfully, spill your guts. She did. "Rob was wounded but that's healed. He has more of a...well, you know."

They did, or thought they did. Their eyes dropped back to their plates. Battle fatigue, Rob thought, quick diagnosis. He longed to blurt it out, shock them from their smug labeling. Not battle fatigue with that bloody war. More of a combination of drug addiction, soul sickness, guilt, and an obsessive hatred of self. Go on, mom, make more excuses for a big strapping son who won't go back to the beautiful American way of life.

"He's an engineer," she told the Quillers. "Graduated and all. In time he'll be building bridges and putting up buildings and..." Her voice trailed off.

"Of course he will," Rayburn said tactfully. "May I have a little more of that delicious chowder, Mrs. Brome? Far the best I've ever tasted and I fancy myself a connoisseur of chowder."

Her face split in a wide smile. "'Course. If you like good food you're going to be happy with Holly Amos doing for you. She's a better cook than I am."

"Come now, I can hardly believe that."

"We-ll, maybe not better, Mr. Quiller, but Holly does fancier cooking than me. 'Course she has lots of time out there to read cookbooks and all."

Dorothy turned to her father-in-law. "This island—tell us more about it."

"In the first place, let me assure you that we'll be comfortable. There's a big house waiting for us, with all the modern amenities. I've laid in a supply of good food and fine wine. There's a game room there with enough entertainment to amuse the younger ones. I checked the weather and quite often at this time of year there's a spell of Indian summer that may have us in bathing suits. Even if the weather isn't too good there'll be hiking and brisk walks to be enjoyed. Of course, the main thing is that it's a private place where we can really be a family."

Dorothy forced a rather wan smile. "It won't be for that long anyway. Jim said maybe a week."

Leaning forward, her husband touched her hand. "I told you dad would see to a nice place. It sounds wonderful." He glanced at his father. "You said a big house. Is it a hotel?"

Rayburn shook his gleaming gray head. "I don't believe it was ever used for that purpose. Mr. Brome can fill you in on the history of the place."

As Wilfred Brome cleared his throat, Rob smothered a grin. Let's see dad field that one. What a history! His father said slowly, "Island isn't exactly a popular vacation spot, Mr. Quiller. Never been much interest in it. Even in summer it's kind of bleaklike."

Thelma Thaler lifted her head. "How old is this house?"

Wilfred ran a hand over his stubbly chin. Mom had overlooked making him shave again, his son noticed. "Winchfields built it after the turn of the century. Started kind of a school there. Then, after they was all done in—"

"Done in?" It was Tammy's clear voice.

Swinging around, Wilfred looked down at her. Dark lenses looked back. "Holly and Jeb Amos can fill you in on that. Their favorite story. Gruesome tale, but supposed to be true."

His wife came happily to the rescue. "Holly and Jeb come from families that were here than. Fishermen, mainly. One time Amoston was a bustling place. Don't look like it now but that's what Holly says. 'Fore her marriage she was a— what was her maiden name, Wilfred?"

"Cranston."

"That's right. Her dad and Jeb's were in the gang went to the island and punished the Winchfields though I always think Holly lays it on a bit thick about what happened. Trying to sound important like folks do, y'know."

Jim glanced at his stepdaughter. "Let's not go into grisly details, please. What happened to the island after that?"

Minnie's mouth tightened. The story wasn't only Holly's favorite. It appeared Minnie was going to be cheated out of recounting it. She said shortly, "Couple of rich families had it, one after the other. Didn't stay long. Didn't like it."

Holding out his cup, Rayburn turned his sunny smile on her. "The coffee's excellent, Mrs. Brome. May I have more, please?"

Incredulously, Rob watched his mother melt. As she pushed past him to the coffee urn, she continued more expansively, "Few years ago some company in New York bought the island. Planned to make it into a resort. Kinda petered out so they hired Holly and Jeb to caretake it and rent it out occasionally. Worked out well for the Amoses. Holly's a hard worker but Jeb's kinda no account. Lost his little farm and with both their boys killed in Nam it looked like they'd have a tough time. Nice fellow though. You'll like Jeb. Weakness is drink. Can't leave it alone and him with a pipe never outta his mouth. Passed out twice and set his chair alight. Keep warning Holly that Jeb'll do for both of them with that pipe. Tell her, Jeb should either give up the pipe or the drink." Minnie put the coffee cup in front of Rayburn. "Got some blueberry pie here if anyone wants a piece."

Rayburn Quiller rubbed his hands together. "A large piece for me, Mrs. Brome."

She started to dish up the pie. "Got a light hand with pastry if I do say so myself."

Lighting a cigarette, Rob glanced through the cloud of smoke at the table. Most of the guests were doing justice to his mother's cooking. The exception was the girl called Tammy. She hadn't even loosened her jacket in the heat of the cafe. Was she cold? She looked it, the way she crouched over the table, pushing her food around on her plate. He wondered what she looked like, what the eyes under the sunglasses were like. Probably like her mother's, on the small side. His eyes wandered the length of the table and settled on Philip. He'd finished his pie and was lounging back, his eyes wide and candid, a smear of blueberry at the corner of those thick lips. The boy's hidden hands must be busy. As Rob watched he saw Thelma, next to the boy, jump and glare at him. Philip must be taking his grandfather literally. He *really* was getting to know his relatives. Thelma didn't look displeased. With that chunky build and that broad face she should have looked placid. She didn't. Her mouth was tense and she had a barely discernible tic under one eye. Perhaps it was only Philip's sneaky attentions doing it. Funny, Thelma still hadn't even glanced at her little son. Buddy was on Ruth's lap, docilely chewing the food his grandmother put into his mouth. Again Rob was struck by the child. He was a handsome boy but he was quiet. Maybe he was overawed by all the adults around him.

Wandering back to the window, Rob cleared another spot in the steam and peered through it. He swung back and addressed Rayburn. "If we wait much longer, sir, you'll have to bed down here for the night. Looks like the wind is shifting."

Shoving back his cuff, Rayburn glanced at his watch again. Looks like a Rolex, Rob though. If it is it matches the tailored tweeds, cashmere turtleneck, and expensive brogues. For the first time since his arrival, Rayburn's black brows drew together in a frown. "I was hoping to take the others out with us. This will mean two trips for you, Rob."

Minnie moved closer to the table. "If they arrive later we can put them up in one of the cabins, Mr. Quiller, and Rob can bring them out tomorrow."

Jim lifted a brow. "Micah's wife?"

His father's frown vanished. "And his son."

"*Son.*"

"Thought that would surprise you. We always guessed, of course, that Micah's wife had a child but she's steered clear of us all these years. I heard from her some time ago and she offered to bring her son to meet us. Best news we've ever had. Ruthie was delighted too, weren't we, dear?" Ruth nodded, soft hair brushing the soft mink collar.

"A son," Jim muttered. "Micah's son."

Pushing back his chair, Rayburn got to his feet. "We'll accept Mrs. Brome's kind offer. When Nadine and Nigel arrive they can remain here until Rob can bring them out. Now, we must get the luggage down to Rob's boat." Dorothy started to rise and her father-in-law waved her back. "The men will handle it. You ladies stay in here where it's warm until we're ready to leave."

The men rose, milled around, and then headed toward the door. Ruth and Buddy, Dorothy, and Thelma obediently remained in their places but Tammy followed the men. Without waiting for them to lift the luggage from the four vehicles, she wandered down to the dock. Rob followed her. His boat, an ancient fishing trawler, breasted the freshening waves. He regarded the old boat affectionately. Not really much to look at, stubby in the bow and broad in the beam, but she glistened with fresh paint and her metal work gleamed. He tried to strike up a conversation. "Not very impressive, is she, Miss Quiller?"

"Syles."

"Sorry, Miss Syles. She's more seaworthy than some of the

bigger, prettier craft that are here in the summer. She's not fast either, but she's sure. Can weather most gales."

Tammy didn't appear interested in his boat. Her head was tilted back and she seemed to be watching a couple of gulls. "Are there birds on this island?"

"Swarms in the summer. Right now about the only ones you'll see are gulls." Stepping onto the deck, he picked up a coil of rope.

She called, "Do they pipeth?"

He dropped the rope. "Pipeth? Well, they squawk a lot, if that's what you mean." He held out a hand. "Might as well come aboard. Here come the rest."

Taking his hand, she leapt lightly to the deck. Leaning against the rail, she watched the Quillers, all the men but Rayburn laden with luggage, straggling down to the dock. The three women were following. Dorothy was talking to Thelma and Ruth held the little boy's hand.

Rayburn was directing the workers. "That's right, Philip, you get aboard and the rest of you hand him the baggage. As soon as that's done we'll assist the ladies. Ah, Tammy, I see you're looked after already."

Dropping the matched pigskin cases he was carrying, Andy Thaler rubbed his arm. "Strange name your boat has, Rob. Any significance to it?"

Rob laughed. "That was her name when I bought her. I didn't bother changing it. Now I kind of like it."

Dorothy left Thelma Thaler and wandered over to her husband. She peered around his shoulder. "What is the name?"

"Caravan," Andy told her. "Odd name for a boat, isn't it?"

"Caravan," Rayburn Quiller echoed. "Well, camels comprise caravans and they're called ships of the desert. Rather fanciful though."

Rob wasn't listening. He glanced toward Dorothy and noticed that under the heavy tan the fresh color was ebbing from her face. She grasped her husband's arm but he paid no attention to her. Jim Quiller was staring at the girl leaning against the rail. Tammy's shrouded eyes seemed to be looking at her mother and a smile played at the corners of her mouth.

Ye gods, Rob thought, this is shaping up as a great family reunion. Dorothy Quiller was looking terrified at the name of a boat, Philip was hungrily watching his cousin's buxom wife, and a girl who wondered if gulls pipeth was leaning against his rail. Shrugging, he turned away and reached for the ignition. None of his business. He'd get them to Winchfield and then Jeb and Holly Amos could take charge.

Three

The *Caravan* was a sturdy little craft. Under Rob Brome's skillful hands she plunged through seas that might have daunted larger boats. Despite the heavy plunging motion and the icy spray, most of the passengers remained on deck. Only Ruth, snuggled in rich fur, her grandson, and Dorothy had taken shelter in the cabin. Ruth and Buddy were still there but moments before Dorothy, pale green under her tan, bolted out and was now bent over the rail, being violently sick. His face anxious, Jim supported her.

Paying no attention to her seasick mother, Tammy stood beside Rob at the wheel. She was an excellent sailor. With her feet firmly braced on the heaving deck, her hair blowing back from the clean lines of her face, she stood, gazing ahead.

Rob glanced at the spray-moistened hair. "You'd be warmer and drier in the cabin." She made no response and he asked, "You like the sea?"

"My father used to take me sailing."

All the advantages, he thought, poor little rich girl. Casually wearing a jacket and jeans from some New York salon, two rings on her hands that were probably worth a small fortune. Sheltered and spoiled. What a tough life the kid had. But she was a client and that's how he made his dubious living. He tried to draw her out. "You in university?"

She shook her head and he probed further. "Do you work?"

"No."

"Oh. Then you're still at home. Mom said Mr. Quiller told her your parents have a ranch in Florida. Funny, I've never known there're anything there but beaches, casinos, and hotels."

"The Kissimmee prairie is cattle country."

"Where's that?"

"South of Orlando."

"And that's where your ranch is?"

"Uh-huh."

Not only spoiled but rude, Rob thought. She was making no effort to even act civil. "Must be nice lazing around a ranch."

She turned her head toward him. "I don't really know. I haven't been on a ranch in three years. I attend school."

"I thought you said—"

"You asked if I went to university. This is a special school."

"For the rich," he grunted.

That strange smile he'd noticed a while before played around her lips again. "That's true. But to enter it you must have other special qualifications. It's called a school but actually it's a mental institution."

Well, Rob thought morosely, you asked for it. Goaded her into an answer. "I'm sorry," he told her. "I'd no right to pry."

"Don't be. I like it there. In fact I didn't want to leave to come here."

"You *like* it?"

"It's safe, I like to feel safe."

"Look, this is none of my business either, Miss Syles, but do you have to wear those glasses?"

"If you mean for my sight, no."

"Take them off."

To his surprise, she turned her face directly to him and flipped off the glasses. He stared into violet-blue eyes. Rob thought, she's lovely, a beautiful girl. "You're not mad," he said quickly and immediately knew he'd spoken too fast. He also knew why. He'd just lied. He had a hunch she probably was disturbed. A girl like this, what a damn shame.

She gave him her mocking little smile. "Ah, but I am. It's safer."

"Safe," he blurted. "What are you talking about safety for?"

Sliding the glasses back into place, she turned away. "You should know. You're hiding yourself."

There was no answer to that. Biting his lip, he gave his full attention to the *Caravan.*

Thelma leaned against the rail and watched the helmsman. Quite a chunk of man that Brome was. Good shoulders under that pea jacket, nice build too. Must be well over six feet. Wasting himself in this desolate spot. Boy, what a place to spend a winter in. Her thoughts about Rob were interrupted by a hand placed over the one she was resting on the rail. She didn't have to look to know the identity of the man beside her. Funny how big her husband's hands were for his size and no matter how cold it was they were always sweaty. She could feel moisture from his palm wetting her knuckles.

Norman's voice was a hoarse whisper. "Good news, Thel. Granddaddy says he's giving us a room together."

"Great."

"Aren't you happy about it?"

God, she thought, will Norm ever stop asking if I'm happy. Here I'm toying with the idea of blowing my brains out and this idiot wants to know if I'm happy.

His sweaty grip tightened. "Well, Thel, aren't you?"

No use blaming it on Norm, Thelma thought, not the poor devil's fault. As usual the only person I can blame is myself. Marry in haste, repent at leisure. Shit! Aloud, she said, "It was nice of Ray, Norm."

"I don't like them, Thel, do you?"

Intrigued, she tore her eyes away from the gray swells. His face was only inches from her own and she examined the tight orange-red curls, the skimpy beard, the pale eyes earnestly fixed on her own. "We've just met them, Norm."

"That Philip. I saw him looking at you. You don't like him, do you?"

"No, I don't like him." Silently, she admitted, but I lust after him.

"I don't mind at all, Thel, as long as you don't like him better than me."

"I don't like him, Norm."

"Good. I don't like the rest of them either."

"But Jim's your uncle and you should like him. Dorothy seems nice. She's your aunt now, Norm, and I guess that makes Tammy some kind of cousin."

His free hand yanked at his beard. "Jim's my uncle so I guess I have to like him. But not those others."

She patted his scrawny arm. "Maybe you will in time. Why don't you tell Ray I'm happy about the room?"

"I will." His voice rose. "I'll go tell granddaddy you're happy we'll be together."

As Norman scurried down the deck toward Rayburn, Thelma sighed. Her relief was short-lived. Someone else was behind her. Again she had no difficulty guessing whose hand was on her. This hand was firmly grasping her buttock. Without even glancing around, she drove her heel into a leg. The hand was hastily removed. "Enough of that, you twerp!" she said.

Philip's scalp lock dangled over one shoulder as he bent to rub his calf. "You pack an awful wallop, lady, but what a gorgeous ass you have." Straightening, he grinned at her. "Overheard the good news. You and hubby are sharing this trip. Think it will cramp our style?"

"For a jerk I met a couple of hours ago, you're pretty sure of yourself."

"Sure of you, lady. Minute I saw you I thought, wow! that's for me."

"You've proved it. My rump's black and blue." She turned away from him. "Get lost."

"No way. I was going to ask—your room or mine. Guess yours is out but I'm bunking alone. Tonight?"

"From the looks of that head of yours, Phil, I'd take it you're on a religious trip. What about your vows?"

"Haven't made any. I'm the kind of guy who needs lots of tail. Like you're the kind of girl who does. And you're not getting much, are you?"

She turned a flushed face to him. "My private life is none of your business."

"What have you against me? We're practically kissing cousins."

"You're no relative of mine."

"That makes it even better. You didn't answer. Why do you dislike me?"

The deck heaved and she fell against him. His arms went around her and he pressed his long body to hers. She wrenched away. "You remind me of every fresh young intern I've ever know. Every on-the-make, come-across-baby in my past. No wining, dining, or wooing. Let's get down to cases, get your pants off and we'll do it against the wall."

Throwing back his shaven head, he roared with laughter. "Great! We understand each other, lady. See you tonight."

She didn't bother watching him move away. Her hands were grasping the rail until the knuckles whitened. Damndest part of it was that she *would* sneak into his room tonight if she got half a chance. And he knew it. If only she could set time back, she thought wistfully, set it back six years. Never have met Norm, never have given in to a stupid impulse and married him.

Out of habit, Rob Brome was keeping an eye on his passengers. Landlubbers sometimes did stupid things on boats. He saw Philip moving away from Thelma, giving her one last squeeze, and grinned. Then he glanced at the girl beside him. All he could see was the wildly blowing hair and the glasses. Tammy didn't seem to know or care that he was near her. His eyes swept the deck again and what he saw this time brought a warning shout from his lips. "The kid! Someone grab him quick."

Buddy had pulled himself up on the rail and now hung over it, his short legs thrashing wildly. Andy Thaler started toward him but Rayburn, with speed amazing for his age, reached the child first. Grabbing one of the boy's feet, he heaved the small body backward. Andy put out a steadying hand and in a moment the boy was squeezed against Rayburn's chest. The other passengers were scurrying toward them. Now, Rob thought, we'll see Thelma and Norman finally act like parents.

He was wrong. Thelma stopped a few feet away from Rayburn and her son and simply looked at them. Norman, paying no attention to Buddy, grasped at his grandfather's arm. "Granddaddy, should I have—"

"No, it's all right," Rayburn reassured. "It's all right, Norman." He raised his voice. "Ruth!"

His daughter came bolting out of the cabin. "What's wrong, dad? Buddy—did something happen?"

Rayburn glared at her. "Something happened all right. Buddy was just about over the side."

Ruth sagged against the rail, looking down at the waves. "Oh God. I was reading. Buddy was right with me a moment ago. Playing with his coloring book. You know how fast he moves, dad."

"And so do you. All the more reason to keep a good eye on him." His voice softened. "Don't look so stricken. Buddy's safe. Better get him inside out of this wind."

Ruth took the boy from her father's arms, cradling her cheek against his hair. "Don't cry, Buddy, it's all over now."

All over, Thelma thought, and moved away. Buddy safe, everybody happy. What would Ray have done if the boy *had* gone over the side? Only one answer knowing Ray. He'd have gone right over after the boy. Ray was good at many things and he was an excellent swimmer. She saw Rob Brome staring at her with hard eyes. She didn't have to guess what he was thinking. What a lousy excuse for a mother. She shrugged. What the hell difference did it make what Brome thought about her? What the hell difference did anything make?

Holding on to the rail tightly, she made her way to where Andy was standing. Funny, Thelma thought, Norm looks like his dad but they're about as different as two people can be. Andy's eyes only mirrored intelligence and a trace of sadness. His hands and feet were long and slim and shapely. Norm's were like his mother's, oversized, ugly, dangling from scrawny wrists and ankles. But there was terrible strength in those hands.

Andy looked down at her. "That was close."

"The kid moves like greased lightning, always has. Of course, Ruth lets him have his own way too much."

"I wouldn't say he's spoiled," Andy said dryly, vainly trying to smooth his blowing hair down. "Saw Philip with you a while ago. Is he giving you a bad time?"

"Nothing I can't handle." She changed the subject. "Looks like we're just about there."

Silently, they both contemplated the island. It loomed out of the sea, an ungainly, unattractive mass of rock, one higher pinnacle rearing against the bleak sky. Directly ahead was a long rock pier jutting out into the turbulent water. Beyond the pier the rocky slope was studded with patches of waving sea grass and stunted pines.

"I've seen better resorts," Thelma grunted. "Andy, why a family reunion here?"

"No idea. It's Ray's idea."

"And that says everything, doesn't it? Big daddy has spoken." She pointed. "Look, on the pier. Must be that Jeb Amos they were talking about."

A man was waiting on the pier, hunched into a shabby tartan jacket. He wore a cap with a long bill and under it was a bulbous nose, an unshaven chin, and a stubby pipe firmly clenched in his mouth. "Now that's the nose of a heavy drinker," Thelma pointed out. "What's that with him?"

Andy squinted. "Looks like a cat."

It was. At the man's feet a large, blue-gray Persian stood, its tail curled in a feathery plume over its back, golden eyes unblinkingly watching as the *Caravan* drew closer.

Four

Rob Brome had decided, rather smugly, that he was proof against any further surprises from the Quiller party. As he turned the bow of the *Caravan* toward Winchfield again, he glumly admitted he'd been mistaken. Granted, the group he'd delivered the previous day had been interesting but they paled in comparison with his present passengers.

He sensed eyes fastened on his back and wondered if they belonged to Nadine Quiller or to her son. He found himself hoping they belonged to the man. Nadine was a handsome creature but her face looked as though it had been carved from agate and she had a baneful, Sphinx-like stare. Enough to freeze the blood in the veins was that stare.

Behind the helmsman, Nigel Quiller lounged and guessed with amusement the direction of the man's thoughts. Nigel found he liked Brome. At least Rob had sense enough not to try and pretend that the visitors who'd arrived late the evening before were exactly normal. Mrs. Brome had made a valiant effort and had managed to make a fool of herself scurrying around making vapid, and at time, hilarious conversation. Rob simply looked, noted and accepted. This morning, when the time came to board this old tub, Rob had matter-of-factly swung his own light body up and handed Nigel to Nadine's outstretched arms. Nigel also guessed Brome found his mother more upsetting than he did himself. Nadine sometimes had that effect on people. Since they'd left Boston to join the Quillers, she'd worn what he termed her Romany look. With the look had not come the silence he yearned for but a flood of words, words he'd heard all his life, the very repetition dulling whatever impact they originally had had. She raved on until he signified he had enough and she knew better than to argue. Nadine retreated to a dark brooding silence, unsettling to the Bromes but a much needed rest for him.

Nigel's long-lashed eyes moved upward, seeking his mother's profile against the cloudy sky. The sky made a fitting frame for that profile, dark and ominous, with her nose and brow cutting cleanly across it. How had she managed to keep the passion going all these years? He wondered. Could the love for her young husband have been strong enough to keep those fires flaming? Or had love been smothered and lost in a frenzy of hatred and revenge? Lines from Shakespeare brushed his mind. How had the great bard put it? Something about patience on a monument smiling at grief. Nadine had patience, long enduring and as hard as her expression, but smiling— no way. She positively glowered at grief. And was that hatred any more genuine or was it on a par with her pretensions about having gypsy blood? Nigel was certain his mother was not descended from gypsies, that she'd started that particular fiction to strengthen the image she created for her profession. But now she was thoroughly convinced that her ancestors had traveled in gaily painted wagons, gathered around campfires, and made strong magic with chicken bones and tatters of bright cloth. Poor Nadine. He sighed. And poor Nigel. Raised and trained with only one goal in view. When the time comes, Nadine always repeated, when you're fully ready. When she'd told him she finally had come out of hiding, finally written to Rayburn Quiller, Nigel knew his mother had decided the time was ripe. We'll see, he said to himself, we'll see.

The boat lurched and Nadine automatically stretched out a protective hand to steady him. Smoothly, he avoided it and moved away from her, down the deck, grasping the rail, and peering ahead. The *Caravan* was plunging through a trough of waves, turning her stubby bow into a cove. He could see a boathouse, a stone pier dotted with a number of figures. The welcoming committee, he decided, and his relatives

42

seemed to have turned out in force. How would the fabled sire of the family handle this meeting? Rayburn Quiller might have seen Nadine years ago but Nigel knew he'd never been introduced to her.

As the boat drew closer to the pier, Nigel tried to sort the Quillers out. That big, bulky man in tweeds would have to be Rayburn. He cut quite a figure and looked like a man of substance. Another man, tall, younger, with a faint resemblance to Rayburn, was standing beside him, his arm around a good-looking blond. As Nigel watched the younger man— it had to be Jim—turned to his father and said something. I can guess what Jim's saying Nigel thought wryly. Jim is insisting they've been had, brother Micah has been dead for over a quarter of a century, this is no son of his.

Two other men were trotting down the steep slope. The tall one in the short overcoat must be Ruth's husband, Doctor Andrew Thaler. He was trying to hold thin red hair down on a gleaming scalp. Must be sensitive about going bald. Andy wasn't as handsome as Rayburn but he seemed to have presence. At the doctor's heels was a thin young man with a beard. From the resemblance this had to be Andy and Ruth's son, Norman.

His eyes moved away from Norman and Andy and were caught by a girl, standing behind and to one side of the group of relatives. It was her stance that caught his interest, the way her shoulders were hunched forward, her arms clasped across her breast. Like a turtle, Nigel thought, a female turtle halfway out of her shell and with no desire to come any further. His gaze slid over her face but with the wildly blowing hair and the round dark glasses he caught only a glimpse of a pointed chin, the pure line of cheekbone. The blond woman clinging possessively to Jim's arm must be his second wife and this girl had to be Miss Tamara Syles. Marc Syles's daughter. He caught his breath. Tammy Syles. He changed the metaphor he'd used. Not a turtle but a rabbit, crouching, immobile, praying the hunters would pass without seeing her. No use, Tammy, Nigel told her silently, hunters always have rabbits pegged.

A man detached himself from the huddle of people, a boat-hook clasped in one hand. He stood waiting for Rob to cut the motor and throw a rope. Again Nigel had no trouble sorting this chap out. Jeb Amos, drinker and smoker, the one Mrs. Brome had feverishly babbled on about to cover her own dismay when she'd made her first goof and patted his own head and told him he was a fine little fellow. Nigel grinned. Mrs. Brome had been right on about Jeb. His nose was a fine shade of drinker's red and, as the caretaker caught the rope, he staggered. No doubt deep in his cups again. Jeb must be obstinate, the controversial pipe was firmly clenched in his mouth.

Rob helped Nadine to the pier and Jim Quiller caught her arm and steadied her. Turning back, Rob swung Nigel up and handed him to Jim. Jim nearly dropped him. Searching with one foot, Nigel found rocky surface under it, and grinned up at the man towering over him. "Easy does it. I'm fine now. You can turn loose. Uncle Jim, I presume."

Jim opened his mouth and then shut it but another voice broke smoothly in. "That's correct, Nigel, and I'm your grand-father." Bending from the waist, Rayburn solemnly extended a hand. Nigel's tiny hand was engulfed in the massive strength of that huge one. Rayburn continued, "You must forgive us. We had no warning you are a—" He faltered and then continued manfully, "We didn't know you are a midget."

"I prefer the term dwarf," Nigel told him.

"Ahem...of course. Whatever you wish. The main thing is that you're here. And your mother, of course." Rayburn moved down the pier toward Nadine, and Nigel had a clear view of his massive grandfather. Yes, a distinguished-looking man. Tactful too, but Rayburn would soon find tact was wasted on Nadine.

"My dear," Rayburn said softly. "How wonderful. We had despaired of ever meeting you and then to think you'd contact us yourself. Quite right, too. A family must not allow old griefs and grudges to separate it. Life is far too short."

Quite a stirring speech, Nigel thought, but Nadine simply stared at her father-in-law with her best Romany stare. Her lips parted. "You said there was a house. I don't see one."

Everyone started to talk at once, telling Nadine where the house was. Although they were speaking to her, most of them covertly studied her son. Nigel was well aware of the scrutiny. Go ahead, he told them under his breath, stare your fill, I'm used to it.

Behind him, the engine of the *Caravan* roared throatily into life. Turning, Nigel waved good-bye to Rob Brome. Rob lifted a hand from the wheel but Nigel noticed that the man's gaze wasn't on the group on the pier. Nigel swung around
44

and followed Rob's eyes. Tammy was still standing apart from the Quillers and, as he looked at her, she ducked her head and turned away from the sea. Nigel was aware that his grandfather was introducing Jim's wife, Dorothy. For some reason he found, like Rob Brome, that he was more interested in the girl scuttling up the slope.

Hunching even further into her jacket, Tammy was aware of that interest and of Rob Brome's. She didn't want to go back to the house but she certainly had no desire to linger and watch the reunion. A tide of oddly assorted thoughts brushed her mind as she hurried away as though hoping that distance would dim them. Keep the barrier up, she warned herself, you've learned how to do it, don't let it slip. Control, that's the word Doctor Thule always used, but she thought of it as a barrier. Control that imagination, he always repeated, as though repetition would do the job. Now that you understand your problem you must handle it.

Tammy concentrated on small physical things—the chill of the wind at her back, the feel of suede against the hands jammed into her pocket, the sharp, sliding pebbles moving under her boots. Against her will, the images of the two arrivals shifted across her mind. The woman with the hard, cold face and the tiny man-creature. What would it feel like to be that small? She wondered. Nigel Quiller barely reached his grandfather's waist. At first she decided, as had all the people waiting for the boat to dock, that Nadine's eagerly awaited son was a child, about the same age as Buddy. Only when Rob had lifted the child-sized figure to the pier had she seen her error. Nigel was diminutive but there was no doubt he was a man. He wore a leather jacket fringed along the sleeves, well-cut brown trousers, and tiny, beautifully polished boots. He was handsome, easily the best looking of the male Quillers, with vibrant, red-gold hair, thickly lashed, wide-spaced eyes, good features, and a firm chin. Nigel also had poise and had faced the staring eyes with a tiny, ironical smile playing around his mouth.

Tammy paused to catch her breath. She had reached the cut through the cliff that led first to the Amoses' cabin and then curved upward to the main house. By lifting her eyes she could have seen the great pinnacle that towered over and enfolded most of the main house in its cold arms. Even Rayburn had seemed surprised and slightly dismayed when he'd seen the house's situation. He had questioned Jeb Amos. "Isn't that a dangerous place to build a house? One earth tremor and it looks as though that whole mass would bury the building."

Removing his pipe, Jeb pondered. He was as slow speaking as he was slow moving. "Looks that way, don't it?" he'd finally drawled. "But safe as churches that house is. Stood there nearly seventy years and nothin's happened." He added, "Best shelter there for it, most sheltered spot on this island."

The Amoses' cottage was directly ahead of the girl. She stopped and regarded it. Like the main house, this was built of clapboard but the wood was neatly painted white and the shutters and door were a bright blue. It was a warm, homely looking dwelling with crisp curtains at the windows, the gray-blue Persian sitting placidly on the doorstep, its fluffy tail curled around its body. There was no sign of life around it though. Probably Holly was at the main house going about her duties. Wistfully, Tammy stared at the blue door, at the brass knocker shaped like a mermaid. The cottage looked warm and comfortable, a place of potted plants and warm fires. It didn't resemble in the slightest the ranch house she'd been born and raised in but something about it brought back vivid memories of her home. Did her home still look the same? She wondered. Did it still lie in sprawling, dozing warmth under the shade of old oaks? Did moonlight still spill softly over gleaming wood floors and reflect from white plastered walls, did muted sounds still drift through open windows on a summer evening, the murmur of voices, the whinny of a horse in the corral, the lowing of cattle from one of the near fields? Memories of the house brought memories of her father, warm memories of strong arms, a smiling face, comfort... safety.

With a shiver she turned away from the beckoning blue door and continued up the winding path. She was chilled to the bone and there was nowhere else to go but back to the main house. Her own home was gone, the ranch sold three years ago by Jim Quiller. Her mother had taken her for a weekend to what she called "your new home, Tammy" and that was the only time Tammy had left the school. I won't go again, Tammy had told Doctor Thule, not to that sterile glass and plastic horror that my mother's husband calls home. They've taken my home away, my past, my memories. Hush, Doctor Thule lectured in his soft, mushy voice. Your parents

46

did it for your sake, Tammy, look what those memories do to you.

I wish I could cry, Tammy thought, I wish I could feel salty moisture flooding my eyes, dripping down my face. I wish, she thought miserably, I were dead. No, you don't! If you did you wouldn't fear to lose life, you wouldn't be afraid now, afraid and alone. Mother...mother, couldn't you at least— Tammy's mind searched back through those forbidden memories. Had her mother actually been different through her childhood or had those memories been tinted by what she wanted her mother to be? She remembered her mother when she was...how old had she been? Perhaps four. Her mother bending over a tiny sweater she was knitting for Tammy's favorite doll, Tammy standing against her mother's knees, watching intently. Her mother's laughing face as she held up the knitting so Tammy could see it. The sound of her mother's voice, the tenderness of her mother's arms. Such a short time to know love. Then the long cold years with a wall between them that neither could break through. Every attempt made to breach that wall ending in quarrels, accusations. Dorothy had turned away from her husband and daughter and, after she was widowed, she had turned to Jim Quiller. Tammy had turned inward, away from all human contact.

Grimly, she thrust everything but the present moment away from her. She was walking up a path. Soon she'd make a turn and the house would be in front of her. It was neatly enclosed with a metal fence, the gate dangling by one hinge and wide open. A path of crushed shells led whitely through a small plot of land where at one time a valiant but unsuccessful effort had been made to landscape. The wind and sleet and cold had destroyed everything but a few stunted shrubs and a forlorn chrysanthemum plant that labored to survive.

Reaching the last turn in the winding path, Tammy paused, curiously reluctant to look at that house. Everything about it repelled her. She tried to laugh. Nowhere else to go but back to the pier and the welcoming committee for the latest guests. Might as well return to the house and the rest of the Quillers. Despite the cold wind that morning the only ones who hadn't gone down to the pier had been Ruth and Buddy, Thelma and Philip. Buddy had begged to go down with his great-grandfather but Rayburn decided the boy was safer away from water and Ruth had agreed to stay with the child. When Tammy had left the house Buddy had been playing with a fleet of toy trucks in the drawing room with Ruth fondly watching him. Neither Thelma nor Philip had put in an appearance. Tammy's mouth quirked. Knowing her step-brother's reputation, she figured Philip was probably finding better ways to put in his time.

She lifted her head. Philip must have left his room. She could hear a man's voice drifting down from the direction of the house. She caught a few words. "Playing hide-and-seek, eh? Come out, come out wherever you are." She listened and then she heard the same voice, closer this time. "Gotcha! Thought you could get away, did you?"

Tammy frowned. Hide-and seek? Was Philip playing with the little boy? But Buddy had been forbidden to leave the house and Philip was hardly the type to waste his time play-ing with a child. She took a couple of steps and then a shrill cry cut across the silence. More of a muted scream, it sounded like an animal in agony. And on top of the cry, drowning it out, laughter. Laughter, dark and disturbing. Laughter and a few more words. "Rosemary, my little Rosemary."

Tammy was running, running around the curve of rock, up the path. She stopped dead. No one. No one on the path, no one around the house. The only sound now was her own ragged breathing and the moan of the wind. Clutching her head in both hands, she rocked back and forth. Have to gain control...have to fight this. There was no one on this island but the Quillers. Setting her mouth, she forced herself on.

The house loomed over her. It was a tall, high-shouldered structure with tall, lean windows. The clapboards might once have been painted but now were a uniform silver-gray that showed no touch of paint. Lashes of gingerbread trimming crept along the roof line, hung like fungus from the wide veranda. It was a stern no-nonsense house that made no effort to look pleasant. It stared coldly from tall windows from the barren garden, down over the windswept Atlantic to the dark smudge that was Amoston—a house that turned its back to the weather and avidly accepted the stony embrace of the cliff that looked no kinder than it did.

The house, Tammy silently told herself, that the Winch-fields, who had been done in for some mysterious reason in some unknown way by a mob of fishermen from the hamlet across the water, had once called home. School? What kind of school had been in this grim house? Immediately she knew she had no wish to know anything further. The previous

evening Holly Amos had been only too willing to tell all and
Rayburn had been encouraging her when Jim had taken a
hand. For Tammy's sake, her stepfather had pleaded, please
don't discuss it. Hasty agreements had sounded and eyes
looked askance at the girl in the shadowed corner of the big
drawing room. Tammy had nearly laughed aloud. What did
the Quillers expect? That an ancient, grisly tale might un-
hinge her delicate mind and she'd run amok in their midst,
maybe frothing at the mouth? No, she said silently, not that
kind of madness, my dear Quillers. My kind of madness is
silent, the vision of a bloody club, the agony of that club
crushing into her own skull, the swirl of thoughts all around
her she must close out.

She hadn't noticed the door opening, that huge, preten-
tious door crowned with an arc of brightly stained glass.
Thelma Thaler stepped out onto the warped boards of the
veranda. "Tammy," she called. "I thought it was the others.
Did Nigel and his mother arrive?"

"They're here," Tammy told her, and forced herself to
mount the sagging steps, to cross the wide veranda, the
boards creaking dismally under her boots.

Shivering, Thelma retreated into the hall. "What are they
like?" she asked.

Tammy was tempted to tell her to wait and see, but she
hesitated. A feeling of kinship with Nigel stirred, after all,
in different ways, both of them were freaks. It might be easier
for him if the people in the house were forewarned, perhaps
they wouldn't stare at him so openly. She told the older
woman, "Nigel is a dwarf."

Thelma's mouth sagged open. Her lips looked swollen and
her hair was tousled. She wore a blue-and-white checkered
shirt and denim pants. Tammy noted the zipper in the pants
hadn't been closed and she caught a glimpse of plump, pink
belly. As Thelma moved, her large breasts surged loosely
under the shirt. No bra, the girl decided, and thought immediately of Philip. "Wow!" Thelma exclaimed. "A midget
Quiller."

"He said he prefers to be called a dwarf."

"Midget or dwarf—still wow. How did big daddy take it?"

Tammy shrugged and loosened her jacket. The hall was
as bleak as the exterior of the house. It was paneled in gloomy
wood, the floor was covered with carpeting, so old that the
pattern, swirls of purple and blobs that looked like yellow

pineapples against a dingy brown, was faded and in places worn right through the nap. A fine grandfather clock ticked away beside the closet where their coats and jacket hung. As Tammy squeezed her jacket onto a hanger, she saw Ruth's lustrous mink carelessly draped near it.

Tammy gazed around. The Winchfields hadn't bothered with any beauty or grace in lines or contours. The staircase marched straight up in an uncompromising line, paused for a square landing, and then lunged off again to the third floor. Even the bannister was square. She thought the ornament at the foot of the stairs had been put there by later tenants. It provided one touch of relief from straight lines. A bronze Atlas, with a graceful, strongly muscled body, held a bronze globe on his massive shoulders. For some reason his face reminded her of Nigel Quiller.

She glanced upward and the ugly staircase was momentarily beautified. Making her dainty way down was Ruth, holding up a flowing silk skirt. "Are they here?" she asked.

It was Thelma who answered. "Safe and sound. Better brace yourself. Your nephew is a midget."

Ruth paused beside the bronze Atlas. Her mouth sagged open as Thelma's had moments before. Thelma grinned at her mother-in-law. "Your mouth is open."

"So is your fly, dear," Ruth said sweetly.

Hot, unbecoming color flared across Thelma's broad face and she groped for the zipper. Without lingering, Tammy continued down the hall, past the arches that led to the big drawing room and the equally large dining room. The doors to the library and the game room were closed. She pushed at the swinging door to the kitchen and, as she'd hoped, saw Holly Amos. Holly was bending over the oven, taking out a cookie sheet. The mingled odors of hot bread, sugar, and cinnamon filled the room. Holly glanced up, her cheeks flushed even pinker from the heat of the oven. "Come in and sit, Tammy, you look half frozen."

"I am." Tammy sank down at the scrubbed pine table.

This room was the only one she could honestly say she liked in the entire house. It was an odd mixture, a blend of the modern and the ancient. A hotel-sized freezer-refrigerator towered in one corner near a huge gas stove, stainless steel counters and sinks contrasted with old oak cupboards, a large chopping block, its top gouged and cut, sat in another corner, and the floor was covered with worn linoleum. Some color had been introduced, no doubt by Holly, in the form of brightly patterned curtains and rows of geraniums on the window sills. Tammy carefully avoided looking through those windows. Gray light filtered in but only three feet away the rock wall of the cliff reared up.

Wiping her hands on her apron, Holly bustled over. She was a plump woman with a mop of crisp gray hair and eyes as bright and blue as the color she'd chosen for the door of her cottage. She hovered over the girl, gently brushing back the windblown hair. Her hand lingered on Tammy's head in a caress. "Your cheeks are like ice. I just brewed a pot of nice strong tea. You're having a cuppa and some hot buns and no arguments. You just picked at your dinner last night and hardly touched a bite of breakfast."

Meekly, Tammy accepted a plate of cinnamon buns, a steaming mug of dark tea. She spooned sugar into the cup and munched a bun. Holly put some jelly on a saucer and thumped it down beside the girl's plate. "Mind you eat every bite. Made this myself—quince jelly. Thought when I saw the food young Rob brought out for Mr. Rayburn that he'd relish some good homemade preserves. Stuff you buy now is nothing but filler and artifical flavoring. Fine gentleman, Mr. Rayburn, took to him right away. He understands about this house and all the work, y'know." One thing that Tammy really liked about being around Holly was that the older woman did all the talking. She neither waited for nor seemed to expect any sort of reply. Her words continued to tumble out. "Minute he looked at this big barn last night he says right away, 'You just do what you can, Mrs. Amos. We'll look after our own bedrooms and Thelma will be glad to help you with the housework. All we really require is your cooking ability.' Have to admit the way he dug into his dinner made me proud. Relishes good food, Mr. Rayburn does. Took to him right away."

Holly paused to catch her breath and Tammy silently admitted that it was obvious that Holly had taken immediately to the oldest Quiller. He had a way with aging women. Look at Mrs. Brome's reaction. Younger ones too; her mother appeared quite overwhelmed with the man's charm. Tammy had a hunch the recent arrival, Nadine, might not be quite as taken.

Pouring a mug of tea for herself, Holly sat down heavily opposite the girl. "Must admit you're a welcome bunch.

Should see some of the folks rent this place. Figure me and Jeb is slaves to them. Used to rush around trying to please them but we're getting no younger and I got this rheumatism now. Got fed up a couple of years ago and I sat down and wrote that bunch in New York. It's a company owns this place and not the same as trying to talk to a person, but I told them flat that Jeb and me was hired to caretake this place, not be slaves. Wrote me right back and told me to do what I wanted. Said if the folks who rent want servants they can bring them." Blowing on her steaming tea, Holly took a cautious sip. "'Course the extra money comes in handy and I'm glad to do all I can for nice folks like you. Told Mr. Rayburn this morning I'd get a good hot lunch on with his kin coming and all. Told me not to bother, lay out a cold buffet, he says. We'll have a sit-down meal for dinner. Not many as considerate as him."

She paused for breath again and this time Tammy felt compelled to say something. "Does your husband help you with the work?"

"Does what he can. Jeb looks after the generator for power and the pump on the well. Good hand with machinery, Jeb is. Keeps the place in some kind of repair. Old house like this always needs something. Good man Jeb is, though some people would argue that. But he was a steady worker at one time and never touched a drop of spirits. Started on them after the boys was killed in the war. He took Pat's death—Pat was the older, y'know—not too hard but couldn't seem to get over it when young Tommy was killed. Tommy was a cheerful lad, a great one for laughing and joking. Real nice to have around, Tommy was."

Lulled by the warmth of the kitchen and Holly's chattering, Tammy had let the barrier slide. Suddenly she had a flash of a laughing, round-faced boy and she winced at the depth of grief that came with that face. A round-faced boy who had died in a steaming alien land without even knowing why he had to die. Poor Jeb, left with his bottle and pipe, waiting for two boys who would never return. Blank it out, she told herself; the barrier. The barrier slid up and she was safe in the warm, sweet-smelling kitchen. She pushed back her plate.

"More?" Holly asked and when the girl shook her head, the caretaker reached out a plump hand and placed it over Tammy's. "Going to cook a good dinner tonight. Lamb and all the trimmings. You try to eat. Got no more flesh on those bones than a bird has."

For a moment Tammy left her hand cradled in Holly's, fighting a strong urge to fling herself into the older woman's arms, bury her face against that matronly breast. A mother image, she told herself, a desire to return to the comfort of childhood. But she was no longer a child. Gently she removed her hand and stood up. She pointed at the window. "Does that bother you?"

Swinging around, Holly looked at the rocky wall. "Not me, but Jeb hates it. Don't come into the back part of the house if he can help. People in Amoston used to call it Kat's Rock."

"Cat? It isn't shaped like a cat. It's more like a huge cone."

"K-a-t," Holly spelled. "Folks called it after Kat Winchfield. She was the daughter."

"How many Winchfields were there?"

"Four. Mother and father, son and daughter."

"What kind of school did they have here?"

Holly's flood of words seemed to have dried up. Folding her hands on the table, she looked down at them. "Can't talk about it, Tammy, your dad told me—"

"My father is dead."

"Well, Mr. Jim told me, don't talk about it to Tammy, he says. Told him I wouldn't."

"That's all right, Holly. I won't ask any more questions."

"Can't see myself why it would hurt you. Happened a long time ago." The older woman swung around. The swinging doors were pushed wide and Buddy, balancing a bright red airplane, entered the kitchen. He leaned against Holly, staring longingly at the plate of buns. Holly laughed. "Young ones are always hungry. Like a hot bun, Buddy?"

He nodded and clattered the toy on the table. She lifted him to a chair, took a plate, lifted a bun onto it and put it down in front of him. "Only one, mind you. Spoil your lunch if you eat more. Mind you don't get crumbs on the table. You remind me of my own boys when they were tykes. Always relished hot buns, they did." She sighed and then asked, "Where you going, Tammy?"

The girl paused by the door at the end of the room. "Up to my room."

"Better use the front stairs. Bulb's burnt out on that rear one and the stairs are pretty steep anyway. Got cartons piled

53

on them too. Told Jeb to get some new bulbs in and clean them up but he hasn't got to it yet."

Taking Holly's advice, Tammy turned back to the swinging door. As she neared the arch to the drawing room she could hear the murmur of voices. A hearty laugh resounded that could only be Rayburn's. They must have come up from the pier, Tammy thought, and are now entertaining the new arrivals. As she passed the archway she caught a glimpse of her mother. Dorothy beckoned to her but Tammy slid hastily past and hurried up the staircase. At the top she paused and looked down the long hall. It was as gloomy as the lower floor, a motley of dark paneling and worn-out carpeting. Doors opened from each side of it and at the far end was the door to a huge old-fashioned bathroom, the only room she'd entered on this floor. She understood there was a second, more modern bathroom but that one was situated between Rayburn's and Ruth's rooms and shared by the father and daughter.

Whatever heating system was used in the house managed to heat the first floor adequately but the higher one went, the cooler the air got. This second landing was far from warm but one flight up, where she slept, was frigid. Turning, she made her way up to the third floor. She stopped again and the chill struck. There were two small bedrooms facing each other and at the end of the hall a set of heavy double doors. Jim Quiller hadn't managed to silence Holly about the Winchfields when the caretaker had brought Tammy up the night before and Holly had told her a little about this floor.

"Don't know why they stuck you up here," Holly had said. "Still an empty bedroom downstairs."

"They're probably saving that for one of the people arriving tomorrow. I don't mind anyway, Holly, it's less crowded up here. There're only three bedrooms."

"Two. Those doors back there lead to a big room, takes up most of this attic. These two little rooms was used for the children and that there's a kinda schoolroom and playroom the Winchfields took folks to if they come to look at the place 'fore sending their youngsters here. Crowded those youngsters into these two rooms here."

Holly said no more about either the schoolchildren or the Winchfields. Now, as Tammy opened her door, she wondered for the second time how many children could have been squeezed into this tiny room. The attic ceiling sloped and
54

there was only one window looking down over the cove and the sea. The schoolroom at the rear must look directly into the rock wall. This was a stark place but she didn't mind. The floor was covered with faded linoleum but an oval rag rug had been stretched over part of it. The walls were more cheerful than the rest of the house and were painted white. A large wardrobe took up one corner and in the other was a massive chest of drawers. The bed was narrow but comfortable and covered in the same gingham that hung at the window. Other than these the only other furnishings were an armchair in front of the window and a portable heater. She had added a few touches of her own—a pile of books on the rug near the window, a sketchbook balanced on top of them, her dresser set on the chest, and her father's picture in its center.

Tammy took a step into the room and then stopped, her nostrils quivering. What on earth was that smell? She took a deep breath and then took a step backward. It was faint but it was sickening, alien. No, not alien. She'd smelled something similar before. Back in her home in Florida. That terrible smell of decaying flesh when the rat had crawled under the floor of her bedroom and died there.

She clung to the door, feeling sick and cold, cold with a fear that touched her spine, that seemed to freeze her muscles. Ridiculous! She'd only left this room a short time before. There was no way....

She moved. She ran to the window, threw up the sash, stood in the stiff wind that rustled the gingham curtains and blew the hair back from her brow. Shivering, she turned away from the window, took an experimental and shallow breath. Nothing. Whatever her mind had conjured up this time was gone, gone like the voices on the path, the round-faced boy in Holly's kitchen. I shouldn't have left my sanctuary, Tammy thought, Dr. Thule should never have let me leave. But she was here and she'd have to make the best of it. She thudded the window down and sank into the chair.

Kicking off her boots, she extended her feet to the heater. The coils were glowing cherry-red and she felt welcome heat against her stockinged feet. She picked up the sketchbook and examined it. This morning she'd started a sketch of the scene from her window. It wasn't bad. She'd caught the pier and the cove. Beyond them danced the waters of the sea. Her hand moved and she started shading in the background, glancing occasionally from the book to the window.

A brisk knock splintered the silence and she swung around. It was her mother, a smile carefully arranged on her lips. The smile didn't reach her eyes. "Didn't you see me when I beckoned you into the drawing room, Tammy?"

"I saw you."

"Then why didn't you join us? You haven't even bothered to say hello to Nadine and her son. At least you could do that for Jim and Rayburn if not for me."

"I like being alone. You know that, mother."

Dorothy's lips tightened into a bitter line. "You're making excuses. Using your...illness as an excuse for rudeness. Like you were rude to Rayburn in the cafe yesterday. Making Jim and me look like fools before his relatives."

Shooting her mother a look, Tammy turned back to her sketchbook. For a moment Dorothy eyed her daughter's back and then she took a few steps and looked over the thin hunched shoulders. "What are you drawing? Oh, the cove. My, that really is well done. Doctor Thule tells me you're doing well in oils too." When there was no response, Dorothy turned back to the bed and perched on the side of it. She gazed around the room. "This is a cramped little hole. If you'd like, I'll speak to Rayburn and have you moved down to that room next to Jim and me." She shivered. "Cold, too."

"I don't mind it." Tammy's pencil moved swiftly over the paper. "What do you want?"

"To talk, I suppose. It's a long time since we've had a talk."

"Our talks generally end the same way."

"It doesn't have to be like that," Dorothy said eagerly. "We're both adults. We can try."

Putting down the pencil, Tammy swung around. "Very well, let's try."

"It's about Jim. The way you feel about him. I know how much you loved your father, Tammy, but he's dead. You resent Jim but he's never tried to take your father's place. He's only tried to be kind to you. Jim is fond of you, dear, he wants you home with us. Doctor Thule told us, and he probably has told you, it's time to come home—"

"Mother, try to understand. My home is gone."

Dorothy's mouth tightened but she said evenly, "Did you ever consider how hard it was for me to stay on at the ranch?

56

The memories? Have you ever stopped thinking of yourself long enough to realize *I* might miss your father?"

"You must have," Tammy said slowly. "But you couldn't have missed him for long. Four months after his death you were remarried. As soon as you could you sold the ranch, the place he worked so hard to make a home."

Dorothy sprung up, her face contorted.

"I was alone, Tammy, all alone. I have no living relatives and Marc was an only child. All I had were you and Marc. He was dead and you..." Dorothy hesitated and then said abruptly, "You might just as well have been dead. I'd go and see you and you wouldn't even know I was there. Jim was kind, Tammy, he lost his wife in that accident—"

"Accident," Tammy said slowly, and her lips curled.

Shivering, Dorothy moved closer to the heater. "The doctor told us about your hallucinations about your father's death. I think it's time you know the truth. Shielding your father is only injuring Jim. You father and Vinnie Quiller were lovers. Tammy, look at me! They'd sneaked off to Pensacola and were sharing a motel room there, the bed was rumpled from them, Vinnie's nightie was tossed across it. The bathroom shelves were crowded with her cosmetics. Marc and Vinnie had been out for dinner and they'd had a great deal of wine. There was a half-empty bottle of liquor in their room. Vinnie and Marc went for a drive. The car went out of control, crashed, a d they both were killed—"

"And the bodies burnt."

"Yes, and the bodies were burnt. They weren't *murdered*. Just a sordid little affair, too much to drink, and an accident." Dorothy's chin lifted. "You expect me to mourn a man like that?"

The round glasses were fixed squarely on Dorothy's flushed face. Tammy's voice was only a whisper. "You were glad that father died. From the time father hired Jim Quiller and he started to come to the ranch, you wanted *him*."

Dorothy backed toward the door. Blindly, her hand sought the knob, found it. She flung the door open. Over her shoulder she threw furious words. "You *are* insane. You're mad, Tammy, right out of your mind!"

"Mother, wait! I'm sorry—"

"I'm sick to death of it. Sick to death of you saying these terrible things and then saying you're sorry. Sick of your delusions about your father's death. Delusions, Tammy. You're mad!"

The door slammed behind her and Tammy whispered hopelessly, "Mother."

For a time she stared at the blank panel and then she turned back to the window. Removing her glasses, she rubbed her eyes, and picked up the sketchbook. She stared down at it. While her mother had been in the room she'd finished the scene, her mind not even on it. It wasn't the sketch she'd started. Charcoal had changed the seascape to a night scene. A full moon peeked eerily out of a bank of clouds. The pier, stretching deep into the cove, now had a fishing boat drawn up beside it. Minuscule figures tumbled from the craft, the lines of their figures transmitting a feeling of stealthiness. One figure was part way up the pier. Bending closer, Tammy studied it. She could discern a long shining coat that looked slick, wet—like oilskin. The face, under a tall top hat, was only a blur. One arm was raised, the tiny hand clenched. She shut her eyes. Then she picked up the pencil and carefully filled that clenched fist. Now the hand brandished a short club.

She threw the sketchbook from her. It hit the corner of the heater and fell to the rag rug. Bending foreward, Tammy buried her face in her hands.

On the second landing, Thelma met Dorothy. She opened her mouth but Dorothy brushed by without looking at her. Thelma caught a glimpse of the woman's expression. Jim's wife looked as though she were ready to bite. She'd come bolting down the stairs from the attic and that's where her daughter's room was. Probably a family fight. Great little family reunion. Nigel Quiller was down in the drawing room making polite conversation while his mother stared off into space. Nadine looked like an ice sculpture. Momentarily, Thelma wondered why the woman had agreed to come. She soon lost interest. Other people's problems really didn't interest her.

She looked down the dim hall stretching out in front of her. Ray sure had a talent for picking houses that looked and felt like mausoleums. She started briskly toward the room she shared with Norm but as she passed Philip's door she noticed it was ajar. A pale blue eye stared through the aperture. The eye closed in a wink and the door swung wide. All he was wearing was jockey shorts.

"Hi, lady," Philip said in a hoarse whisper. "Got time for a quickie?"

"Lunch is ready and you'd better get your butt moving. Ray's expecting you to put in an appearance. Told me to drag you out of bed."

"Not hungry for food. Only one thing I hunger for."

Her eyes avidly traveled down the length of his body. "Better get down and meet your new relatives. Doesn't pay to cross Ray."

Reaching out, he tried to pull her to him. She avoided his hand. "What are they like?" he asked.

"Go down and find out."

"I suppose I'd better. Wouldn't want to get on the wrong side of granddad. How about tonight?"

She grinned. "Don't hold your breath."

His hand groped down to his crotch. "I'm holding something else, lady." The door closed in her face.

A hand grasped her shoulder and whirled her around. Through her thin shirt she could feel the hot wetness of that hand. "Do you like him?" Norm demanded.

"I told you I don't."

His other hand grabbed her breast. "There's time before lunch. Thel, can we?"

She was about to refuse when both his hands tightened. She winced. The strength of those hands! "If you want to. But only a few minutes, Norm."

Nodding eagerly, he drew her across the hall to their room. Thelma threw herself across the unmade bed and her husband lowered himself beside her. She felt him fumbling at her shirt and then his lips on her breasts. His wiry beard tickled her but she didn't move away. His mouth sought her nipple and he suckled, making small, contented grunts. She stood it as long as she could and then she shoved his face away. He didn't argue. Curling up against her, he whispered, "You're my mommy and I'm your little baby."

"Yes," she said automatically, "you're my little baby."

Despite herself, his lips on her nipples had excited her. Mentally, she drifted away from him, picturing the night before, the hour she'd spent in Phil's bed that morning. She imagined Phil's hard young body and drew her breath in

59

sharply. Tonight, as soon as she possibly could, she'd seek that bed again, that body again.

Damn Ray Quiller, she thought, double damn all the bloody Quillers.

Much to Dorothy's relief her daughter dressed for dinner that evening. Rayburn had made it clear at lunch that informal attire was permitted through the day but denims and sweaters were not tolerated in the evening hours. After Dorothy's argument with Tammy that she refused to return to the girl's room to tell her, but she admitted, as she watched her daughter take her place at the table, as usual it wasn't necessary to tell Tammy anything. The girl was wearing a silk blouse the color of daffodils and a floor-length, matching skirt. Her long hair had been pulled back and fastened with gold clips. If she'd just take those awful glasses off, Dorothy thought, the girl would be an asset.

The dinner proved to be delicious. Holly deserved Mrs. Brome's glowing recommendation. The conversation was lively with Rayburn, Jim, and Nigel carrying most of it but even Doctor Thaler and young Philip joined in. Thelma hunched morosely over her plate and Ruth, always quiet, attended to the needs of her small grandson. She seemed to anticipate the child's desires. Nadine ate with a good appetite but except for darting glances at the rest of the diners, she kept her attention on her plate.

After they had dined, Rayburn, rendered expansive by the excellent food and wine, invited the Amoses to join the family in the drawing room. Jeb appeared reluctant but Holly accepted with alacrity and plumped herself down on an armchair in their midst.

A wood fire had been kindled on the hearth of the stone fireplace and a few lamps were scattered around the room, their mellow light kind to the shabby furnishings. Brandy and coffee were served and Jeb's unshaven face brightened as he accepted a generous amount of the liquor. His wife divided a glare between his snifter and the pipe he was pulling from his sweater pocket. She shook her head and Jeb pushed the pipe back. Nigel avoided the chairs and selected a footstool near the hearth. The flickering light gilded his flaming hair and handsome features. He was regarding the caretakers intently.

Taking a sip of brandy, Nigel asked, "Is it true what Mrs.

Brome was telling us, that you both are descendants of pioneers in this area?"

"'Deed we are." Holly beamed at the tiny man. "I was a Cranston and my dad was minister here at one time. Jeb's folks were farmers, the town's named after them."

"Interesting," Nigel murmured.

Rayburn leaned forward. "You have some interest in Amoston?"

"My hobby, sir. I'm a bit of a buff on history and criminology. Old crimes seem much more—how would you put it?—more colorful than contemporary ones. As a matter of fact, I ran across a story on this island. A family called Winchfield—"

"We decided not to discuss that story," Jim broke in. He waved a hand. "My stepdaughter. Tammy's not been well and we're afraid that sort of thing might upset her."

"Really, Jim." His father tipped a little brandy into his snifter. "I do think you may be a bit too protective. What do you think, Dorothy?"

Dorothy shot an icy glance at her daughter. "I have no objection. I doubt anything could hurt Tammy."

Tammy's clear voice cut across the room. "If you'd like, I'll go up to my room."

"Not necessary, my dear." Rayburn turned to Nigel. "Dorothy doesn't mind and neither does Tammy so we'll override Jim. He's always been something of a fussbudget. I'm curious. Tell us what you've learned about this island."

"Not a great deal," Nigel confessed. "That's the reason I was so pleased to meet Holly and Jeb. The old accounts are sparse. Merely titillating. I'd hoped the Amoses could fill them in."

Holly's blue eyes were sparkling. "What did you find out, Mr. Nigel?"

He gazed into the flames, his long lashes shading the wide-set eyes.

"The Winchfields turned up here from nowhere. There were a mother and father, people in their mid-sixties, and two children, a daughter and a son, probably in their twenties. They appeared to be well-to-do and wasted no time in having this house built. Apparently they got off to a poor start with the villagers and there were hard feelings even before the house was started. Is that correct, Holly?"

"That's the truth. Mind you, I was only a babe in arms at

61

the time and Jeb was a toddler but our dads was in the bunch that came to the island and—"

"Suppose," Rayburn broke into the flood of words, "you tell us the story from the begining, Holly."

Leaning forward, he poured a little brandy into the woman's glass. Jeb held his snifter out and Rayburn tipped the bottle over it. Jeb smiled and fumbled for his pipe but this time his wife was so engrossed she didn't notice. While her husband contentedly packed tobacco into the stubby pipe, she started to speak.

Five

The Winchfields came to the coast of Maine two years before the world was to be convulsed in the first of the global conflicts that would destroy a slow, contented way of life. The inhabitants of the Amoston area had a narrow sphere of interests that encompassed their neighbors, their work, and the sea. Most of them were fisherman, hardy tough men with equally tough women; some were farmers, a few were merchants. They were proud and independent people, they were also inbred and suspicious of strangers. While their better informed countrymen were mourning the loss of the *S.S. Titanic* near Cape Race, the people of Amoston were mourning two of their mates drowned in a storm when their fishing boat capsized. Theatergoers were flocking to see Shaw's *Pygmalion* and his *Androcles and the Lion* while Amoston families were content to crowd into the church hall for a potluck dinner. Jascha Heifetz attracted music lovers from scores of countries when he began his tour as a soloist, and in Amoston men and women of all ages square danced to the lively music of Lonny and Jeff Ware's fiddles. Readers thrilled to the exploits of Scott and the rest of his gallant party when they reached the South Pole. In Amoston people puzzled over a newly arrived family called the Winchfields.

Even before their arrival people began to call them *those*

Winchfields. Barges loaded with lumber, brick, and cement chugged through the bay and unloaded their cargoes on the island. These materials, the locals argued, could have been purchased on the spot with less expense than having them shipped up coast. Also, they pointed out, it would have been to the town's financial benefit. Their anger grew when the masons and carpenters arrived, also by boat from up coast. They were greeted by the villagers with jeers. Eyetalions, the villagers snorted, can't even speak English. Trust those Winchfields, could have hired carpenters from Amoston, but they're too good for that. The workers sent for supplies, camped on the island, and in record time threw up the big, ugly house in the shadow of the rock pinnacle that reared its gray stony head against the sky.

Amoston was prepared to ostracize the family on their arrival but even that pleasure was to be denied them. The Winchfields had their own boat and settled into the house without even visiting the village. It was over a month before any of the family deigned to set foot in Amoston. When they did come it was to pick up food supplies, grudgingly sold to them by Mark Spence, the grocer.

Curious eyes studied the family. There were four of them, Mother and Father Winchfield and Kat and Johnny. Kat appeared to be in her mid-twenties and was a fine-looking young woman with thick black hair and a buxom figure. Johnny looked a few years older and his fair good looks turned many a female head as he strutted by. From the beginning it was noted that Kat had a way with men. Her smiles and glances melted most of the young men immediately and even had some effect on the older ones. Father and Mother Winchfield were brusque and aloof but both Kat and her brother were more expansive. They told the villagers that they were going to start a school for children, boys and girls from toddlers to ten years of age. The villagers soon surmised that the students consisted of unwanted children. The children delivered for the school were either offspring of unwed mothers or children who had lost one or both parents. Second marriages in which the new husband or wife declined to raise step-children were far from rare. Two other facts were noted, mainly from observation. The people who deposited the children looked affluent and they made only one appearance in the village. As soon as the children were delivered, the adult escorts left hastily and never returned.

64

Kat would sweetly explain. "Someone has to take care of the poor little darlings and we're all so fond of children."

Fond of money too, the villagers mumbled to each other, pretty penny those Winchfields were making. The locals still disliked the closemouthed mother and father and they barely tolerated Johnny, condemning him for his foppish looks and his air of arrogance and scorn, but Kat was winning them over. She had a magnetic personality that attracted not only the young men of Amoston but also many of the women. Kat was handsome, stylishly dressed, and seemed pleasant and frank. She confided in the grocer's young wife, Laura Spence, that her family took the children as students with two provisions. One was that full tuition would be paid upon acceptance and would cover the children until they attained the age of sixteen. The other was that the parents or guardians were free to examine the school and its facilities when they delivered the children but that they were never again to come to Winchfield Island. Too unsettling for the little darlings, Kat explained to Laura, only make them homesick. In return, the Winchfields guaranteed to raise the children, clothe and feed them, and give each one as much education as he or she could absorb.

Laura Spence was completely captivated by her new friend. Laura was bored by her aging husband and his family, and she turned more and more to Kat Winchfield. Through Laura, Kat met many other Amoston females and won them over in various ways. She told their fortunes with tea leaves and tarot cards, lent them dress patterns, and even gave them some of her discarded clothing. With envious eyes they ogled her serge suits, ruffled shirtwaists, and glossy, high-buttoned boots. They imitated her hair style, the high-piled wealth of black hair combed up into a charming pompadour over Kat's rounded brow. The women of the village became dissatisfied with their own dreary lots and began to plague their husbands and fathers for money to buy materials to ape Kat Winchfield's clothes.

The young men were even more interested in the girl. The brawny Ware twins, Jeff and Lonny; Austin and Harry Spence; both of Josiah Amos's boys; and even the minister's pallid son, David Cranston, competed for Kat's favors. Gradually the elders of the village found discord and unrest entering their lives. Their sons were neglecting their work, their wives and daughters were full of complaints. Kat had a talent for turning people against each other. Her special friends, of both sexes, changed frequently and, as a result, jealousy and envy erupted. For a time she attended church suppers and dances with one or the other of the Ware twins and then she dropped them and concentrated on the Amos boys. The young men, friends from birth, fought each other behind the dance hall and once on church grounds. Laura Spence, who had basked in her position as Kat's best friend, found herself ousted by the schoolteacher, a tall, raw-boned woman named Piety York.

In a short time Kat Winchfield managed to make many enemies but her most virulent ones proved to be Laura Spence and the Reverend Cranston. The minister was a tall, bony man with a strongly featured face and a long flowing beard. He was a stern, despotic man of God and, although he began by urging Christian charity for the new family on his congregation, he soon learned to distrust and fear the Winchfields. His overtures were spurned by the family, his invitations for them to worship in his church were ridiculed by the Winchfields, his one attempt to visit their island ended in ignominy when they wouldn't even allow him to disembark from his boat. The last straw proved to be his son David. David had early decided to follow his father and become a minister but Kat changed that. After driving the other young men wild, she turned to David and selected him as her companion. David visited the island frequently, sometimes remaining there for days. He used his boat to ferry Kat and Johnny back and forth from the island to the mainland, and he followed the girl like a tame dog. David was a moody, high-strung lad and in time he became even more withdrawn and morose. He wouldn't satisfy the villagers' curiosity about the new house and the pupils at the school and he flatly refused to discuss Kat or the rest of her family even with his own father.

By the time that the Winchfields had been on the island for six months the only friends that Kat retained in Amoston were the spinster schoolteacher and the minister's son. The villagers continued to gossip about their neighbors, rumors began to fly, questions were asked. Those children, the locals asked, why do they never come near the village? Why even in fine weather hasn't a sign of them been seen by the men on the fishing boats? Why won't the Winchfields allow the youngsters' guardians to visit the school? Just what kind of school is this?

From his pulpit, Reverend Cranston heaped more fuel on the growing flames. "Sodom and Gomorrah!" he thundered, alluding pointedly but not yet by name to the Winchfields. "Those ungodly sinners in our midst. Children are denied the word of God, not allowed to attend church or even Sunday School." And, wrathfully eyeing the empty seat in the pew where his own family sat, where David had once been. "Scarlet woman, seducing our young men with her Satan-giving allures, sowing sin and discord in our village."

In a more devious way, Laura labored as hard as the minister did. Gathering the women around her, she whispered about Kat Winchfield, about her brother Johnny, about the school. What goes on out there? she demanded. Why is only David Cranston allowed on their precious island? What do they have to hide?

The Winchfield family couldn't have helped but know about their growing disfavor. When they came to Amoston for supplies they were treated to turned backs, cold stares, and whispers. Finally they started to go down coast for their needs but that didn't diminish the whispers. In fact, it spurred on their detractors. Reverend Cranston threw all caution to the wind. "Those Winchfields," he intoned, leaning over the pulpit and fixing steely eyes on the congregation, "this nest of vipers in our midst. Satan walks among us, dear friends, Satan holds sway on an island only a short distance from our homes, from our families. This abomination cannot continue to flourish! The day of reckoning must come!"

The day of reckoning was fast approaching. After a week's absence from his home, David returned to it one evening and went directly to his room. His face was white and drawn, his eyes looked haunted. His father, wild with anxiety, went to his son's bedside. In one thin hand he clutched his Bible.

"I'm ill, father," David told him. "Leave me alone."

Blazing eyes examined the boy's face. "Bewitched, my son, sick in your soul." Cranston grasped his son's hand and placed it on the book. "Swear on this that there is nothing amiss on Winchfield Island."

Wrenching his hand loose, the boy refused to speak. Finally, his father left him alone.

The following day two children arrived who were to spell doom for the Winchfields. They were brother and sister, a girl of fourteen and a tiny boy of five. Their names were Rosemary and Robert Fiscall and they were dumped in Amoston by a stepfather, obviously delighted to rid himself of them. The weather was bad and a boat couldn't come immediately for them and so Laura Spence took them into her home for several days. Rosemary was a pretty, plump child with blond ringlets and a body already rounding into womanhood. Laura wondered about the girl's age—all the children at the school were ten or under—but Rosemary explained that the Winchfields had kindly agreed to take her so her little brother wouldn't be lonely. On the fourth day after their arrival the weather cleared and Father Winchfield and Johnny arrived to pick the children up. As soon as they'd left her house, Laura sought out Mrs. Cranston. Leaning close to the minister's wife, Laura confided, "I feel terrible about that girl. You should have seen the way those two men looked at Rosemary."

"What exactly do you mean?" Mrs. Cranston asked.

"They looked at her with—with lust."

"To speak ill without proof is deadly sin," Mrs. Cranston murmured automatically, but her brow furrowed in thought.

A month passed. David pulled himself from his bed and returned to the island. His father helplessly watched the boy go, his own brow furrowed. Drawn like he is powerless to resist, the minister told his wife, as though he's been hypnotized by that Jezebel. His wife agreed and told her husband what Laura Spence had told her about Rosemary. No, Reverend Cranston said decisively, I can't believe that, not even about those Winchfields.

Three weeks later the storm broke over Amoston. Again David dragged himself home and this time he was deathly ill. His Bible in his hand, his father again went to his son's bedside. This time David didn't take refuge in silence. With the book clasped between his thin hands he confessed. Horrified, his father listened to a story of blood and murder, of children starved and butchered, of incest among the Winchfields, of Kat's unnatural relationship with both her father and her brother.

"Why?" David's father moaned. "Why, after all this time of silence, are you speaking now?"

"The new girl," David sobbed. "I can't stand it...what they're doing to her."

Under the barrage of questions from his father, David told

the fate of Rosemary Fiscall. Shared, he moaned, between the father and son, used as a grown woman might be used. Kat and her mother watching while the child was abused. Kat forcing him to watch also. "I can't stand it!" the boy cried.

Getting to his feet, his father looked coldly down at the boy. "Did you partake of these acts, son?"

"I swear I didn't!" David clutched the leather-covered book until his knuckles whitened. "I did not sin!"

"You are guilty of sin, the sin of omission. You may not have actively partaken of this but you did nothing to stop it. You are as guilty as those fiends. For this you must atone."

"How?"

Seizing his son, his father dragged him from the bed. "Dress. I will summon the congregation and you will confess to them as you have to me."

"No!"

"Yes, son. That is your first penitence. There will be others."

The church bell was tolled and the villagers flocked from their houses. It was a cold, windswept autumn night and they were bundled in oilskins, caps drawn down over their faces, their mittened hands clutching lanterns. The lanterns bobbed and glimmered as they filed into the church. David, supported by his stony-faced father, leaned against the pulpit and told them about the school on the island. They heard the boy out, their expressions as grim as their minister's, their fists clenching and unclenching, some of the women weeping, many of the men swearing under their breaths. Finally, David's voice wavered and he was silent. Flinging the boy into a chair, Cranston faced the congregation.

"Well?" he asked.

The blacksmith, Edward Ware, a huge, powerful figure, lumbered to his feet. He rumbled, "I'm going out there. Right now!"

Near Ware, Mark Spence jumped up. "I'm with you, Ed!"

"So am I!" Josiah Amos raised a clenched fist. "My boys too."

The minister lifted his own hand. "All in favor, rise."

With the exception of one person, the congregation rose. Cranston looked down at Piety York. "You don't agree these devils should be stopped?" he asked icily.

Impassively, the gaunt woman stared back. "If this is the
69

truth, they must be stopped. But not by a mob. Send for the sheriff and his deputies. This is work for the law."

Her face wild, Laura Spence turned on the teacher. "You're only trying to protect *her*, Piety York! That harlot, you're trying to save her precious skin! We should start on you!"

"Mrs. Spence," the minister chided. "Please remember you're in the house of the Lord." He turned his gaze back to Piety. "It would take time to summon the law, Miss York. In the meantime think of the agony of that little girl. Every minute is precious."

"Now. Right now!" Ed Ware bellowed.

Voices were raised in agreement. "Let's go!" "Now!" "Give those devils what they've earned!" "Kill them!" one woman shrieked. Cranston raised his voice against the clamor. "Be seated. We must select a committee—"

"I'm going!" Laura Spence shouted.

"No, you're not," her husband told her. "This is men's work. Listen to the minister, Laura."

The minister said slowly, "I will lead you. With me will go Ed Ware and his boys, Josiah Amos and his sons, Mark Spence and Austin and Harry—"

"And me, Reverend." A big fisherman was on his feet. "Don't leave me out. And my boy too."

Cranston nodded. "We'll take your boat, Charlie. So, that's Charlie and Jack Vance."

The schoolteacher drew her long frame from the pew. "I'm going too."

"No!" Laura Spence turned hate-filled eyes on her rival.

"If I have to take a boat and go by myself I'll be there," Piety said.

Cranston examined the teacher's set face. "Very well. Piety York will accompany us." His eyes shifted. "What's the matter, Ed?"

Twisting his cap, the blacksmith looked sheepish. "That's thirteen, Reverend. Not that I'm superstitious but some of the other boys may be."

"Fourteen will be going, Ed. My son is coming with us."

David raised a ravaged face. "No, father, don't make me. I can't stand it...I love her. I can't help it. I love—"

His father struck him so hard the boy crumpled and slid to the floor. "Don't say that. Never again!" He raised his eyes. "Forgive me, Lord, for using violence in Your house." Having asked forgiveness, the minister hauled his son violently up.

"You are going." He turned to the congregation. "Men, we will go about the Lord's work."

Dragging his son, the minister walked down the aisle. The men fell in behind them and Piety York strode along at the rear. Lanterns were retrieved and oilskins buttoned. Huddling on the church steps, the women of Amoston watched their men trot down the winding trail that led to the wharf. Their lanterns twinkling like fireflies, the men went about the deadly business of the Lord.

As they sailed across the bay to Winchfield Island, it appeared that the elements were against the group from Amoston. Shortly after they embarked in Charlie Vance's trawler, the wind rose to a shrieking gale, driving sleet before it, and whipping waves into white-capped frenzy. That didn't stop them. They were sailors, their life was the sea and they bore it both love and hate. They fought the waves with the instincts of generations of seamen, and they won. Eventually the trawler was docked at the rocky pier the Italian workmen had thrown out into the cove and the men jumped onto its rocky surface.

In their hands they clutched at makeshift weapons. There wasn't a firearm among them, in fact it is doubtful if there was a gun in the village. They held the tools of their trades, the implements used in daily life. The fishermen grabbed marlin-spikes and boathooks, the burly blacksmith and his twin sons had mallets, Josiah Amos and his sons had cattle prods, and the minister, the only one without a ready weapon, clutched a short length of stove-wood like a club.

Once on the pier they milled around, some of their earlier rage dissipating now that they were actually on the island. The minister sensed this and his voice was low and firm as he told them, "Men, you are acting as extensions of the Lord's hand. Follow me."

They followed his tall figure up the path that wound through a cut in the cliff, stumbling along in the darkness, cursing under their breaths until a couple of men stopped to try and light their lanterns. The rest of them clustered around, shielding the lanterns from the gusts of wind with their bodies. Josiah Amos took the opportunity to grunt in Ed Ware's ear. "Whatta you figure we do when we get in that house?"

The blacksmith, like many big men, was slow to anger but

71

when it came it was terrible to see. His face was set like granite as he said, "What we have to, Jos."

"I dunno, Ed. Do you suppose young David could have been dreaming this? He's always been a queer one. Think he could be—" Breaking off, Josiah tapped one chapped finger against his brow.

"Tetched? He's that all right but we know who did it to him, don't we? Those Winchfields drove him plumb outta his skull."

The lanterns were finally lit and Reverend Cranston waved his club up the path. "Onward, men."

They surged forward but Piety York had circled them and now barred the path. Holding both arms spread wide, she looked from one face to another. The eyes in her thin face fixed firmly on the minister's. She asked the same question that Josiah Amos had moments before. "I think you'd better tell us what you plan. We aren't killers. Do you intend to harm the Winchfields?"

In the flickering light the men's faces turned toward Cranston and he read unease in those faces. "We're here to stop them, that's all. We're not a lynch mob. We're going to take them and the children back to Amoston. We'll keep them there until we can send for the law."

Piety nodded and stepped aside, allowing the men to proceed. They filed up the narrow path, turned the last bend, and then they could see lamps from the tall windows of the house shining through the darkness. Cranston set a fast pace and soon they were mounting the steps and crossing the wide veranda. Cranston lifted his club to bang on the door but the blacksmith lunged past him and kicked it open. Wind and the men from Amoston rushed into the hall of Winchfield School. From the drawing room, Kat came running and her parents and brother crowded out behind her.

Kat was consumed with fury. "What are you doing? How dare you break into our house like this?" Her dark eyes flew from face to face. She caught sight of David Cranston cowering behind Jack Vance and his father. "You! What are you doing here, you little worm?"

Cranston towered over the girl. "Back. The four of you, into that room."

The Winchfields slowly gave ground, retreating to the drawing room. The men moved after them, their wet oilskins dripping on the carpet, gleaming in the light from the lamps

72

and the lively fire leaping on the hearth. Their eyes traveled around the large room, taking in the comfortable chairs, the velvet drapes, the remains of a lavish supper spread on a low table before the fire.

"Do yourselves well," Mark Spence grunted, pointing at the platters on the table. "How do you feed the little tykes?"

Drawing herself up, Mother Winchfield looked disdainfully at the grocer. "That, my man, is none of your affair."

"We'll have the law on you," her husband threatened. "Breaking and entering—"

"Silence!" Cranston ordered. "We are here on the Lord's business. My son has been corrupted by you demons but he is entering the fold of the gentle Shepherd again and he has told all."

Johnny turned on his sister, his face furious. "I told you about playing games with that weak fool. Told you he was gutless."

"Will you shut your mouth!" Kat spun away from her brother and confronted the intruders. "Anything David has told you is nothing but a pack of lies. He's trying to get even because he wants to marry me and I turned him down."

The minister stroked his flowing beard. "So...you say my son lies. You say he swears on the Sacred Book of God and he lies. Prove David a liar. Bring down the children. Let us see them"

"We can't do that," Father Winchfield told them.

His daughter touched his arm. "Let me explain, father." Her anger seemed to have disappeared and she was relaxed, smiling. The smile was charming, displaying even white teeth and a deep dimple on her left cheek. One hand went to her pompadour and she patted glossy hair into place. "Gentlemen," she said demurely, "I'm afraid this is a misunderstanding. David has told you some wild tale and brought you out on a night like this for nothing. As a matter of fact, there are no students here now. We found the school was too much for us, too much of a burden—"

"*Where* are those youngsters?" the blacksmith cut in.

"I'm trying to explain. " Kat turned her smile on him. "It just didn't work out, Mr. Ware. We tried for months but it was too much for mother and father so we decided to return the children to their guardians and sell this house. In fact, we're packing to leave—"

"How?" Mark Spence blurted. "None of them was brought

back to the village. We haven't seen hide nor hair of them since you put them in your boat."

Kat transferred her smile to the grocer. She straightened her shoulders, the movement tightening the shirtwaist and outlining jutting breasts. "We haven't been exactly welcome in your village, Mr. Spence. So we took the children down coast and delivered the little darlings into their guardians' hands there. If you like, I'll show you the schoolroom. Completely fitted up for work and play at great expense to us. We've lost money, Mr. Spence; we had to return most of the children's tuition."

The men were mumbling to each other. They seemed suddenly conscious of the weapons they held and Jack Vance was trying to hide his boathook behind his back. Piety York pushed through their ranks and went to Kat. Kat's wide eyes swept over the tall woman. "Piety! What on earth are you doing here?"

"Trying to talk some sense into those fool men, Kat. I knew David was telling a pack of lies." Piety looked at the minister. "Well, are you satisfied now?"

Grabbing his son's arm, Cranston hauled him forward. "Did you lie on the Good Book, son? Did you put your immortal soul in danger because of this woman's refusal to marry you?"

David hung limply in his father's powerful hands. "Leave me alone. Please...all of you, leave me alone."

Johnny took a step toward the miserable boy. "I've a mind to give you a thrashing, you young pup. Couldn't take no like a man—"

"Johnny, don't blame David." Kat slid an arm through her brother's. "He took it so hard. Forgive him. I do." She beckoned her mother. "Perhaps these people would like a cup of tea and some food, mother. Something to warm their stomachs before they make that trip back to the mainland."

A deep voice cut across the girl's. The blacksmith was striding toward the hall and he spoke over his shoulder. "Don't know about the rest of you but I'm taking a look around. Don't trust her and that smarmy way of talking. Don't think David made it up."

Moving swiftly, Kat reached the archway before he did. She spread her arms gracefully and smiled up into Ware's bearded face. "If you wish, Mr. Ware, I'll show you around."

"Get outta my way 'fore I break your arm. May have the rest fooled but not Ed Ware."

"Ed," the minister called. "I really don't believe we should compound our error by searching this house. Miss Winchfield has given a reasonable explanation and if we continue we could all be in trouble."

Ware threw the man a look of contempt, pushed the girl aside, and lunged into the hall. "You men or mice?" he called back to his mates.

The grocer hurried after him. "I'm with you, Ed."

The blacksmith turned. "Charlie, you get your back against that front door and have your lad guard the back one." He glowered at the Winchfields. "You stay put till we look around this here house. The reverend will stay with you."

Gaining courage, the other men followed him. Vance and his son went to their posts by the doors and only the minister, his son, and Piety York remained in the drawing room. Kat Winchfield, the florid coloring ebbing from her handsome face, drew the teacher aside and urgently whispered to her. Piety York stared into her friend's ashen face and then slowly she shook her head. Putting out a hand, Kat gently caressed the woman's bony shoulder, and, after a time, Piety nodded. Then Kat left her and went to stare into the burning logs on the hearth. David tried to break loose from his father to go to the young woman, but Cranston held him firmly.

The men tramped up the staircase and milled around in the upper hall. Ware waved his mallet at the rows of closed doors. "Have a look," he told them.

Doors were flung open and from one doorway, Lonny Ware called to his father. "Have a look at this room. Must be Kat's. What a place! Canopy and frills on the bed and one of them lounging couches—"

"We're not here to gawk, son." Ware raised his voice. "Find anything, men?"

The men hurried back. The grocer's older son, Austin Spence, said, "Nothing here, Ed. Just the old people's rooms and Johnny's and Kat's. Rest of them rooms ain't even furnished. Kat was telling the truth about moving. Couple of trunks half packed."

"Think we're on the wrong track," Josiah Amos volunteered. "That sissy boy of the minister's must have gone loco."

"Hey," a voice called. "Looka what I found in one of them trunks."

It was the other Ware twin, Jeff. He rushed down the hall, holding out a metal box. "Full of money. Kat was lying about giving back them tuitions. Looka the pile of bills in here."

Mouths fell open in bearded faces as they stared at the contents of the box. None of them had seen that much money in their lives. Mark Spence broke the stunned silence. "Could be their savings. Those Winchfields never seemed short of cash. Hired those workmen to put up this place and always paid for their groceries on the spot. Carried thick rolls of bills too."

"That ain't savings," Ware said. "That there's a fortune. Still think David was telling it straight. Them devils coulda been getting ready to cut and run. There's another floor above this one. Let's have a look."

They crowded up the staircase to the third floor. Only three doors faced them. Spence raised his lantern and it threw shuddering shadows on the white walls, the linoleum floor. He headed down the hall toward the double doors at its end. The rest followed him. Swinging wide the doors, he exclaimed, "This is the schoolroom Kat talked about."

It was a huge room and an impressive one. Small desks were set in two rows facing a dais where a larger desk sat. A bookcase held an assortment of books, piles of slates, and boxes of chalk. On the wall behind the teacher's desk hung a blackboard and several brightly colored maps. One side of the room was crowded with toys. Lonny Ware touched the mane of a rocking horse and his twin picked up a doll with a waxen face and golden curls. Jeff turned it in his big hands. "Kinda reminds me of the Fiscall girl," he mumbled. He fingered a ringlet. "Same kind of hair she has."

Mark Spence's narrow face was drawn in a worried frown and he fingered his balding head. "Got a feeling the whole bunch of us is in trouble. Looks like Kat was telling the truth and those Winchfields can sure have all of us behind bars for this night's work."

Even the big blacksmith was looking doubtful. Picking up a brightly colored ball, he frowned down at it. Then his mouth, in the midst of the wiry black beard, firmed. "Could be, Mark, but we still got two rooms to look at."

Josiah Amos headed toward the door. "Think we'd better let well enough alone. If that preacher don't beat that lying boy of his within an inch of his life, I'm gonna do it. Fine mess he's got us in."

Ware grimaced. "I'll help you, Jos, but I ain't leaving here without looking at them other rooms."

One of Amos's sons was opening the bedroom door to the right. "Bunch of cots piled up in here, that's all." He turned to the door on the left. "This one's locked, Ed."

"Break it open," the blacksmith ordered.

The boy shuffled his feet. "Don't think we better, we—"

"Outta the way." Shoving the boy aside, Ware put a brawny shoulder to the flimsy panel. Under his weight the lock splintered and gave and he pushed the door open. "Gimme that lantern, Mark." He held the lantern high and then strode into the room. "Figured this was a wild goose chase, eh? My God!"

The other men stared and sniffed the sickish odor that filled the tiny room. A ragged blanket was drawn over a cot near the one window and it humped slightly in the middle. On the other cot another filthy blanket was spread. Across a soiled mattress tangled hair framed a sunken, grimy face. Eyes in that face stared wildly up at the men.

Josiah whispered, "Is that...is it..."

"Rosemary Fiscall," Mark Spence said heavily. "Can hardly recognize her. What did they do to you, child?"

He moved forward and his foot touched something. He glanced down and then pointed. "While those Winchfields was eating that roast beef and them potatoes and gravy, see what they fed this tyke." At his feet were a pitcher of water and some ragged crusts of bread. He held out a hand to the child. Cringing away, she crawled to a sitting position against the wall. The blanket fell away from her upper body. "Oh, dear God in heaven," Spence moaned.

With disbelief they gazed over the bruises on the girl's budding breasts, over the rib cage standing starkly from her chest. Her body was covered with scratches, some of them festering. Sinking to his knees by the child he and his wife had sheltered in their home, Mark Spence pulled the blanket gently over the thin torso. "Rosemary," he whispered. "Where's your brother? Where's little Robert?"

"Right here," Ware said from behind them. He had pulled the other blanket back from the cot by the window. Robert Fiscall lay on the bare mattress, his eyes wide open staring at the ceiling, but seeing nothing. "He's long dead, men. Looks like he died from starvation. Those *bastards*."

"I can't believe it," Spence cried. "Can't believe anyone could do young'uns like this. Girl's been abused right outta her mind. Looka them eyes." He turned to Ware. "First thing we gotta do is get this child into a woman's hands. Get a doctor for her."

Austin Spence said, "I'll go get the schoolmarm, dad."

"No! Leave that one outta this." Ware shouldered in beside the grocer. "Had her way those Winchfields woulda had time to kill this girl too. Get some decent blankets from those rooms on the second floor. Wrap her up and, Austin, you and your brother get this girl over to your mother. Laura will know what to do. Then you get back here."

Josiah Amos spoke up. "Might's well use those Winchfields' boat for getting us back, Ed."

The blacksmith tapped the mallet against his calloused palm. "We'll be needing that boat, Jos. Austin and Harry will have to bring Charlie's trawler back here for us. No hurry, boys, we'll be busy for a spell."

"What are you planning to do about—" Breaking off, Josiah jerked his hand toward the floor.

Lonny Ware chimed in. "You heard Mr. Cranston, dad. Said we was to take the Winchfields back and call for the sheriff."

"We generally look after our own, son."

Lonny's chin, as stubborn as his father's, jutted. "Can't say these Fiscall youngsters are our own."

Mark Spence stepped up beside the blacksmith. "Them young'uns stayed in my house, ate at my table. I'm with you, Ed."

"The minister and Piety will try to stop us," Lonny insisted.

The mallet rose and fell against his father's hand. "Time's wasting, men. Austin, you and Harry wrap that girl warm and bring her on down."

Muttering, the rest of the men followed the grocer and the blacksmith.

In the drawing room, the Winchfields, Piety, and the minister and his son waited. Johnny and his mother and father clustered near the hearth, talking in low voices. Kat waited near the archway, glancing occasionally down the hall to where Charlie Vance was leaning his bulky form against the front door. Her eyes flew toward the staircase and she watched as the men from Amoston, Ware in the lead, clattered down the steps.

"Well," she called, "satisfied now? I suppose you looked all through our private possessions, too." She added viciously, "You're going to pay for this."

Ware approached her and she retreated from him. Ignoring the Winchfield family, he went directly to the minister. "Found a metal box upstairs bulging with money."

"That's not our business, Ed. We'd better get back to the village."

"Not yet, Reverend. Got something to show you. Bring her in here, Austin."

Austin Spence, a blanket-wrapped bundle in his arms, came through the archway. Mother Winchfield clutched at her husband's arm and Johnny drew his breath in sharply. Kat glared at her brother and hissed in his ear, "This is your fault, you fool. I told you we should have got rid of that brat days ago. But no, you and father had to have your own way."

With a trembling hand the minister folded back a corner of the blanket and peered down at the pitiful face. "Who is this?"

Mark Spence shouldered his way through the knot of men. "Rosemary Fiscall."

"What's wrong with the child? Her eyes...she doesn't seem to see me."

"Crazed," Ed Ware rumbled. "Beaten and starved and abused. We found her in an attic room. Her little brother's still up there. Dead, and he's been dead for days. Long enough to start to smell."

The minister swung on the huddle of Winchfields. "How could you do this? What matter of humans are you?"

"Not humans," the blacksmith told him. "Beasts. Worse than beasts. Get that girl outta here, Austin. Take her to your mother." He walked over to the Winchfields. "Where'd you bury the rest of them tykes? Where are their bodies?"

Kat threw her head back. "Bury? This island is solid rock. No place to bury anything. I can explain about the Fiscalls. They had pneumonia. Robert died, we couldn't save him..."

"Shut your lying mouth!" Spinning around, Ware fixed David Cranston with flaming eyes. "Well?"

The boy whispered. "They weighted their bodies, took them out to sea and dumped them."

"How they kill them?" Ware asked.

Young Cranston covered his face with both hands. His voice was muffled. "Bashed their heads in. Most of them soon after they arrived so they wouldn't have to waste food on them."

"A murder factory," Ware grunted. "Take the money from them rich folks who didn't want their own young'uns, kill the tykes, and clear out. My little Pearl is about the same age as Rosemary Fiscall. Mark, you got a couple of little girls, and Mr. Cranston, you got your Holly. How do you feel about these child killers?"

It was Piety York who answered. "They must be punished but this is a job for the law."

"Miss York is right," the minister said heavily. "These people must have justice."

"Like they showed these youngsters?" Ware called over his shoulder, "Charlie, you and Jack get in here." He waited until the Vances came through the archway. "Men, you all seen that girl. All the youngsters that came here are dead, murdered in cold blood. The schoolmarm and the minister here think we oughtta turn these Winchfields over for trial. Maybe they'd get what's coming to them, maybe not. Can't see a jury hanging Mrs. Winchfield and Kat. Good-looking women and that smarmy way Kat talks might save her from having her neck stretched. I vote we give them Amoston justice. Settle it for once and all. Let's have a show of hands. All in favor of doing it ourselves, get your hands up."

The men mumbled among themselves and then Mark Spence's hand shot up. "I vote for my sons too. Austin and Harry would've voted yes."

Other hands went up. Ware took a count. "So...only Miss York and the reverend and David against." He grimly eyed the cowering boy. "Seems to me you should be over with them." He jerked his head at the Winchfields.

"He didn't do anything," Cranston said quickly. "David didn't do a thing."

"He kept his mouth shut, didn't he?" Josiah Amos growled. "Let them children be killed. He's as guilty as the ones who done it."

Pointing a long finger at Kat, Cranston intoned, "That witch put a spell on him. David was bewitched."

"All right, he can live." Ware raised his mallet. "'Nough talking, men. Let's get it done."

80

The men surged forward, boathooks, marlin-spikes, mallets ready. Mother Winchfield screamed and ran toward the archway, her son and daughter at her heels. "Let 'em go, men," Ware bellowed. "Can't get far." As he ran toward the old man, Father Winchfield fell to his knees. He raised his hands. "Mercy," he gasped. "Mercy!"

The men were on him. A mallet battered his hands down. A hand stabbed down with a marlin-spike. Boathooks were hammered into him. He screamed once and then the only sounds were the thuds of weapons against his body. Finally the men stopped, moved away. Piety York took one look at the mashed thing on the hearth and she opened her mouth in a wild shriek. She flung herself headlong at Ware. "No," she implored, "Johnny—yes. Don't kill the women. You can't do this!"

She was wasting her breath. The men were out of control. Their eyes flaming, they shoved the teacher aside, raced into the hall. "Find them, men!" Ware howled. David crumpled to the floor but his father, his club clenched in one fist, hauled the boy along after the others.

They found Mother Winchfield in the kitchen, vainly trying to hide her plump form behind the chopping block. Rough hands hauled her off the floor, stretched her screaming across the block. Blades rose and fell, and in moments her body was cut and mangled.

"Johnny and that bitch!" Lonny Ware shouted. "Let's get 'em!"

It took longer to find Johnny. The men ranged through the house, shoving furniture aside, flinging doors open. The dreadful game of hide-and-seek was ended with a shout from one of the Amos boys. "Got him! Here, in the hall!"

Men surged into the hall. Johnny had pushed the grandfather clock away from the wall and was wedged behind it. They tore him from his hiding place. He was tall, strongly built, and he fought. His fists lashed out and he caught Jeff Ware on the bridge of the nose. Blood streamed down the man's face. Lifting his hook over his head, Jeff brought it down and viciously dragged the tip through Johnny's face. Cranston, as blood-mad as the rest, battered Johnny's head with his club. More blows hit their mark and Johnny slumped. They clawed his body into a bloody pulp.

Panting they stood back. Jeff Ware wiped at his streaming

nose and tightened the grip on his hook. "That whore," he grunted. "Where is she?"

His twin wiped wet hands off on his sweater. "Saw her running up the stairs."

"The harlot!" the crazed minister brayed. "Kill the harlot! *Kill the spawn of Satan!*"

The men, their rough clothes smeared with blood, surged up the stairs. Pulling his whimpering son along, the minister followed them. He raised his gory club and they went after Kat Winchfield. They found her—

Six

"*Stop it*." **Dorothy Quiller was** on her feet, her lips quivering. "How could you do this, Rayburn? Hou could you bring us to this...this filthy place? A minister joining in on that butchery. This house is soaked in blood. That hall out there, the block in the kitchen where our food is prepared, that spot there—" She pointed at the footstool where Nigel perched before the fire.

"Darling, calm down." Jim put his arms around his wife's shaking body.

Bewildered, Holly Amos was staring at the younger woman. "I'm sorry, ma'am. It happened so long ago. I'd no idea anyone would take on so."

Rayburn joined his son and patted his daughter-in-law's shoulder. "I assure you I had no idea of this house's history when I rented it, my dear. As Holly says it was long ago, such an old violence."

Holly flushed. Above pink cheeks her bright eyes were indignant. "That isn't the same chopping block in the kitchen! Think I'd prepare food on the one where they hacked Mother Winchfield—"

"Stop it!" Dorothy clapped both hands over her ears.

"Come on, darling," her husband said soothingly, "you're overtired. I'll get you up to bed."

He led her from the room and Rayburn, shaking his head, returned to his chair. "I had no idea this would affect Dorothy like that. I suppose I shouldn't have insisted on you telling us about it, Holly." He glanced in Tammy's direction. "Are you all right, my dear child?"

"Fine," Tammy told him in her clear voice.

"It would appear Jim was worrying about the wrong person. Any of the rest of you ladies disturbed? Thelma... Ruthie...Nadine?"

Nadine simply gave him a blank stare but Thelma chuckled. "I'm a nurse. Going to take more than that to bother me."

Ruth gave a tinkling little laugh. "You know better than that, dad. Funny, Dorothy didn't strike me as the delicate feminine type."

"Mother has always loathed violence," Tammy told them.

Nigel's eyes shifted from the shadowed corner where Tammy sat, to Ruth. His aunt was comfortably reclining in a chair near her father. Part way through Holly's recital she'd sent her husband for her coat, complaining of being cold. The mink was draped gracefully over her long silk dress. She seemed to have a preference for loose, concealing clothes, Nigel thought. Perhaps she was self-conscious because of her hands and feet. Dirty trick nature had played on her. She certainly managed to drape her clothes so one caught glimpses of those ungainly feet and hands. With interest, he regarded the boy at her side, perched like himself on a footstool. As Nigel wryly admitted, the kid wasn't much smaller than he was. Buddy was a handsome boy, giving promise of a build that would some day measure up to his oversized hands and feet. Nigel glanced back toward Tammy. Lovely bones that girl had, a pity her eyes were hidden behind those black discs.

Leaning forward, Rayburn lightly touched Nigel's arm. "Did Holly's account agree with the one you read?"

"To some degree. As I said the details were sparse. They covered the school, the murders of the children—a head count of twenty-two—and that was about it. My account said the villagers from Amoston, hearing rumors that something was amiss at the school, sent a group of their prominent citizens to investigate. When they arrived on the island the group found evidence that the students had been killed but when they tried to arrest the Winchfields they fled in their boat and perished at sea."

Rayburn turned his head, the smooth gray hair burnished by firelight. "Holly?"

"That story was my dad's idea, so's they wouldn't get in trouble over what they had to do. It was partly true too. The men took the bodies and tied them to anchor chains on the Winchfields' boat. They used Charlie Vance's trawler to tow it out to sea and they opened the sea cocks." She added soberly, "They give the little Fiscall boy a decent burial in the church graveyard."

"What happened to Rosemary?" Thelma asked.

"Her stepfather came and got her. Never heard how she made out. Guess she never was the same."

Andy Thaler ran a hand over his thinning red hair. "I don't imagine she was. Horrible experience for an adolescent. David Cranston—he was your brother, wasn't he?—how did he survive the ordeal?"

"He didn't. I never knew my older brother. 'Bout a month after the Winchfields were punished, David borrowed a little skiff from Jack Vance. Never came back. They found the boat, drifting with a sea anchor. Couldn't bear to live, my mother'd say."

Staring into the pattern of flames the fire was shooting up, Nigel said thoughtfully, "And that was the end of the Winchfields."

"Got what they deserved," Holly told him.

Nigel lifted his eyes to her round kindly face. "How do you know about this in such detail? Did your father tell you?"

"Dad never talked about it. Neither did the other men. But that night, they told their wives and, although my mother never said a word to me, the other women did. Laura Spence, she was a great one to tell it over and over."

"What about the schoolteacher—what was her name? She talk about it too?" Philip asked from where he sprawled on the carpet at Thelma's feet.

"No idea. Piety York was long gone when I got old enough to hear about the Winchfields. Left Amoston a couple of weeks after the punishment."

Andy Thaler shifted restlessly. "You keep saying punish or punishment, Holly. Hasn't it ever occurred to you that the mob from the village were no better than the Winchfields? Granted that family did a terrible thing but that was a lynch mob who murdered them."

Holly's plump body stiffened and the pink in her cheeks

deepened to an angry red. Her husband put a hand on her clenched fist and answered the doctor's question. "Folks around here never thought about it that way. Figured their men did a good night's work getting rid of those Winchfields."

Jerking her hand loose, his wife sputtered, "With her last breath that harlot cursed them. Even dying she didn't repent her sins. I'm proud, we all were proud, of what our dads and brothers did that night." Stiff backed, she started to rise.

Rayburn waved her back. "There, there, Holly, now don't take offense. Andy didn't mean any insult. Just professional interest." He shot a look at Nigel. "So, Kat Winchfield cursed them, did she?"

Rayburn had his usual calming effect. Holly managed a smile as she said, "Some folks swore Amoston was cursed. Jeb and me never thought that though, did we, Jeb?"

Shaking his shaggy head, he muttered around the pipe, "There was a lot of dying but had nothing to do with a curse. Started with Holly's brother David. Then Piety York cleared outta this area. Never heard where she went. One of the Ware twins, Lonny, had his foot almost cut off with an axe when he was chopping stove-wood. Guess in a way that accident saved his life. Lonny Ware was wild to get into the first war and couldn't on account of that foot. His twin, Jeff, was killed in the war. Lots of boys from the village died in that war. Both my brothers and Austin and Harry Spence were killed. Jack Vance too. After the war, people began to move away from Amoston. Families scattered until only my folks and Holly's was left. The Reverend Cranston wouldn't leave and my dad wouldn't budge off the farm. Now, Holly and me are the only ones left. Dad held onto the farm and I took it over but that's gone too. Not that it matters much. Both my lads dead."

In the silence that followed the caretaker's words the clear voice of Tammy Syles startled them. Heads turned in the direction of the shadowy corner where she sat. "What was your father wearing that night, Holly?"

"My dad? Don't rightly know what you mean?"

"How was he dressed?"

"'Spose the way he always was. Neat dresser, dad was. Always wore a dark suit and I guess he had oilskins on. It was a bad night."

"Did he wear a hat?"

Holly laughed. "Bless me, the questions you ask, child.

Long as I can remember dad wore a top hat. One of them shining ones, y'know. Lotta folks laughed about that hat behind his back, not to his face though. Nobody dared do that with dad."

Rayburn's head swiveled toward Tammy. "That *was* an odd question, my dear. My, we're certainly keeping Jeb and Holly up late tonight. Has anyone any more questions?"

Nigel shook his red head. "She answered mine. All the Winchfields were killed that night."

"Not all," Jeb blurted.

"Hey," Philip cried, "you're changing the story." He counted on his fingers. "Mother and father. Brother Johnny in the hall. Do you mean they let Kat live?"

"They did Kat in all right. This was just a rumor when I was growing up. Don't know if there's any truth in it or if folks was just making it up."

"Not much use of telling it," Holly chimed in. "Like Jeb says it coulda been just Laura Spence trying to make Piety look bad. Fierce jealous of that teacher, Laura was. Bad-mouthed Piety for the rest of her life."

"Holly," Nigel said, a note of excitement in his voice. "What was this rumor?"

"Laura always claimed her husband told her there was a baby—"

"A baby!" Nigel exclaimed. "Whose?"

"Mark Spence said it belonged to Kat. Just an infant. While the men were upstairs, Kat begged Piety to save the child, not to let the men—"

"One moment," Rayburn broke in. "You said the house was searched. How could they have overlooked a baby?"

"The tyke was supposed to be in Kat's room. Back in a corner in a cradle. The men looked into that room but they missed the baby. After Kat was punished, Piety went and got the little one and hid it under her skirt. The men was so fired up she figured they might bash its brains in. Baby started to cry and the men found it. Ed Ware was all for finishing it off on the spot but Piety faced him down. Mark Spence told Laura that the teacher looked into Ed's face and told him straight that he'd gone mad with killing and if he wanted to murder an innocent child he'd have to kill her first. Mark Spence said him and Jeb's dad and mine sided with Piety, and Ed didn't get his way. Folks said Piety left town so fast to protect the child from Ed Ware and see Kat's baby was raised proper." Holly lifted her brows as she stared at Nigel's intent face. "Bless me, Mr. Nigel, it was only hearsay. Laura coulda been making it up."

"So," Nigel said, "one of the Winchfields did survive."

Philip licked his thick lips. "Whose kid was it?"

Shaking her head, Holly pursed her own lips primly but her husband said, "Don't rightly know. Some said it was David Cranston's, others held out it were either her father's or Johnny's. Doesn't bear talking about."

"Most unpleasant," Rayburn agreed. "This Kat must have been an exceptional woman."

"Yes," the doctor said. "Interesting. One of those women who attract not only men but women. Laura Spence and Piety York. Hmm...sounds as though both of them had latent lesbian traits. This jealousy over Kat's favors—"

"Doctor," Thelma said with a grin, "you're sounding like a doctor. I doubt in a place like Amoston that lesbians would have been tolerated."

"Never been anything like that here," Holly blurted.

Andy raised a long hand. "Whoa. I said latent, not active. Anyway, Kat must have been a woman of intense magnetism."

"She was a devil," Holly said grimly. "Killed my brother as sure as if she'd stuck a knife in his heart."

"Do you and your husband ever feel nervous?" Nigel asked.

"What do you mean? Nervous? What of?"

"There may still be a Winchfield alive somewhere, Holly. From the description of that family they sound like a tribe who would never forget a wrong done to them."

Throwing back her head, Holly laughed. "Bless me, Mr. Nigel, you are a one."

"I can't see why Holly and Jeb should worry," Philip broke in. "Even if a Winchfield did survive—this happened before the first world war—that baby would be too decrepit now to even raise a weapon."

Holly bridled. "Younger than me and Jeb," she said tartly.

"Was it a boy or girl?" Rayburn asked.

"Don't know. Guess Piety was the only one who did. Laura Spence never said and if she'd known she sure would have told."

There was a rustling from Tammy's corner and the girl was on her feet. Rayburn peered at her. "Are you off to bed, Tammy?"

88

"Yes, I'm tired. Goodnight, all."

They watched her leave the room and then Holly said to Nigel, "Still don't rightly see what you're getting at."

Pulling himself off the footstool, he stood before the hearth, firelight silhouetting his diminutive form. His face was shadowed as he said softly, "Keep in mind that it doesn't have to be that surviving Winchfield. Children grow up, have children of their own. Grandchildren. I'll say goodnight now too."

He slipped through the ring of chairs, his child-sized figure moving swiftly toward the archway. "Wait," Holly called. "Nothing lasts that long. This was years ago."

His words drifted back. "Hate lasts, Holly, and so does revenge."

In the dark hall, Tammy had lingered. She heard what Nigel said to Holly Amos, then she turned and started quickly up the stairs. Nigel was right behind her. "Wait, Tammy, I'll walk you up to your room. I'm up in that deep freeze too."

She looked down at him. He was so short all she could see was the top of his head. "I thought you'd be in that room on the second floor."

"Our host saved that for my mother." Trotting past her, he switched on the light over the second landing. "Have to watch this next flight. It's steep."

Tammy found the switch on the third floor. The single bulb did little to cheer the dismal hall. She glanced at the double doors at the rear. Nigel followed her gaze. "I'm curious about the schoolroom too. Let's have a look, Tammy."

"It's been so long. I doubt there'll be anything left there now."

"Can't tell. This is the attic and it doesn't look as though any of the owners ever put improvements up here." He scuffed a shining boot over the worn linoleum. "Looks as if this is the original floor covering." Swinging open one of the doors, he fumbled along the wall. "No switch."

Tammy passed him. From the darkness, her voice drifted back. "There's a cord dangling from the ceiling." Another bare bulb glimmered down.

Looking up, the little man grinned. "Good thing you were here. I'd never have reached it." He looked around. "See, no renovations here. Looks like the Amoses have been using it as a storeroom."

Tammy followed his eyes. The tiny bulb cast enough light to see a pile of cartons and two old steamer trunks in one corner. Against the far wall a number of small wooden desks were stacked. On a dais at the front of the room a larger desk sat. On its dull top were a stack of magazines, a lamp with a broken china shade, and pruning shears.

Standing under the bulb, Tammy slowly revolved. On the dusty floor near her were two rocking horses, one white with a rearing head, the other a dappled gray, this one with an arched neck and a dingy red saddle. Some toys were piled behind them. She could see a couple of large dolls and several rubber balls.

Nigel waved an arm. "Most of the equipment is still here. Must have been pretty impressive at one time. The blackboard's still in place and there's the bookcase Holly mentioned. Good Lord! The slates and books are still on the shelves." Leaving the girl, he wandered toward the bookcase.

Putting out a hand, Tammy touched the mane of the gray horse. Dust flew up at her touch. Her hand moved down, along its flank, and stopped dead. She blinked.

The room was pitch black. She swung around, her back touching the rocking horse. She could feel it rocking against her body in the darkness. Had the bulb burned out? Her lips opened to call to Nigel but no sound came out. Her hand brushed her long silk skirt—it wasn't silk. It was coarser, some kind of tweed. Her fingers closed on the skirt. Serge. She was wearing a serge skirt. Her hand explored. The silk blouse was gone. Crisp cotton ruffles covered her breast. Then she understood and tried to fight free. She fought to move away from the rocking horse but not a muscle moved. This wasn't her body. Part of her was in it, but another mind was directing the movements of that body. Helpless, she probed that mind and found terror, terror and agonized waiting.

The waiting was over. Double doors flew open and a lantern was held high. Light from it threw wavering shadows over the room. Two rows of little desks were drawn up in front of the dais. The top of the large desk was bare, its polished surface gleaming. Behind it a number of brightly colored maps hung.

Men crowded into the schoolroom, some of them grasping lanterns. She could see them clearly. The man in the lead was huge, holding aloft a bloodstained mallet. In a stern bearded face, small eyes flamed redly. His mouth was moving but there was no echo of a voice. Yet she knew what he was saying, what the other men were shouting. They were swearing, calling vile names at her. Above rough clothes spattered with blood, their eyes were mad, their mouths writhing. So many of them!

A tall man, older than the rest, with a gaunt face and fanatical eyes was brandishing a club, pulling forward a cringing boy with his free hand. The minister and David, the big blacksmith, Ed Ware. That short, balding man with the sly expression—Spence, the grocer. All of them closing in on her. One of her hands moved, it was searching for something under the shirtwaist. She felt something under the cotton, something hanging from a ribbon around her neck.

Then they were on her. Hands clutched at her, ripping at her clothes, tearing the shirtwaist into shreds, hauling her serge skirt down. One of her hands tried to protect what she wore around her neck. Ware reached for it, pain in her throat as he wrenched the ribbon loose. He threw it over his shoulder. They were pushing her down, down to the floor. The body she was in was fighting, fighting for more than its life. She felt her fingers twisting, clawing into a bearded face. She smelled the rank odors of the men she was fighting—fish, sweat, blood. Foul breaths gusted into her face. She clawed at another face, her nails raking at flesh and then agonizing pain in that hand. A boathook! The grocer had driven a boathook through her wrist.

Her mouth opened and although there was no sound, she knew she was screaming. The hands abruptly fell away. A tall woman was fighting the men. Piety York. Tammy felt the body she was in pull itself up on an elbow. The fingers of the uninjured hand were pointing. She caught the other woman's wild eyes. She pointed. Piety jerked her head in a nod before Ed Ware's fist drove into her chest and knocked her backward. But she'd understood, Piety had understood!

The men were swarming over her again. Kill me, she begged, get it over with! Oh God, they were fumbling at her clothes, unbuttoning shabby pants. Punish you, they were howling, give you what a whore deserves. Hands were brutally pinning her down, others were forcing her legs apart. The pain! Jesus God, no! *No.*

She still fought...she still... "Tammy!" a voice was crying. "Tammy! Stop it!"

Tammy blinked and looked up at the ceiling. A light bulb glowed with a dull, yellowish light. Nigel's head, his red hair blazing, was silhouetted against the light. The nightmare forms were gone. But the pain! She curled in a ball, whimpering with pain, both hands clasping her stomach.

Nigel stared down at her. "I'll get your mother and Andy—"

"No," she moaned, "give me a moment."

"You need a doctor. I was at the bookcase and heard a thud. When I turned you were on the floor. It looked like a convulsion."

"No, I'll be all right." With his help, she pulled herself up and braced her shoulders against something hard, something that cut into her flesh. The rockers on the gray horse were cutting into her back. She squirmed around. "This is where they murdered her. Right here."

His eyes narrowed. "Kat?"

The girl buried her face in her hands. "No matter what she did, she didn't deserve that! No woman deserves a death like that."

His arms were around her shaking shoulders. "I still think I should get your mother."

Her hands fell away from her eyes and she looked into the face close to hers. "Not my mother. She doesn't like anything unpleasant." Tammy fumbled at her face. Her glasses were missing.

"Here," Nigel put them into her hand. "They fell off while you were fighting. Whew, can you fight!"

"Did I hurt you?"

"I'll have a few bruises. Nothing serious." He peered down at her. "What did you see?"

"What does it matter?" She pushed the glasses back on her nose. "Don't you understand? I'm a patient in a mental institution. I'm subject to hallucinations." She added brokenly, "Usually I can control it but tonight...the way Holly told that story I could see it." She shuddered. "See them. Feel them."

Nigel's face was now expressionless, cold. "Tell me."

She shrugged. "If you enjoy hallucinations, all right. They beat her and they raped her. Even the man of God was in on it. The brave group of avengers from Amoston, like a bunch of mad dogs."

"Did you see Piety York?"

"She tried to stop them. The blacksmith hit her."

"Kat—did she have a piece of jewelry on?"

Tammy frowned. "Jewelry? I don't know. There was some-

thing she was worried about, even when they were...
something around her throat."

"What?"

"I don't know. It seemed to be on a cord or ribbon. When they stripped her the men tore it off. Threw it in that corner." Tammy pointed to a corner and Nigel looked around as though expecting to see something there. She forced herself to try to remember. "Kat was trying to show Piety where it was." Her voice was mocking as she asked, "Satisfied?"

"More than you'd believe. Tell me, was it your psychiatrist who convinced you about these hallucinations?"

Tammy struggled to her knees and Nigel put a hand under her elbow and helped her up. He grinned up at her. "Now would be a nice time to sweep you up in stalwart arms and carry you to your room." He spread his short arms wide. "Alas, that is beyond my simple powers. Now, if it were the other way around—" Breaking off, he said sharply, "You didn't answer my question."

"You haven't given me a chance to." She brushed dust from her skirt. "I've never had a psychiatrist."

"What about good old Doctor Thule?"

"How do you know about him?"

"I know a lot of things, Tammy."

"Then you must know he's an M.D."

"Of course Thule's an M.D.," Nigel said patiently. "A psychiatrist has to have that degree."

"A medical degree is the only one that Dr. Thule has."

His eyes widened. "Are you telling me a man who isn't a psychiatrist is running a place for disturbed young people?"

"It's a small, very exclusive one. More like a resort. He's most reassuring to the parents. Tell them exactly what they want to hear."

"Sounds like a quack."

"No, not that. Dr. Thule is sincere, kind. He does do some good."

"And his so-called school?"

"A resort," she repeated. "Very posh. We play tennis, take courses. Our parents visit and play games with us. Cosy."

"What sort of treatment does he use?"

"Mainly tranquillizers. And he talks to us."

"Cosy indeed, and he's convinced you that you hallucinate."

"Over imaginative. A nice way of saying loony." Her

mouth tightened. "I've no idea why you're so interested in insanity."

Putting both hands behind his back, he quoted solemnly, "'Teach me half the gladness/That thy brain must know,/Such harmonious madness/From my lips would flow/The world would listen then—as I am listening now.'"

"Shelley, and not even appropriate."

"An, so you enjoy quotes too."

"I read a lot." She gazed down at the tiny man. "Try this one—'One gets into situations in life from which it is necessary to be a little mad to extricate oneself successfully.'"

He clapped his hands. "Bravo! La Rochefoucauld! We must have a contest one day. I see you have an extraordinary memory too."

She moved away from him, toward the doors. He called after her. "Tammy, would you get the light?"

He waited while she tugged at the cord and stayed close to her as they moved through the darkness. Tammy found she was glad of his company. As she opened the door to her own room, he tugged at her sleeve. "There's a bar on my door. Do you have one on yours?"

"Yes."

"Pull it to, that's a good girl."

"Why?"

His smile was impish. "Never can tell. I might walk in my sleep. Goodnight."

He watched her door swing to and then turned to his own room. Tammy quickly pulled off her clothes, shivering in the cold air, and donned pyjamas. The thought of Rosemary Fiscall imprisoned in this room with the decaying body of her little brother brushed Tammy's mind but she resolutely pushed it away. The barrier. After her experience in the schoolroom she could stand no more. Climbing into bed, she reached for the lamp. As she did she heard a clicking sound. Perhaps a branch scraping at the window. Then she remembered there were no tall trees on the island, certainly none outside her own window. Later that night she awoke, remembered Nigel's words, and switched on the lamp. The bolt to her door was pulled across. She buried her head in the pillow again. She must have barred the door without even realizing it. Somehow it was reassuring, and she drifted off into a sound, peaceful sleep.

* * *

Across the hall from the girl's room, Nigel stretched his stockinged feet toward the circle of warmth from the electric heater. His mother, perched on the sole chair in the room, frowned down at his reclining figure. "I still don't know how you guessed I was here. I didn't make a sound and the light wasn't on."

"No mystery. Your perfume is rather heady. What I can't guess is why you were lurking in here."

"Waiting for you, but you were busy. What were you and that girl doing all that time?"

"Having a look at the schoolroom."

"I saw you eyeing her all evening. Even while Holly was talking you were watching her." She leaned over him. "Nigel, you're not here for idle flirtation."

He regarded Nadine. When she allowed her face to relax she was a fine-looking woman. One could almost believe her pretensions to gypsy blood. She had the right coloring. Her olive skin was unblemished, her dark eyes magnificent under arched brows, hardly a thread of white showed in thick black hair. As a girl, when she'd captivated Micah Quiller, she must have been startlingly lovely. "Don't tell me what to do," he warned her. Then he pushed himself up on an elbow. "After I left the drawing room—"

"Chasing that girl."

"Did Holly say anything about Kat's death?"

The arched brows drew together in thought. "Both Rayburn and that queer-looking son of Jim's—what's his name? Philip? They both questioned Holly but she seemed to close up. She did say Kat was killed in the schoolroom."

"I know why she was reluctant to give details. Kat was raped before they finished her off and Holly's daddy was in on it."

"How do you know?"

"The very best authority." He stretched his small frame. "I'm bushed. At the risk of sounding rude I'm going to ask you to spit it out. What do you want now?"

Nadine took a deep breath. "When are you going to act?"

"We had it out about that, mother. When I'm good and ready. If I act at all."

Her mouth twisted. "Nigel, my son...my son. They murdered your father."

"Don't turn on the dramatics and for God's sakes, don't

cry. I told you when you got this harebrained idea that I'd come and have a look. I didn't promise I'd act."

"But you've seen them!" She flung her arms wide. "Your father's blood is crying out for vengeance!"

Sitting up, he hugged his knees to his chest. His face was set in cold, remote lines. "Not only did I never know my father but there's no real evidence that he died any way but by his own hand. I tracked down his death certificate, mother, he hanged himself."

"Who signed it?" she shot back.

"Doctor John Andrew Thaler."

"Ruth's husband. I told you of Ruth's power over men."

"You've told me everything, time and time again. Andy Thaler wasn't even married to Ruth then. He'd just met her."

"But that's *how* he met her. When Rayburn called him in because of Micah. Ruth can twist men around her finger. Whatever they wanted, that doctor would have done." Jumping to her feet, she loomed over her son. "*When* will you act?"

"Be reasonable. We only got here this morning. Sit down."

"You haven't the guts. Admit it." She waved her arms wildly. "I demand you act! I raised you for this. I want those monsters—"

"I—always *you*. What about *me*? Now sit!"

The chair, behind the woman, lurched, catching her behind the knees. She collapsed into it, tears streaming down her cheeks. She whispered huskily, "Would you use this against your own mother?"

His voice was as cold as his expression. "Be quiet, mother, and stop that crying. I want to think."

"Rayburn?"

"Something like that."

Rayburn was two floors down from Nadine and her son, sitting at the pine-topped table in the cavernous kitchen. Light streamed from the center fixture on his smooth gray hair and the assortment of small dishes on the table. Dipping a spoon carefully into one dish, he smeared a dark substance on a cracker. When the door swung open, the cracker was halfway to his mouth.

"Jim," he called, "have you settled your wife down?"

His son took the chair opposite him. "She's not in good shape. I had Andy give her a sedative."

"I'm sorry. I had no idea...why did Holly's story hit her so hard?"

"Must have been the minister in it. Dorothy's father was a minister and, from what I've heard, the same type as the Reverend Cranston. A real hellfire and brimstone man. Dorothy's mother died when she was just a kid and her father raised her his own way. Practically kept her in jail and drummed in sin and sex until she was close to frigid."

"How did Syles meet her?"

"Dropped into her father's church and spotted Dorothy in the choir. She was only seventeen. Marc was extremely wealthy, years older than Dorothy, and a man of the world. All sins in her father's eyes. Dorothy ran away with Marc and they were married but her father disowned her."

Pointing at a dish, Rayburn said, "Like some?"

"Caviar. And I'll bet it isn't lumpfish."

"Iranian and delicious."

Jim touched the goblet in front of his father. "Vintage wine?"

"Latour, '64."

"You're cultivating expensive tastes, dad."

Rayburn's heavy shoulders moved in a shrug. "I've always had them but most of my life I haven't been able to gratify them. But that's changed now, hasn't it?" Without waiting for an answer, he continued, "I suppose Dorothy had emotional scars from her early years."

"She still has."

"Yet she seems so well balanced, a thoroughly modern woman. I notice she even swears."

"Deliberately, still trying to rebel against a father who's been dead for years. But she found marriage with Marc a hell, thought sex was sinful and filthy."

Sticking a cracker heaped with caviar in his mouth, Rayburn spoke around it. "You thawed her out nicely."

Dull red flooded into his son's face. "I'd rather not discuss my wife," he said stiffly.

Throwing back his head, Rayburn bellowed with laughter. "Touchy, eh? I've a hunch you had a yen for her long before her husband died. That was a convenient accident, wasn't it? At one crack disposed of a wife you couldn't stand and the husband standing in your way."

"I won't gratify that with an answer, dad. Anyway, you read about their deaths."

"Relax, Jim, I was only needling. You have a soft shell. You look like me but that's a lot of your mother in you."

The younger man's expression softened. "I wish she'd lived long enough for me to be able to remember her. She looked like Ruth, didn't she?"

Rayburn was gazing past his son, his eyes focused as though they were searching back through time. "Yes, my gentle Jenny looked much like Ruthie but she was even more beautiful."

"You've never got over her, have you?"

"I never wanted to." Rayburn put a hand on his chest and his eyes snapped back to his son's face. "I have her right here. Jenny didn't have to die. I protected her from everything else but I couldn't protect her from herself. Keep in mind it was that infernal softness that killed your mother...and your brother. I lost them through it but I won't have it harm you." He lowered his voice. "Remember something else too, Jim. You've enjoyed being a wealthy woman's husband, the country club existence, your importance in the community, but you are my son. Despite the waning of parental authority I'm the head of this family. When I'm gone the Quiller family will be your responsibility. Until then you'll obey me."

"Unquestioned obedience," Jim said bitterly.

"Exactly. You owe everything to your family. We sacrificed to educate you. If you pride yourself on your success, put credit where it's due."

"Which brings me to a question. You insisted I bring Dorothy and Tammy too. What do you have in mind?"

Scooping up the rest of the caviar, Rayburn spread it on a cracker. "What a convenient memory you have, Jim."

"I want to know."

"I don't come to hasty decisions. In time I'll let you know." Rayburn's big hand tightened on the knife. "You've fallen for that woman, haven't you?"

"I'm fond of her," Jim muttered.

"Tammy?"

"The girl's suffered, dad, she's gone through hell. Yes, I'm fond of her too." He scraped back his chair. "I don't want them hurt."

Jim lunged toward the door and his father's voice followed him. "Remember Micah."

"How can I forget him? Especially with his weird widow and a dwarf son among us!" Jim banged through the swinging door. Behind him his father sighed and reached for the wine bottle.

Stepping into his daughter's room, Rayburn nudged the bathroom door closed with his foot. He wore a woolen robe, his hair was still damp from the shower, and he carefully balanced two frosted glasses.

Ruth was curled up under a satin comforter on the four-poster bed. Sitting up, she reached for a glass. She took a sip and said, "Superb."

"I pride myself on my Gibsons." He sank into an armchair beside the bed. "Buddy asleep?"

She glanced toward the large crib in the corner. "Hours ago. What kept you so long?"

"Having a conversation with your brother." He stirred the icy liquid with a speared onion. "Long overdue."

"Trouble?"

"Might be. Jim's grown away from us." Setting his empty glass down, he stretched out both hands. "Come to papa."

She shook her head, her hair swirling around her face. "Too cold. Must we always be in a house full of drafts?"

"Not for much longer, my love." He stood up and took a couple steps to the bed. "If the mountain won't come to Mahomet—move over."

She moved over and he stretched his long frame beside her, an arm sliding around her shoulders. He cradled her head on his shoulder. He whispered in her ear. "I think it's about time you get to know your brother better. Families shouldn't grow apart."

Her eyes sparkled. "Mirror, mirror on the wall..."

With a finger he traced the lines beside one of her eyes. "Crow's-feet, Ruthie, we all grow older."

She wrenched away from him. "Cruel! Must you be like this?" Pulling herself up, she faced him. Her nightgown slid down, baring the luscious curve of a breast. "Three of you gloating over that girl as though she were a piece of raw meat."

"Three?"

"First that Brome boy and then Nigel. You—I've watched you eyeing her. Why I can't see." Hunching her shoulders, she put one hand over her eyes. " A long stringy kid who can't be more than sixteen."

"Nineteen, Ruthie, and despite your caricature of her a

very delectable female. You can't stand the company of lovely women, can you? Unfortunately for you, every woman isn't as plain as your daughter-in-law. Tammy's mother isn't bad, either."

She clawed at his face. Laughing, he grabbed her hand and pulled her back into his arms. Holding her in a powerful grip, he caressed her hair. After a moment she stopped fighting and smiled. "So...Jim's giving you trouble. I told you he'd fallen for Dorothy."

"You were right." Rayburn sighed heavily. "The boys looks like me but he's like Micah with some of his mother's nature in him. You're the one who takes after papa. Too bad you hadn't been a boy."

"You really wouldn't have wanted that." Her teeth flashed. "Don't worry about Jim."

"Use discretion, Ruthie. I've a feeling where her husband's concerned that Dorothy is on a short fuse."

"Does it matter?"

"For the next few days I'd prefer a harmonious atmosphere. After that..."

She pulled the comforter over him. "Six," she murmured. "Six little lambs."

"It may be only five."

"Nigel makes me uneasy. He's no lamb."

A frown drew her father's dark bars of brows together. "Nigel's a complete enigma. He's witty and intelligent and he's also too sure of himself. As though he knows something we don't. I don't like the way he researched this island."

"He explained that, dad. His hobby. Let's forget about them for now."

"Even the delectable Tammy?"

She slapped him and, laughing, they struggled. In the shadowed corner there was furtive movement in the crib. Between the bars, wide eyes stared as unblinkingly at the bed as Holly Amos's Persian cat had at the *Caravan* as it entered the cove.

Seven

Toward morning the wind veered and when the people in the Winchfield house rose they found sunlight streaming in their windows. With brighter weather their spirits lightened. Only Holly Amos seemed out of sorts that morning. Rayburn Quiller watched her serving breakfast and noticed she was limping.

"The rheumatism," she complained. "Always acts up when there's a change of weather."

"You'd better take some time off and get off your feet," he told her genially.

With professional interest, Andy Thaler regarded her drawn face. "Would you like me to give you a painkiller, Holly?"

"No, sir, I have some pills. A little laydown and I'll be good as new. What about lunch, Mr. Rayburn?"

"We'll cope and for dinner too. Thelma can manage. Can't you, my dear?"

"You know how well I can cook," she muttered.

Rayburn's eyes moved to Dorothy. "How are you at culinary arts?"

"I can make a decent cup of coffee and throw together a salad but I've never really done any cooking."

He chuckled. "Well, you and Thelma take care of the washing up. Perhaps make sandwiches for lunch. We'll deal with dinner later."

He sent Holly, leaning heavily on her husband's arm, to her cottage. Thelma and Dorothy started to clear the table and the rest of the Quillers drifted away. Taking her brother's hand, Ruth led him toward the staircase. Dorothy called after them and Jim swung around. "Ruth and I are going to have a game of chess, darling. We used to play when we were children."

"I thought we might go for a walk, Jim."

"Later, maybe this afternoon."

Dorothy gazed after them, wondering about her own resentment. Silly, she told herself, begrudging Jim's spending time with a sister he hasn't seen in years. Picking up a stack of dishes, she followed Thelma to the kitchen. Thelma stood at the sink, gazing morosely around. "With that fridge and stove you'd think they'd have a dishwasher, wouldn't you?" She banged open a cupboard and pulled out a bottle of liquid soap. Turning on a tap, she watched the soap bubble up. "Always a workhorse is good old Thelma."

Dorothy searched through the drawers until she found the one where dishtowels were piled. She pulled a couple out. "Does the family work together?"

"Andy and Norm and me work. Ruth's ornamental and Ray charms the old ladies."

"Jim says you run a nursing home for the aged."

"That's right." Thelma plunged her hands into the soapy water.

"Profitable?"

"Not so's you'd notice. Not much money in them on a small scale. But we're through with that now. Ray's retired."

On Marc's money, Dorothy guessed wryly. She tried to divert her thoughts. "Will you and Norm stay on with his dad?"

A cup slipped out of Thelma's hands and crashed against the edge of the counter. Gingerly, she picked up the pieces of china. "We haven't decided."

Dorothy regarded the younger woman's broad back. "How did you meet Norm?"

"In a hospital. He was doing janitor work and I was nursing." Without looking around, she said, "Better have a look in the fridge. We'll have to find something for lunch."

Opening the fridge door, Dorothy peered in. "Some lamb

left from last night. Cooked ham too. Pickles, mustard. Yes, lots for sandwiches."

Tammy called from the swinging door, "Need any help?"

Her mother ignored her, but Thelma smiled and said, "Not now. Just about done."

Swinging the door to, the girl walked down the hall. She stopped to get her jacket but when she stepped out on the veranda she found she didn't really need it. The air was close to balmy. As she passed the forlorn chrysanthemum, she paused. The tight buds were starting to uncurl and she gently touched a bronze petal. Walking swiftly away from the house, Tammy turned down the rocky path. Jeb was making his slow way up toward her. He plucked the pipe from his mouth. "Going for a walk?"

"I thought I'd stop in and see Holly."

"She'll be glad to see you. Walk right in."

Tammy didn't walk in. She lifted the bright mermaid and let the tail clatter against the blue door. Holly's voice drifted out. "Come on in. Oh, Tammy, how nice of you to stop in."

With pleasure, Tammy gazed around the room. It was much as she'd pictured it, snug and warm, sunlight falling across a polished wooden floor, plants arranged along the window sills, the big cat curled up in front of the potbelly stove. Holly was reclining on a sofa, an orange-and-brown afghan pulled over her plump body.

"Sit down, child. That rocker there is comfortable."

"What a lovely home you have."

"Kinda old-fashioned but we like it. Bits and pieces from both our family homes. That desk in the corner was my dad's and that little spinet belonged to my mother. That chair there—" Holly pointed at an aged morris chair near the stove, "—that came from Jeb's home. Belonged to his dad. Should be recovered but never seem to find time to do it."

The old chair was shabby with several burn marks on the seat and arms. The narrow table beside it was crowded with pictures, some in frames, small snapshots propped up against them. Holly followed the girl's eyes. "That's my dad there and next to it is a picture taken when our lads were in school. Got a better one of them but Tommy and Pat are in uniform in it and Jeb won't let me put it out."

Wandering over, Tammy examined the collection of family pictures. She avoided the Reverend Cranston's pictured likeness. That narrow face, blazing eyes, and tight mouth she'd seen before. Pat Amos had his grandfather's features but his expression was milder. The other boy she merely glanced at. She'd glimpsed that round, laughing face before. "Tommy looked like you," she said.

"Picture of me, coloring too. Wish I could offer you a cuppa."

Tammy turned around. "Could I make tea for you or do you need—"

"Jeb gave me some before he left. But you might stick a couple of pieces of wood in that stove. Feel the chill when I'm like this. My hips, y'know. Ache something fierce."

Leaning over the wood box, Tammy told the older woman, "Empty. Where is the wood kept?"

"In the shed out through the kitchen. Don't try to lug too much. Jeb'll be back soon and he can get a load."

Following the pointing finger, Tammy wandered into a kitchen as bright and cheerful as the living room. She glanced through a doorway into a tiny bedroom with a patchwork quilt covering a double bed and an old-fashioned dressing table crowded with more pictures. The shed, tacked on to the end of the building, was as neat as the rest of the house. Hoes, rakes, and shovels hung on the walls, cordwood was piled in orderly rows against the outer wall, and two large metal drums sat near the door. As she bent for the wood, she saw a cardboard box filled to overflowing with empty liquor bottles.

Back in the living room, she stepped around the cat to dump her armload of wood. Gingerly, she stuck the metal lifter into the hole on the hot lid and poked a couple of chunks of wood into the stove. Then she bent to pet the cat.

"Careful," Holly warned. "Old Blue's ornery." As the animal arched his back against the caressing hand, she said, "Bless me, he takes to you. You got a way with animals."

Scooping the cat up, Tammy returned to the rocking chair. Old Blue touched her chin with his moist nose and started to purr. She ran a hand over his soft back. "How old is he?"

"Can't rightly remember. He was Tommy's. Just a kitten when the boy left. Powerful fond of cats, was Tommy. Last thing he said was, 'Look after Blue.' Jeb and me look after him too." Shifting, Holly rubbed at her hip. "This dang rheumatism. Sure hope I haven't put Mr. Rayburn out."

"He's an expert at allocating work," Tammy told her drily.

"Don't worry, Holly. By the way, what are those drums in the shed. Oil?"

"Gas for our old boat. Jeb's set in his ways. Carries a pail down to refuel but won't leave the drums in the boathouse."

"Isn't it dangerous keeping it there?"

"Not with my Jeb. May be careless with his pipe but watches hisself close around that gas." Her plump hand left her hip and massaged her temples. "Got a headache too. Didn't sleep peaceful last night. Mr. Nigel kinda bothered me. Still can't see what he was getting at." The blue eyes searched Tammy's face. "You think there's anything in what he said?"

"Hate and vengeance? I really don't know, Holly."

"He said they last. Sent cold shivers up my back. Told Jeb, if'n anyone was going to come after us, they'd done it years ago. Anyway, Jeb and me had nothing to do with it. Just young'uns at the time. Sure, our dads did but they been dead and gone a long time."

Tammy's eyes were fixed on the cat curled up on her lap. "When they left Amoston, where did Ed Ware and the Spence family go."

"Ed's wife died in the 'flu epidemic after the war. Jeff never came back from the trenches and Lonny moved out to Utah. Married there, we heard. Ed got old and couldn't look after hisself so he and his daughter Pearl went to live with a cousin. Don't rightly know where. Mark and Laura Spence?" Holly frowned. "Haven't thought of them in years. Both Mark's boys was killed in the war. Mark was a lot older than Laura and he died...guess it were in the twenties. Laura kept the store on for a time but she couldn't make a go. Folks had moved away and then the Depression come. Seems to me Laura and her two stepdaughters went out to the west coast, maybe Washington."

"And the Vances?"

"Charlie was a widower. His son Jack was killed in the war. Charlie had a stroke about '28. Think he was in a hospital somewhere when he died." Holly waved a hand. "Over half a century ago. Hard to remember." She rubbed at her brow again. "I think Mr. Nigel was just talking. Too long ago, nothing lasts that long."

Vendettas do, Tammy said under her breath. Aloud she said, "I must be getting along. I don't want to tire you."

Holly pushed her plump body up on an elbow. "Mind you

eat a good lunch. Tell Mr. Rayburn I'll try to get back in the morning. Some roast lamb left from dinner last night and—"

"Stop worrying, Holly, we're not helpless. Take care now."

Carrying the cat over, Tammy put it down beside the older woman. Purring, old Blue tucked his front paws under his chest. She paused at the door, waved at the caretaker, and then she stepped out into the sunlight. Perched on a rock near the door was a small figure. It was Nigel, idly swinging his short legs. He pointed at a wicker basket near his feet. "Like to share my picnic lunch?"

"Do you have enough?"

"Plenty. I made some sandwiches and a thermos of coffee." He grinned. "The cooks are acting like sorcerer's apprentices and that dining room is like a morgue. What about a jolly lunch under the sky?"

"I accept. Where will we eat?"

Jumping off the rock, he picked up the basket. "This way, madam. Jeb tells me there's a good spot down thisaway. We'll find some shelter from the wind and dine in style."

Tammy followed him. Instead of turning through the cut in the cliff leading to the pier, he continued straight on. They rounded a rocky outjutting and before them was a tiny half-moon beach. A few stunted pines sheltered it and gulls wheeled overhead. They found a large, flat rock and Nigel opened the basket. He spread out bundles wrapped in waxed paper, a red thermos, two plastic cups, a jar of sweet pickles, and some paper towels. "Couldn't find napkins. Poor man's serviettes." He sketched a bow to the girl. "Dig in."

Tammy dug in. The sandwiches were good—rye bread, lots of mayonnaise, slices of Spanish onion, ham. Around a mouthful of food, her companion said thickly, "You're with a friend. How about taking off the shades?"

She hesitated and then shrugged and snapped the glasses off. His wide-set eyes moved over her face. "Eyes like that shouldn't be hidden, Tammy," he told her softly. "'Was this the face that launched a thousand ships?'"

Tammy thought for a moment. "'And burnt the topless towers of Ilium?'"

He applauded. "I've met my match! Oh, vanity. Another of my accomplishments equaled. What other accomplishments have you?"

She wiped her hands on a paper towel. "I'm a good swim-

106

mer, a fair tennis player. I play bridge adequately but I don't like it. I sketch and work in oils and read a great deal. What about you?"

He threw some crusts and watched gulls glide in to fight over them. "I'm a history buff and I study old crimes."

"I know that. What do you do for a living?"

He fingered the bridge of his well-shaped nose. "How mundane. Are you really interested or are you making polite conversation?"

"Curious."

"An honest lass. Wondering how a man merely thirty-nine inches high and about ninety pounds soaking wet makes out in this world of giants. Actually, very well. I started working at a tender age. Of course the milieu was perfect. A circus—"

"Surely not a sideshow?"

"Hardly. Mother paved the way for me. She started out as a waitress, began reading teacups in a cafe, and became enamored of fortune telling. By the time I was in my early teens she was working as a gypsy fortune teller with a circus, one that toured small towns in the midwest. I became a clown, great on pratfalls and driving kiddy cars. When mother left the circus and started as a medium in Los Angeles, I worked in movies and TV bit parts. There are generally no meaty roles for dwarfs. Of course, there are possibilities. Think of the great hobbit I would make if they ever filmed Tolkien's masterpiece with live actors." Springing up, he faced the girl. "Some hair on my heels, a brightly colored suit, and lo! A perfect Frodo!"

"How about Gollum?"

Immediately he hunched forward and wiggled. Slanting his head, he peered slyly up at her and whispered throatily, "Gollum, gollum. What's in your pockets, precious. Nice fresh f-fishes?"

Throwing back her head, Tammy roared with laughter. He touched her knee. "That's the first time I've heard you laugh. Nice sound, should do it more often. Back to my life history. Money was scarce and then I stumbled on my true vocation. Standing before you is none other than Lila Linder, Polly Paren, and Martha Cerne." Jutting his jaw, he stuck out his chest. "Also that red-blooded, muscle-bound hero— Tex Rocher."

"Lila Linder...Tex Rocher?"

"I thought you were a reader."

Her eyes widened. "Are you a writer?"

"Using the term loosely...yes."

"I'm sorry. I don't believe I've read any of your books."

He scrambled up and perched on the rock at her side. "Don't be sorry, you haven't missed anything. That's why I use pseudonyms. Potboilers. Nursie bedpan stories. Light romances where the heroine always sports a pert nose and three tiny freckles. Never could figure out why three instead of two or four."

"And Tex Rocher?"

"The author of the Rock Stone books. Westerns. Tall in the saddle and blazing sixguns."

"Why do you write this sort of thing?"

"Why not? Fair money and only one plot. Twist it a little, add a few gimmicks and for the faithful readers—yet another pot of harmless drivel."

Tammy started to gather up the debris from their lunch. Picking up scraps of waxed paper, the thermos, cups, and paper towels, she packed them back into the basket. Leaning back she enjoyed the warmth of the sun on her head, her shoulders. "Funny," she said dreamily, "a full stomach, a sunny day. Does wonders, doesn't it?"

"To say nothing of a bright, sparkling companion."

"Modesty is certainly not one of your accomplishments."

He stretched languidly. "Honesty is, to a certain extent."

"What are the others doing?" she asked drowsily.

"As I said the two cooks were bumbling around, trying to make lunch. Jim and Ruth and that kid Buddy are closeted in her room. In fact, that's what Thelma was grouching about when I was working in the kitchen. They'd sent down for their meal and she had to make up a tray for them." He shot a look at the girl's relaxed face. "Your mother had an expression like a storm warning."

"She's jealous of her husband."

He smiled. "Should be a husband here who's jealous of his wife. Cousin Philip was hanging around the kitchen devouring Thelma with his eyes as though she was *his* lunch."

"Where was Norman?"

"Following his granddaddy around. Rayburn's doing a little manual labor."

"You're joking."

"Uh-uh. All togged out in working gear—checked shirt,

Levi's, even a Stetson—chopping firewood beside the house. Norman was stacking it. Rayburn told me he likes to sweat occasionally. Keeps him fit."

"He does look in good shape. How old would he be?"

"No idea." Nigel stretched out beside her on the warm rock. "Young enough to have an eye for a pretty lass."

"I've felt the eye."

"No harm in looking. Can't blame him either. You'd be something to look at if you'd throw away those glasses and straighten up."

Her eyes snapped open. "Why don't you mind your own business?"

"Haven't got much of my own. Enjoy poking into other people's." Without changing his tone, he asked, "Did you know Kat Winchfield *did* die in the schoolroom?"

"So?"

"Still trying to tell me you hallucinate? Let's discuss old Doctor Thule—"

"Let's not." She jumped off the rock. Picking up her jacket, she walked away from him.

He called after her, "Tammy, come back."

"Go poke your nose in someone else's business."

Angrily, she stalked across the sand, located the beginning of the path and marched up it. Nigel was the same as everyone else, picking and poking at her. Her glasses dangled from her hand. She started to lift them toward her face and then she jammed them in a pocket. Her anger was fading and remorse was taking its place. She shouldn't have been so curt to Nigel. Why did she constantly react with such hostility? She kept blaming her mother because she couldn't or wouldn't sit down and discuss her problem and yet when Nigel tried to she flared up and walked away. I'm *afraid*, Tammy admitted, afraid of someone getting past the defenses I've built up, afraid of becoming fond of anyone. Afraid of suffering from another loss of a loved one as I've suffered for my father.

Automatically she started to turn toward the Amoses' cottage and the main house; then she changed her mind and continued down to the cove. She stumbled and rocks flew noisily down the path before her. Folding her jacket, she put it down on the pier and sat on it, her long legs dangling over the water.

The cove stretched out, the water calm and pale blue. Hard to remember it as it had been for the last few days, gray, capped with white, whipped into raging waves. She shaded her eyes. A boat was making the turn into the cove, coming around smartly, and heading for the pier. She recognized the stubby lines of the *Caravan*. As it drew closer she could make out Rob Brome's unruly dark hair and wide shoulders. He drew the boat expertly in until it nudged at the pier.

"Miss Syles," he called and tossed her a line.

"Let's make it Tammy," she called back.

"It's a deal." Jumping onto the pier, he took the line and snugged it around a stanchion. "Enjoying the change in weather?"

"Love it. I hope it lasts."

"May hold for a few days but don't expect it for long. Not on this coast." He scrambled back on the deck and picked up a small carton. "Grab this."

She took it from him. For its size it was heavy. "What is it?"

"No idea. Found it in the storeroom and figured I'd forgotten it when I brought out the supplies Mr. Quiller ordered. I thought I'd better bring it out." He eyed her slender figure, the hair blowing brightly around her face, the beautiful blue eyes in that face. "Now that I'm here, would you care to come out for a while? Nice day on the water."

Amazed at her own eagerness, she scooped up her jacket, unwound the line, threw it onto the deck, and jumped after it. Rob moved to the wheel and clicked on the engine. Standing at his side, Tammy watched the pier recede. His hands were deft and sure, turning the boat out of the cove, making a wide circle and then heading out to sea. The water was choppier but Tammy braced herself, welcoming the plunging motion under her boots. Spray blew back across her face and whipping hair and she enjoyed that too. He eyed her. "You really like boats, don't you?"

"Perhaps some day I'll have one of my own." He has sailor eyes, she thought, deep, graven wrinkles around them, clear, the look of facing into long distances. Nice eyes. "How long have you been handling boats?" she asked.

"I spent most of my boyhood on the sea. Dad was a fisherman until he hurt his leg. We moved here and mom and he started the cafe and motel. During summer vacations I used to help out by taking tourists out to fish."

"Charter boat?"

"Uh-huh. Made enough money to help put me through the

110

university. Plus what I made waiting tables and so on during the term. Mom and dad got away yesterday and they were glad to go. Climate's tough on them here during the winter now. They headed south, into your state, to soak up a little sun." He paused and then added, "They won't be coming back this time. Dad's looking around for a piece of property in Florida."

"What about the motel and cafe?"

"It will be on the market next spring."

Pushing her hair away from her face, she looked up at him. "Have you made any plans yourself?"

His mouth set. "No," he said curtly.

Lord, Tammy thought, hit a sore point. I'm as nosey as Nigel. She turned around to look back at the island but it was out of sight. She felt a touch on her arm and Rob said slowly, "Sorry, didn't mean to snap you off like that. It's just...well, everyone keeps after me. 'Do something with your life,' they say. 'Use that degree you worked so hard to get.' Take my mother for instance. She means well but she's been difficult. She's forever explaining to perfect strangers— like she did with you people—that her boy's not really lazy, just nuts."

"I know how you feel. There's still a type of shame people feel about mental problems, but my mother is the direct opposite. She prefers to think I'm mad."

"Why?"

"Because if she believes I'm sane it will mean facing unpleasant facts. Mother takes the safe course. Tammy is mad."

"Safe, that's the word you used the other day. You said you wanted to feel safe."

"Don't we all?"

He gave a bitter laugh. "Right. Here I am hiding my head like an ostrich too. It isn't that I haven't tried. God, but I've tried. You were right when you said I was hiding, mainly from myself, I guess. But unless you were there, you can't know what that goddamn country was like, what that war did to a guy. When I enlisted, I was a hundred percent patriot. Off to war so we wouldn't be fighting on beaches in California. What a bunch of bullshit! I watched some of my buddies killed, others going to pieces, everyone trying to stay juiced up...drugs were so easy to get and tempting to use. That steaming, rotten place. Fighting shadows, not knowing who we were fighting or even why—" He stopped abruptly, took

111

a long, gulping breath, and said, "Sorry, Tammy, I shouldn't be dumping this on you."

She looked compassionately at his tortured face, his baffled sailor's eyes. "Perhaps it will help. Did you get into drugs?"

"I held off for a while. There was a girl—"

Tammy had let the barrier slip. Without warning, she was ripped from the sunny deck of the *Caravan*. It wasn't pleasantly warm, it was hot, a fetid heat she'd never felt before. Sweat ran from her body, soaking through the combat jacket. The helmet on her head dug into her brow, her hands were slick with sweat against the metal of the rifle. Rifle—she looked down at the hand clutching the weapon. A man's hand, hair curling against tanned wrists. She probed the mind of the body she was imprisoned in. Fear . . . anxiety . . . Sally?

Other soldiers were around her, jackets dark with sweat, weapons at the ready. Steaming jungle, vines, creepers, clammy green growths reaching out. They forded a stream, knee-deep in murky water, the muck at the bottom sucking at boots. Ahead—a clearing with smoke rising in sluggish columns. Cautiously, she sent a tendril into the man's mind and caught agony—agony and a girl's face. Black, almond-shaped eyes, glossy ebony hair cut straight across an amber brow, a soft, pink, tender mouth . . . Sally.

A body sprawled across the trail, a shapeless mass of flesh. Male? Maybe. Skirting the body. The smell drifting with the smoke, sickening! A few huts on poles. Most of the village smouldering piles of ashes. More mutilated bodies, mockeries of humans dotted across beaten earth. The man she had become was running, racing down what had once been a lane. A man in an officer's uniform trying to stop the maddened body. Not heard words but sensed. "For God's sakes, Brome, don't. Don't look!"

Brome's eyes looked and through them Tammy saw the thing lashed to the stake. The thing that once had been a pretty fresh girl with a tender pink mouth. Madness swirled through the mind of the man she was trapped in, red, blazing madness. Let me go! Please, she begged, let me go!

Hands were on her and she sagged weakly against them. Her exhausted eyes lifted to Rob's puzzled face. She buried her head against his chest. "Sally. Oh God, what they did to her," she moaned.

"And to the child she was carrying. My child." The arms holding Tammy stiffened and Rob pushed her back, staring

112

down at her white face. "What's going on? For God's sakes, I never said anything about Sally. I've never told anyone about her. All I said to you was that there was a girl." He shook Tammy roughly and she moved in his grip like a doll. "*What are you?*" he whispered, and there was fear in that whisper.

"Please, you're hurting me." His hands fell away and she braced herself against the rail. "I don't know...what I am. I only know at times...I see things. I told you I am in a mental institution, Rob."

He forced himself back to the wheel, his knuckles whitening as he grasped it. "I called her Sally because I couldn't pronounce her name. I was going to marry her, bring her home, bring our baby home. The Cong got to her first. That was when I went on drugs, swallowed anything I could get my hands on. In time, I suppose they'd have killed me but I caught a bullet, was invalided out. The army shrinks tried to straighten my head out. Finally I was discharged and came back here." He added bitterly, "I wish that bullet had been two inches to the left. No more dreams. No more guilt, no more living hell."

Her hand moved to cover his fist as it gripped the wheel. "Did you kick the drugs?"

"I'm not on them now. It's a day-to-day business. At times I nearly give in and take some. What difference does it make? Sally's dead. If I'd got her to some place safer, if I'd made an effort to see she was okay, the kid was okay." He tried to smile but it was more of a snarl. "Aren't you going to say something? Tell me time heals all? Be consoling?"

"No, I'm afraid it's up to you."

"Thank God for that! I think you understand. Most people have glib answers—glib and easy because they don't have to do it." He took a deep breath. "Funny, I feel as though I've shared the whole nightmare, that for the first time I've said it aloud." He spun the wheel and her hand fell away from his. "Better get you back." He draped an arm around her shoulder. "I don't know what you are, Tammy, and I don't care." His arm tightened. "You're okay."

Tammy made no effort to pull away from his embrace. The warmth of his body, the arm around her shoulders were comforting. She darted a look at his profile, at the thickly lashed sailor's eye, the clean line of his jaw. He's as starved as I am, she thought, as hungry as I am to break out of his mental

113

cage. Both of us emotional cripples. But for this moment at least, both of us *are* okay.

As the *Caravan* sliced cleanly through the gentle swells of the cove, Rayburn watched from the pier and felt rage surging through him. Carefully, he composed himself, arranging his lips in a genial smile. Under the brim of his jaunty Stetson he eyed the two young people so close together behind the wheel. Brome was hugging the girl to his side and both were smiling. Rayburn moved heavy shoulders under his plaid shirt, feeling sweat trickling down the powerful muscles. As Brome docked the boat, he moved to take the rope. "Ahoy," he called cheerfully.

He caught a glimpse of the girl's eyes and then their beauty disappeared behind the dark discs of the glasses. Apparently she saved those eyes for younger men, Rayburn thought wrathfully. "You had us all worried. Your mother's been frantic," he told her evenly. "We had no idea where you'd disappeared to." He stretched out a hand to help the girl but she avoided it and jumped onto the pier. He turned his attention to Rob Brome. "What's this?" He aimed a kick at the carton on the pier.

"Found it in the storeroom and I figured it must be yours."

"You were wrong. Canned peas!"

"Must have made a mistake. Mom must have ordered it."

"You made a mistake, all right." Some of Rayburn's anger seeped into his voice but the look he turned on Tammy was still bland. "Get along now and see your mother. She's worried. I want a word with Brome."

Tammy didn't argue. Lifting a hand in farewell to Rob, she turned up the rocky path. On the way to the house, she met Jeb Amos. His baseball cap was pushed to the back of his head and his nose was redder than ever.

"How's Holly feeling?" she asked.

"More comfortable now. She's napping."

Jeb waited until the girl was out of sight and then he pulled a pint bottle from his hip pocket. It gurgled as he tipped it up and took a long pull. As he screwed the cap back on, he heard loud voices from the direction of the pier. Silently he padded down toward the sounds. His brow furrowed. Old Mr. Rayburn was sure giving Rob Brome hell about something. Changing his mind, he wheeled and returned to his cottage.

Eight

Much to Thelma's relief, Holly recovered from her illness
and returned the next day to take the cooking and house-
keeping back into her capable hands. The weather appeared
to have relented and for a full week the sun shone and the
air was balmy. Most of the party sought the beach and the
rambling paths that covered the bleak island, basking in the
warmth of the Indian summer. The exceptions were Jim, his
sister, and Buddy. Most of their time was spent in Ruth's
room and when they did go outside they walked together,
Buddy clinging to the two adults' hands. Thelma and Philip
ranged over the island, carrying picnic lunches and a couple
of blankets. Seeking the sun, as they told everyone who would
listen. No one seemed that interested.

Norman certainly showed no interest in his wife's sun-
bathing. He followed his grandfather around, assisting with
wood chopping and other chores. Nadine seemed less grim
and spent hours strolling with her son. The time that Nigel
could steal from his mother he spent with Tammy. The girl
was content to sunbathe, sketch, and chat with the little man.
Nigel didn't press her further about either her doctor or the
school she attended and, as she admitted, he was amusing
company. Tammy didn't see much of her mother. She didn't
try to avoid her but she had a feeling Dorothy didn't want

to be bothered. Daily, Tammy would spend a little time on the pier, sitting on the hard surface, and, as she admitted, hoping to see the *Caravan* breasting the waves toward her. There was no sign of the boat or Rob Brome.

After lunch on the seventh day of sunshine, Tammy, clad in shorts and a halter, her sketchbook in her hand, ran down the austere staircase. The front door was open and silhouetted against the strong light, she could see her mother's slim figure. As Tammy neared the door she caught a glimpse of Jim's tall figure as he moved down the shell path. Buddy was riding piggyback on Jim's shoulders and the child was bouncing up and down, his arm flailing as though whipping up a horse. Beside them, her head reaching only to her brother's shoulder, was Ruth. She wore a pale green caftan and seemed to float along rather than walk.

As Tammy started to step around her mother, Dorothy said, "Just a minute, dear." She added contritely, "Let's make up. I'm sorry I said those awful things to you. I shouldn't have."

The girl shrugged a bare brown shoulder. "We both said things we shouldn't have."

Dorothy pushed her heavy hair back and her daughter noticed that her mother's face looked thinner, her eyes faintly smudged and tired looking. "Aren't you feeling well?"

"I'm all right. No...I'm not all right. I'm miserable. Will you talk with me for a few minutes, Tammy?" Tears welled up in Dorothy's eyes. "I'm lonely, lonely and confused."

Putting an arm around the older woman, Tammy turned her toward the archway of the drawing room. "Come sit down, mother."

"Not in there. I hate that room. Let's go to the library."

"That's Rayburn's private domain."

"He's outside with Norman." Dabbing at her eyes, Dorothy walked down the hall. She pushed open the door. "Not very cheerful but it's private."

The library was far from cheerful. The sole window, draped in dusty velvet, looked directly into the rock wall. The walls were papered in dingy red, picked out with tarnished gilt. Several glass-fronted bookcases held a small assortment of books and a dainty, spindly legged French desk contrasted oddly with the bulky club chairs. As Tammy urged her mother into one, she noticed the leather was cracked and

116

worn. Perching on the edge of the desk, she looked with concern at Dorothy's forlorn face. "What's wrong, mother?"

"Everything! We shouldn't have come here. I never should have let Jim persuade me to come. I don't like this place, Tammy, and I don't care much for Jim's family. He said I'd love them but I don't even like them." Tears started to her eyes again and she wailed, "Jim doesn't pay any attention to me. He's too busy with that sister of his."

Tammy felt a surge of compassion for her mother. For a moment the memory of a younger Dorothy knitting a doll's sweater came back to her. She must put aside her own uneasiness about this house, her instinctive distrust of the Quiller family, and reassure her mother. "Jim's been separated from his family for years. Probably he's only getting acquainted with them again."

"Ruth! She's the one he's getting to know again. And Rayburn, he seemed so courtly, so kind. Have you noticed his eyes? Like pebbles. Sometimes I think he's laughing at me—" Dorothy broke off. "I've really got to get a grip of myself. Maybe it's just this terrible house. Jim and I—we've been so close. Why, he never even goes golfing without me. When we were married he told me he wanted to do everything with me. And for this last week he hasn't even glanced at me!"

Placing her sketchbook on the desk, Tammy locked both hands around a knee. "How much do you actually know about Jim and his family?"

Dorothy fumbled for a cigarette case and tried to strike a match. Taking the box from her mother's trembling hand, Tammy held flame to the cigarette. Regarding the glowing tip, Dorothy said slowly, "If you'd asked that a week ago, I'd have flown at you. I thought I knew everything about him. Now...I'm not so sure. The way he's been acting....Anyway, Marc hired him about a year before he died." Her brow wrinkled in thought. "Philip wasn't with Jim and Vinnie then. I think the boy was with a commune at that time. In addition to the business relationship, Marc insisted we see Jim and his wife socially; he said they didn't know many people in Orlando and they were lonely. Marc was always so kind. We played bridge together and golfed a bit. I played tennis with Vinnie but, to be truthful, I never paid much attention to the woman. I don't think anyone did. Vinnie was colorless, no personality. I had an impression that she and Jim didn't get along well. Marc always felt sorry for her. Why, I don't know."

117

"What about Jim's background? He must have told you something about the Quillers."

Dorothy stubbed her cigarette out in a glass ashtray. Her teeth nibbled at her lower lip. "He talked some about his family. Told me how hard they worked, how poor they'd always been. He never knew his mother but he said Rayburn loved her dearly." A ghost of a smile touched Dorothy's mouth. "The way Rayburn met his wife was rather romantic. During the Depression. Her name was...oh yes, Jenny. Jenny's father was a doctor and after he retired from active practice he began looking after some elderly patients in his own home. He only took a few and Jenny and he did all the work. Rayburn turned up at their door, looking for work and Jenny's father hired him as handyman. Jim said his mother was beautiful and Rayburn must have been an attractive young man. In a short time they married and the twins, Ruth and Micah, were born. The old doctor died soon after their birth and Rayburn and Jenny ran the rest home. Jenny didn't live long, she died soon after Jim was born and Rayburn never remarried. He raised his children with the help of a housekeeper. Gertrude? A name something like that. Jim hated her, said she was a despot. The Quillers moved around a lot. Jim laughed and said he had a patchwork education, a new school nearly every year."

"What about his brother?"

"Nadine's husband? Jim seldom mentioned his brother. All he told me was that Micah was his father's favorite but the boy was unstable, a dreamer. When he was seventeen, Micah ran away and married Nadine. Rayburn disapproved and then Micah committed suicide."

"Anything else?"

Dorothy frowned. "Jim said when Micah died, Rayburn called in Andy as the doctor. In a way, it was as romantic as the meeting between Rayburn and Jenny. Ruth was in bad shape, she was so close to her twin, and Andy took care of her. They were married and—" Dorothy broke off, her face cleared and she smiled, this time the smile was genuine. "That's about it."

"Feel better now, mother?"

"Much. Everything's back in perspective." She gazed around the shabby room. "It must be this house and that awful story about the Winchfields. It's perfectly natural for Jim to want to be with a sister he hasn't seen for years, and

118

with her grandson. He just doesn't realize how lonely I've been. I'll talk to him tonight. It was nice of you to listen to me ramble, Tammy."

Tammy pushed herself away from the desk and picked up her sketchbook. She felt closer to her mother than she had in years. Impulsively, she said, "It was thoughtless of me to worry you the other day. I won't do it again. I'll let you know if I leave the island with Rob."

"Rob?" Dorothy raised fair brows. "Were you boating with Rob?"

"Didn't you know? Rayburn said you were worried."

Dorothy laughed. "I didn't even know that Rob was here. I wouldn't have been concerned anyway. The young man seems reliable. Go out with him any time you want to, Tammy."

Tammy's eyes widened and then she moved toward the door. Over her shoulder she told her mother, "Somehow I don't think I'll have another chance to."

Stalking out of the house, she turned toward the sounds of an axe striking wood. She stopped and watched the rise and fall of that axe in Rayburn Quiller's powerful hands. Norman cast one incurious look at the girl and then continued piling chunks of firewood. Rayburn stopped, leaned the axe against the chopping block, and took off the Stetson. He wiped his damp brow and smiled at Tammy. Her mother was right, she thought, that smile never reaches his eyes. "Looking for a job, my dear?" Rayburn asked pleasantly.

"What did you say to Rob?" she demanded.

The smile vanished. "That's between Brome and me. You've been hanging around the pier waiting for him, haven't you? Well, my girl, you'll have a long wait. He won't be back."

"*What* did you say to him?"

"I told him exactly what he is. I also discharged him and told him under no circumstances was he to try any further fortune hunting with a member of my family—"

"I'm not a member of your family! You lied to me! You had no right to interfere in my business."

Norman's pale eyes bulged and he dropped his armload of wood. "Don't you talk to my granddaddy like that!"

"Whoa, boy. Easy." Rayburn caught at the younger man's arm. He told the girl coldly, "Norman's right, Tammy, you need a lesson in respect. You're Jim's stepdaughter and that

119

makes you my responsibility. I'm an old-fashioned man and I'm head of this family. Don't force me to discipline you."

His voice was calm and even, but Tammy felt a chill breath of danger. She backed away and hurried around the side of the house. Releasing the boy, Rayburn picked up the axe. "Spirited," he muttered. "Spare the rod and spoil the child."

"I hate her," Norman blurted. "She shouldn't talk to you like that. I hate that Phil too!"

Quizzically, his grandfather examined the boy's sullen face. "What's wrong, boy?"

"Thel—she doesn't pay any attention to me since she met that Phil. She won't play games when I ask her. Granddaddy, you told me she'd always play with me."

"She will, boy. You run in and have Holly make you a cool drink. I'll be back soon."

"And Thel—"

"Thelma will be good to you. I promise, Norman."

Obediently, the boy headed toward the back door of the tall house, and Rayburn circled the house and headed down the path toward the broken gate. Jim and Ruth, her arm linked with the man's, were coming up the path. Buddy tagged along behind them. "Have you seen Thelma?" Rayburn asked them.

Ruth waved a hand. "Down at the beach with Phil as usual. Why?"

Without bothering to answer, Rayburn brushed past them and trotted down past the Amoses' cottage. When he reached the beach he could see the pair sprawled out side by side on a blanket. Both of them wore shorts and above his, Philip's slender body was bare. Thelma's back was bare too, she'd unhooked her halter and lay on her stomach. Beside them a picnic lunch had been spread on a folded blanket. Turning his head, Philip looked sleepily up. "Hi, granddad."

"Make yourself scarce, boy."

Taking one look at the older man's face, Philip got to his feet and hastily walked away. Thelma hugged her halter to her big soft breasts and heaved herself to a sitting position. Rayburn glared down at her. "What do you think you're doing?"

"You damned well know what I'm doing."

"Norman tells me you haven't been showing him any affection."

"Affection!" Her mouth twisted. "Look, Ray, I'm a normal

120

woman. I have needs and Philip is filling those needs. Norm isn't losing anything. What in hell do you care anyway?"

"I'm not concerned with who you lay or how often. This isn't hurting young Philip, probably doing him good. But I won't have my grandson neglected. You know your role in the boy's life."

"He has a mother. Tell him to go to Ruth."

With one swift movement, he hauled the woman to her feet. The halter fell away and her breasts bobbed loosely against his rough hands. "You forget easily, Thelma. I think I'd better suggest to Norman that you need a little reminding."

"Don't do that!" She winced away from him. "He nearly killed me, Ray."

"Then get up there and give him what he wants. Sex it up with Philip all you want but no more complaints from my grandson. Understand?" Nodding, she edged around the man. He snapped, "Get yourself covered."

He watched her running awkwardly up the path, trying to fasten up the halter as she ran. Her buttocks jogged loosely and the shorts had ridden up so he could see the bulging curves of her big rear end. Chuckling, he sat down on the blanket and reached for one of the thick sandwiches. He flipped the bread back, eyed the egg salad filling, scowled, and threw the sandwich away. Three gulls, who had been circling over the beach, dove on the food and started squabbling over it.

On the path behind the beach, Andy Thaler paused, saw his father-in-law's broad back, and turned away toward the pier. Near the end of it he saw Tammy, a sketchbook balanced on a rounded bare knee, gazing toward the mainland. Such a lonely figure, Andy thought, so many lonely people. Tammy's eyes were hidden by the glasses and her slender shoulders hunched forward. As he came up behind her, he cleared his throat. "May I join you?" He gestured toward her sketchbook. "Am I interrupting?"

"No." She held the book up so he could see the untouched page. "I can't seem to get started."

He lowered himself beside her, his long legs dangling near hers. She glanced at his profile. His cheeks wrinkled, his balding head making him seem older than he was. Looks older than Rayburn, she thought. Andy had the colorless brows and lashes that often went with that carrot-colored hair. His pale eyes were the same shape as his son's but where Norman's bulging eyes made her uneasy, his father's affected her the opposite way. She had an impression of Andy's sadness, sadness and infinite weariness. He said nothing further and she found herself relaxing. Silence didn't hang awkwardly between them, it was peaceful, almost a dreamlike quiet. Neither the man nor the girl attempted to break that peace.

After a time, still without looking at her, he said, "He'd come if he could."

Yes, Tammy thought, Rob would come if he could. She wondered at the intensity of her desire to see him again. Was it this solitude, this forced interlude with a group of strangers? Was it something deeper than that? She'd seen Rob only twice and yet there was a bond between them. She retained the warmth of his body against hers, the feeling of security he'd given her. Two emotional cripples, walled off from the world, but perhaps not walled off from each other. Perhaps they could help each other. Perhaps....

"If it's destined," the doctor said gently, "it happens. I know. When I met my wife I never dreamt she could care for me." As though talking to himself, he continued, "I was such a clod of a young fellow, fresh out of medical school, one of those people who're never noticed." He chuckled. "Girls didn't notice me anyway. I don't know why Rayburn called me; maybe it was because I had a room in the house next to the one they were renting."

"A rest home?"

"Not at that time. Rayburn takes—took—what he called breaks from rest homes and this was one of them. Jim had gone away to school and Micah...that's why I was called in. He took his life in his attic room. Cut-and-dried suicide, there was a note, but such a waste. Even in the horror of that kind of death there were signs of his physical beauty and such talent—"

"Talent?"

"The walls were covered with drawings and Micah wrote poems. Rayburn let me read some. Young and raw, I suppose, but gripping. Rayburn was a broken man, sick with heartbreak, and Ruth. Ah, Ruth. Even in grief she was the most breathtaking girl I'd ever seen. I never dreamt she would want me. A girl like that and Andy Thaler."

How he loves Ruth, Tammy thought, and I've never heard

her speak to him except to demand something—her coat, a drink, a scarf. Gently and deliberately, she probed at his mind. There was a glimpse of Ruth, a younger Ruth, her eyes swollen and red, her hair spread across a pillow. Other sensations blurred that lovely face. Hints of grief, shame, fear. The sensations came faster and then hunger, sharp longing. An image again. His arm bare, scarred. A needle poised over a swollen vein. Hastily, she pulled back from that mind.

Drugs. Was she transposing Rob's addiction on this man's mind? Glancing down, she saw one of Andy's hands massaging the sleeve of his other arm. He moistened dry lips with a quick dart of his tongue. Casually, he pulled himself up. "Enough sun and exercise for today. I'll get back and finish my book."

She stared at the shimmering water. "Good?"

"No," he told her. "Terrible, but with a fascination. Once you begin, impossible to stop."

That was true enough, Andy told himself grimly, impossible. He speeded his steps, his fingers opening and closing as though he already were holding the needle case in his hands, as though the rubber strip were already biting into his eager flesh.

As Andy passed the half-moon beach, he noticed that Rayburn was no longer alone. A woman, ramrod straight beside his father-in-law's bulk, was standing beside Rayburn. Nadine. Andy shook a puzzled head and then hastened his steps. Nirvana was waiting.

Nadine caught a glimpse of the doctor and hoped he would join them but Andy trotted up the path toward the Amoses's cottage. Sighing, she forced herself to stand her ground. Rayburn's voice was as unctuous as it always was. "Delighted you sought me out, my dear Nadine."

"Don't flatter yourself. If I'd known you were here—"

"You'd have avoided me as though I have the plague." He gave a throaty chuckle. "My dear Nadine—"

"Forget the soft soap. I know you."

"How can you? Until you set foot on this island we'd never met."

"Micah told me all about you."

Stooping, he unwrapped another sandwich and threw it to the waiting gulls. "Like people. Greedy. Have you heard about the trick some sailors play on gulls? They attach a string to a fishhook and jam the hook into a ball of bread. When the bird swallows the bread they yank—"

"Too bad you didn't bring a hook."

"Cruelty for cruelty's sake has never appealed to me. Enigmas, on the other hand, always excite me. You and your son are enigmas. Nigel has tried to be pleasant but you've kept your distance from us. Why did you come?"

"I had a reason."

His hand closed on her arm. He didn't seem to exert strength but she winced. "Sit down, we're going to have this out. No, don't try to pull away."

She had no choice. Her face stony, Nadine sank to the sand. He knelt before her. "Say it," he ordered.

"You murdered my husband."

"Murdered? I never laid a hand on the boy. He was dear to me, dear to Ruth. When Micah came back to us I'll admit I was stern with him. I considered your hasty marriage a grievous mistake. I suggested an annulment but when Micah told me you were with his child I urged him to bring you to us, to his family. Micah was always...overly emotional. He was less than eighteen, Nadine. The pressure of your marriage, the responsibility of a child, my own disapproval...he lost his mind. He took his own life." Rayburn's voice broke. "You fancy you loved him but the depths of my grief even you could never comprehend."

For the first time since she'd arrived at the beach, she looked directly at the man. For a moment, uncertainty stirred. Then her mouth firmed. "You're like an actor. The grief-stricken father. If you loved Micah, why was he so deathly afraid of you? When he first came to the cafe, when I first saw him, I adored him. And Micah loved me. He was so...so beautiful, so gentle. Like a prince. We ran away and married. We must hide, he told me, hide from my father and sister. We only had four months together. Neither of us had any savings so I worked as a waitress to support us and then I found I was pregnant. Micah said that might change your mind about me. Another Quiller might, he told me. He seemed so sad when he said it. I begged him not to go back to Saint Louis, but Micah said he had to. He told me to stay hidden. If anything happens to me, Micah told me, take the baby and run. Stay hidden."

Rayburn averted his head. "His mind giving even then. Delusions."

124

"He never came back to me. I waited and waited. Nigel was born and I did what Micah told me to. I ran and hid. I'd no money to find out what happened to my husband. It took time to save enough to hire a private detective." She took a deep breath. "Micah was dead. Murdered by you."

"We go round and round. I'll never convince you. Just why did you come here?"

"To destroy you. I brought the weapon to destroy you with me."

Lunging to his feet, he looked grimly down at her. "If anyone killed my son, you did."

"What do you have against me?" she cried. "Was it because I was a waitress? Wasn't I good enough for you?"

"You were unsuitable."

"Who do you think you are—God?"

"You're hysterical!" His voice altered and became mild and benign again. "You must consult with Andy. Perhaps he can give you something to calm you." He stretched his long frame. "Now, I'm off to see what Holly has for dinner." Without glancing at Nadine, he strode away, his heavy boots kicking up clouds of sand.

It was getting chill. The sun was sinking against a dark bank of cloud. Shivering, the woman crouched on the blanket, looking unseeingly at the sunset. She didn't move when the hand gripped her shoulder.

"What did you tell him?" Nigel demanded.

"The truth."

"All of it?"

"Do you think I'm a fool? I told him I would destroy him."

"Wonderful." He ran a hand over his thick hair. "I suppose you blurted out the weapon."

"No. And I didn't tell him who controlled the weapon."

"Thoughtful of you."

"*When* will you act?"

On her shoulder, his hand tightened. "It's a two-bladed weapon, mother. It could destroy me. Is it worth that much to you?"

She didn't answer. After a moment, his hand fell away.

Shortly before midnight, the good weather broke. A gale whipped in over the Atlantic, driving clouds across the dark sky. Dorothy watched the wind lashing the stunted shrubs in front of the house, then she allowed the curtain to sag back

125

into place. In the wavery mirror over the dressing table, she could see her reflection. All the ritual preparations done, she thought. A bath in that damned awkward bathroom with the old marble fixtures, two inches of tepid water puddling on the bottom of that monstrous, claw-footed tub. Then back to her room to peel off the sensible wool robe and slip into this short, flimsy nightie with the matching negligee.

She peered at her reflection. Thank God her legs were still good. Critically, she examined them. Long, shapely, tanned to a golden brown. She pulled the chiffon tight so it outlined her small breasts, the indentation of her waist, the swell of her hips. Not bad. The perfume that Jim liked dabbed behind her ears, between her breasts, a touch at the parting of the long legs. She grinned wryly and her image grinned back at her. Nice, even teeth and her hair was still glossy and attractive, but the years hadn't been as kind to her face. Leaning closer to the mirror, she touched the slight sag below her jawline, the wrinkles at the corners of her eyes. When she got home she might consider a face lift. God, what she'd give to be home right now.

Resentfully, she stared at the twin beds. When Marc had been alive she'd insisted on twin beds but since her marriage to Jim this was the first time they hadn't shared a large bed. With Jim it had been heaven, feeling her flank pressed against his, turning to rest spoon style against his warm back, her fingers tracing a delicious path across the muscles of his chest, down across the flat stomach to the crisp hair around his—

Convulsively, her hand clutched the parting of her legs and felt moisture against her fingers. One hell of a long time since they'd...but it hadn't been long. Only a week. Seemed a lifetime. She pictured Jim's hands on her body, knowingly touching all the hidden, delicious places, and her hand tightened. Well, she grinned again, tonight was the night.

She picked up the thermos she'd filled in the kitchen before she came upstairs. Carefully and secretively. Martinis. The way Jim liked them—Beefeater and a touch of Italian vermouth. Beside the thermos, a dish of olives. All the trappings of seduction. Only the principal missing. She glanced at her traveling clock. Nearly one. Damn that sister of his. And how could she be jealous of a sister?

Impatiently, Dorothy took the cap off the thermos and filled a tiny stemmed glass. Dropping an olive in it, she
126

sipped. Good, but so icy. In this cold house perhaps a hot rum would've been a better idea. She walked to the window, carefully balancing the glass. Near it two armchairs faced each other across a low table. On the glass top, artlessly arranged, were a magazine, an ashtray, cigarettes. She glanced back at the thermos. Should she move that over too? No, it might look contrived.

In her mind, she practiced the seduction. Jim would open the door. He'd be surprised to find her still up. Every night for this last week, he'd softly entered the room, taken off his clothes in the dark, and crawled into bed. She waited for him to come to her side, pull back the covers, slide his long body in beside hers. He hadn't. After a time, she could hear his breathing change to the heavy sound of sleep. She'd been acting like a child, Dorothy told herself, thank heavens she'd talked to Tammy that afternoon. Saying all those things aloud showed how silly she'd been acting.

So...soon Jim would open the door. He'd say something like, can't you sleep darling? and she'd smile at him and raise her glass. Having a drink, Jim, reading. Then he'd come over and maybe have a drink first, maybe he'd scoop her up and carry her to bed and—

The door creaked open. Jim, his tie loosened and his hair rumpled stood in the doorway. "What's wrong?" he asked abruptly. "Decided to sit up and do your sulking for a change?"

Her welcoming smile weakened but she forced herself to hold it in place. "Having a drink. Your favorite. Like one?"

"Uh-uh." He sat down on the side of his bed and pulled his shoes off.

Putting down the glass, she reached for a cigarette. He'll light it for me, she thought, he always lights my cigarettes. He wasn't even looking at her. He was unbuttoning his shirt. She found a book of matches and lit it. "Jim," she said hesitatingly.

"I'm bushed. I'm going to bed."

"I can't sleep, darling."

"That's no reason to keep me awake." He pulled off his pants and draped them over the end of the bed. "Take a pill."

"You know I hate pills."

Peeling off his shorts, he tossed them on the floor. He stood up, yawned, his arms lifted, the muscles across his chest outlined against the tanned skin. One hand fell and fingered

127

his flaccid penis. "You're out of luck tonight, I think I feel a headache coming on. Better try a vibrator."

Her eyes were wide with disbelief. This wasn't Jim, this wasn't the man she'd lived with for five years. "What's wrong?" she whispered.

"Now? Nothing." He smiled but it was an ugly smile, merely a baring of the teeth. His words were spaced and coolly deliberate. "For five years I've earned my keep. Fetched and carried, acted like a stud. That's over now, Jim won't jump for the bone any longer. Time for you to understand I'm head of my own house. Not a rich woman's bought toy."

She was rigid with shock. "I thought you loved me."

"I thought so too." Flinging back the covers, he got into bed. "Then I got here and my sanity started coming back. I suddenly saw what you'd done to me. At your beck and call. Jim do this. Jim do that. I'm ready to be serviced, Jim. Doling out your money as a sweetener—"

"I never did that! You used money as you wished. Even those checks you sent to your father—I didn't say a word about them. I only wanted...want you to be happy. You and me, happy."

Reaching out, he switched off the lamp beside him. "I'm happy now. So, you snooped into my checkbook too? Begrudging a little of your lousy money for a father I owe everything to. Always letting me know who held the purse strings."

Her shock was turning to rage. How dare he! She was on her feet, the glass falling from her hand, liquid splashing against her bare feet. "I still hold the purse strings!" she shouted. He didn't respond. In the shadows around his bed, she couldn't see his face. She lowered her voice. "What about Tammy? You love Tammy, Jim."

"Another spoiled little bitch for Jim to have to coddle. She's your daughter, all right. What Tammy needs instead of sweet talk is a touch of the belt. And maybe I'll give it to her."

"You won't lay a hand on Tammy! She's sick—" Breaking off, she moaned, "Jim, let's get out of here! Now! This place—these people—they're doing something terrible to us, Jim!"

His voice came from the shadows. "Shut your mouth and get to bed. One more word and I'll use my belt on *your* pampered ass."

The voice was low but there was violence in it. She didn't recognize it. *There's a stranger in this room*, she thought
128

wildly, *a man I don't know.* Her breath caught in her throat and cold fear washed over her, as icy as the spilled drink on her flesh. Creeping across the room, she crawled under the comforter. *Tammy*, she thought, *what am I going to do?*

Nine

Thelma grapsed the arm beside her. "What's that? Do you hear someone outside the door?"

Rolling over on his side, Philip raised his shaven head and listened. After a moment he relaxed, grinned, and patted the woman's bare belly. "Simmer down, lady, that there is my daddy making his way back to Dorothy after another session with the gorgeous Ruth." He punched his pillow into a more comfortable shape. "Can't figure out why with a sexpot like his wife waiting, dad spends so much time with a sister for."

"If you knew the sister you'd understand," Thelma said darkly.

"Hey, you're always doing that."

"What?"

"Taking snide little digs at the Quillers and then clamming up. Come on, dish up the dirt."

"Anything you're curious about, twerp, go right to the top."

"Granddad? No way! That look on his face down at the beach today told little Phil all he wants to know. No way I'm tangling with granddad."

"I noticed you didn't stick around. Took off like a pup with your tail between your legs."

He tickled her. "What a tail, though. Must suit you."

She rolled away from his searching hand. Her whole body

was dripping sweat. Phil was right about one thing—no complaints about his lovemaking. She made a move to get up and Philip caught her arm. "Hey, lady, didn't anyone ever tell you it's rude to fuck and run. Let's rap for awhile."

"What about?" she asked, but she allowed him to pull her back in his arms.

"Like what did granddad want today? I thought when he came storming down and booted my ass out, he was going to break up our dandy arrangement."

"Ray's broadminded," Thelma told him drily. "Doesn't mind what we do as long as Norm gets his share of attention."

Picking up a roach clip, Philip dexterously slid a hand-rolled cigarette into the alligator clamp. He lit it, drew smoke in, and exhaled with a satisfied sigh. "Want a drag?"

"Not now, not in the mood."

"About Norm—"

"I don't want to talk about him."

"Come on, Thelma. What goes with cousin Norm? How'd you ever marry that moron?"

"It's a long story."

"So? From what I've seen of the man, I'd figure he's mentally about eight."

She turned her head and her voice was muffled. "In some ways, even younger."

"And he can't get it up, can he?" When the woman didn't answer, Philip drove a rigid forefinger into her ribs. "Give."

"All right. Norm's retarded and he's impotent. Does that answer your questions?"

"All except the most important ones. How did a nurse come to marry a guy like that? Especially a hot-pants one like you."

"I was stupid, that's how, and conned." Rolling over, she looked into the boy's pale blue eyes. "I've had six years of absolute hell with the Quillers and don't try to pretend to sympathize. You're like all the rest of the dudes, all you give a damn about is your cock. But you're curious, so okay, here's how it was. I was fed to the teeth with guys like you. From the time I was in high school I earned my way by putting out. Other girls got the dates and proms. I got quick tumbles in back seats of cars. I thought it would change in time. It never did. Every intern or orderly on the make had a piece of me. When they married they picked a pretty girl and
132

Thelma just kept on working and screwing. Then Norm came along."

"Like a knight in shining armor."

"More like a janitor with a push broom. But he was different."

"That's no lie." Philip was smiling broadly.

"If you want to hear anymore, wipe that smirk off your face."

"Okay, go on. Norm was different."

"He wasn't fresh, made no passes. He followed me around looking at me as though I was something special. Finally, he worked up the nerve and asked me out. I went—"

"What'd you do? Play tiddlywinks?"

Rolling off the bed, she stood up. Her eyes were bright with unshed tears and, as she bent to pick up her clothes, one rolled down her cheek. Coming lithely off the bed, Philip threw his arms around her. "Hey, baby, I'm sorry. Come on." He urged her back and they sat down on the rumpled blankets. "I won't make any more cracks. Go on."

Picking up a corner of the blanket, she wiped at her face. "Norm took me to a movie and then we had a milkshake. He treated me as if I was made of china. Didn't even try to hold my hand. I felt as though time had turned back, as though I was a school kid again. I liked it. Norm didn't say much, just listened to me talk, staring at me as though I was important."

Philip hugged her thick waist. "You should have tumbled."

"Sure, in no time I would have, but it all happened so fast. Norm brought his grandfather and mother to the cafeteria to have lunch with us and they were handsome and well dressed and Ray did all the talking."

"You figured you were really making a match."

"Yes, I thought they were wealthy and Norm...I guess I figured he was just shy and quiet. He took me out a couple more times but Ray and Ruth went along and then Norm asked me to marry him."

"You jumped at it. You didn't stop and wonder what a wealthy kid would be pushing a broom in a hospital for."

"If I'd had time—yes." Her wide brow wrinkled in thought. "Something triggered me. There was this new intern, a good-looking guy, and pretty polite. I was eyeing him, y'know. Thought, well, this could be the main man. The morning after Norm proposed—"

"With his granddaddy's help?"

"Ray sure must have rehearsed him until he was letter perfect. Anyway, this new intern cornered me in the dispensary and without a word rammed his hand up under my skirt. I tried to play coy and then he told me what all the men called me. The bicycle, they called me. Because—" She wiped at her eyes again, "—because they said I was easy to mount and anyone could ride me."

"A real dirty bastard."

She shrugged plump shoulders. "I'd earned the name, Phil. They say when you're drowning your whole life passes before you. That happened to me. Standing there with that guy groping me, I saw the whole scene, all the years, all the guys, all the gropes. I figured if I turned Norm down, that's all I'd ever have so I marched out of that room, found Norm mopping a floor, and I asked him if he really wanted to marry. He nodded and...that was it."

"Again, only part of it. Why, when you found out about Norm, didn't you have tha marriage annulled?" Putting both hands on the sides of her head, he turned it so she was forced to look directly at him. "Most important of all. Who's Buddy's father?"

She pulled his hands away, and stood up. "Don't mention that brat to me," she said evenly. Stooping, she bundled her clothes up. This time Philip made no effort to stop her.

Wind howled in across the island, swirling through the black night around the Amoses' cottage, catching a loose shutter and chattering it against the clapboards. The sound woke Holly Amos and she tensed under the warmth of the patchwork quilt. A loose shutter, she thought, have to get Jeb to fix it in the morning.

Stretching out a hand she reached for her husband. The other half of the bed was empty. She sat up and switched on a lamp. Jeb's pillow was undented. Sighing, she pushed back the quilt, swung her feet to the floor. It was icy and she slid her feet around hastily until one touched the pink plush slippers Jeb had given her the previous Christmas. Shivering, she lifted the matching robe and pulled it on over her flannel nightgown. He must have let the fire go out, she decided. When she'd come to bed he'd promised not to sit up late, not to do any drinking. At the kitchen door, she paused to rub at her hip. Dratted rheumatism, acting up again. This getting chilled wouldn't help either.

Light from the living room spilled softly across the kitchen tiles. She could see Jeb from where she stood, his chin drooping forward onto his chest, a bottle clutched in one hand, the boys' school picture moved around to where he could look at it. Holly felt no resentment. He just can't get over it, she told herself, just can't believe they're gone. She moved through the dark kitchen toward the lighted doorway surely, knowing the way so well she didn't bother turning on a light.

His pipe was on the floor and she bent over to pick it up. It had charred a hole in the rag rug by his chair, the one her mother had made the year she'd passed on. Holly felt tears well in her eyes as she rubbed at the ugly mark. Ah well, it was only a rug, her mother was long gone. Tomorrow she'd shift it around, get it further away from Jeb's old chair. Safer that way. Wouldn't do much damage if he dropped his pipe on bare boards.

Sadly, Holly looked down at her sleeping husband, trying to find in his elderly, whiskered face the features of the man she'd married. A stench rose from him, a smell of body odor, smoke, cheap whiskey. Didn't bathe often enough. She kept after him to get in the tub and shave but only so much you could do without turning into a nag. Looking at Jeb now, few would believe he once had been a young fellow with a slim strong body and a ready smile. Ah well, he was hers, all she had left.

Gently, she shook his shoulder. "Jeb. Time to get to bed." He grunted and his chin waggled loosely. She shook him again and his head snapped up.

"Whatcha want? Holly?"

"Time to get to bed," she repeated. "It's cold in the house. You let the fire go out."

Lifting the hand clasping the empty bottle, he blearily regarded it. "Sorry, old girl, broke my promise again. Started to think of the boys when they was youngsters."

"I know, but don't do no good. This won't bring them back. Only hurting you and me."

He set the bottle down beside the wood box. "Won't do it again. Never again." He rasped a hand over his stubbly chin. "What's the time?"

She glanced at the clock on the spinet, squinted, and then she went closer. Pretty little thing, that clock, had belonged

135

to her mother. But the numerals were so tiny. Her mother said it had come from France and it was painted real pretty, flowers all over it. When it struck the hour, a little ivory girl came out and curtsied. As she moved, music tinkled from a box in its base. The little figurine looked something like Tammy, long hair like her. Maybe she'd give it to Tammy. Holly rubbed her eyes with the back of one hand. Eyes not so good now. When the Quillers left, she best get over to the mainland and have them checked. Lifting her head, Holly swung around, and listened.

"You hear anything, Jeb?"

He pulled himself up and came to stand beside her. He cocked his head. "Wind. Bad night. Looks like the good weather is all over for this year."

"Must be that shutter banging that woke me up. Better put a couple of nails in it in the morning. Know you got a lot to do but—" She stopped and then said abruptly, "I do hear something. Sounds like it's right outside the door."

He squeezed her arm. "You getting spooky, old girl? Who'd be out on a night like this?" Looking at her intent expression, he chuckled. "I'll have a look, just to keep you happy."

She stretched out a hand. "Jeb, don't!"

He chuckled again. He was still chuckling as he padded across the room to the blue door and drew back the heavy bolt. He swung the door open. "Well, I'll be! You and Holly scared stiff. Come on in outta that wind."

When Holly saw the figure standing in the doorway she relaxed and smiled broadly. "Bless me, sure had me going there. What are you doing at this time of night?"

The figure stepped into the room and another followed. Holly and Jeb both wore broad smiles. Holly kept on smiling until she saw the club. Jeb didn't have a chance. It was brought down with such force that he was driven to his knees. He died quickly.

The killer stepped over Jeb's body, and advanced on Holly. Before she died she heard three things. One was the intruder's voice shouting, "*Dies irae!*" The second, incongruous in that room of death, was the clock striking two and the tinkling music box in its base. The last was her own voice, prompted perhaps because of the fancied likeness of the ivory figurine to the girl in the main house.

Her bulging eyes fixed on the bloody club, Holly made only one sound. "Tammy!" she shrieked.

Tammy found herself on the edge of her bed, one leg thrown over its side, as though preparing to run. Her eyes stared into the darkness of the room unable to pick out even the silhouette of a piece of furniture. Against her leg, the air was chill, chill enough to shock her fully awake. Pulling her leg back, she curled up in a ball in the warm hollow under the blankets.

I don't dare close my eyes, she thought. That vision of a hand holding a club, that ripping sensation of horror and shock—had she been reliving her father's death? Or—in the darkness her lips moved in a grim smile—her hallucination of her father's murder. The club had been stained with blood as the club that had killed her father had been stained.

Tammy forced calmness on her racing mind. A nightmare. Only a bad dream. Resolutely, she made herself relax in the warmth of the bed. The house was still, the night silence broken only by the creaks of ancient boards, by the rush of the wind against the window. Lulled by the silence and the warmth, the girl dozed off.

Later, and she had no idea how much later, she came wide awake again. This time there was no violent picture hanging against her mind, simply the cold darkness of the attic room and a lingering sensation of a rocking motion. Gently, she thought, as though she'd been on the *Caravan* with the deck moving under her feet.

She made no effort to go back to sleep. Her hand moved to the bedlamp, found it, and switched the light on. The light flooded the room, reflecting from the mirror over the chest, from the window panes framed in faded gingham. She glanced at the clock her father had given her, standing primly in its green morocco case beside the lamp. Half past two, hours yet to daybreak. She was reaching for the book she'd been reading earlier when a soft tap sounded at the door.

"Who is it?" she called.

"Your sleepwalking neighbor. Only I'm wide awake. Can I come in?"

She was about to tell Nigel to open the door and come in, when she saw the bolt was pulled snugly across the panel. She frowned. She'd no memory of barring that door. This was the second time she'd done it without realizing.

"One moment," she called.

Wincing from the cold, she located her slippers and robe.

The bolt was stiff, she had to use both hands to pull it back. Fleetingly, she wondered how she could have closed it without remembering. Nigel was nattily attired in a camel's hair robe and striped pyjamas. His red hair was rumpled and he was combing it with his fingers.

"I noticed light under your door and took a chance," he told her.

"Come on in, I'm glad to have some company."

Bending, he plugged the heater in. "Better climb back in bed, Tammy, this attic is like Siberia."

She took his advice and pulled a blanket over her shoulders. Nigel tugged the heater over as far as the cord would stretch and hoisted himself onto the foot of the bed. As the coils started to glow, he swung his legs around in front of them. "You hear anything a few minutes ago?"

"Something woke me. I've no idea what. Not so much a sound as a...a motion."

He nodded. "Vibration. It woke me too." Restlessly, he jumped off the bed and walked over to the window.

"See anything?" she asked.

He turned away from the window. "Only my reflection and yours. Beastly night." Picking up a sheaf of loose pages from her sketchbook, he idly thumbed through them. He held a charcoal sketch up. It was the one she'd done of the cove, the night scene. "Damned good work, Tammy. You certainly caught it. The men from Amoston disembarking from the trawler, even the top hat on the minister's head. When did you do it?"

She opened her mouth to reply but they both froze. The silence was shattered by a shout, several shouts. By the time she reached the door, Nigel had wrenched it open and was trotting toward the head of the stairs. The light in the lower hall was on and they could see Andy Thaler, a coat thrown over his pyjamas, at the foot of the stairs.

"Fire!" the doctor was shouting.

"Where?" Nigel grasped the girl's wrist. "What part of the house?"

"Not here. Saw it from my window. Must be the Amoses' cottage."

Gasping, Tammy tried to pull free from Nigel. With a strength surprising in his tiny hand, he held her back. "*Holly*," she told him.

138

"That's pneumonia weather. Won't help for you to get sick. Get some clothes on."

As she raced back to her room, she could hear men's voices from the second floor. Hastily, she pulled jeans and a sweater on over her pyjamas, rammed bare feet into boots. She threw open the wardrobe door and tore a trench coat from a hanger. Fast as she was, she found when she reached the landing that Nigel had been even faster. She could see his hair flaming in the light over the second landing. The lower hall seemed to be a mass of milling people. Rayburn, his usually smooth cap of hair a disordered mass, was trying to calm them down.

"All right," he shouted. "Don't lose your heads. Who sounded the alarm?"

"Andy." Jim stepped up beside his father. "And he's right. From our window I could see flames shooting up."

"It might be the boathouse," Philip pointed out.

"Not a chance," his father told him. "Too far from the cove. Has to be the cottage."

"Where's Andy?" Thelma called.

"Gone down to see what he can do," Jim said. "Norm went with him. We better all get down there."

Tammy didn't wait to hear more. She ran down the staircase with Nigel close behind her. She fumbled at the front door, found the catch, and raced across the veranda. Behind her, she could hear voices, someone shouting for a flashlight and then she was through the gateway, heading down the path. She slipped and fought to regain her balance. Nigel shouted, "Wait up. Going to break your ruddy neck." He caught up with her and flashed a beam of light down the path.

"Holly!" she gasped.

"Okay, but watch the footing."

They moved as fast as they could. Nigel's short legs pumped to keep up with her strides. As they turned toward the shore they could see the cottage. It was a raging inferno. The wind was whipping flames toward the night sky, sparks were flying in all directions. Silhouetted against the glare was Andy's bulky figure, leaning heavily on Norm. Tammy reached the two men first. Andy's face was beet red and one side of his face looked badly scorched. He cradled one arm against his chest. Andy grunted, "Keep clear, Tammy. No use. Tried to get to the door—"

"You hurt yourself, daddy," Norm cried. "Your hand."

Tammy glanced at the doctor's raw hand and then she turned back to the cottage. A window pane gave and glass sprayed out. With his sound hand, Andy pulled her further back. "Holly?" the girl asked.

"No sign of either Holly or Jeb," Andy told her grimly. "Doesn't look as though they got out."

Nigel was standing beside the girl, the flashlight dangling from his hand. He clicked off the light. Tammy stood immobile, her eyes on the blue door. In the light from the flames the mermaid knocker glinted. Confusion surrounded Tammy, a babble of voices, the sound of a woman sobbing, Rayburn shouting.

"A battering ram," a man's voice shouted. "Let's get that door open!"

"Buckets," someone called wildly, "Water."

As though caught in a nightmare from which there was no awakening, Tammy numbly watched. Philip came charging up from the direction of the beach, a bucket clutched in one hand, his scalp lock flying straight out behind his head. He got as close to the flaming building as he dared and tossed the bucket toward the blue door. A few drops sprayed out, sizzling as they hit the hot wood. Upending the bucket, Philip peered into it. "Jes-sus," he said and started to giggle. "A hole in the bucket." Throwing back his shaven head, he brayed with hysterical laughter. "A drop in the bucket. Water, water, everywhere—"

"Stop that!" Rayburn's big hand cracked across the young man's face.

"Too late," Andy moaned. "Too late."

Heat from the flames drove them further back. Nigel climbed part way up the rocky cliff and he stood there, shading his eyes. He stretched his other hand down and helped Tammy pull herself up. She collapsed at his feet. *Hell*, she thought, *a scene from hell.* The lurid light cast its glow across the ring of faces below her, redly highlighting cheeks and jaws, leaving the eyes and mouths in darkened hollows. The figures looked demonic, a company of imps with empty eye sockets and grinning mouths.

Small, inconsequential details gripped her. Andy nursing his burnt hand, his hair singed, a red, puckering mark on one cheek. Rayburn's skinny bare flanks protruding from under the skirt of a three-quarter-length raincoat. Dorothy's coat gaping open disclosing a chiffon nightie. Ruth bundled in her luxury fur, her big feet in silken slippers. Tammy noted the way they were grouped. Andy was standing alone. His son had moved to Rayburn's side. Ruth was clutching Jim's arm and Buddy was clinging with both hands to her coat. A few feet away from them, Dorothy gazed with shadowed eyes from the burning cottage to her husband's face. Thelma had an arm around Philip's waist and he'd buried his face against her plump shoulder. Nadine was standing alone, her head thrown back, dark hair spilling glossily down her back. Turning, Tammy gazed up at Nigel. His eye sockets looked empty too, flames gilded his hair and played redly over his cheekbones. Another demon, the girl thought.

Smells drifted up—burning wood, hot tar, another sickening one that jarred her stomach. Barbecues, pork spareribs sputtering on a grill. The smell of burning human flesh. *Holly*, she thought, *Holly and Jeb*. Bright blue eyes, crisp gray hair, pink cheeks. Charring into a black, greasy mass in that furnace.

She stifled a scream. Something cold and moist was touching her hand. She felt softness pressing against her side. She fumbled shaking fingers through a silken fur. Old Blue, pressing against her. Lifting the cat, she buried her face in him. His fur smelled of smoke. Tommy Amos's cat, Tammy thought, take care of Blue. Old Blue alive, Tommy's mother and father dead. She prayed for tears, there were none. With dry eyes she saw the blue door enveloped by flames. In their midst, the little mermaid writhed as though she were dying too.

In time they straggled back to the house. The massive door had been left open and wind tore down the hall, clawing with avid fingers at the tall clock, swinging the door to Holly's kitchen to and fro. They gathered in the drawing room slumping in their hodgepodge of hastily donned clothing. It was bitterly cold but no one complained or suggested lighting up the logs on the hearth.

Thelma, a scarf bound over her hair, was competently treating Andy's burns. She'd brought a bowl of ice from the kitchen and was holding a compress against his cheek, placing wet cloths over his hand. Norm had fallen and twisted his ankle. He was rubbing at it and watching his wife, but Thelma didn't spare a glance for him. Rayburn had pulled on a pair of trousers but he still wore his coat and his gray hair stood on end. The remains of Ruth's frail slippers, now torn and wet, had been kicked off and she sat in an armchair, her feet curled up under her. Jim perched on his sister's chair arm, one hand on Ruth's fur-clad shoulder. Coffee had been made and a tray sat on a table near the archway. Nigel handed Tammy a cup and sank down on the carpet at her feet. The big cat huddled on her lap, his head buried under the folds of her trench coat.

The silence in the room stretched out broken only by the small sounds of shifting bodies, the clink of a cup against the saucer, the tinkle of ice as Thelma bent to wring out a strip of cloth. Finally, Rayburn straightened and put his cup down. He looked around the room. "A tragedy," he sighed. "We're all shocked but we must pull ourselves together. Decide what has to be done."

Philip rubbed at his cheek, smudging it with soot. He gazed down at his grimy hand. "If we'd got there faster—didn't anyone but Andy know?"

Heads were shaken and Andy mumbled around the edge of the sodden cloth pressed against his face, "Something woke me. Felt like a giant hand shaking the house. Couldn't figure it out. Got up to check and then I saw the flames."

"The mainland," Nadine said quickly, "wouldn't they see the fire from the cafe? Rob Brome?"

"No way, mother," Nigel said. "Even if Brome were awake, I doubt it. That rim of rock along the shore hides everything but the cliff and this house. Noticed that when Brome brought us over."

Dorothy tore her eyes away from her husband's face and looked at his father. "Rob! Even if he didn't see it...we've got to get help. When is Rob due again?"

Rayburn cleared his throat. "As a matter of fact, young Brome won't be back."

"What?" Thelma dropped the cloth she was holding.

"I was forced to discharge the young man." Rayburn darted a look at Tammy. "I found his attentions to my granddaughter unbecoming and I told him to get out of here and stay clear."

"You did *what*?" Dorothy's voice was shrill. "Tammy's *my* daughter. I'm quite capable of deciding who she should see and—"

"That's enough," Jim said flatly.

As Tammy gazed at her stepfather, her eyes narrowed. Jim looked different than he had a few days before. The resemblance to Rayburn, which she had thought slight, was more pronounced. The set of his jaw, the lines of his mouth, a shadow of a mustache above that mouth—ah, that had to be it. Jim was growing a mustache. But he even sounded like Rayburn as he continued speaking in an even, measured way. "Dad had a perfect right to decide who will come on to this island and who won't. The point now isn't what has happened but what we must do."

"Thank you for the firm defense," Rayburn said drily. "And you are quite correct. I may have acted rather hastily but what's done is done. You needn't look so downcast. Do you believe I'd not give some thought to our welfare? We're certainly not dependent on Brome and his boat."

Nigel raised his head. "How do we raise the alarm, sir?"

"Jeb Amos has a boat. I've seen it in the boathouse and perhaps some of you have too. Old and only an open motor boat but quite seaworthy. We have two men here whom we can press into sailors' duties. Andy used to tinker around boats and Jim, while he's lived in Florida, has had some experience with pleasure craft. They're certainly not experienced in these waters but I'm sure they can make it to Amoston and a telephone."

Several heads nodded in agreement, and Ruth gave her father a brilliant smile. Tammy was watching Nigel's profile and she saw his russet brows lift. "Good thinking, sir. Jeb was showing me around the boathouse yesterday. Said the boat was adequate to get back and forth in. But..."

"But what?" Jim barked.

"Jeb told me as a safety precaution he drained the tank when the boat wasn't in use. Had some trouble a few years ago with a gang of hoodlums who stole it for a joy ride."

Rayburn chuckled. "I think we'll be able to fuel the boat without too much strain."

Nigel cocked his red head. "With what?"

"Gas, of course. Jeb must have kept a good supply of gas at the boathouse."

"What do you think caused the explosion at the cottage, sir? An explosion that was strong enough to make Andy think a giant hand was shaking this house. Strong enough to wake me too."

"That hadn't occurred to me." Rayburn frowned. "I thought it probably was the fuel the Amoses used in their stoves."

For the first time since they'd come back to the house,

Tammy spoke. "The stove in Holly's living room burns... burned coal and wood. So did the range in her kitchen. The gas for the boat was kept in drums in their shed."

Dorothy moaned and Ruth stiffened. Lifting a hand, Rayburn tried to smooth his hair. "I'll admit it's a serious situation and I'll take my share of blame but we can handle it. After all, we're not actually marooned here. Perhaps we can use a signal fire, there're piles of wood." He swung toward Nigel. "Did Jeb say anything about distress flares? Surely he had some."

"Didn't mention any but it's an idea."

Philip laughed, the ragged note of hysteria still in it. "Probably kept them in the shed with the gas."

His grandfather gave him a sharp look. "In the morning we'll organize and decide on a course of action. Now, we'd better get to our rooms and try and get a couple of hours of rest." He added soothingly, "We're in no serious trouble. We have a couple of weeks supply of food and there's plenty of fuel—"

"What kind of furnace heats this house?" Thelma broke in. "What about power? With Jeb gone how are we—"

"In the morning, Thelma." Rayburn stood up.

"Funny," Nigel said softly, "no one's even speculated on how the fire got started."

Philip gave his shrill laugh. "That's no mystery. Jeb and his booze and his pipe. Remember Mrs. Brome telling us he'd do for his wife and him?"

"Yes," Nigel admitted. "Now I remember."

Most of the people headed toward the hall. Rayburn scooped Buddy up and Ruth, limping slightly, clung to Jim's arm. Tammy remained where she was and Nigel made no move to leave her. The last person to pass them was Dorothy. She clutched her coat tightly around her slender body. "Are you coming up?" she asked her daughter.

"Not for a while, mother."

"Can I... would you mind if I spent the rest of the night with you?"

Tammy stood up, still clutching the cat. "Are you all right?"

"Shaken up." Dorothy tried to smile but her lips quivered. "I guess we all are. Do you mind?"

"Of course not. You go on up. I'll be there shortly. Better

144

plug in the heater." She held out old Blue. "Would you take Blue up with you?"

Taking the cat, Dorothy hugged him to her breast, and left the room. Nigel pulled himself up. Instead of heading toward the staircase, he walked toward the front door.

"Where are you going?" Tammy called.

He picked up a heavy flashlight. "Thought I'd go down to the boathouse and see if there are any flares there. I won't sleep anyway."

"I'll go with you."

"Going to be cold."

She buttoned the trench coat to her throat. "Can't be much colder than this house."

As they headed down the path toward the cottage, the wind wasn't gusting as fiercely as it had earlier. The flames were dying down but there was still enough glow to see clearly and the ruins of the building radiated a fierce heat. Nigel called over his shoulder, "Better wait here. I'm going to circle around behind it."

Tammy didn't wait. She followed him around the edge of the shell, picking her way cautiously around charred boards and splintered glass. As she rounded the ruin, she saw Nigel clambering up on the rocks behind it.

She gazed up at him. No longer did flames make him appear demonic. As he looked down on the wreck of the Amoses' cottage his expression was brooding, a remote sadness and a hint of weariness touching the corners of his mouth. The light from the dying fire cast a gentle bronze glow over him. Again she was stuck with the elusive resemblance to the young Atlas holding aloft the polished globe at the foot of the stairs in the tall house behind them.

"What are you looking for?" she called up to him.

Leaning down, he pulled her around so her back was to the building. "Trying to see if Holly and Jeb made any effort to get out."

"Can you...can you see anything?"

His hands tightened on her shoulders. "Their bedroom—where was it located?"

She thought, trying to take shallow breaths. In this sheltered spot the stench was terrible. "Right off the kitchen, next to the shed."

"A common wall. Probably they didn't have a chance.

145

There's a mass of twisted metal there, could be bedsprings, and a couple of . . . Looks like they died in bed."

She buried her face against his body. "Do you think they suffered terribly?"

"If they were in bed and made no effort to get out, I'd guess they probably suffocated from smoke before the flames hit them. Depends on where the fire started. From Mrs. Brome's report, Jeb could have dropped a spark on his chair. With upholstered furniture it might have smouldered for hours before breaking out." Gently, he shoved her back and climbed down. "Let's get out of here."

This time she went first, keeping her eyes on the ground. As they left the area around the ruins, Nigel clicked on the flashlight and they followed the circle of light down to the pier. The boathouse wasn't locked. Nigel sent the light beaming around the interior. The circle caught and settled on a work bench. "There's a flash of Jeb's back there, Tammy. You check those cupboards and drawers and I'll search the boat."

Tammy obeyed, her nose crinkling from the damp, mildewy smell of the place. She heard the boat in the bay creaking as Nigel jumped down into it. Then, methodically, she started to search. Over her shoulder, she called, "There's nothing back here but tools, some fishing gear, a couple of bottles of whiskey."

"No gas? Not even a gallon Jeb might have overlooked?"

"Just a minute. Some cans on this shelf. Turpentine . . . some paint cans. No gas or flares." She followed the light of her flash back to the boat. Nigel was bending over a locker. "Any luck?"

Straightening, he dusted his hands off. "Two blankets, a tarp, some rags, another pint of whiskey, a can of oil. That's it." He shook his head glumly. "If Jeb had any flares they must have been in the cottage." He sank down on a seat. "Might as well catch our breaths before we start back. Come aboard."

She crawled down while the boat rocked under her weight. Taking the seat opposite Nigel, she flashed her light around. It was a fair-sized boat, but old and showing signs of neglect. The paint was scaling and the engine cover was dull and tarnished. "Even if we could locate fuel, Nigel, I doubt this boat would get us to Amoston."

"She'd make it. Not pretty, but sound, and the engine is in good shape." Reaching into the locker, Nigel pulled out a

146

dark bottle. He tilted it up and took a swallow. Shuddering, he held it out to the girl. "Jeb's private stock is pretty raw but try to get a gulp down. At least it warms the stomach."

She took a drink and coughed, "Provided it can get past the tonsils."

He reached up and set the flashlight on the floor so the beam hit the wall behind them and cast enough light to see by. "This is shaping up as a wonderful reunion. Think next time I'll settle for Disneyland."

Tammy hunched forward, her collar pulled up around her throat, her hands jammed into her pockets. Nigel's eyes wandered over her face. "You were fond of her," he said softly.

"Holly was motherly. The way she touched me, pushed back my hair, or patted my cheek. The way she worried about how much I ate. Holly has been the only woman who touched me like that in years and I wanted to respond. I wanted to touch her too, put my arms around her. But... I couldn't. Too many years of being a creature cowering in a shell. Afraid to let that shell open even a crack. And now I can never touch her, put my arms around her." Tammy's hands tightened into fists. "It's so horribly unfair! Holly and Jeb weren't young, they didn't have much time left anyway. But to die like that!"

"I know, Tammy." He shifted on the hard seat. "Isn't there anything left between your mother and you? Wasn't she ever motherly?"

"At one time she was. I have memories of her when I was very young, of her holding me, loving me. A silly little episode when she was knitting a sweater for my doll. But as I grew older I started to frighten her. She couldn't understand me and she withdrew." Lifting her head, Tammy stared at the bright circle of light against the splintered boards of the wall. "It's not her fault. Mother has always wanted *all* of a person. I think as a child she must have been lonely, felt unwanted, unloved. I believe she tried to possess my father and he loved her deeply but he wouldn't be swallowed whole. Maybe at one time she tried to possess me. I do know she resented the attachment between my father and me, thought somehow it closed her out of our affections. When she married Jim she found exactly what she's always wanted—someone who belongs only to her."

"And your father?" Nigel prompted.

Tammy smiled, a smile of quiet radiance. "Wonderful. Warm, generous, giving. He understood."

"Did he understand about your visions?"

"Don't start that again."

Tammy made a move to get up but Nigel leaned forward and pushed her back. His voice was firm as he said slowly, "We have to start that. For your own sake, Tammy."

"Why?" she whispered. "Why are you doing this to me?"

"Because maidens in distress have always appealed to me. Don't you realize what's being done to you, what you're doing to yourself. You've been sheltered behind walls—"

"My school has no walls. It's low-key, even the attendants don't wear uniforms."

"Symbolic walls. You've lost part of your childhood, all your adolescence. Life passes quickly, Tammy. One of these days you'll look up and find you've wasted your life."

"It's secure, Nigel, safe."

"So is death," he said soberly, "and that's what you're living in that so-called school. No sorrow but no joy. No hate but no love. Safety but no happiness. Sure life is terrifying, but at least, it's *something*. A lovely girl like you..." His voice trailed off and then he said so softly she had to strain to hear, "You were meant to live, to love. I picture you running along a beach in the sunshine. Free. Your hair streaming out behind you. Alive."

For an instant she could see the same scene, felt sand spurting up under bare feet, the sun and wind warm against her skin. She saw a man waiting for her, bronzed, with rough dark hair and sailor's eyes. His arms stretched out. Rob. She blinked and was back in the dim light in the boathouse, the wind brushing at the walls with icy fingers, the smell of rot and mildew in her nostrils. "Why do you care, Nigel? You don't even know me."

He smiled, but there was weariness in that smile, the same hint of sadness and compassion she'd noticed earlier. "Don't you know, Tammy, inside every dwarf there's a seven-foot warrior struggling to get out? I care. Tell me about your father and your visions. Did he know about them?"

She was too weary, too emotionally exhausted to fight him any longer. She bowed her head and told him, "From the time I was tiny I got flashes. Hard to explain. Mother hated it, wouldn't even admit that it existed. I remember she spanked me for being naughty when I tried to tell her about things I'd seen. Perhaps it was because of her background, her early life."

148

"No doubt. That religious fanatic of a father of hers would call this sort of thing black magic. Associate it with witchcraft and Satan."

Tammy's eyes widened. "You know about mother's father?"

"I'm a writer. Good at research. I've looked into the background of everyone connected with the Quiller family. Your father took a different attitude, didn't he? Explained to you what those visions really are. You know you're a telepathist, don't you?"

"Yes," she admitted. "I've known that for years. Father explained it and he helped me develop it. There was a bond of the mind between us. He was going to take me to Duke University to be tested. He told me I wasn't a freak, that I had been given a gift. He taught me how to blank out thoughts, to stay sane." Lifting her head, she looked directly into Nigel's eyes. "Have you any idea of the torture, the constant swirl of thoughts around me? The images I see, the bodies I'm trapped in—"

"Bodies?"

"I don't just catch thoughts, I live in the bodies of people. Feel what they're feeling, see what they see. Helpless to look away. Now, can you understand why that symbolically walled world of mine offers security?"

"But you have learned how to close thoughts out?"

She nodded and her hair swung loose against her cheeks. "Except when I'm very tired or off guard. Once in a while there's no warning, I'm just there."

He asked abruptly, "You went into that school of Doctor Thule's shortly after your father's death. What happened to force you into a catatonic state?"

"Father died in a car accident. Jim's first wife, Vinnie, was killed with him."

"This mental bond between you and your father—did you witness Marc Syles's death?"

There was no way she could fight this man. Docilely, she told him of the evening of her father's death. She and her mother had been in the big ranch house in the Kissimmee valley. Jim came out to the ranch that evening to bring some papers that required her father's signature. When Tammy went to bed she left Jim and her mother in the living room, drinking coffee and chatting. Later she wakened, heard the wind gusting around the house, and crawled out of bed. Tammy tiptoed to the kitchen with the white plastered walls

149

and the rows of hanging copper pots. She peeked into Maria's bedroom and saw the plump Mexican housekeeper sound asleep, snoring gently, the bedlamp still glowing beside her. Cautiously, Tammy eased open the fridge, poured milk into a glass, took a handful of cookies and retraced her steps. Softly, she opened her mother's door and saw the spread of blond hair across the pillow. The other twin bed was neatly made up. Tammy could feel the coolness of the flooring under her bare feet, the drift of the thin nightie around her body. She sat up against a pile of pillows, thinking of her father, wondering when he'd be home. She wondered what this parapsychology center at the university was like, whether she really wanted to go and submit to tests. So ordinary, so peaceful. Then her name called, not aloud, but searingly across her mind and she wasn't in her bed any longer. She was standing with blood trickling down her face, her eyes fastened on a club in a hand, the stained club ripping and crushing her life out—

"I died," she told Nigel brokenly. "I experienced my father's death."

She'd wrenched her hands from her pockets and Nigel was gripping both those hands in his. He fumbled in the locker, found the pint of whiskey, and held it out to her. She accepted it and took a burning swallow. "Hold on there, Tammy," he told her.

"I want to go back to the house. Please, Nigel, no more."

"There has to be more. I'm sorry."

"Why? What good will it do?"

"I need help," he told her soberly. "You're the only one who can help me. So...you went into catalepsy and stayed that way for months. After you came out of it you meekly accepted the diagnosis—hallucinations."

"I was only a child. It was easier. Mother preferred to believe me mad rather than telepathic. Doctor Thule was only too willing to give her what she wanted. I didn't...I just didn't care."

Nigel sat forward and his voice was crisper. "Did your father have enemies?"

"I suppose so. Most rich men do have."

"Jim Quiller and your mother wasted no time in mourning, they were married in a few months."

"I'd had flashes from both of them before father died. They were attracted to each other but mother never would consider
150

divorce. Her religious background forbids that and in many ways she's a product of the nineteenth century, not the twentieth. Anyway, father and Vinnie died near Pensacola and both Jim and mother were at the ranch that night. They couldn't have had anything to do with the murders."

"There's such things as hired killers."

Shocked, she looked at him. "Mother would never do *that*."

"Jim might have. An attractive woman, a big estate. Think back, Tammy, you say you see and feel what the person whose body you're in sees and feels. Did you get even a glimpse of the killer's face?"

She nibbled at her lower lip. "I saw a hand holding a club. There were stains on it. It wasn't in a building, it was in the open. My hands were tied together...I mean, my father's hands. This is difficult, Nigel."

"Do your best. Speak as though it were you, not your father. Could you smell anything, hear anything?"

With a fingertip, she touched her cheek. "My face was bleeding, under the eye here. There was wind, gusting against the open gash, stinging it. Light from somewhere behind me, strong light."

"Any sounds?"

"Surf, I think, breaking against a beach." Her eyes widened. "A shout. Someone shouted a few words."

"What words?"

"*Dies irae.* That's what they were. I'm so tired, Nigel."

"Only a little longer, Tammy. So...day of wrath. Strong light—maybe headlights from a car. Not in the motel, on a beach somewhere." Under the cap of ruddy hair, his wide brow wrinkled. "Send Vinnie Quiller on some pretext to join Marc Syles in Pensacola. Catch them in the motel. There must have been a struggle. Marc's face cut during it. Bring Vinnie's clothes and cosmetics from her room and mix them up with Marc's. Rumple up the bed to make it look like a love nest. Take them out to some quiet spot and kill them. Load the bodies in Marc's car, arrange an accident, and a convenient explosion of the gas tank. The perfect crime! Everyone concerned wanting to hush it up because of scandal. The only witness a little girl who the world considers mad." He struck his tiny hands together. Numbly, the girl stared at him as he continued, "Anything else, Tammy, anything since you got to this island?"

"The schoolroom and Kat Winchfield. You were there."

She thought of Rob Brome and his Sally. No, that was none of Nigel's business. She wondered fleetingly where Rob was, if he was thinking of her. Nigel touched her arm and she told him, "A brief look into Andy Thaler's mind. He's on drugs."

"I know that. Anything tonight." Pushing back his jacket cuff, he glanced at his watch. "I mean last night. It's nearly six."

"Only a dream. It seemed to be about my father's death. A hand with a club and 'Dies irae' shouted. I must have been reliving it again."

"Are you certain, Tammy? Could it have been something that was happening at that moment?"

Her brow wrinkled. "Something that happened last night?" She gasped. "You mean *Holly*."

"That's what I'm getting at. Isn't it possible that Holly might have called you? That you might have been in her mind when she died?"

"No! I was dreaming, reliving the whole terrible thing again. Who would want to kill Holly and Jeb? They had nothing...no money. Nothing for anyone to gain. They were harmless and old and nice." Her mouth set in tight lines. "You frightened Holly when you asked her if she was nervous because of the Winchfield child. What are you trying to do to *me*? Are you a writer in search of a plot? This is cruel, Nigel."

"Face the facts, Tammy. Another fire, the bodies pretty well destroyed. Your vision of a club—"

"I told you that was a dream." Her voice sank to a whisper. "You're suggesting that Jeb and Holly were murdered by the same person who killed my father and Vinnie Quiller. That's insane."

"That's exactly what good old Doctor Thule and your mother thought when you tried to convince them that your father didn't die in an accident."

"There was some reasonable motive for my father's murder. He was wealthy. Jeb and Holly Amos were poor. They had nothing."

The tiny man stood up and stretched the stiffness from his body. Crawling out of the boat, he picked up the flash and held a hand out to help the girl. "They had their lives, Tammy, maybe that was motive enough. But enough of this. Let's get back to the house. Too bad we couldn't find those flares. Getting off this island wouldn't be a bad idea."

Tammy jumped up beside him. She listened. "The wind has dropped. Rayburn's suggestion about a signal fire. Perhaps we can light one now."

"I'm afraid not." He pointed the flash toward the double doors at the end of the boathouse. There was a gap between the bottom edges of the doors and the water. Whitish tendrils were curling under the doors, edging along the water of the bay. "Fog," Nigel said grimly. "If it's the usual pea souper they get here it will be some time before a signal fire would be worth the effort. In a thick fog a fire couldn't be seen from the mainland."

She laughed but it was only a sound. "Then we are marooned here. You called my school a prison and here I am in another one. Haven't you a suitable quotation, Nigel?"

"One." He hesitated and then said solemnly, "If this dread isle my prison be, I thank who made my cell mate thee."

"You win the contest. I can't place that quote."

Opening the door, he stepped out onto the pier. A wall of white greeted them. He took her hand and led the way up the path. "Still no contest, Tammy. I made that one up on the spot."

Behind them, fog crept steathily up toward the house under Kat's Rock.

Ten

The fog enveloping Winchfield Island had already blanketed the cafe at Amoston. Tugging a heavy pullover over his shirt, Rob Brome circled the counter and the tables, their chairs upended on them, and gazed morosely at the mass of fog huddling against the wide window facing toward the sea. Looked like it was settling right in. Must have started in the early morning hours, he decided, when he'd gone to bed a little after midnight the night had been still clear, windy but clear.

He rasped a hand over his chin. Need a shave. Better have one after breakfast. No sense in getting like dad had in the last few years, slouching around unshaven, wearing old carpet slippers. He certainly wasn't entering his dotage yet, no excuse for him.

Rob went back to the hotplate he'd moved out beside the stove. Cost too much to turn on the grill for one person, though it did a better job. He missed his mother's cooking. Granted he was pretty fair at frying bacon and eggs and chops, but mom could sure whip up a tasty pie and that chowder of hers—now that was rib-sticking food. He also missed her chatter. The place seemed so damned quiet now. He shrugged. Might as well get used to it. From the looks of that fog it would be a while before there was even any traffic to break the monotony.

Turning the sizzling bacon, he stacked the strips in one corner of the frying pan and broke a couple of eggs in the hot grease. Reaching under the counter, he pulled out half a loaf of bread, and stuck two slices in the toaster. He wondered if he should check and see if there was more bread in the freezer. Should be. Mom would never leave without seeing everything was stocked up.

He shoveled bacon strips and eggs onto a plate, buttered toast lavishly, and slid the plate onto the counter. Coffee, strawberry jam—homemade, thank God—pepper, salt. Ah, that did it. Perching on a stool, he wondered how the Quillers were making out for fresh food. He'd carted over lots of frozen stuff and canned goods, but they might be running short on milk, butter, bread, maybe eggs. Savagely he speared a rasher of bacon. Wonder how Holly and Jeb are getting on? Probably Holly is as impressed as mom had been with Rayburn Quiller but from what he'd seen of the man that charm might be wearing thin. Last week, Rayburn had certainly dropped the charm with him. What in hell had gotten into the man? Rob admitted he'd known the carton of canned peas wasn't for the island, used it as an excuse to see Tammy, but what the hell. All he'd done was take her out for a ride on the *Caravan* and she'd been willing to go. He hadn't twisted her arm or kidnapped the girl.

Across the bridge of his nose, Rob's dark brows drew together in puzzled thought. The insults that old goat had spat at him had been out of proportion. Rayburn had acted...jealous. Ridiculous! The man had to be at least as old as his dad and mom were. For God's sakes, he had a great-grandson! Fortune hunter! Taking advantage of a disturbed teenager. At first he tried to reason with Rayburn, tried to use some common sense. Sure, his temper had finally snapped. Whose wouldn't? He'd driven the poor old *Caravan* at top speed away from Winchfield Island, determined if he ever saw another Quiller it would be too soon.

Swiveling the stool around, he gazed at the fog-shrouded window. Still...that island was cut entirely off. Right now it might as well be in another world. Mentally, he shook himself. Jeb and Holly were out there. Jeb knew the sea and the weather and he had that old tub. Like the *Caravan*, Jeb's boat didn't look like much but it wasn't a bad craft. As for

156

the Quillers—one of them was a doctor, another was a nurse. As for Tammy with her hunched shoulders and eyes as shrouded by those glasses as that window was by fog...her mother was with her and that stepfather of hers seemed to have a good head.

He thought of Tammy on the deck of his boat, his arm around her slender shoulders, the warmth of her long body pressed against his side, that lovely face tilted up to him, those deep blue eyes. What was Tammy? She said herself she didn't know. How in hell had she pulled the name Sally out of his mind? No possible way she could have heard anything about Sally. The shock and horror of her expression as she doubled up against the rail, her hands balled into fists. Had she pulled the whole thing from his mind? Seen what the Cong had left of Sally dangling from that stake?

He rubbed a hand over his shaggy head. He'd had another rotten night, waking drenched with sweat and the bed a tangle of sheets and blankets, both pillows on the floor. Only part of his dream had lingered when he came awake. Generally, he dreamt of Nam, of the jungle and the village where Sally had lived. Last night he'd been on the deck of the *Caravan* near the pier at Winchfield Island. On the pier there'd been some sort of stake and lashed to it was Sally, not Sally dead and mutilated, but Sally as she once had looked. Jet black hair blew around her amber face, long almond-shaped eyes gazed imploringly at him. Her pink mouth was open as though she were screaming. He was trying to dock the *Caravan*, struggling to get to her, and every time he brought the boat up close something seemed to slap it away. The lines of her tiny, full-breasted figure blurred and became long and slim. The hair brushing her amber cheeks was longer, finer, a sun-streaked blond. The long eyes rounded and turned to violet-blue. The figure on the stake kept changing, one minute it was Sally, the next it was Tammy. He fought to get ashore but he couldn't...then, mercifully, he awoke.

Rob tried to grin. The army shrink would sure have fun with that dream. Probably put it down to transference, a veering of feeling from a dead girl to a live one. Rob admitted he disliked the idea of Tammy on that island. He'd never liked the place himself, never cared for that cold, dank house. He'd been in it a couple of times with Jeb, helping the caretaker fix some wiring, and it had given him the willies. Of course from the time he'd been a kid Holly had talked about

157

the Winchfields. His mom liked to hear Holly tell and retell that grisly tale, although mom always said privately she thought Holly was doing a lot of embroidery on it. Had to admit one thing, Holly Amos was a natural-born story teller. Could make your flesh creep.

Rob pictured Tammy wandering around that house, the fog eerily pressing in on it, walking down the hall where Johnny had been slaughtered, sitting before the fireplace where the old man was supposed to have been clubbed to death, working in the kitchen where the old woman was chopped to bits.

With a start Rob realized that until a short time ago he wouldn't have been at all concerned about Tammy. Other people had just been a blur to him and he'd had no interest in their welfare. Oddly enough it was his father who had managed to break through his son's indifference and apathy. Mom was the talker of the family, running on and on but somehow managing to skirt the main issue—what exactly was wrong with her son. Wilfred Brome had said nothing, merely watched, until that night. It was late in the evening and Rob had left the living room and retreated to a table in the dark cafe, sitting at the window, moodily smoking and drinking a beer. His dad shuffled out in his carpet slippers, opened the fridge and got out a can of beer.

"Sitting in the dark, son?" he called. "Want a light on?"

"Doesn't make any difference. Mom gone to bed?"

"On her way." Sinking into a chair opposite his son, he looked out over the sea. "Your mother's not getting any younger, gets tired pretty fast these days. Worrying about you isn't helping her any either."

"If she's worried she sure as hell manages to hide it."

His father darted him a quick look. "Wouldn't hurt *you* to worry about someone else occasionally."

"Look, dad, if I'm not welcome here, say so."

"How would you like to shut up and listen for a change? Didn't say a word about your not being welcome. Just want you to stop acting like a spoiled kid and start acting like a man. Think you're the only one who ever went to war? Think you're the only one who ever watched people die?"

Rob smashed his beer can down on the table. "Going to give me a lecture, eh? Tell me all about *your* war. Let me tell you something. At least you knew what in hell you were fighting *for*."

158

His father set his own can down softly. "Sure, and you were hurt far worse than anyone else ever was. Hurt so much you won't even try to live. Walking around like a robot. Hiding out here like a kid, scared to get going again. Saying to your mother and me and to the world, 'Hey, this is what *you* did to me.'" Pulling himself to his feet, he placed a hand on Rob's shoulder. "Think about this. Your war lasted for two years. Two years from your life. You had all those years before and you got lots of them ahead. Are you going to waste all those good years for a lousy two? Think about it, son."

Before his father had shuffled back to the living quarters, Rob was out of the cafe. For hours he walked the beach, gazing out across the moonlit sea, forcing himself to retrace those years before Nam. In so many ways those had been good years. Before he went to school his mother had had a tendency to coddle her only son but his father had combatted that in his own quiet way. Wilfred Brome took Rob with him on his boat, taught him about the sea, fishing, handling boats. The sea had been Rob's first love but his third term in school had given him his second. She was his teacher and to him she always personified a mermaid. Miss Cutter, such a prosaic name for a creature of moonbeams and sea-green eyes and spindrift hair. The mermaid drifted from his life, the years passed, and high school had arrived. His third love was not a creature of moonbeams but a very earthy Joyce Carlson. As Rob thought of Joyce his lips curved in a smile. He'd been a big-boned boy, tall for his age, but too light to make the school football team. God! how he'd tried to make that team. For Joyce. Not only was she the prettiest girl in school but an avid cheerleader. He could still see her in that skimpy little uniform excitedly jumping at the edge of the field. Ash-blond hair streaming out under the pert cap, shapely breasts jiggling, a fine neat bottom holding his covetous gaze. There was nothing spiritual about his feelings for Joyce—he lusted after her—but Joyce Carlson never knew he existed. Her time and attention and affection were only for football players.

Rob's reminiscent smile faded. A few years ago he'd seen Joyce again and the high school sex goddess had vanished under excess poundage, the gleaming hair was fading, the large blue eyes were pouched and empty. Joyce had got her own dream and married the captain of the team. She'd produced four children, put on weight, and watched her handsome husband turn into a fat slob making a precarious living selling insurance. So much for dreams.

Rob stooped and picked up a pebble from the beach. Tossing it overhand as far as he could, he watched it slice into the water in a spray of silver foam. The university had come next. His parents had tried to help, but Rob had had to dig in and earn as much of his tuition as he could himself. He'd been busy and as he wasn't an exceptional student he'd had to work to get grades. Somehow he'd found time for Jennifer. Ah, Jennifer. Neither a sex goddess nor a mermaid. Somewhere in between. She was a wispy little girl wearing granny glasses and limp calico dresses drifting around bare grubby feet. She called herself a radical and perhaps she was. Her background was middle class and she never suffered from lack of money but she despised her parents and all they stood for. Jennifer was a person of conflicting values. She ached for the starving children in Asia, agonized for the slaughter of baby seals, but appeared to be blind to the suffering in her mother's face. She despised war and violence but during a demonstration had attacked a policeman with a broken bottle. He'd needed thirteen stitches to close the gash she'd inflicted but it didn't bother her. She just couldn't see him as a man simply doing a job.

Rob had been fascinated by her, infatuated with the body under the cotton dresses. He'd consumed pounds of wheat germ and yogurt and nuts with her, listened to her theories on self-involvement and self-identity, made passionate love to her, and lost her when his draft number came up.

"Tear your card up," Jennifer raved. "Go to Canada, go to jail. Don't go to Vietnam."

Good advice but Rob couldn't take it. He went to war. The last word his love had said to him was uttered as a curse. "Murderer!" Jennifer had shrieked.

Picking up another pebble, Rob hurled it into the water. He found himself shouting over the sea. "Not murderer, Jennifer. Not on your life!"

He pulled himself together and headed back across the beach. Two years in that alien land, two years of death and horror and destruction. Stinking jungles and fetid swamps. Feeling his sanity slipping and then, like a miracle, love came to him again. Sally. Tiny Sally with her understanding and her compassion, with her amber skin and long dark eyes. Finding salvation in those soft arms, in that gentle body. But
160

he'd lost Sally and with her death had lost the best part of Rob Brome. All that had been left was a hollow, echoing shell. A creature who cowered away from affection, from any commitment, who spent his days helping around a motel, taking out charter boats. A thing that walked like a man but wasn't one.

He opened the door of the cafe. Light still spilled out through the doorway of the living quarters and he could see a dark form huddled on one of the counter stools. For a moment he thought it was his dad and then he recognized the shabby woolen robe. Mom.

He called to her. "Home is the sailor, home from the sea."

She didn't speak and it was only when he was closer that he saw tears trickling down her cheeks. "Mom," he said, and wrapped his arms around her.

Her voice was muffled against his chest. "I thought...."

Without further words Rob knew exactly what she'd been thinking. "No, mom, not that. No worry about me casting myself into the sea." He tried to laugh. "Couldn't drown anyway, not the way I swim."

"Ever since you came back I've worried for fear you'll do something...dreadful."

His arms tightened around her plump body. God, he thought, and this she's lived with. Never let on by a glance or a word, babbled cheerfully on about inconsequentials, and wondered every time I went out if I'd ever come back. And I thought *Jennifer* was blind. Mom and dad are aging; they should retire. The only reason they're hanging on here is to give me a place to stay, a place to pretend I'm working in. And I've never seen it, never looked past myself long enough to see it. He told her gently, "Come to bed, mom. It's all right, everything is all right now."

It wasn't all right, but at least it was better. Before his parents left to winter in Florida he told them his decision. "You don't have to come back here. I'll see to selling the business. You find a place in Florida to live."

His dad lifted his bushy brows. "What will you do, son?"

Rob gave him a reassuring smile. "Haven't a clue right now but by spring I'll know."

Brave words. He still didn't have a clue to what he'd do, where he'd go. But some emotion had seeped back into the empty shell. What his mother and father had started, Tammy

161

Syles had finished. When she'd probed his mind, shared Sally's death, the door opened a little wider. He owed Tammy.

Abruptly Rob jumped up, and stacked the plate, cup, and utensils. Carrying them over, he dumped them into the sink. What a mess. The remains of last night's dinner were congealing in a pot, dishes coated with dried food were stacked on the counter, crumbs and dabs of butter and jam encrusted the plastic area around the sink. He grimaced and turned on the hot water tap. As he worked, his mind wandered back to Tammy Syles. Wasn't there a book his mother had found in one of the cabins? Some traveler had forgotten it. He could remember mom bringing it to him, asking him what it was. He glanced at the title and told her, "Another of those things on ESP."

Leaving the sink, he opened the door to the living quarters. When he returned to the cafe he poured a second cup of coffee and carried the cup and a thick book to the counter. He gazed down at the title page. *All About Psychic Phenomena*. After a moment, he flipped the pages until he reached the chapter on telepathy.

Eleven

The pine-topped table in the kitchen was littered with the remains of the breakfast Thelma had thrown together. There was a platter of overdone bacon and undercooked eggs congealing in grease, a box of prepared breakfast cereal, and the remains of a stack of toast.

The only person missing from breakfast was Dorothy who still was in Tammy's bed. Although it was past nine the ceiling fixture beamed harsh light over the table and the people around it. Thelma picked the coffee pot up. "Anyone want more?" she asked.

Philip held out his cup. "Your coffee's fair but that bacon!" Shuddering, he poked at the rasher on his plate. "What'd you do—cremate it?"

"Do you want to drink this coffee or wear it?" She filled his cup and sat down in her own chair. She glowered at Rayburn. "Told you I was no good at cooking. Didn't even have Dorothy to help."

Rayburn made a placating gesture. "You did your best, Thelma. Anyway, we managed to fill up on toast and cornflakes. Tammy, how is your mother? Does she want Andy to look in on her?"

Tammy shook her head. "I think she got a chill last night.

163

I took her up aspirin and a couple of hot water bottles. She's sleeping now."

Jim moved restlessly. "Don't you think we'd better try and get organized, dad? Thelma made a good point last night. I don't know about the rest of you but I haven't a clue what the setup is here for fuel and power. I do know Jeb seemed to spend most of his time tinkering in those sheds out there."

"Right." Rayburn glanced at the fog-coated window. "It looks like we'll have to keep lights on in here even during daylight hours while this weather lasts. An extra drain on the power. We must be methodical. First things first. Thelma, while she's a fine nurse, is really not able to handle the cooking. Tammy, have you knowledge of even simple cooking?"

She shook her head again. It was Nadine who spoke and her voice was heard so seldom that all heads swung in her direction. "I can do plain cooking," she told them.

"Fine," Rayburn said heartily. "Nadine volunteers as cook."

"That was the last of the bacon," Thelma said. "And there's only a dozen eggs left. We're low on bread too."

Filling his cup, Rayburn spooned sugar into the steaming coffee. "I have a list of provisions in the library, Nadine. I'll see you get it. I believe there's canned bacon and some tinned ham. There are roasts and steaks in the freezer and frozen vegetables." He cast a reassuring smile at his relatives. "We may be a bit short on some items but we're certainly not going to go hungry. With Nadine acting as cook that will free you, Thelma, for household duties. We'll care for our own rooms but you will have to vacuum and dust and then there're the bathrooms to look after."

Thelma's voice was as sullen as her expression. "What about Ruth and Tammy?"

Ruth gave her daughter-in-law a sweet smile. "You know I have Buddy to look after."

Her father nodded his smooth head. "That's all I can ask from Ruthie. She's never been strong, you know. As for Tammy, right now she has Dorothy to care for. Perhaps, if you have any spare time, my dear, you can give Thelma a hand."

"What about those motors?" Jim asked impatiently.

"I've given that some thought. I understand young Philip has some knowledge of mechanics. Is that correct?"

164

"That's right. I've tinkered with cars and a motorcycle." Philip fingered his scalp lock. "I've built a couple of radios too. But that doesn't make me an expert."

"You're the closest to one we have. Unless...Nigel?"

Nigel grinned at his grandfather. He was perched on a chair with a sofa cushion bringing him to table height. "Not my field, sir."

Rayburn nodded. "That leaves it up to you, Philip."

"I don't even know where they are."

Nigel's grin widened. "In those sheds east of the house. Jeb dashed in and out with great authority. I think you'll find the water pump there and the generator for electricity."

"Where's the furnace?" Philip wailed.

Playfully, Thelma tugged at the boy's scalp lock. "In the shed tacked on to this kitchen, genius. The furnace, hot water heater and tank, the old washing machine. Waiting for the touch of your skilled hands."

Rayburn frowned. "This is no joking matter, Thelma. If this fog doesn't lift we could be here for several days, perhaps a week. Think of the hardships if we lack heat and light."

"Or water," Nadine pointed out. "Even drinking water."

"Correct." Rayburn turned to Philip. "You have an important task, my boy. We're counting on you."

The young man leaned toward his grandfather. With his shaven head and wide, clear eyes he looked like an acolyte seeking blessing from an abbot. "Do you think I can do it, granddad?"

"Assuredly. Check it over this morning and try to give me a report by lunch time. Remember, our welfare is in your hands."

Pushing back his chair, an inspired Philip jumped to his feet. "I'll get right on it!"

"Do you want me to help him, dad?" Jim asked.

"There's a job for you. Nigel and you had better see if you can find the best place to light a signal fire. As soon as this fog lifts we must be ready. Nigel, you've explored this island. Have you any ideas?"

Bracing his elbows on the table, Nigel said slowly, "The rock behind this house is the highest point on the island. There's an outcropping about halfway up it that's fairly level. Only problem is that the cliff is pretty straight up and down. Even in clear weather, to lug that wood up would be difficult."

"And in fog too hazardous. We can't afford anyone being hurt. Can you think of another spot?"

"How about the beach area?" Ruth asked.

"Too far west of Amoston," Nigel told her. "Second best after Kat's Rock would be the end of the pier. It's almost directly across from the cafe. Good chance that Rob would spot a large fire there."

"Fine," Rayburn approved. "You and Jim start carrying wood down to the pier. Take your time and watch the footing."

Tammy had been watching the doctor. Andy Thaler showed more signs of exhaustion and strain than any of the rest did. The bandage on his cheek was chalk white against lead-colored skin. His burnt hand rested in an improvised sling and he had barely touched his breakfast. Ignoring Rayburn, she spoke directly to him. "Shouldn't we do something about... about Holly and Jeb. We can't leave them there like that."

Andy opened his mouth but it was Rayburn who said heartily, "We've discussed that, Andy and I, earlier. I wasn't going to mention it in front of the ladies. Andy and I are going down now. We'll need some sort of wrappings. I suggested a tarp but Andy tells me no. He says, for obvious reasons, we must have something airtight. Time, you know."

For a moment silence fell over them as they contemplated time and the charred remains of the caretakers. Wiping the traces of milk from Buddy's mouth, Ruth said brightly, "What about plastic garment bags? I've two covering my dresses. They have zippers."

Thelma stood up. "Something better right here." Opening a drawer, she pulled out a sheaf of folded green plastic. "Heavy garbage bags. Use them double and tie the necks tight. What about it, Andy?"

This time the doctor had a chance to answer. "They'll work. Better give us half a dozen, just in case."

Nobody asked in case of what. Norman, who'd stolidly been eating cornflakes, dropped his spoon with a clatter. "What about me, granddaddy? You've given Phil a job and Jim. Even Nigel." He asked eagerly, "Can I help you and daddy?"

Stretching out a long arm, Rayburn affectionately rumpled the boy's carrot-colored curls. "I haven't forgotten you. You start bringing firewood into the house. There're three fireplaces, one in the drawing room, another in the library, and a third in Ruthie's bedroom. In case anything happens with the furnace we must be prepared to have all three ready. That's an important job, my boy."

"As important as Phil's?"

"Fully." Pulling himself up, Rayburn looked around the table. "Everyone get to their jobs. No dawdling. And don't look so downcast. This fog can't last long." He rubbed his hands briskly together. "Let's imagine ourselves as a modern Swiss Family Robinson. Approach our tasks with cheer and optimism. Come, Andy, bring those plastic bags and let's set an example for the younger people."

Except for Thelma, everyone in the kitchen rose. Nigel, Jim, and Norman followed the two older men, and Nadine started to gather up the dishes. Ruth trailed out with little Buddy at her heels. Locating a tray, Tammy put it on the counter and opened the cupboard.

Thelma stared transfixed at the door. "Now I've seen everything, folks! Big daddy going out to stuff a couple of charred bodies in garbage bags and practically telling us to whistle as we work. He missed his calling. Should have been a cheerleader." She pulled herself off her chair.

"Are you going to start the housework now?" Nadine asked.

"Hell, no! Going to milk a couple of goats." Thelma smiled broadly. "Just in case, where is the damn vacuum?"

"Holly kept it in the cupboard in the front hall," Tammy told her.

"Swissfamilyfuckingrobinson," Thelma muttered, and pushed through the door.

Tammy found she was smiling. How could she smile? She asked herself. Her mother was up in bed looking like death, Holly and Jeb were lumps of burnt flesh, fog was shrouding the island so she was a prisoner in this house. She glanced at Nadine and was surprised to see that the older woman's lips were twitching. Nadine's smile turned into a laugh.

"It does happen, Tammy," she told the girl. "I remember a funeral years ago. A dear friend. I was desolate, grief stricken, and then the minister said something. I can't remember his exact words but I found I was laughing. Something about life being thorns and roses and implying that the dear deceased was a prick. There I was crying and laughing at the same time."

"Reaction, I suppose." Tammy took a clean cup and put it on the tray. She plugged the toaster in.

Competently, Nadine piled the dishes and brought them to the sink. She stood beside Tammy. "I like working around a kitchen," she told the girl. "Funny, in this year of the liberated woman with every housewife struggling to get away from the domestic grind and do something meaningful, I'd still give a lot to have a home. All my life I've worked and at any point if I'd been asked what I'd really like to be, I'd have answered—a housewife. A woman with a home and children and a husband."

"Have you never had a home?"

Turning on the tap, Nadine poured soap into the sink. "A couple of rented houses, apartments, once a condominium. Never a home."

I mustn't pry, Tammy thought, and heard herself asking, "Did you ever consider marrying again?"

"Once. But it wouldn't have been fair to the man. Some women love only once. I had my love." Her voice didn't change as she said, "There's orange juice in the fridge. Might taste good to your mother."

Nodding, Tammy filled a glass. She knew the conversation was over. Picking up the tray, she went up the stairs. The second floor was so dark she slowed for the next flight of steps. In her room the heater was pulsing, sending a little warmth into the frigid air. Fog shrouded the window and the room was so dim that Tammy switched on the lamp. Her mother was curled up with the big cat resting against her stomach. Dorothy lifted her head.

"No food," she said faintly.

Tammy cleared a place for the tray on the bedside table. "You're going to drink some coffee and juice, mother." She put a hand on her mother's brow. "Are you feverish?"

"A bit. Mainly exhausted. I want to rest."

"It's so cold up here. You really would be more comfortable in your own room."

"I'd rather stay here...with you. You don't mind, do you?"

"Of course not. But the bathroom's on the lower floor. I don't want you getting chilled." Pushing Blue over, Tammy perched on the edge of the bed. She held out the orange juice. "Drink this and take some more aspirin."

Meekly, Dorothy swallowed the pills and the juice. "Is Jim with Ruth?" she asked.

"He's with Nigel, carrying wood down for a signal fire."

"Did he ask about me?"

168

For a moment, Tammy considered lying. Neither Ruth nor Jim had appeared to notice that Dorothy was missing at breakfast. Rayburn was the only one who'd shown any interest. While she searched for some tactful answer, Dorothy's head moved from side to side on the pillow. "Never mind, Tammy, I know he didn't. At home, even if I had only a headache, Jim would hover over me. And Maria would cook my favorite food and..." her voice trailed off and she started to cry.

Plucking the glass from her mother's limp fingers, Tammy went to the chest and took out a box of tissues. She handed some to her mother. "If I was home," Dorothy sobbed, "it would be warm and comfortable and maybe Alice and Hank would be coming over for dinner and bridge. Maria would be taking care of everything and I'd be trying to decide what to wear. And Jim would be...Jim. Kind and attentive." She grasped Tammy's hand. "When we get home it will be like that. It's just this island, those people. I feel like I'm in the middle of a bad dream and can't wake up."

Tammy squeezed the clutching hand. "Did you and Jim have a quarrel?"

"No, not really a quarrel." Dorothy dabbed at her streaming eyes. "Hand me a cigarette, Tammy." Finding her mother's package, Tammy shook one out. Lighting it, she handed it to her mother. "Jim was terrible to me last night. Accused me of being spoiled, pampered, possessive. Tammy, *am* I like that?"

Wordlessly, Tammy stared at her mother. After a moment, Dorothy murmured, "Don't try to answer that. I know the answer myself. I married Marc when I was so young and he was...Marc was lavish. He did pamper me, I am spoiled. But possessive? I've never had anyone to possess. Marc loved me but he kept telling me I mustn't cling. After you were born, Marc moved even further away from me. You preferred your father to your mother, and there was something between you and Marc, something I couldn't understand." Dorothy gave a harsh laugh. "Perhaps I didn't want to understand. If only you had been a different type of girl. If only you'd been normal—" Dorothy broke off, and cried, "Tammy, I'm sorry! I didn't mean that."

"It's okay, mother." Tammy shrugged thin shoulders. "What's normal?"

Dorothy took a deep breath. "It's not too late. I can change."

169

Standing up, Tammy tried for a lighter note. "You're going to have to. That nightie has soot all over it and so do these sheets. Take my robe and go down and have a hot tub. While you're gone I'll find fresh linen and make the bed up." She scooped up the cat. Curling up in her arms, he started a low, ragged purring. "Better feed this poor old puss and let him outside for a while."

Dorothy sat up. "How many are still in the house? Is Ruth—"

"Shut up in her room with Buddy. Nadine's working in the kitchen and Thelma's vacuuming the first floor. You won't see anyone."

Competently, Tammy herded her mother to the bathroom. Then she took the cat down to the kitchen, poured canned milk diluted with water into a saucer, broke a piece of bread into it, and asked Nadine, "When he's eaten, will you put him outside?"

Nadine was mixing up dough in a blue bowl. "I don't like cats."

Squatting, Tammy stroked the soft fur. "This one is old and there's nowhere else for him to go."

"I'll see he gets out but you better come back and let him in. I don't want him around when I'm cooking."

When Tammy returned to the hall, she found Thelma vacuuming the dingy carpet. "I'll be down in a few minutes to give you a hand," she told the older woman. "As soon as I get mother settled."

"No rush." Thelma grimaced. "This ruddy machine must have come over with the *Mayflower*."

Running up to the second floor, Tammy found the linen closet next to her mother's room. There was a plentiful supply of linen, neatly folded, smelling faintly of lavender sachet. She swung open her mother's door and went in. The twin beds were unmade, clothes were tossed around, it smelled of smoke and alcohol. Tammy located a clean pair of pyjamas and found the housecoat she could remember her father giving Dorothy on their last Christmas as a family. It was an opulent, slightly theatrical garment of crushed velvet, lined and collared in white fur. But it was warmer than her own woolen robe. Scooping the linen and clothes up, she returned to the attic room where she found Dorothy crouching in the armchair, the heater at her feet, gazing unhappily at the

170

shrouded window. She'd washed her hair and it clung damply to the fine contours of her head.

"Here we go," Tammy said, and tossed her mother the pyjamas.

As she stripped the mattress and put fresh linen on, she watched her mother from the corner of her eye. Dropping the robe, Dorothy pulled the pyjamas on. An attractive woman, Tammy thought, her figure was still firm and youthful.

She helped Dorothy into bed, put tissues and cigarettes on the table, and handed her mother a couple of novels from her pile of books. "I'll have to bring Blue up here again, mother, Nadine doesn't like cats and I don't know what else to do with him."

"Do that, Tammy. He's company. I like having him with me." She watched her daughter bundling up the soiled linen and as the girl reached for the doorknob she asked, "You'll be back, won't you?"

"Soon. I'll bring Blue up."

"And then?"

"I should give Thelma a hand with the work but I'll bring your lunch tray."

As she opened the door, her mother whispered, "Tammy, they're corrupting him. They're doing something to Jim. Ruth and Rayburn. I feel it. I'm afraid, Tammy, for the first time in years, I'm afraid."

There was a sound in that voice that Tammy had never heard in it before. A sound that reminded her of the look on Nigel's face in the reflection from the flashlight as they'd sat in the dawn hours in the boathouse. She said slowly, "It's what happened to Jeb and Holly. It frightened all of us. As soon as the weather clears we'll be leaving, mother. Once you're home Jim will be fine."

"I hope so. I'll show him I can change. It's never too late, is it?"

Tammy closed the door. She bit her lower lip. Her mother wrapped in crisp white linen, her hair clinging damply to her cheeks, had recalled a few memorized words. She clattered down the stairs, deliberately trying to make noise, trying to break the stillness of the old house. At the foot of the stairs she paused, resting a hand on the bronze shoulder of the Atlas. The words were still running through her mind. She repeated them aloud. "'How swift the shuttle flies, that weaves your shroud.'" She was surprised at the surge of feel-

171

ing that came with those words, the feeling of protectiveness toward her mother. There has to be something left, Tammy thought fiercely, some lingering remnants of love that existed between us when I was a small child.

Thelma, dragging the vacuum behind her, bumped into the archway. She looked up at Tammy. "Talking to yourself?" she asked. Tammy found she was glad to see her, glad to hear her voice.

"Something like that. What can I do?"

Thelma jerked her head. "Finish up the drawing room. Hearth needs to be cleaned. So...dust and oh...tidy up. Okay?"

Glad to have something to do, Tammy started to clean up the room. As she worked she thought what an ugly room it was. No attempt had been made to soften its square lines, even the furniture was square, heavy, dark. She did what she could. She picked up magazines, emptied ashtrays, dusted the ancient tables. She was on her knees before the hearth, sweeping it, when Thelma pulled the vacuum back down the hall and clicked it off. Rubbing her hands off on her denim pants, the older woman walked to the window and pulled back one of the heavy lace curtains. "Here comes big daddy and his band of merry men," she told the girl.

"Is Nigel with them?"

"Yeah, and Jim and Andy. Gad! Norm's got another arm-load of wood. Sure trying to show his granddaddy what a good boy he is. Notice the mess he's dragged in?"

Tammy smiled. There was no way anyone could miss the mess. The wood box was full to overflowing and Norman had piled more logs back against the wall.

Thelma grumbled, "Every time I got that bloody hall floor clean, Norm came pounding in again. Spraying chips and stuff all over the carpet. Never will learn to wipe his boots off." She laughed. "Must have been driving Ruth crazy. Heard her screaming at him to get out of her room. Said he was turning the place into a woodyard."

The front door creaked open and men's voices resounded from the hall. Norman's high-pitched voice predominated. "See what I did, granddaddy? Look in here."

There was a flurry of movement behind Tammy, and she glanced over her shoulder. Norman was staggering across the room, his arms piled high with logs. Bits of bark and sawdust marked his path. He dumped the wood on the carpet.

172

Rayburn smiled approvingly. "Good work, my boy. That should be enough, I think. Ah, Tammy, how charming you look. Like Cinderella before the arrival of her prince."

"Where's Andy?" Thelma asked.

"He went up to his room. He's not feeling well."

"I'm not carrying any trays up. Ran my feet off this morning."

"Don't get huffy. We've all done our share. Andy said he isn't hungry, anyway."

"I'll bet you are."

He looked at his filthy hands. "My appetite has always been good. Beastly job though. I'm going to wash and change my clothes. Will you tell Nadine she can get lunch on?"

Grunting, Thelma followed Rayburn through the archway. Norman trotted along behind, still chattering about how much wood he'd carried. Jim stood in the archway and Nigel moved over near Tammy. Hanging the hearth brush back on the metal stand, Tammy asked Jim, "Are you interested in how mother is?"

"No need to ask. Dorothy always wallows in illness. Even a hangnail is the signal for frenzied attention."

Behind the dark lenses, the girl's eyes searched Jim's face. The resemblance to her father was more definite. The budding mustache was going to be black, his eyebrows were the same dark bars, his brown hair was smoothly brushed back. All the vague, indecisive planes of his face appeared to have hardened. He'd even adopted Rayburn's enunciation, slow and clear and slightly pedantic. I've never liked this man, Tammy admitted, and I like him even less now. Aloud, she said crisply, "I stopped in your room to get some clothes for mother. It's a mess. Better take the time to at least make up the beds before an inspection is pulled."

"When Dorothy gets tired of languishing in bed, she can do it." He added, "Wise little girls should learn to watch their mouths." Turning on his heel, he walked down the hall.

Stretching out a hand, Nigel helped her up. "Cinderella," he said with a grin, "your prince is here to take you away from your ashes. Jim seems to be a new man, doesn't he?"

"Very masterful." She brushed ashes from her pants.

He crooked an elbow and she bent down to slip an arm through it. "Let's join the rest of this charming family in the dining room."

"Kitchen. Your mother said it was too much work to use the dining room."

On the long kitchen table, a good lunch had been arranged. A large bowl of potato salad was flanked by a plate of tinned ham and a bowl of hot rolls. Nadine had set out bright red place mats and she'd put one of Holly's geraniums on as a centerpiece. At the sink Philip, his sleeves rolled to his elbows, was splashing soap and water over his hands. There were grease marks on his shirt and he wore a broad smile. As Rayburn, closely followed by Norman, took his place, Philip's smile widened even more. Thelma came in, sat down, and scowled as Ruth, fresh and lovely in apricot silk, helped Buddy onto his chair. Thelma transferred the scowl to the child who immediately stuck out his tongue at her.

Rayburn rapped the child's knuckles lightly. "Naughty, Buddy." He watched Philip as the young man nonchalantly reached for a dish towel and dried his hands. "How did it go, my boy?"

Sliding into a chair, Philip heaped potato salad on his plate. "You know, granddad, after years of searching for my mission in life, my reason for being—"

"Hallelujah!" Thelma cast her eyes upward. "The world is saved. Junior has finally found his own identity."

"After," Philip continued manfully on, "years of searching—"

"Including a commune, a motorcycle gang, and every offbeat religious sect you could find," Jim said caustically as he swung the door open.

"I find I am contented and fulfilled doing manual labor." Philip paused as though to add significance to his next words. "I'm going to become a mechanic."

"Thank God!" Thelma dropped her fork. "I was afraid our boy had decided to become a brain surgeon. Tell on, great mechanic."

Turning sulky, Philip lifted a heaping forkful to his mouth.

"Suppose," Rayburn suggested, "you tell us what you found."

Brightening, Philip started to speak rapidly through a mouthful of salad.

His father frowned at him. "Either eat or talk. Don't do both."

Swallowing, Philip spoke directly to his grandfather. "Do you want the bad news first or the good?"

174

"Let's have the good." Rayburn grinned wryly. "We haven't had much lately."

"There's a deep well, spring fed, I think. The house is heated by propane and that stove and the generator for power are run on it too. The storage tank is huge and about three-quarters full so we shouldn't run short of fuel. Jeb has some spare parts out there for the machinery."

"That is good news, my boy. Now the bad."

"Archaic, granddad, positively medieval. I can see why Jeb had to spend so much time tinkering. Practically held together by bailing wire."

"All of it?"

"The water pump and the generator. The furnace is newer and in better shape. But the fan on it is too small for this house. That's why everywhere above this floor is so damned cold."

Selecting a roll, Rayburn broke it open and dabbed butter on it. "Can you handle the necessary repairs if something goes wrong?"

"It'll go wrong. Depend on it. Can't help but." Taking a deep breath, Philip inflated his narrow chest. "I can handle it."

"Whoopee!" Thelma cried. "We're saved."

Philip twisted his head to glare at her. "Shut up!"

"I agree." Leaning over, Rayburn rapped her knuckles as lightly as he had Buddy's moments before. "Your levity, considering the tragedy last night, and our own plight now, is unbecoming. You must behave with more decorum, Thelma."

"If I want to joke it up I can't see why I shouldn't." Thelma glanced around the table. Seeming to gain courage, she said, "I'll talk any way I damn well want."

Rayburn lifted dark bars of brows and looked at Norman. "I think it's time you explain a few things to your wife, my boy."

Eagerly, his pale eyes bulging, Norman grasped his wife's wrist. "Now, grandaddy, now?"

"No," Thelma mumbled.

"Later," Rayburn told his grandson. He swiveled his head toward Tammy. "How is your mother, my dear?"

"Resting."

"Quillers don't coddle their women." He leaned back in his chair. "Jim tells me Dorothy has a habit of malingering. If she is ill enough to remain in bed she must consent to an

175

examination by Andy. We can't tolerate malingering. There are hardly hands enough to do the necessary work. Tell you mother that either she is up and about tomorrow or Andy will have to certify she is ill enough to remain in bed."

"I'll do no such thing. My mother will remain in bed until *she* decides she's well enough to get up."

Slowly, Rayburn drew his long frame from the chair. Thelma, her hand over her mouth, watched him with apprehensive eyes. He walked around the table and stopped behind Tammy's chair. One large hand ran caressingly up the girl's arm, touched her shoulder, lingered there for a moment, and then suddenly grabbed at her long hair. Brutally, he pulled back until the girl's head was bowed backward. She tried to pull free but his other hand went around her breast, holding her immobile. The cords in her neck stood out tautly from the pressure. He's going to break my neck, she thought, and not one person here will interfere.

Philip was staring at them with his mouth sagging open and Jim was smiling. It was Nigel who moved. He jumped down from his chair, the sofa cushion falling off one side, the chair skidding across the floor. One of the wooden legs caught Rayburn below the knee with such force that he lurched, his hands falling away from the girl. He grasped his leg, moaned, and turned pain-filled, furious eyes on the tiny man.

Nigel grasped at his grandfather's elbow and steadied the other man. "Sorry, sir, chairs are damned awkward for anyone my size. Did it do any damage? Let's have a look."

Hoisting his pant leg, Rayburn examined his calf. Bending his bright head, Nigel ran a small hand over the older man's leg. As Rayburn winced, Nigel managed to work around so he was between Tammy and Rayburn. "Doesn't look serious, sir. Probably be bruised. I *am* sorry," he repeated.

"No real harm done." Rayburn straightened. "However, in the future, be more careful. A heavy chair like that might break a bone."

Moving forward, Nigel edged his grandfather toward the door. "I was meaning to ask—what did you do with the Amoses' remains?"

"That was a problem, my boy. Andy and I discussed it and decided there were two possible locations. One was in the shed opening off this room but we decided against it. Too grisly for the people in the house. So we took them down and put them in the boathouse."

176

At the swinging door, Rayburn paused and looked back at the group still at the table. "Back to work. All the men, with the exception of Philip and Andy, will help carry wood for the signal fire. Thelma, I noticed that you haven't accomplished much this morning. The bathrooms are messes and so is the library. Try to be more industrious this afternoon. Nadine, dinner will be served in the dining room. We mustn't let down. Needless to say, we will dress for dinner. No denims and the ladies will wear skirts." His eyes fastened grimly on Tammy's rigid back. "And you, my girl, will watch what you say in the future. Give Dorothy my message."

As the rest of the people filed out of the kitchen, they ignored Tammy. She sat, her head bowed, willing herself not to touch her aching head. When she started to pull herself up, Nadine pressed her back in the chair.

"Rest for a moment, Tammy. I'll make a tray for your mother. I've kept some rolls warm for her."

Bending over the oven, Nadine pulled out a foil-wrapped plate. Quickly, Tammy pushed up her glasses and rubbed her sleeve over her eyes. Tears of rage, pain, and humiliation were trickling down her face. Putting the tray on the table, Nadine started to fill a plate with ham and salad. Then she left it and sank down beside the girl. Gently, she took Tammy's tight fist, spread the fingers and held the palm up. "Let an old gypsy tell your fortune, Tammy."

With the warmth of the older woman's touch, Tammy felt some of the tension draining from her. As Nadine bent over her hand, she examined the face so close to her own. A handsome woman, Tammy thought, with those remarkable eyes and that wealth of raven hair. All the coldness was gone from Nadine's face, all the bitter lines smoothed away. She wore the expression of a young girl, her mouth soft and vulnerable. Marking time, the girl thought, suspended permanently in girlhood. That frozen mask Nadine wore was simply a mask to hide an adolescent. How old would she have been when she met and married Micah Quiller? Perhaps eighteen, maybe only seventeen. So young, so startlingly lovely, so in love.

Tammy forced herself to ask, "What do you see?"

"A man, tall and dark."

The girl felt her lips relaxing into a smile. The usual beginning. "Handsome?"

The glossy head shook. "That I can't see, but young. Young and hurting. His path joins yours and stays with it."

Tammy entered into the spirit of the game. "Do you see a journey?"

"Yes. One across water."

"Maybe it's Rob. The trip across water could be when he takes us away from this island. Are there other people with us on this trip?"

"One...no, wait. There's something with you, another life. But faint, very faint. I see another man in your palm."

"Tall and dark and handsome?"

"Tall, yes. An older man." She lifted magnificent eyes to the girl's face. "Don't cross this man," she said urgently.

Pulling her hand away, Tammy said stiffly, "You're talking about Rayburn." Her rage came flooding back. "What right does he have to put hands on me, order all of us around as though we're in bondage? What right does he have to tell my mother what to do?"

"Ask yourself a question. Thelma is a strong-willed, rebellious woman. Rayburn didn't even raise his voice and she wilted. She looked terrified. There has to be a good reason for her fear."

Abruptly, the older woman stood up and finished fixing the tray. Tammy silently took it from Nadine and walked slowly down the hall. The doors of both the game room and the library were closed but there was the muted throb of the vacuum. Thelma must be obeying and cleaning up the library. The house was so quiet, the fog seemed to wrap the walls in a cocoon of cotton wool, muffling all sounds. She started up the stairs. The landing on the second floor was shrouded in shadow and she didn't see the small figure there until she was directly below it. Her hands tightened on the tray. "Nigel?" she asked.

A whisper floated down. "Rosemary."

Peering through the shadows, she recognized the figure. "Buddy." She told him. "My name is Tammy."

She regarded him. A small boy dressed in short gray flannel pants, the white collar of a shirt open over a navy pullover. Feet stuck in black oxfords, knee socks reaching to chubby knees. Only a child. Then why did she feel cold fear touching her? Shrouding her in a fog as clammy as the one pressing in against this house?

She forced herself to take another step. Above the white

178

collar a young boy's thin neck. She was so close she could see minute pores in the tender skin, his brown hair growing back in a low brow in a line as straight as though it were drawn with a pencil, brows as straight but jet black, a snub nose and a wide mouth. The eyes under those straight brows were deep set, gray, as expressionless as chips of stone. But he was only a well-nourished, well-dressed little boy.

She looked beyond him, down the dark expanse of the hall. Standing on shabby carpet, wavering against gloomy paneling, she saw a host of children. Children from toddlers to ten, children not well nourished or warmly dressed. White-faced wraiths with terror-filled eyes. Over twenty children had died in this house. Had they known they were to die? Had they run along this hall seeking refuge from the pursuing murderers? Those adult figures must have loomed over them like grotesque giants. Transfixed, she stared at the host of children. They were lifting small arms, opening their mouths, waving her back, back down the stairs. They were trying to warn her. "Rosemary," a whispering chant assailed her ears—

A sharp voice cut across the whisper. "Buddy! What are you doing?"

Ruth, apricot silk gleaming, came hurrying down the hall. The door to her room stood open and a shaft of light fell across the brown carpet. The ghostly ranks of children swayed and then were gone like mist before a strong wind. Buddy was only a little boy turning a sheepish face up toward his grandmother. Ruth rested an ugly, large-knuckled hand on his slight shoulder. "Has he been bothering you, Tammy? Buddy, have you been naughty?"

Tammy couldn't speak and Ruth peered down at her. "Why, you look ill. You aren't coming down with your mother's sickness, are you?"

"Yes," Tammy heard her own voice say. "I think I may be."

She hurried across the landing and almost ran up the steep flight of stairs. The coffee sloshed over the rim of the cup but she didn't stop until she reached her room. Her mother was sleeping, one hand tucked under her cheek like a child. Putting down the tray, Tammy touched Dorothy's shoulder. "Wake up, mother," she said softly. "I've a message for you."

In the late afternoon the fog seemed to be settling down even thicker than it had earlier. The men cautiously groped their way up and down the uneven path from the woodpile to the pier. Pausing by the chopping block, Rayburn mopped at his wet face. A man's form came rushing out of the fog, hurtling straight at him. Rayburn caught at his grandson's arm. "Easy, boy, I told you to slow down. Jim's fallen once already. Don't try to carry so much either."

Norman's face was flushed and beaded with sweat and his rusty curls were moistly clinging to his head. "When should I do it, granddaddy?"

"Before dinner, my boy. Remember, don't get carried away this time. And nowhere where it will show. Keep away from her face and arms."

"I like to do it."

"I know, and it's absolutely necessary. She's been getting out of hand again. It's also contagious. Look at Tammy's rebellion, that was sparked by Thelma."

Norman rubbed his big hands together. "I'll teach her not to be bad. That Nigel too. He hurt you, granddaddy, he threw his chair at you."

"No, that was an accident. Nigel isn't strong enough to have done it deliberately." Bending, Rayburn stroked his leg, and winced. "Leave him alone, boy, you just take care of Thelma. No racket either. I don't want her bringing down the house. Muffle her mouth."

Clapping a hand over his lips, Norman allowed a liquid giggle to seep through his spread fingers. After a moment, his grandfather threw back his head and started to laugh.

Twelve

All of Rayburn's instructions were obeyed without argument. Dinner was served in the dining room by an uncomplaining Nadine. She produced a dinner that rivaled in excellence those cooked by Holly Amos, and Rayburn supplied two bottles of superb Beaujolais. The women were in dresses and the men wore slacks and either turtlenecks or shirts and ties. Nigel and Rayburn were dressed almost identically in dark tailored slacks and silky white turtlenecks. On their feet both wore well-polished Gucci loafers. To complete the look-alike attire they wore, suspended from heavy chains, medallions. These too were similar, featuring lions' heads, haloed by rays resembling formalized suns.

During dinner, conversation was carried on almost exclusively by Nigel and his grandfather. Rayburn was gently teasing the tiny man on his insistence on the term dwarf instead of midget.

Twirling the stem of his wine glass, Nigel told the older man, "It's a matter of usage, really. Midget brings to mind exploitation, sideshows come immediately to mind. Then there was poor General Tom Thumb. A sad figure."

"And dwarf?" Rayburn asked.

"More dignity. The folklore about dwarfs as workers in magic and precious metals. Also, the fabulous painting by

Diego Velazquez of the hunchbacked dwarfs at the court of Philip IV of Spain. In many cases, dwarfs were extremely powerful men and influenced many monarchs. Then there was Alberich immortalized by Wagner in the opera *Siegfried*."

"Most interesting, Nigel. Do you know what the medical explanation is for their births?"

Nigel inclined his bright head toward Andy Thaler. "Andy could probably explain better than I can."

Slanting a smile at the little man, Andy said solemnly. "Dwarfs, ah yes. Cretinism. A disease of the thyroid gland is the commonest. Then there's mongolism and, of course, achondroplasia."

Ruth turned to her husband. "What on earth is that?"

"A disease where the cartilaginous tissue is absorbed during the fetal stage. Generally characterized by extreme shortness of the extremities. Then there are rickets, spinal tuberculous, and deficiency of the secretion of the pituitary gland—"

"Enough," Rayburn interrupted. "Sorry I asked."

"The medical reasons for dwarfs are not as unpleasant as some of the practices used to produce them by man-made means." Nigel's eyes were fixed on his wine glass. "Court jesters were much in demand during the days of the Roman Empire and mechanical devices were used on normal babies to produce suitable dwarfs."

Turning glowering eyes on him, Ruth asked, "Do you mean Buddy could be dwarfed?"

Nigel glanced at the boy. "I think he's a bit old for it now. Probably kill him."

"Yes," Andy agreed drily. "If you wanted a dwarf as a grandson you should have started when Buddy was an infant."

Ruth pouted. "What a deliciously ghoulish conversation."

"I agree," her father said. "All from one simple question." He looked suspiciously at Andy who was chuckling. "What's so amusing?"

"You are. Don't you realize Nigel's having you all on?"

"What do you mean?"

"There are real differences between dwarfs and midgets. Dwarfs are misshapen, usually with abnormally large heads. As you can see, Nigel is perfectly proportioned. He's not only a midget, he damn well knows it."

182

Rayburn's head swung toward Nigel. "Is that true?"

Nigel looked demure. "I never claimed I was a dwarf, sir, all I said was that I preferred the term to midget."

With a wide smile, Rayburn flung up his hands and turned to Nadine. Her gown outshone Ruth's and was a floor-length creation of garnet velvet. She'd braided her hair into a thick coronet that framed her handsome face. His glance lingered on her. "You were modest about your cooking ability, Nadine. Seldom have I tasted as good roast beef and Yorkshire pudding. My compliments."

"Thank you," she said demurely.

"Now, we will have an hour to follow our own pursuits and then we'll all gather in the drawing room. Ruth, Buddy has had too many late nights—No, Buddy, don't shake your head like that. Put him to bed immediately. Thelma, you will give our lovely cook a hand with the washing up. I imagine Tammy will want to take her mother's dinner up—"

"Aw, granddad," Philip interrupted. "I'd planned to get in a few games of pool with Jim. I've been slaving all day."

"You have an hour, my boy. One reason I'm so happy to have you here is the blessed absence of television and radio. People quite forget the art of conversation." Pushing up his sleeve, Rayburn checked his watch. "One hour."

There were no further arguments. Thelma hauled herself to her feet and began to help Nadine to clear the table. Tammy lingered, watching the stocky nurse. All during dinner, she'd covertly eyed Thelma, wondering what was wrong with her. Thelma's face was as leaden as Andy's except around the eyes, where the skin was blotched and reddened. As she moved around the table, she appeared to be limping. Tammy said to her, "I'll help Nadine if you're tired."

Thelma mumbled, "Ray said I was to."

Shrugging, Tammy went to the kitchen and made up a tray. When she brought it down from upstairs the room was empty, the sinks and counters shining and clean. The odors of beef and cauliflower still lingered. The big Persian had followed her down and he meowed as his nose quivered, testing the air.

"You're more like a pig than a cat," she told him. "This is the third meal today."

Hastily, she washed the few dishes and wiped the tray off. She glanced at her watch. Only a few minutes left from the hour Rayburn had allowed. She'd better close the cat and the food into the shed. One thing she didn't need was a lecture from Rayburn about letting the animal run loose. Opening the fridge, she took out the milk and some scraps of beef. She opened the door to the shed. "Chow time, Blue." The cat eagerly followed her and purred while she put the two saucers on the floor. "You'll have to stay here," she told the animal as though he could understand her. Ignoring the milk, he was gobbling the meat. She knelt and patted his head. When she left this island, she'd take old Blue with her. For Holly, she thought, and a boy named Tommy. "I'll be back later," she promised.

As she stepped back into the kitchen, she heard a faint sound and glanced around the room. It had sounded like a door closing. She glanced at the swinging door but there wasn't a quiver in the panel. Tammy turned toward the far end of the room where the door leading to the back stairs was located. No one ever used that staircase. As Holly had said the steps were covered with cartons and there was no light over them. She found the silence oppressive, a waiting, listening silence. Eagerly, she left the room and hurried along the hall toward the drawing room. Company, even that of the Quillers, would be welcome.

As she drew near the archway, she could hear the rumble of voices and a shrill laugh that sounded like Philip's. As she entered the room she saw she was the last one to get there. Looking up, Nadine patted the seat beside her and Tammy sank down between Thelma and Nigel's mother. Again she was struck by Thelma's appearance. The woman's clothes didn't help. Thelma had picked a bright pink dress with a plunging neckline and then had arranged a scarlet silk scarf to conceal the decolleté.

Tearing her eyes from the nurse, Tammy looked around at the rest. Rayburn had selected his usual chair, the largest and most comfortable, and near him Nigel perched on a footstool. On the far side of the hearth, Ruth, lovely in a caftan shot with silver thread, lounged. At her feet, his sleek brown head resting against her knees, Jim sat. Ruth shifted position and the girl had a glimpse of the woman's foot, bare, a yellow rind of callus thickly ringing the ball of it. With feet like that, Tammy decided, it would be best to keep them covered. In a shadowed corner, Andy had found a chair and near him, on a nest of pillows, Philip sprawled. On a straight chair near the door, Norman was perched. His color was high and his pale eyes roved from his wife to his grandfather.

On the table beside him, Rayburn had arranged a bottle of Rémy Martin and a number of balloon glasses. As he filled them, Nigel passed them around. When he handed Tammy a glass, Nigel winked at her. Leaning back in his chair, Rayburn held his glass up so firelight danced through the cognac. He inhaled deeply. "Wonderful bouquet." Taking a sip, he smacked his lips. "Heavenly!" He shot an amused look at the little figure near him. "I notice, Nigel, you appreciate a fine cognac too. It would seem we have many tastes in common." One hand fingered the bright medallion on his chest. "You're a Leo too."

"That's my birth sign."

"Mine also and quite a distinguished group of people share it with us. The most powerful sign of the Zodiac, its members excelling in leadership qualities."

"The negative side of a Leo isn't so great, sir. Leos can be dictatorial, flamboyant, and prone to extremes of egotism."

"True, my boy, but it's also the sign for creative talent. Many painters, sculptors, and writers share our birth sign. Which brings me to something I find most intriguing. I understand you are a writer."

"Who told you that?"

"As a matter of fact, it was our late housekeeper. Holly told me you'd sworn her to secrecy but she considered that was because of your modesty. She was thrilled and flattered by the interview you conducted with her on the Winchfields. Said you'd even used a tape recorder." Rayburn took a careful, measured sip. "It shed light on a couple of points I'd found puzzling. The first was why you agreed to join us here, and the second was the research you'd done on the Winchfield family. Do you intend to write a book about them?"

"Something like that." Nigel fingered his medallion. "At least, I hope to feature the family in a book."

"Ah, then it will be a book of various crimes."

"Related ones, yes."

"Related?" The thick brows rose. "In what sense?"

Nigel took a sip of cognac. The way he held his glass, the way he tilted his head, was close to a mockery of the older man. "A theory of my own on crime, sir. One I've formulated over a number of years."

"Please expound." Rayburn made an expansive gesture. "As you can see, you have us all enthralled."

"In that case I'd better get my notebook and recorder." Setting his glass down, Nigel sprang to his feet. As he passed Tammy, he winked at her again.

She looked after him, wondering what he was up to. With his memory he hardly needed to consult notes or use a tape recorder. And what could he possibly have asked Holly about the Winchfields? She'd covered all the facts that night in this very room. For an instant Tammy could see Holly, sitting where Andy was sitting now, firelight gently falling over her placid face and crisp hair, sparkling in her bright blue eyes.

In a short time, Nigel took his place on the footstool again, a notebook balanced on a knee, a leather-covered tape machine at his feet. He glanced around at the circle of faces. "If anyone gets bored, just holler. This is a bit of a hobbyhorse I'm riding and I tend to get carried away. Now . . . my theory. Families, as we all know, carry in their bloodlines qualities unique to them. The first thing that comes to mind is— Tammy, make a guess."

"Physical resemblance, I suppose. Rayburn, Jim, Buddy. All three of different generations but with similar features and coloring."

"Right. Philip?"

He tugged thoughtfully at his scalp lock. "Birthmarks, I guess, and some small deformities. I have a friend whose right thumb is much longer than his left. He told me that every male in his family has the same thumb."

"Good point. Andy?"

Wearily, Andy rubbed his brow with his sound hand. "I really can't see much point in this."

"Kindly answer the boy," his father-in-law said sharply.

"Certain genetic diseases come to mind. Various types of heart diseases, kidneys, diabetes. Blood diseases, the most famous being hemophilia, the one that plagued the royal families of Europe, and eventually was blamed for helping to topple the tsars."

"And again only inherited by male members," Nigel said slowly. "My theory and the one I'll try to prove in my book is that certain families—rare, thank God—carry through their bloodlines another trait."

"Which is?" Rayburn prompted.

"Murder." Nigel's voice was cold and clear. "Mass murders.

An appetite for bloodshed, for violence. Sadism, killing for killing's sake."

Philip shook his head. "Ridiculous! An occasional person like that I can see but right through a family—no way!"

"My boy," Rayburn chided, "your cousin has simply stated his theory. He's offered no proof yet. Instead of condemning him out of hand, let's give him a hearing." He turned his head toward Nigel, his profile outlined against the golden and scarlet tapestry of the burning logs. "I take it you are going to try to link the Winchfield family with others through history. To try and prove that they descended from like monsters."

Through lowered lashes, Nigel shot him an admiring glance. "You catch on quickly, sir."

"I pride myself on an agile mind. Were the Winchfields the ones who started you on this trail, or was it an earlier family?"

"Which came first—the chicken or the egg." Nigel's shoulders moved in a shrug. "I don't really know. But I have established links leading from the Winchfields back through the centuries to the Sawley Beans. Have you knowledge of the Beans, sir?"

"I'm afraid I haven't." Rayburn gazed around at his relatives. "Anyone?"

"I do," Andy said. He seemed more interested. "Intriguing, Nigel. Playing at historical detective, I mean. I read a story of the Beans a few years ago. Grisly tale, but it seems to me you could be on a cold trail. In my book it called the Bean story legendary."

"What is legendary? A story passed down by word of mouth." Crossing his knees, Nigel shifted the notebook and flipped through the pages. "The Bean story was passed down by more than oral accounts. While in London I was able to come up with an unpublished account of it in the archives—"

"You went to England for this?" Rayburn cut in. "Writing must pay well."

"A trip to England doesn't cost all that much." Nigel turned his attention back to the doctor. "Do you recall enough of the tale to fill us in on details?"

"I think so. It caught my attention." Andy rubbed at his brow again. "Sawley Bean was supposed to—" He stopped abruptly. "I'll speak as though it actually happened. This

187

took place in the fifteenth century, in Scotland. Bean was a hedger and ditcher by trade and by nature he was lazy and vicious. The woman he took as mate was as vicious as he and they went to live in a cave in an isolated area near Galloway. For a quarter of a century they lived there without going near cities or towns, or indeed, without seeking the company of others. During this time the Bean family swelled to forty-eight in number and—"

"Hey, hold it," Philip interrupted. "One minute you say the Beans kept to themselves, avoided everyone else, and then you tell us there were forty-eight in their family."

"Sawley Bean, his wife, eight sons, six daughters, eighteen grandsons, and fourteen granddaughters. Forty-eight." The doctor made a grimace. "Incest, Philip. The Beans were like a tribe of rats and had all the moral fiber of rats. But, like vermin, they had a certain amount of cunning. They preyed on travelers but never attacked more than six at one time. Some of the family went directly after the victims while the rest waited in ambush to make sure none escaped. They finally made a mistake. They attacked a husband and wife and while they were fighting for their lives another large band of travelers came to their aid. The wife had been killed but the husband survived to tell his story to a magistrate in Glasgow. The king ordered out four hundred soldiers and some bloodhounds." Andy paused, caught his breath, and continued, "The caves were so well hidden that the soldiers would have missed them without the dogs. But one dog caught the scent and led them into a cave. All the Beans were in hiding there and they all were taken alive. These were rougher times, people were more callous then but those soldiers, hardened as they were, were sickened with what they found. The main cave was described as a 'charnel house,' with pickled limbs and lumps of human meat hung from its roof. Like rats, the Beans were cannibals."

Nadine gasped. In a muffled voice, she asked, "What happened to the Beans?"

"First they were taken to Edinburgh where they were committed to Tolbooth, then they were taken to Leith for execution. There was no trial, justice was swift and almost as inhuman as the crime. The men had their hands and feet chopped off and bled to death while the women were forced to watch. Then the women were burnt alive in three fires.
188

The Beans, so the story goes, never repented but continued cursing until they were dead."

As Andy's voice died away, Rayburn said, "That account *must* have made an impression on you." He turned toward the small man on the footstool. "You intend to prove this tribe of human rats were the ancestors of the Winchfield family?"

Nigel tapped his notebook. "I do."

"Aha! Got you." Rayburn beamed. "None of them escaped. The Bean family was wiped out in Leith."

Flipping open the notebook, Nigel said slowly, "That's what most accounts would lead one to believe. But this account, more of a diary really, that I found in the archives was written by a sergeant who commanded one of the troops of soldiers who captured the Beans and took them first to Edinburgh and then to Leith. Strangely enough for that era, he had a bit of education and was able to read and write. His name was Angus Harker and he insisted that there were forty-nine members of the Bean family, not forty-eight."

His mother was staring at her son. She asked him, "But if they were guarded closely, how did one escape?"

"Love, mother. Sergeant Harker had in his troop a recruit who was the son of the sergeant's best friend. The boy was young and 'dull witted,' the kind of lad the girls wouldn't exactly flock after. Harker said the Beans were a 'wild, ugly, ragged bunch' with one exception. Her name was Kitty and she was around fifteen, pretty enough in a filthy way, and quite a girl. She told the soldiers she had never tasted human flesh, had tried to run away from her horrible relatives, and had been restrained against her will. She also entertained them with songs and cast some of their fortunes. Most of the men shied clear of her but the dull-witted recruit, John MacDurrant by name, became infatuated with Kitty. Sergeant Harker admitted she was 'a pretty jade' and if she'd been washed and put in different clothes, would have been even prettier. He said she had flashing black eyes, very red lips, and although her hair was matted, it was long and dark."

"So," Philip said, "the young soldier fell for Kitty Bean."

"Head over heels," Nigel told the boy. "Despite the fact that Kitty was obviously pregnant. The sergeant warned MacDurrant away from her, told the lad that Kitty was 'lying through her teeth' and 'was just as rotten as her relatives.' It didn't work. Shortly before they reached Edinburgh, the

189

boy and Kitty Bean disappeared. They'd escaped during the night. Harker was wild with rage and the soldiers fanned out looking for them, convinced that a pregnant girl and a soldier couldn't get far. MacDurrant didn't. They found his body in a ditch. He'd been stabbed in the back with his own knife, his throat had been cut, and his chest had been ripped open. His heart was missing and, as Sergeant Harker wrote, 'it took no great thought to know what had been done with that organ. The likes of Kitty Bean would consider a human heart a delicacy.'"

"Jes-us!" Philip whistled softly between his teeth. "I take it Kitty wasn't tracked down."

"Vanished along with the unborn Bean she was carrying." Closing the book, Nigel said to Rayburn, "First link in the chain."

"Still very much supposition," Rayburn said. "However, I'm keeping an open mind. What is the next link?"

"There were a number of crimes I considered but in each case one vital factor was either not there or not recorded. My next positive link is a woman called Mary Bateman. That skips a long period of time—from the mid-fifteenth century to the late eighteenth." Nigel glanced around the room. "Does the name ring a bell?"

Everyone was looking hopefully at Andy Thaler, but he shook his head. It was Tammy's clear voice that asked, "Was she the one called the Yorkshire Witch?"

Nigel stared at the girl. Her hair was loose and fell forward against her cheeks. As usual, dark glasses masked her eyes. "That's the one. What do you know about her?"

"As Sergeant Harker might have said, she was a nasty piece of goods. The story I read about Mary Bateman concluded that she was a sadist. She worked as a domestic but actually she made most of her living by tellinq fortunes and swindling. On occasion she acted as midwife. How many people, particularly young girls, she managed to maim or kill while pretending to help them, is anyone's guess. Finally, she tried to poison a husband and wife who came under her influence. The husband survived but the wife died in torment. Mary Bateman was arrested and tried for murder. She was executed and her body was exhibited to make money for charity. Thousands of sightseers came to see it and finally the skin was stripped off and sold in pieces for charms."

"Very succinct," Rayburn complimented. "Also very grisly,

my dear. I must admit I fail to see any connection between the Beans and Mary Bateman. Nigel?"

"Tammy has the basic facts but again, in the archives, I was able to read an unpublished account about the Witch of Yorkshire. This was written by Mary's only friend, a woman named Aggie Chambers. Aggie sounded like a decent kind of woman, not overly bright, but intensely loyal. She refused to believe that 'her cherished friend' was guilty of the crimes she was executed for. Completely hoodwinked by Mary Bateman, was Aggie. But one of the interesting facts was that although Mary Bateman was supposed to have died without issue, Aggie Chambers insisted that Mary had two children, youngsters at the time of her execution. Aggie had boarded and raised the children because 'her dear friend was so busy with her charitable work.' One was a boy, John, the other a girl, Kate—"

"I see what you're aiming at," Rayburn interrupted. "You're going to make a case on names."

"Partially, sir. You see, although the Yorkshire Witch's name was Mary, she preferred to be called Kate. That is the name that Aggie called her."

"Flimsy, my boy, but continue."

"Shortly before her execution, Mary Bateman called her dear friend in to see her and instructed Aggie to find a family to adopt the children and take them to the colonies where 'they wouldn't have to bear the stigma of a mother unjustly accused as a murderess.' She disclosed to Aggie the hiding place of a sum of money to pay the surrogate parents. Aggie took this last task seriously and located a childless couple, German people, who were embarking for the new world. She paid the money to them and they took John and Kate and left England before Mary Bateman was executed. Their name," Nigel paused and looked at Andy, "was Bender."

"Bender," Andy echoed thoughtfully. "The bloody Benders of Kansas."

"Exactly, the bloody Benders. A tale of horror that should be known to any American. Not only a family of human rats, but one that dropped from sight and whose whereabouts to this day are a mystery."

Thelma muttered, "I've never heard of them."

"I've heard the name," Philip said, "but that's all I know."

Rayburn moved restlessly. "Again I fail to see any tangible connection with Mary Bateman's children. Bender isn't an uncommon name." Pouring a little cognac in his glass, he inhaled. "But carry on. What about the Benders?"

"The Bateman children left England with the Benders about 1808 or '09. In 1871 a family turned up in Labette County, Kansas, and took a homestead in an isolated spot near Independence. There were four members of the Bender family, Mother and Father Bender, a son John and a daughter Kate, both in their early twenties. They threw up a log shack and started to run a kind of rude inn. Kate Bender claimed she was a psychic and lectured in nearby towns. One of the contemporary prints shows a handsome, wasp-waisted young woman declaiming on table-tapping to an admiring audience. In the meantime she was also raising havoc with the young men of the district. Kate was dark and good-looking with 'flashing black eyes.' She was reputed to have been intimate with both her brother John and her father."

Philip was no longer lounging against the pile of pillows. He was sitting bolt upright, his wide eyes fixed on Nigel's face. "And I figured this was going to be dull. So, she was screwing—"

"Watch your language, boy!" his grandfather snapped.

"Sorry. What were the Benders doing besides running an inn and playing at being psychic?"

"Murdering travelers," Andy said.

"Right," Nigel agreed. "Eventually they overplayed their hand and a brother came looking for a missing man. Suspicion focused on the Benders and eleven bodies were exhumed from their orchard. Nine were men, one was a woman, and the other was a small girl. The adults had been bludgeoned to death but the child had been buried alive under the body of her father. The Bender family and their stolen hoard of money disappeared. After April of 1873, nothing more is known about them."

For a moment, there was dead silence. Then Norman, at a signal from his grandfather, quietly piled logs on the embers of the fire. The wood caught and blazed up. Draining his glass, Rayburn set it down. "Most ingenious. You feel that Mother and Father Bender were actually Mary Bateman's children. The Benders, I presume, lead us directly to the Winchfields. But my arithmetic is fairly reliable and I'm ready to dispute. By 1912, when the Winchfields came here, Mother and Father Bender would have had to be ancient. The elder Winchfields were people in their sixties. As for John and Kate Bender—" He stopped abruptly and rubbed at his mustache. "You're theorizing that Mother and Father Winchfield were actually your handsome young Kate Bender and her brother John and that—"

"Kat and John were their children, again products of an incestuous union," Nigel said flatly.

Throwing back his sleek head, Rayburn laughed. "Mother Winchfield, described as 'closemouthed and brusque' was actually vivid Kate Bender who drove young men wild."

"Yeah," Philip chimed in. "Sounds kinda farfetched."

Andy leaned forward, firelight glinting ruddily over his face, giving it an illusion of color and throwing the white gauze on his cheek into vivid relief. "You're both forgetting one thing Holly Amos said about the mother. She quoted Ed Ware as doubting that either of the Winchfield women would ever be hung for their crimes. If I'm not mistaken the exact words were 'good-looking women.'"

"Nice going!" Leaning over, Nigel tapped the tape recorder with his finger. "In a few minutes, Andy, I'll back you up on that. You know you have the makings of an historical detective yourself."

"Even with Andy's worthy support," Rayburn said drily, "there's enough holes in this theory to sink it instantly if it were a boat instead of an idea. To be blunt, my boy, it's a crock of shit."

"Language," Philip chided, grinning broadly.

Rayburn grinned back. "Indeed, I was carried away. Writers are so glib, so demanding at times. Put it in black and white and they expect instant credulous belief. Now, Nigel, what you have here is a clever but shaky linkage through the centuries of families or, in Mary Bateman's case, an individual who committed foul crimes. I know you're going to lean heavily on two points. One is the similarity of names, the repetition of the name 'John' and various forms of 'Katherine.' The second is the number of times the women in question practiced fortune telling or like psychic phenomena. Am I on the right track?"

"Partially, sir."

"Allow me to ask a few questions to show what a shaky theory this is. Nadine, I understand you've made your living at times by telling fortunes."

"I still do. At least, I'm in a similar field. Now I'm operating as a medium."

"What is your professional name?"

She moved her head and the dangling earrings glinted. "Madame Katryn. I thought it sounded better than Nadine and besides, it's my second name."

Rayburn spread his hands out, palms up. "See my boy? Your own mother dabbles in fortune telling and calls herself Katryn. Andy, what's your first name?"

"John," the doctor mumbled.

"Hey," Philip cried. "John's my second name."

"So," Rayburn said triumphantly. "Two Johns in this room and a Katherine. Katherine and John are common names. Fortune telling is far from rare. What else have you?"

"Several points, sir. The crimes themselves—vicious, sadistic mass murders. In each case I've cited although financial gain appears to be the motive for the murders—" He broke off and said firmly. "Let's examine them in turn. All the money and valuables taken from the Beans' victims were found discarded in the caves. They actually had no interest in that type of profit."

Andy pointed out, "But the Beans did use the bodies as a food supply."

"True," Nigel agreed. "But think how much simpler it would have been for them to have a flock of sheep or some cattle. They picked a dangerous way to get their food. I contend their motive was sheer blood lust. The Beans *liked* killing. Mary Bateman—here again is a motiveless murderer. She could have made more money by pursuing her ordinary work, by being a midwife and a fortune teller. She loved to play with her victims, watch them suffer, acting like a cat with a mouse. The Benders...the tipoff there is the little girl they buried alive. How long would it have taken them to knock her head in? They *enjoyed* the child's agony. Then we come to the Winchfields—"

"One moment," the doctor broke in. "I'm on your side, Nigel, but I'm afraid I can't go along with the Winchfields being in the murder game for anything except profit. That description of the cash box bulging with money that was found by the men from Amoston—it had to be the children's tuitions. A cut-and-dried case of murder for profit."

"Was it really?" Nigel drawled. "Take a second look. The family arrived here with plentiful funds and they were expensively dressed. No lack of money. In the interim, from the time they fled Kansas as the Benders and turned up here

194

under another name, they must have parlayed their ill-begotten gains into a small fortune. How they did it, we can all make an educated guess about. Okay, they buy this island, have this house built and furnished, then they bring in a total of twenty-four children. I figure they spent far more in settling here than they gained in tuitions. Now, why didn't they go to a larger center, one where they could have rented a house cheaply, set up their school, and actually made some profit?"

"I'll bite," Philip said. "Why?"

"Because they wanted an area they could control, a place their victims had no chance of escaping from. Which brings us to the conclusion that they wanted to toy with those children, terrorize them, watch them die slowly—"

"Sorry," Andy said. "I'm sticking my nose in again. Holly said that her brother, David Cranston, told the posse that the children had been killed almost as soon as they'd arrived. Had their heads knocked in so they wouldn't have to be fed."

Nigel shot the doctor a searching look. "David Cranston was already in a tough spot. Ed Ware was as ready to butcher the minister's son as he was the Winchfields. Suppose David had regaled that bunch of irate men with tales of the children tortured, slowly killed. He would have been clubbed to death on the spot for not telling the truth sooner." He gazed past the doctor, his eyes strangely intent. "A quotation comes to mind. 'For murder, though it have no tongue, will speak.' Those children had no tongues to tell of their torment, but if these very walls could speak I know all of us would stop our ears for the words they'd say would be unbearable." His eyes snapped around and fastened on Rayburn's intent face. "My contention is that the Winchfields murdered for the love of killing, the love of torture. They left the body of the little boy, Robert Fiscall, in the room where his sister was locked for days. They must have known it was risky and they could easily have disposed of the dead child. Why? Because it was vile and disgusting, because it added to Rosemary's torment. The Winchfields were worthy descendants of the Beans."

Thelma pulled herself unsteadily to her feet. "I think I've had enough of this."

"Sit down, Thelma," Rayburn ordered. "I suppose you're tired but so are the rest of us. Here, Philip, take Thelma a little more cognac." Without waiting to see the nurse take the glass, he said eagerly to Nigel, "Fascinating, my boy!
195

What an amount of research you must have done, what a tremendous amount of reasoning. You almost have me convinced and I've a feeling that you have the—as the younger generation would put it—the clincher."

"Here's the clincher." Nigel opened his notebook. "First I'll quote from the diary of Sergeant Angus Harker. 'Around her grubby throat, Kitty Bean had a thong supporting a strange shaped pendant. At first I thought it a crucifix and pondered on what an unlikely ornament that was for the ungodly Kitty to wear. On closer inspection I saw it was carved from bone, two snaking pieces forming a rough cross. There were two pieces of ruby-colored glass, one set at the extreme top of the upright piece, the other at its extreme bottom. It looked like two snakes embracing and filled me with repulsion. Some of my men whispered it had been carved from the finger bones of one of their victims.'"

Nigel flipped through the pages. "Aggie Chambers wrote this. 'When I entered the cell where my darling Kate Bateman was imprisoned, she embraced me warmly and pressed into my hand a little cross made from bone with two red stones embedded in it. "For my little girl," she whispered. "Give it to my Kate."'"

Andy Thatcher shifted his injured arm in the sling. "The Benders?"

Nigel nodded his bright head. "One of young Kate's lovers, and she had several, testified that while making love he had seen at her throat a fine gold chain with a 'crooked cross set with two pieces of red stone' attached to it. Kate Bender told him it was a talisman that had been in her family for a long time and that it aided her with her psychic powers."

"Very well," Rayburn said. "You've conclusively linked the Beans, Mary Bateman, and the Benders. What of the Winchfields?"

Sticking the notebook into a pocket, Nigel picked up the tape recorder. "That interview with poor Holly. I found her in the kitchen two days before the fire, and explained I needed more information for a book I was writing. Holly was flustered and nervous so I started the tape before I began questioning to calm her down a little. I'll run it through for you." He lifted his head. "Anyone getting bored?"

Philip laughed. "Are you kidding? Wild horses couldn't drag me away."

As Nigel switched the machine on, Tammy jumped. Holly's voice sounded as though she were still in the room with them.

"Bless me, Mr. Nigel, I'll do what I can. But I told you everything I know the other night. So, you're writing a book about the island. My dad would sure be flabbergasted if he knew. 'Course he's been gone these—"

Nigel's recorded voice broke in smoothly, "Relax, Holly, this mike won't bite. It'll make it easier for me than taking notes. Now, my questions. I don't want you to repeat what you told us the other night. I want you to tell me more about the Winchfields—what they looked like, how they dressed. Things like that. Think you can do it?"

"I'll try. Like I told you Laura Spence did rave on about them. Father Winchfield, she said he was a tall chap on the thin side. Had been fair but was losing his hair, going bald. His eyes were pale blue and Laura said he was a fine-looking man but had a funny look around his eyes. 'Course, like I said, Laura was a great one for doing those Winchfields down."

"You're doing well, Holly. Now, about the mother."

"Good-looking woman. Getting on in years but well set up with dark eyes and a lot of white hair. Laura said Mother Winchfield must have been the spitting image of Kat when she was a girl."

"Johnny?"

"Favored his dad. Fair hair and blue eyes and tall and thinlike. Laura said he had a bad twist to his mouth and looked down his nose at the people of Amoston. Kat was the best looker in the family. Like I told you, she had a lot of black hair and dark eyes. High color and olive skin. Sounded as though she looked something like your mother, Mr. Nigel. Tall like her too with a good bust." Holly's voice had gained confidence, she sounded as though she'd forgotten she was being taped. Her next words bore this out. "Would you like a cuppa, Mr. Nigel? I got some spice cake here I made this morning."

"In a while, Holly. Now Kat. Did she wear jewelry?"

"Bless me, yes. Laura was forever raving on about all the gewgaws Kat wore. Said they was bought with blood money. Kat always had a couple of wide gold bracelets on her wrists, one set with diamonds, the other with pearls. Wore a garnet brooch in a heavy gold setting too. Let's see... oh, yes. On the lapel of her jackets she always had this watch pinned. Pretty

197

little thing, Laura said, tiny watch set in enamel with flowers shaped like forget-me-nots. How's that?"

"Great! You have a marvelous memory."

"I listened close. When I was a young 'un it was my favorite story."

"Now, think back, Holly. Did Kat ever wear anything around her throat? Beads or a locket, maybe?"

There was a pause and then Holly said hesitantly, "Laura told me about one thing. She kinda wondered why Kat never wore a necklace of some kind. One hot afternoon Kat was visiting the Spence house and Laura made up some iced lemonade. Kat spilled some of it on her shirtwaist and Laura told her if she took it off, she'd sponge it out with cold water. Kat said she'd do it herself, 'cause she could stand a sponge-off in cool water account of the heat. Laura was a real nosy one, Mr. Nigel. Took a couple of clean towels as an excuse and flung open the door of the washroom. Kat was standing there stripped down to her corset cover, washing herself. Laura only got a quick look 'fore Kat covered herself with a towel but she said it looked like it was made of ivory. Real small it was and had a couple of rubies in it. Laura told me that Kat fair flew at her, called her all sorts of names. Said she figured that's what turned Kat against her. Kat started to see Piety York right after that afternoon."

"Thank you, Holly, that was a lot of help. Now about that cup of—"

Nigel switched off the recorder. "Well?" he asked Rayburn.

"I surrender." Rayburn laughed and threw up his hands. "The names, the rest of it—could have been coincidence. But this—you've got a book there and I'd like a copy when it's in print."

"You can depend on it, sir. With a suitable dedication."

"Have you a title?"

"*The Family That Wouldn't Die*. You see, there's one other strange thing. Even when the entire family was taken, some member always managed to escape. Kitty Bean and her unborn child lived on. Mary Bateman's children were saved. All the Benders got away and... well, you know about the Winchfields."

Andy was bending forward, his expression serious, almost brooding. "Are you hinting that in some supernatural way this family *can't* be wiped out?"

"At times that old hackneyed idea of being in league with

198

Satan did occur to me. It appears to be one tough bloodline to wipe out."

"Then why the title?" Andy asked. "Shouldn't it be present tense instead of past?"

"You mean I should call it 'won't' instead of 'wouldn't'?" Standing up, Nigel turned with his back to the fire. His face was shadowed. "Perhaps by the time this book is finished, the Bean-Bateman-Bender-Winchfield family will be gone from the face of this world. I sincerely hope so. These monsters we don't need."

"Or very much alive," Ruth said brightly. "You know, Nigel, you're not the only one who can come up with a theory. I have one. Here on Winchfield Island we have a person who absolutely fills the bill for the Winchfield child. She dabbles in the occult, she calls herself a form of Katherine, and she has the same build and coloring as Kat Winchfield. Come on, Nadine, confess. *Are* you the Winchfield baby?"

"Don't be absurd, Ruth!" Jim jerked his head away from his sister's knee. "That child was born about 1912. Nadine would have to be damn well preserved!"

Pouting, Ruth rested a hand against her brother's brown head. "I said a theory. Makes as much sense to me as Nigel's does. Anyway, she could be the daughter of the Winchfield child, couldn't she?"

Nadine smiled and Tammy could see a deep dimple in her cheek. "I might be. Here's a theory for you, Ruth. One person who's been overlooked is Rosemary Fiscall. She was a survivor too. From what Holly said about the girl's stepfather— the way he brought Rosemary and her brother here—makes him sound like a man who would make short shrift of an unwanted stepdaughter. Perhaps he married her off young. What if I was Rosemary Fiscall's daughter? Suppose I'd watched my mother living a life of hell, perhaps madness, because of the torture inflicted on her by the Winchfields? I wonder how a child of Rosemary Fiscall would feel about the Winchfield survivor? I know one thing. If I *were* a Winchfield, I'd be watching over my shoulder for a descendant of Rosemary Fiscall."

"I hadn't thought of that." Ruth stared at Nadine's handsome face. "What was your mother's maiden name?"

Nigel chuckled. "If we told you I doubt you could pronounce it. Mother's father was a traveling salesman out of Duluth. In ladies' underwear, wasn't he, mother? He married a Rumanian girl. Mother is convinced her mother, Magda, was a gypsy."

"She was," Nadine said indignantly. "She was a *tiganca* and traveled in a *caruta*, and she told fortunes too."

"Gypsy woman," Nigel told the room at large. "Traveling in a gyspy wagon. Most romantic. I seem to have started an epidemic of suppositions."

Rayburn beamed at the tiny man. "You have. Got all of us thinking and that's what conversation is all about. Much better for the mind than simply staring at figures on a television screen acting out our fantasies."

"All this thinking is tiring." Standing up, Andy rubbed at his brow. "I'm ready for bed. Anyone else coming up?"

Ruth pushed back her sleeve and the silver threads caught the light dazzlingly. "It *is* late. I'll go with you. Jim?"

He pulled himself off the floor and Nadine rose, glanced at Nigel, but he was staring into the fire. Shrugging, she followed Andy. Philip pushed himself off his nest of pillows, tried to catch Thelma's eyes, failed, and then trailed off after the others. Only Tammy, Thelma, and the two men near the fire lingered. Thelma seemed to be dozing and Tammy watched her. Finally, she roused and shifted position. As she did, Rayburn called, "I think I fancy coffee, Thelma. Would you be good enough to make a pot?"

Nodding, Thelma got stiffly to her feet. As she did the scarlet scarf gaped and Tammy caught a glimpse of the woman's breasts. They swelled lushly against the chiffon and were marked with bruises as bright as the color of the scarf. Tammy made an involuntary sound and Thelma glanced down at her swollen eyes and then turned toward the archway. Tammy sat rigidly, the soft murmur of the men's voices unheeded. So that's what was wrong with the nurse. Beaten, badly beaten. And trying to pretend that nothing had happened. Going like a beaten dog to the task assigned her by Rayburn Quiller. Closing her eyes, Tammy again saw Norman's hand on his wife's arm, the avid look he'd turned on his grandfather. Shuddering, she stood up.

"Aren't you going to wait for coffee, my dear?" Rayburn asked her.

Tammy averted her head. "No," she muttered. "I'll get Blue and then I'm going upstairs."

She reached the archway when a scream cut sharply across the silence, splintering it into ragged shards. She reached the swinging door in seconds, aware that Nigel and Rayburn were close behind her. Under the glaring kitchen lights Thelma bent over the sink, her shoulders heaving as she vomited. Tammy gazed around the room. The dishes and tray were on the drainboard, the counter was shining and orderly. What— then she saw it. Her eyes riveted on the chopping block, she clung to the edge of the table. Dimly, she was aware that others were crowding into the room.

"My God!" Jim said. "How in hell did that happen?"

Lunging from the room, Tammy ran down the hall. Behind her, in the brightly lit kitchen, the Quillers gathered around the chopping block. On it, sprawled in obscene and horrible mutilation, was all that remained of a big blue-gray Persian.

Thirteen

Clustering around the chopping block and its pitiful burden, the Quillers were all talking at the same time, asking questions no one answered, making comments that none heeded. At last, Rayburn tried to impose some order.

"Quiet down," he ordered. "I must find who did this disgusting thing. Despoiling the block we use for our food, making this kitchen into a slaughter house. I warn you, I'm getting to the bottom of this." He glared around at the circle of people. "The one who chopped that animal to bits had better confess and get it over with."

Eyes shifted from one face to another, heads shook in silent negation, but no one spoke. The only sound was the refrigerator motor revving up and Thelma's retching. Moving over to the sink, Nadine put a comforting hand on the younger woman's heaving shoulders. With her other hand, Nadine reached for the tap, turned it on, dampened a dish towel, and held it to the nurse's brow. "You've got everything up," she told Thelma. "Try to stop."

Thelma straightened, staggered, and weakly accepted Nadine's arm as support. Nadine glanced at Rayburn's enraged face. "I'm going to get her to bed. She's exhausted and sick."

"One moment. I told you I was getting to the bottom of this. Thelma, did you do it?"

"Hey," Philip protested. "Look at the way she upchucked. I think that proves her innocence. But earlier today when I was looking at the furnace I heard Nadine telling Tammy that she can't stand cats."

Nadine smiled bleakly. "There's a number of things I can't stand but I don't go around hacking them to pieces. Think back, all of us were in the drawing room together. Who had a chance to do this?"

"She's right," Jim told his father. "And we all went upstairs in a group."

"Thelma came out here to make coffee," Rayburn muttered. "She must have screamed as soon as she reached the kitchen. No, she didn't have time. But there was an hour after dinner when all of us were scattered around the house."

"Won't work," Nadine said flatly. "Thelma and I were out here cleaning up and we didn't leave the kitchen for three-quarters of an hour. There wasn't any dead cat on the block then."

"How in hell was it done so quietly?" Jim muttered. "That was a big, powerful animal. Surely we'd have heard the commotion. It must have fought back."

"Not the way it was done," Nigel called. He'd opened the door to the shed. Near the furnace were a couple of saucers. One was overturned and milk puddled over the floor. The rest of them crowded into the shed, staring at the spilt milk. Nigel pointed to a small mallet beside the saucer. "That was the initial weapon. The cat was peacefully lapping the milk and the killer came up behind it, hit it on the head, stunned it, then carried it out to the kitchen and finished it off with the meat cleaver. Didn't just kill it, disemboweled it. Overkill."

"Tammy must have put the food out for it," Rayburn said. "Where is she?"

"She ran upstairs," Philip told him. "I saw her in the hall when I came down."

"Maybe Thelma and Nadine know what time she fed it. Thelma? Now *where* did they go?"

Andy stepped up beside his father-in-law. "They left when we came out here. Better let them go. Thelma's not in good shape, Ray."

"Ruth went with them," Jim volunteered. "Anyway, dad,

I think you're making a mountain out of a molehill. It was only a mangy old cat."

"It's not the cat, it's the chopping board," Rayburn told him. "But you may have a point. Norman, you clean this mess up. Take disinfectant and scrub that block down. Clean that cleaver off and the mallet too." He shivered. "Let's get out of this shed. It's freezing."

They returned to the kitchen and Jim said, "It's no warmer here than it was out there. Feels like the heat vents are shut." He stepped over to the nearest one. "No, it's wide open. Not a speck of warm air coming through."

Moving to his father's side, Philip felt the grill. "Damn it to hell! Looks like the furnace has gone out."

His father glared at him. "You bungling idiot! Lolling around all evening, making smart remarks instead of attending to your job."

"How was I supposed to know, dad? The fireplace warmed the drawing room and the furnace was working perfectly earlier."

"Now that I think of it," Andy chimed in, "the second floor did feel colder than usual."

"It's always cold there," Philip said indignantly. "How in hell—"

"Arguing isn't going to fix the furnace," Rayburn broke in. "Calm down, Philip, and have a look."

En masse they returned to the bleak shed. Under the bulb dangling from the ceiling, the shed was desolate, a place of unfinished walls and floor, the old washing machine hunching in one corner, the furnace and white enamel hot water tank in the opposite one. Squatting by the furnace, Philip fumbled with the lower section of it. "Pilot light going," he grunted over his shoulder. "Nothing wrong with the fuel intake. Must be that bastard of a fan." He lifted the panel off and got down on his knees. "Now, what the hell is wrong with it?"

Bending down, Nigel held up a thin piece of black rubber. "Would this be the trouble?"

"The V-belt!" Philip swore lustily. "The son-of-a-bitch has snapped!"

"Take a closer look." Nigel held up the belt. "It's been cut."

"Cut?" Rayburn bent over and peered. "You're right. It's cut right through. What's going on? Killing that cat was one

205

thing, but this!" He glared down at Philip's shaven head. "Well, don't just sit there. Fix it!"

Throwing back his scalp lock, Philip glared back. "How?"

Andy touched the end of the belt. "Can't you splice it together?"

Jumping to his feet, Philip said, "This is a V-belt. Runs around a pulley. If it breaks, you've had it. No way the fan will run. If the fan doesn't run, no heat is pumped into the house. Even an idiot knows that."

"Well said." His father grinned. "Now, idiot, you said there were spare parts. Get another belt and install it."

"There isn't another one."

Nigel looked up at the young man. "Are you certain?"

"I sure in hell didn't see one. A belt usually has a long life. Jeb may not have kept a spare one around."

Rayburn groaned. "One thing after another. And no sense to any of them. Cutting the belt and putting the furnace out of commission. Sheer vandalism." He pulled himself together. "Couldn't you make a belt out of a piece of rubber? Jerry-rig something that would last for even a couple of days?"

Philip waved the belt. "Where are we going to find anything like this?"

"How about a tire?" Andy asked. "An auto tire or even a bicycle tire?"

"Sure," the boy said sarcastically. "You find a car or bike on this island and I'll give it a try."

"I *loathe* being cold." Shivering, Rayburn hugged both arms across his chest. "But we can't do anything tonight. Let's get to bed. At least we'll be warm there. In the morning we'll search every foot of this house and those sheds. The boathouse, too. Until we get the furnace in operation we'll use the fireplaces to keep from freezing."

As they left the kitchen, Philip whispered to Nigel. "Somebody in this house is right out of their head."

Nigel nodded. "Looks like it, doesn't it?"

As he reached the third floor, Nigel paused and glanced at the bottom of Tammy's door. No bright line of light showed. She must have joined Dorothy in bed. Just as well. The ground floor was chill, the second floor icy, but this floor—Nigel puffed out and fancied he could discern his breath hanging in a mist. By morning they might well have icicles dangling from their noses. Opening his door, he stopped in his tracks.

206

The lamp wasn't on but a ruddy glow came from the heater. In a chair pulled up to it, a blanket from his bed draped over her shoulders, Tammy crouched. She didn't have her glasses on but, as she lifted her face, the red glow threw her eye sockets into pits of darkness.

Closing the door softly behind him, he took the few steps to her side. He rubbed his hands together, trying to warm them. "Cold, and going to get colder. The furnace is on the blink."

"I know," she whispered.

He switched the lamp on, opened the door of the wardrobe, and pulled his suitcase over to the heater. Perching on it, he asked carefully, "How do you know?"

"I saw the belt being cut. By the same person who... who killed old Blue."

"Yes, no mystery about the wielder of the cleaver. Funny, Rayburn's awfully fast on his mental feet but he hasn't tumbled yet. Pretty obvious it could only be one of two people and I can't see your mother doing it."

"Buddy," she breathed, as though forcing herself to say the name. "He was standing on the landing of the second floor when I came up the stairs. Same place where he was this afternoon and this time I knew he was waiting for me. Just a small boy with tousled hair and white pyjamas covered with tiny blue sailboats."

"You went into his mind?"

"I had to. He called me Rosemary again—"

"*Rosemary.*"

Her eyes held his almost hypnotically. "Nigel, have you ever seen a movie or read a book about a group of people who come together in some spot they've never been before? For a time everything seems fine, quite normal. Then the whole place seems to become distorted, menacing. After a time, although their memories don't function about this, they begin to suspect they're dead." Her voice rose. "They find they're in hell."

He kept his own voice level and firm. "It's a plot that's been overused, Tammy."

"That's the way I feel, as though I've died and gone to hell. That this island is hell."

Leaning forward he gathered her hands in both of his. The girl's skin was clammy, her fingers were limp, lifeless. "Why did Buddy do it?"

The blue eyes closed. Under them faint shadows marred her fine skin. "I was in his body as he relived it. He crouched on the back stairs, among those cartons, the door ajar, watching Thelma and Nadine finish the dishes, eavesdropping on what they said. Buddy likes to eavesdrop. He saw me come into the kitchen with old Blue, get the food ready. When we were all in the drawing room he came out of hiding, got a knife from the rack over the stove. He went into the shed to kill the cat—"

"Why?"

"Because he knew I was fond of it, because he wanted to hurt me. Because he'd listened to the story of the Winchfields' murders and he saw the chopping block and remembered how the posse from Amoston butchered the old woman there. He crouched down beside Blue and he saw the furnace. Buddy was angry at his grandfather because Rayburn had ordered Ruth to put him to bed early and the boy wanted to stay up and listen to us talk, he wanted to hear exactly what we were discussing—murder and torture and blood—" She broke off, took a deep breath, and forced herself to continue. "Buddy knows Rayburn is fond of comfort, hates the cold. So he lifted off the furnace panel, saw the belt on the fan, and sliced through it with the knife. Then he went back to the cat. He was afraid to try to stab it, afraid of its claws. He went to the rack over the stove, got the mallet that tenderizes meat. He hit old Blue on the head as hard as he could, then he carried him to the chopping block...."

As her voice trailed off, Nigel's small hands tightened around hers. "The rest I know. But weren't his clothes covered with—Wouldn't he show telltale marks of the slaughter?"

"He's cunning, not childlike at all, Nigel. Buddy went up, washed, changed his pyjamas. All his pyjamas are the same color and pattern. He pushed the soiled ones back behind the luggage in Ruth's closet. Nigel, I couldn't get *out* of his mind."

"Tell me."

"I can't." Pulling his hands from hers, she covered her face. She couldn't shut out those dreadful moments in that boy's mind. She'd still been trapped in his body, her cheeks pressed against something cool and hard. Bars. At first she thought it was a prison, maybe a cage. Then her hands, chubby but strong, inched up the bars hauling her pyjama-clad body with them. She was in a large crib. The room her eyes scanned, through Buddy's, was large and quite luxurious. There was

208

a four-poster bed near a fireplace and, although no lamps were lit, the room glowed with reflected light from a lively fire kindled on the hearth. The eyes fastened on the bed, on the figures entwined on a rose satin spread. There was a glimpse of misty dark hair, the red, wet slash of a mouth gaping wide in a woman's face, the bottom of a foot, big, ugly with a rind of hard yellow callus. Tammy felt the nausea of an unwilling voyeur, the helplessness of not wanting to see and being forced to. A man's body writhed, wide shoulders, the play of muscles across them, gray hair between the shoulder blades, the gleam of shining gray hair in the firelight. The image wavered, the man's body changed. Now the smooth back was heavily tanned, the gray thatch of hair vanished. The head bending over the woman's wet, red mouth was covered with light brown hair. Tammy felt she was in a sewer, every part of her awash with slime. She fought with all her strength. Then she was free again, standing panting and sick on the stairs, gazing up at a small boy in pyjamas covered with blue sailboats. A boy whispering over and over a name that was not her own.

"It's all right, Tammy. You don't have to tell me. I think I can guess."

"*Hell*. We're in hell, Nigel. If we aren't, Doctor Thule is right, my mother is right. I'm mad!"

"Tammy, look at me. Do you trust me?"

"I do. I don't know why but, yes, I trust you."

"Then hold on to this. You're not mad and this isn't hell. Granted it's hellish but it's man made." His voice softened. "Tell me, if you were able to leave this place now, would you return to Doctor Thule's school?"

Tammy tugged the blanket closer around her. "I don't believe I could. Not now. I know I'd want to run back, I know at times I'd long for it. I'd want to seek sanctuary in it. But you're right. It's a kind of prison. After this island, this ghastly prison, I don't think I could give up freedom no matter what price I have to pay."

His hand tenderly brushed her cheek. "Then trust me. I promise that you're going some place where you'll find that freedom, where you'll run under a glorious sun down a beach. You'll run toward life." His voice was husky and he cleared his throat. "Go to bed now, Tammy, go to your mother."

Obediently she rose, lifted the blanket from her shoulders, and dropped it on the chair. With her hand on the doorknob, she turned. "One other thing I'm now certain about, Nigel. My father's last words were 'your mother.' He didn't have a chance to say more but I know what he meant, what he wanted. He knew her and he loved her deeply. He knew how helpless she is, how much like a child. He was asking me to look after her. I must. Somehow, I feel she's the child, I'm the adult." Tammy smiled crookedly and opened the door. "A tired, very old adult."

Standing in the hall, Nigel watched the door close, heard the rasp as she pulled the stiff bar across it. Lost in thought, he stood motionless, staring at the blank panel. His own name jarred him from his thoughts.

"Nigel," a voice called from the end of the hall.

He spun toward the sound. In the doorway to the schoolroom was a tall figure, a coronet of braids silhouetted like a crown, a velvet skirt softly draping and touching the floor. Nadine smiled down at her son. "Sorry I startled you."

"You scared hell out of me. What were you doing in there?"

"Freezing." She pushed past him and held her hands out to the heater. "Turning blue. Thank God your heater is on. Can I steal some warmth for a few minutes?"

"Sit down and pull that blanket around you."

Sinking in the chair, Nadine eagerly swathed her shivering body in the blanket. "I never," she told him, "pictured hell as cold."

"Listening at the door, mother?"

"Not eavesdropping. I saw the light under your door and paused. Then I heard Tammy's voice and a couple of words. I find I agree with her." Nadine's mouth tightened. "I helped Thelma to bed."

"For a nurse she certainly had an unusual reaction to a slaughtered cat."

"That happened to be the last straw. She was so weak I had to help her undress. Her breasts, hips, and stomach are covered with bruises and what looks like...like teeth marks. Someone did a job on her."

"Doesn't take much conjecture to decide who. Norman, carrying out his idol's orders. Odd we didn't hear her scream."

Nadine shrugged. "Her lips are swollen too. Looks like she didn't have a chance to scream. Nice folks, the Quillers."

Perching on the suitcase again, Nigel searched his mother's face. Her Romany look wasn't in evidence. He noticed, as Tammy had earlier, the soft, naked vulnerability of her fea-
210

tures. "Why did you come up here tonight? Going to urge me to take action again?"

"Just the opposite."

His eyes widened. "I can't believe my ears. A change of heart. What brought this about?"

"Time to think, I suppose. For the first time in years I've really thought. Searched back through the past, back through both our lives. What you said on the beach that day about the two-bladed weapon and if it's that important to me. Gradually, I've come to realize what I did to you from the time you were a baby and I discovered the special talent you have." She sighed. "At dinner tonight you said dwarfs are exploited. Your own mother exploited you. Oh, I didn't put you in a freak show. I wasn't that kind. I did worse. I honed you, formed you, made you into a weapon. You were never my son, only something to use to revenge a man I knew for only a few months. Since I've come to this place, I've wondered how well I really did know Micah."

"Something else must have helped change your mind, mother."

"Rayburn. I pictured him as a bloodthirsty monster who terrorized Micah and killed his son rather than let him come back to me."

"Now?"

She lifted her hands and the blanket sagged away from her shoulders. "At first I couldn't believe that Rayburn's grief and love for Micah were genuine. I thought he was acting. Now . . . I think he did love his son. I don't believe he arranged your father's murder to look like a suicide. That leaves me only two choices. Perhaps Micah's mind was crumbling. I know he had no strength. He was an artist, sensitive, brilliant, but with no actual strength. Or . . ."

"Or what?"

"Or Micah regretted our hasty marriage. He may not have wanted to come back to me. Yet, he was honorable and would have felt forced to. Perhaps his suicide was a way to escape a marriage he didn't want, a woman and child he couldn't stand to live with." Her voice broke and tears started to her eyes. Lifting the corner of the blanket, she dabbed at her face.

With somber eyes, her son regarded her. "What do you want now?"

"Only to leave here. You and me and Tammy and her mother. To put the Quillers out of our lives, out of our minds.

211

I release you, Nigel, your father is long gone. For the first time since you were born I'll allow you to be free."

"You?"

Through tears she managed a smile. "I plan to live too. There's Sam Silverstein—"

"Your manager?"

"More than my manager. Sam's loved me for years, wanted to marry me. I know he's a funny, dumpy little man but he's kind and gentle and capable of deep love. I want a home, a husband. Someone to wait for, to cook and clean for. I want life."

"It would appear," Nigel mused, "that we now have an outbreak of sanity. You're the second person tonight to get your values straight. What about revenge? Won't you miss it?"

"I'll miss it. I've lived on it so long. It's eaten right into me. I've lived it, slept it, dreamt it. Now, I find I've devoted a lifetime to hate for a man who only wanted to be rid of me."

Almost timidly she placed a long hand over his small one. "You know so much, my son. Tell me, am I wrong about your father?"

"Not about Rayburn's emotions about his son. He didn't murder Micah. He loved his son as deeply as a man like Rayburn can love. I think he's experienced only two loves. His wife, who he called gentle Jenny, and his son Micah. He lost both of them to similar deaths. Micah hung himself, gentle Jenny slashed her wrists." Nigel lifted his gaze to his mother's face. "You no longer fear Rayburn?"

Her rounded brow wrinkled in thought. "I thoroughly dislike him. Look what he had Norman do to poor Thelma. Look at the brutal way he handled Tammy. But now I see him clearly. Rayburn hungers for power and hasn't the talent to earn it so he acts as a petty tyrant, rewarding and punishing his family according to his whims. Trying to instill fear, to control. A sad man but not a monster."

Nigel squeezed her hand. "I'll offer you the comfort I can. Micah did love you, mother. He wanted nothing more than to live out his life with you."

"Then why did he kill himself?"

"Because he *did* love you. Don't question me further, mother."

Nigel's face was weary and her voice was gentle as she said, "Only one question, son. You like Tammy, don't you?"

212

"More than like her. It may seem wild but from the moment I saw her, before I even set foot on this island, I felt something for her. I couldn't even see what she looked like, just a poor, hunched kid standing there by herself."

"I know. The first glimpse I had of your father...you love her."

"With all my heart." He gave a harsh, barking laugh. "Which, believe it or not, is a normal size."

"How does she feel about you?"

"How would any woman feel about a dwarf?" he asked bitterly. "I couldn't love someone closer to my own size, not a girl of maybe four eleven or even five feet. No, I have to worship a girl who stands about five ten in her stocking feet, a girl who looks down at the top of my head, whose hands are twice as long as mine. God, to think my arms don't even go around her shoulders!" His voice roughened even more. "Even if Tammy did return my feelings—what would our future be? Constantly mistaken as her little boy, eyes staring at us, a freak show wherever we went. Sly speculations and gross jokes about our sex life. Tell me, dear mother, how long would love last?"

She started to weep again. "I'm sorry, Nigel, so sorry."

"Don't be. It's not your fault. I'm a joke of nature. A miniature man with all the desires, all the longings, all the emotions of a man twice my size. And I *feel* tall. I feel seven feet tall and a warrior." He said sadly, "You can't free me, mother, my body is my prison. But if I can't love Tammy, I can do something for her."

"What?"

He spoke for a long time. As she listened the fresh color drained from her face, her flesh seemed to sag, as though she was visibly aging. When he had finished, she asked huskily, "How long have you been...doing this?"

"For years." Under the burnished cap of red-gold hair, his face looked older than hers. "I started because I hoped to release you from your obsession. I gathered bits and pieces, traveled over this country, and to England. Checking records, reading old letters, talking to people." He laughed, but it was a bleak sound. "Then I found I was hooked. Your obsession had become my own."

"You never let me know."

"Would it have stopped you from coming here?"

"No. And you found my mother's name wasn't Magda, that she wasn't a Rumanian gypsy."

"I've known who you are for a long time."

She bit at her lip. "Nigel, this might destroy you too."

There was a long silence and then he said evenly, "Yes, it could at that."

Fourteen

At dawn, when much of the country was greeting a rising sun, the coast of Maine remained shrouded in a gray fog. Inland, it wasn't quite as thick but there still was a rash of traffic accidents, a populace cursing at the lack of visibility and hoping for a quick release from the clammy blanket of mist.

At Amoston oily waves washed up against the sand, slow, sluggish swells grayer than fog. It was cold, achingly cold, and Rob Brome shivered as he stood on the beach, vainly trying to pierce the fog with his eyes, hoping to see a break, wishing a gale would come along and wrench it into bits. Like that fluffy candy sold at fairs, he thought, only that stuff was spun into vivid pink threads. Coiled into paper cones to be torn apart by sticky childish lips, hardly touching the tongue before it melted into nothing. He wiped his sleeve over his face. Dampness dewed his hair, the collar of his pea jacket, clung to his brows and lashes, moistened his lips, and crept into his nostrils with that smoky tang that was its smell alone.

He turned his back to the sea and walked glumly across the sand. Ice crystals splintered beneath his boots. His boot touched an asphalt surface and he paused, listening intently. Even when the eyes were blinded, the ears were still a protection. There was no sound of a motor and he sprinted across the road, felt sand under his feet again and paused to get his bearings. He brought up short against the wide window, grunted at his own lack of direction, and felt his way along to the steps and the door of the cafe.

Inside, the fluorescent bars in the ceiling poured cold light over the tables with their burdens of upturned chairs, over the plastic counter and the glimmer of nickel-plated sugar containers and the gleaming unused coffee urn. On the hot plate beside the grill, a pot of coffee was bubbling merrily away and he headed toward it. Instead of reaching for the pot he found his hand was firmly resting on the hard black plastic of the phone. Every fiber in him longed to pick that phone up, dial the memorized number, and speak to some ensign or warrant officer at the Coast Guard station up coast.

Common sense stopped him. He imagined the conversation, the crisp, businesslike voice flowing down the line. Polite, and ready to get the facts, sir. Yes, Mr. Brome, you feel we should check on the welfare of this group of people. Have you reason to suspect they might be in an emergency situation, sir? The probing questions, and his own dumb answers. No, ensign or warrant officer or whatever, they aren't short of food. Yes, they have a fully qualified doctor and registered nurse with them. Yes, there is a boat there and a man who knows how to run it. The crisp voice became crisper. Then, Mr. Brome, sir, what is the reason for your concern? Well, you see, Coast Guard person, I had this dream—

Taking his hand off the phone, Rob grinned mirthlessly. They'd be looking for him with a butterfly net! Switching off the burner the coffee pot rested on, he reached under the counter and pulled out a bottle of rye. The sun wasn't over the yardarm, in fact there was no sign a sun was up there or ever would be again, but he needed a drink. Screwing off the cap, he tilted the bottle and took a long swig. As he rubbed the back of a hand across his lips, he grinned again. Real elegant way to drink. Getting just like old Jeb Amos—straight from the bottle.

Yes, sir, he told himself, I sure enough had this dream. Spent most of yesterday reading that book on psychic phenomena, devoured every word, and then went to bed and had this dandy. Last night he hadn't been trying to dock the *Caravan* to get onto the island. Oh no! In his dream he was on the island, right outside the fence around that tall house.

216

No fog in the dream. He could see clearly that monstrosity of a building with the gingerbread trim hanging off the roof line and the veranda that ought to soften the damn place but didn't. The fence was no longer chest high, it towered over his head. He was pushing his face against the gate, not the short gate sagging forlornly from one hinge, but a tall, securely locked gate he couldn't break through. On the crushed shell path two figures were struggling. One was Rayburn Quiller, wearing his expensive tweeds, and the other was Tammy, wearing nothing but some blood streaming down one arm and more trickling down from a gash under a beautiful blue eye. Rayburn's powerful hand was entwined in the girl's long hair and he was dragging her along, caveman style, toward the steps. The massive door, under the arc of colored glass, crashed open and another man appeared on the veranda. A man with curls and a beard the shade of ripe carrots, a man with pale bulging eyes, stretching out his hands, grasping at her naked body, tugging her into that house.

Rob felt his own hands, sore and bleeding from impotently pummeling at the gate. He heard the echo of a woman's screams. He had to get in! He had to stop them! Help, he needed help. Break down the gate, break down that door. He was racing down a rocky path. Jeb and Holly. They'd help him. He turned a corner and felt despair. All that remained of the neat blue-and-white cottage was a pile of rubble, charred and splintered. He could hear his own voice shouting. Jeb! Holly! He jarred himself awake, fighting, his hands aching where he'd clawed at the headboard. In his ears he thought he could still hear his name being called, Tammy's voice, shouting his name.

Taking a deep breath, Rob tilted up the bottle again. The rye burned his tongue, burned his throat. Try telling that dream to a sane voice from the Coast Guard station.

And yet...perhaps there was such a thing as one mind communicating with another. Some of the things in that book had sounded like a bunch of hokum but there were cases, carefully documented, that couldn't be discounted. The way that Tammy had pulled Sally's name out, the look on her face as though she'd seen...Perhaps there was trouble on the island, perhaps—

He set the bottle down so hard the sound splintered the silence of the cafe. Too damn many perhaps. Too much thinking and drinking and no action. He only had a hunch but he'd had hunches before. He'd wanted to get Sally out of her village but his buddies had talked him out of it. She's as safe there as she'd be anywhere, they'd told him. Hell, the Cong aren't anywhere near Sally's village. So, he'd disregarded his hunch and the Cong had got to Sally, Sally and the baby. Rob's mouth firmed. One girl had died, this time he was going to do something.

But what? No possible way he dared try to get out to the island. No radar equipment on the *Caravan*. The Coast Guard could make it but they'd have to have a damned good reason for moving. His brow wrinkled. There had to be someone who could get them moving, someone they'd have to listen to. Someone connected with the Quillers who carried a little clout.

Slumping down on a stool, Rob rested his chin in his hand. When mom was dealing with Rayburn Quiller for supplies and so on, why hadn't he paid more attention? At that time he hadn't given one damn about them, only another group of tourists, only one more headache. But mom was pretty shrewd, she'd keep records of some kind.

He jumped down and opened the door to the living room. It didn't look much like it did when mom was home. Newspapers littered the floor, magazines cluttered the glass-topped coffee table, the ashtrays were full of butts, a couple of cups with coffee dregs in their bottoms flanked a plate with the stale remains of a sandwich on it. Disregarding the clutter, Rob went directly to his mother's desk. It was a beauty, had once belonged to her grandfather, a roll-topped antique with a satiny luster that his mother carefully waxed every Saturday. A couple of tourists had coveted that desk and offered a tempting amount of money for it but mom said, no, it's for my Rob after I pass on. Sitting down on the cane-bottomed chair, he rolled the top back. He ran a hand over the banks of pigeonholes. One thing you could say about mom, her bookkeeping might be kind of peculiar but she was sure neat.

Rob started to pull papers out of the holes. Letters from her sister in Tennessee, more from a girlhood friend who now lived in Scotland, post cards from friends with pictures of Disneyland and swaying palms and blue lagoons on them. Bundling them up, he jammed them back again. He worked methodically from right to left. Bank statements and canceled checks, receipted bills from wholesalers for buns, hamburger, shellfish, relishes. Carbons from receipts given for cabin rentals, a baby picture of himself, a chubby hand grasping a rattle, a color snap of mom and dad taken on their trip to Florida last winter. Picking it up, Rob grinned down at it. It was rather blurry but mom was wearing shorts and a well-filled halter and dad was proudly holding up a fish. He flipped it over. In dad's writing a terse, "fifteen pounds." Trust dad. No mention of where or when, get to the important part, how much the fish weighed.

Rob didn't try to replace the items as he went. Pictures and checks and receipts crowded the desk. He'd sort them out later. Then his hand stopped. An envelope, thick white expensive paper, his mother's name and address in heavy stylized writing. Black ink. No return address. Even before he flipped up the flap and took out the heavy page, Rob knew this was from Rayburn Quiller. Inside, no address, only a date. My dear Mrs. Brome...Rob's eyes flew down the lines. Flowery, exuding even from the page a heavy, calculated charm.

His eyes caught and held. "I'm deeply sorry," Rob read, "that because of my recent retirement I am unable to give you a forwarding address. On the back of this page I've listed more supplies that my family and I will require. I would appreciate it if your good son will take these items out to the island. In the event that more funds are needed, please contact my son, Jim Quiller, who will send a check to you immediately."

Turning the page over, Rob scanned the list of supplies. They were itemized. Scotch—Chivas Regal. Champagne—Dom Perignon. He read faster. Château Lafite Rothschild, Chablis, Rémy Martin. Meat—sirloin tip roasts, New York steaks, racks of lamb, caviar. Rob whistled softly. Nothing but the best for the Quillers. Food and drink to match the English tweeds, the elegant mink, the expensive car that Rayburn and Ruth Thaler and that kid had arrived in. Well, one thing for damn sure. Mom wouldn't have filled this order without the money in hand. So, Jim Quiller's address must have been in her hands too, that and his check.

Rob snapped his fingers. An address book. He pawed through the mass of papers. Had to be one here somewhere. No, didn't seem to be. The drawer. He hadn't opened the drawer. A shallow one. Two pens and a bunch of pencils, notepaper, cheap, with the name of the cafe printed on the top, envelopes, a huge eraser with the legend on it, "I never make missteaks." Ah, a small book with a cover of violent mauve. Gold letters, my address book. The Q's...Quincy...Quimbly...Quitler. But only Rayburn Quiller and in tiny letters, "party of twelve." Thanks mom, that's a real help.

With an exasperated sigh, Rob leaned back. Where would Jim Quiller's address be? On a scrap of paper she'd tossed out? Not mom. Jim...try the J's. He had it! An address in Florida and—thank you, mom—a telephone number. He pulled the extension phone toward him and bills and pictures cascaded to the floor. Never mind, he was dialing the number, listening for the click, for the measured rings. What in hell would he say? Never mind, ad-lib.

A voice spoke in his ear, a lilting female voice, not young but musical. "The Quiller residence." The last syllable lifting as though in inquiry.

"This is Robert Brome. Who am I speaking with?" His very best enunciation.

"Maria Velasquez, the housekeeper for Mrs. Quiller, sir."

It should have been señor, he thought, the soft lilt was Spanish. He cleared his throat. "I'm calling from Amoston, about the Quiller family—"

"Amoston?"

"Maine. A village across from the island where the family is vacationing."

"Maine? Island? I know they go up north but I don't know where." The accent was thickening, the words spilling out. "There is trouble?"

Carefully, Rob chose his words. "I'm not quite sure but the weather is bad here. Fog conditions. The island is cut off— I should explain my position. I was hired as boatman to bring the family back and forth and take them supplies." I was also fired, he thought, and hurried on. "Because of the weather I haven't been able to get out there and I'm a bit nervous. I was wondering if you could give me the name of someone I might speak with about this."

There was a pause and then the soft voice said, "Someone?"

"A lawyer, perhaps, a family friend."

"I know of no one, señor." Spanish all right and the accent was steadily getting thicker. "There is a lawyer who does business but he is in Orlando. I could perhaps find his name but...por favor, señor, I must think." Another pause. "Señora Quiller, I think she not tell many of this trip. She was in hurry, Señor Brome. She tell me, Maria, we be gone maybe
220

ten days but Señor Quiller, when he carry out their suitcases, he tells me, Maria, we be gone maybe a month. He tell me, close up the house and visit your sister if we not back in two weeks. Señor, I was packing to visit my sister when you call. Now, I won't go! I wait to hear how Señora Quiller—" She stopped abruptly, and she spoke he could hear panic flooding into her voice. "*Tammy.*"

Damn it to hell, Rob cursed. What in hell did he think he was doing? Getting a poor old woman shook up, that's what. He forced his voice to be soothing. "No cause for alarm, Maria, I'm sure they're fine. It's just—"

"Tammy! She is such a sweet girl, such sadness she has had. I come to Señor Quiller before Tammy was born. Señora Syles, she was then and her husband, what a good man. I nurse Tammy when she was a baby. In these arms I nurse her. I don't like—"

"Maria," he broke in. "I'm sorry I upset you. Tammy's fine, just fine."

"I tell her mother, I don't like Tammy going away now. Doctor, he doing Tammy good. I go out to see her and she is in that nice place with flowers and a blue swimming pool and she painting."

"Doctor!" Just what I need, Rob thought. Tammy's doctor. "Maria, maybe I should speak with Tammy's doctor. Have you his number?"

"*Sí*, is right here. Speak to doctor. He such a nice old man. Do Tammy good." Speaking more slowly, she said, "Doctor Anthony Thule. Here is number." Carefully, she read the number out. Jotting it down on the edge of a post card, Rob said, "Thanks, Maria."

"You call me if—"

"Anything comes up, you'll be the first to know. Now, don't worry. I'm only taking precautions."

"Adios," the soft voice said. "Take care of my Tammy, señor."

Rob clicked the connection down and before he could change his mind, dialed the number she'd given him. The voice that answered wasn't soft and gentle and accented. It was a feminine voice too but a colder, clipped, no-nonsense voice. "Doctor Thule's office."

Rob straightened. This was like stepping out of the warm tropics into a northern ice storm. "May I speak with Doctor Thule, please."

"Your name, sir, and your business."

Oh boy! "I'm Robert Brome and I'm calling from Amoston, Maine."

"Mr. Brome, the doctor is a busy man. May I ask why you're calling."

Courteous words, but that voice. His own voice chilled, his words became clipped. "A matter of emergency, concerning Miss Tamara Syles."

"Miss Syles?" No warming, but a trace of uncertainty. "Hold the line, please, I'll put you right through to the doctor."

Great, Rob thought, some action. Now, if he could just think of the emergency—

"Mr. Brome, this is Anthony Thule."

Rob's heart sank. A voice as soft as Maria's, an unctuous as Rayburn Quiller's and filled with oily self-satisfaction. He could almost see the man. Elderly, well dressed, stomach flowing softly over his belt. The voice again. "Mr. Brome, what is this emergency concerning Miss Syles?"

Rob spoke rapidly. "I'm Robert Brome, doctor, and I'm calling from Maine—"

"That I already know. Ms. Colburn told me. Now, tell me about Miss Syles."

"Allow me to explain, sir. I'm hired as boatman to provide for the Quiller family's needs on the island that they're visiting. It's a fair distance from Amoston and it has a grisly history. Fog has closed in and there's no way I can check on their welfare. I thought, as Miss Syles's psychiatrist—"

"Doctor." There was a chuckle. "I can't claim that title, Mr. Brome."

Christ, Rob thought, running a mental institution and not a psychiatrist. He rushed on. "With the weather and the isolation and Miss Syles's condition, I'm worried about—"

"Hold on, Mr. Brome. I can tell you're upset but I must have something definite to go on. In the first place, what do you expect me to do from this distance?"

"A call to the Coast Guard, sir, I've the number right here. They have equipment to reach the island, see if the Quillers are all right."

There was a small pause and then the fruity voice said, "I'm afraid to take this step I must have more information, Mr. Brome. Have you reason to believe they may be in some kind of trouble?"

"As I told you, the weather, the grisly history of that island—"

"Factual or legend?"

"Factual, sir. Mass murders, pretty horrible, in the house where the Quillers are staying."

"Hmm. If I'd known that I might have given a different answer when Mrs. Quiller asked my advice on this trip for her daughter. Miss Syles is in delicate shape, abnormally suggestable." The doctor paused and it sounded as though he was drinking something. Coffee? Maybe sneaking a drink of something stronger. Mint juleps? Rob could picture him lounging back in a comfortable chair, a frosted glass in one fat paw, rheumy eyes fixed on banked flowers and that blue swimming pool. The doctor coughed and said, "However, Mrs. Quiller is not only a generous, wealthy woman, but she is also extremely levelheaded. We hold her in high esteem here, Mr. Brome. Mrs. Quiller is community minded and has endowed many worthy charitable institutions... but I digress. Allow me to question you further. Would the Quiller party, because of this fog, be in any discomfort, lack of heat or food?"

"I imagine they're running short of fresh food but there's frozen and canned food out there. Heat? No problem with Jeb Amos around."

"Jeb Amos? I take it they're not alone on the island. Would this be a local man?"

Rob sighed. "A local couple. Jeb and his wife are caretakers. They live on the island."

"Mrs. Quiller assured me that her husband's brother-in-law is a doctor and there is also a registered nurse in the family. Is that correct?"

"It is, sir, but—"

The chuckle resounded in Rob's ear. "So, we come to the conclusion that their physical needs are well cared for, that there are people quite qualified to look after them in a medical emergency. I'm at a loss to understand the reason for this call, young man."

"It seems to me you were alarmed about Tammy for a moment yourself. Could you tell me anything about her background, sir, anything that might assist me if this weather persists?"

"I'll be frank, Mr. Brome. None that is any of your business. It is privileged information."

"If anything should happen to Tammy," Rob said evenly,

223

"and it became known you'd refused to help, I doubt either you or your school would look too good. If I didn't feel concern I'd never have spent money on this call." Hit him where he lives, Rob thought.

"Hmm, you may have a point. After all, you are employed by the Quillers. This is public knowledge in this area, and certainly no discredit to the Quiller family." Having talked himself into it, the doctor continued, "Tammy was very close to her father, one of the warmest father-daughter relationships it's been my privilege to witness. A charming daughter and a wonderful father. Both Marc Syles and Veronica Quiller were killed in a tragic car crash—"

"Would Veronica Quiller have been a relative of Jim Quiller?"

"His wife. Luckily, Dorothy and Jim were able to find comfort in each other. They, too, have a wonderful relationship. The good Lord, Mr. Brome, may take away with one hand but He gives back with the other."

"Not to Tammy."

"Ah, then you noticed her distaste for her stepfather." Doctor Thule added hastily, "Not Jim's fault. He has done everything in his power to help the child but she refuses to accept him. I thought this little trip might...ahem, might assist their relationship. Jim is genuinely fond of Tammy."

"Then her father's death is the reason for Tammy's condition?" Rob probed.

"Partially. There are other factors. She was only fourteen when this double tragedy occurred and she was a high-strung, overly sensitive child at that. Her mind and her imagination went wild. She fancies, has illusions, that her father and Veronica didn't die accidentally, that they were bludgeoned—I'm talking too freely."

Rob pointed out, "You might as well finish."

"Well...keep in mind this is confidential, Mr. Brome. Tammy tried to convince both me and her mother that her father and Veronica were murdered. I hasten to assure you that at the time of the accident, Tammy was miles away from the scene of it, tucked into her own bed. Sheer illusion! It's taken me five years to straighten out her thought processes."

Fine doctor, Rob thought disdainfully, spilling his guts to a voice on a phone. He kept the disdain out of his voice, forced it to be admiring. "You've done a remarkable job, doctor."

224

"I think, in all modesty, I can say that Tammy now admits she *is* overimaginative, that she does hallucinate."

Rob picked words carefully. "Have you ever considered, Doctor Thule, that Tammy might be telepathic?"

"Claptrap!" The doctor's voice sharpened as much as it possibly could, booming down the line like dull claps of thunder. "Mishmash, Mr. Brome. To think that even eminent universities are now seriously researching in this superstitious nonsense!" He gave a most unprofessional snort. "Paranormal, indeed!"

Rob held the receiver away from his ear. "The mere fact that serious research is being conducted indicates that there may be something to this. Up until a few days ago I would have agreed with your sentiments, but Tammy pulled something from my mind, something she couldn't possibly have known about, a name I never even said to my psychiatrist—" He cut himself off abruptly, cursing under his breath.

"You were saying, Mr. Brome? No, don't bother answering. So, you're undergoing treatment." The oily voice trailed off and Rob waited hopelessly. Now he's going to tell me to take aspirin and get bed rest, he thought. What the founder of Doctor Thule's school actually said was, "This explains much, Mr. Brome. Let me reassure you. The young girl you are so worried about is in good hands. Her mother and stepfather are the salt of the earth and I would imagine Jim's family is much the same. Now, compose yourself and leave this in my hands. If, by the end of the month, they have not returned, I shall certainly make inquiries."

"But the weather—"

"Good-bye, Mr. Brome."

There was a muted click in Rob's ear. He smashed the phone down. Trust old Doctor Thule. Couldn't even hang up with a bang. Rob touched his face and found it running with sweat. He fumbled for a handkerchief, couldn't find one, and used the sleeve of his sweater.

My damned big mouth, he thought, had that chicken-livered excuse for a doctor on the run and then I have to blurt out the one word that would convince Thule he was talking to a raving maniac. Probably didn't place much more stock in psychiatry than he did in the paranormal. So, he'd blown it. No more leads either. Rob cursed helplessly. One phone call from that fruity old bastard and the Coast Guard would've been on the way.

225

Rob left the mess on his mother's desk and went back to the cafe. The coffee was cold. Reaching for the bottle, he poured himself a stiff belt. Might as well get bashed. He took the cup, circled the counter, perched on a stool and swung it around so his back was braced on the counter. Gloomily, he stared at fog pressing against the window.

Maybe Doctor Thule had a point. God knows he wasn't all that stable himself. Working himself up about what? A couple of nightmares. Should be used to them by now, he'd had dandies for years. Maybe he was only reacting to his dislike for Rayburn Quiller. He didn't like Quiller and he didn't trust him. The look Quiller had given Tammy when she'd jumped off the deck of the *Caravan*, the old goat's unreasoning anger because she'd come out with him.

Okay, Rob decided, let's pretend you're not a mess yourself. Let's look at this objectively. Oily Doctor Thule had let a few things slip. Dorothy Quiller was wealthy, rich enough to donate money to worthy causes, no doubt Doctor Thule's school was one. Rob had figured the money was on the Quiller side. The supplies Rayburn had ordered, the way he and his daughter dressed, their cars—but what about the shabby old station wagon that had brought the rest of his family? The one that Andy and Thelma and that creepy-looking Norman had ridden in. Their clothes looked as though they'd come straight from a rummage sale. And the bills for the liquor and meat and caviar had gone to Jim Quiller.

Rob took a sip of rye. One step further. Dorothy had the money, probably had inherited from Tammy's dad...what was his name? Marc Syles. Marc and Jim's wife dead five years ago in a car accident which Tammy insisted was a double murder. A kid, a telepathic kid, miles away in bed. A strong bond with her father. If Tammy could read the mind of a stranger, it wasn't too far-fetched to figure a message might have been sent from that man's mind to his daughter's. If it was a double murder, who would gain? Jim Quiller, marrying the wealthy widow, would gain and, if Jim was a dutiful son, so would his relatives. Now, if Jim would kill his own wife and Dorothy's husband to marry money would he balk at killing his wife and stepdaughter to get the whole caboodle?

Rob shook his head. Didn't quite square up. From the little he'd seen of Jim and Dorothy he'd swear they were much in love. Of course, Jim could have been acting. Not his wife.

226

That emotion in Dorothy's face had been genuine. Any estate she had *would* be Jim's. Murder had been committed lots of times for far less money. Rob grinned mirthlessly. Already he'd accepted the idea that Tammy and Dorothy had been taken to that island for only one reason—to knock them off.

Restlessly, he slid off the stool and wandered over to the window. Rayburn had gotten rid of him neatly but what about Jeb and Holly? And what about the rest of those people? He hadn't liked any of them, not even the haggard doctor and the chunky nurse with the tic under one eye. No...wait a minute. That midget, Nigel, was a decent little guy. Little was the key word. What could a runt who only came up to his own belt buckle do to protect a couple of women?

Rob touched the chill glass. What about himself? He'd been responsible for a girl's horrible death. Was he only conjuring up danger to try and save another girl? By convincing himself that Tammy needed help was he trying to expiate his guilt of omission in Sally's death? No! This feeling he had was more than a tidbit thrown to an uneasy conscience. Granted he hadn't seen that much of Tammy Syles but he knew one thing. He wanted those years stretching ahead, he wanted children, he wanted...he wanted Tammy. His lips moved in a grim smile. Just his luck to want a girl just as battered and bruised and vulnerable as he was.

Never mind the future now. He had a hunch, and this hunch he was going to ride. As soon as this fog lifted even slightly, he was going out to that island. Rayburn could throw him out again but first he was going to see if Tammy was okay.

Balling his hand into a fist, he brandished it at the fog. "Lift," he shouted, as though speaking to an enemy. "For God's sake, lift!"

Fifteen

Nadine had turned all four burners on and around the stove there was a tiny lukewarm circle of warmth. Crouching as close as he dared to the heat, Rayburn sipped his coffee, both hands clasping the hot mug. Over the rim of the mug he eyed the other people in the kitchen with a jaundiced gaze. None of them made any move to sit at the table and they stood around it, shoveling down their breakfasts, gulping scalding coffee, and grumbling. They were bundled in layers of clothing. Philip had pulled a toque over his shaven skull and his scalp lock dangled under the edge of it. Nadine was wearing gloves that she'd snipped the fingers and thumbs from, her glossy hair was swathed in a bright scarf, and her lips were blue with cold. None of the men had bothered shaving and neither Nadine nor Tammy wore any makeup.

"What a night," Philip complained. "When I did get to sleep I dreamed I'd volunteered for a mission to Antarctica."

"Talking about it won't help," his grandfather snapped. "Where's Thelma?"

"Still in bed," Norman told him.

Nadine flipped a pancake. "I'll take her breakfast up."

"Said she wasn't hungry." Norman shivered. "Sure wish I was Ruth, up beside that nice fire."

A voice from the door called merrily, "Good morning, all."

229

Their eyes turned toward Dorothy. Not only was her voice cheerful but her expression radiated the same cheer. Her hair was freshly washed and fell in a tawny, leonine mane around her smiling face. She wore a heavy blue sweater, matching slacks and her suede jacket, but she was expertly made up. Eye makeup made her eyes appear larger, skillful lipsticking almost straightened the crooked line of her mouth. She radiated vitality and good spirits.

Rayburn's eyes traced the lines of her face, lingered on her pert breasts outlined against blue wool, and swept down over rounded hips and long legs. For the first time that morning his mouth relaxed in a smile. "Nothing like a smiling face to raise the spirits. And a pretty one, too. I don't have to ask how you're feeling, my dear."

"Wonderful." She accepted a mug of steaming coffee from Nadine.

"Let's hope bed rest does as much for Thelma. Who are you looking for, Dorothy? Jim?"

She tossed back the mane of bright hair. "No. I met him taking a tray up to Ruth and Buddy. I was wondering if old Blue had come back. Tammy tells me he wandered away last night."

Behind her mother, Tammy was urgently shaking her head. Nadine shoveled sausages and pancakes on a plate and handed it to Dorothy. "Cats do that," she told the other woman. "You can't depend on them. Probably hunting."

Dorothy took the plate. "I've never been around a cat before. Oh, we had cats on the ranch, of course, but they stayed around the barns, never came near the house. When I get home I think I'll get a couple of kittens. I find I enjoy old Blue."

Involuntarily, Tammy found her gaze wandering to the chopping block. The top of it was now scoured and clean. She moved around to where she could see her mother's face. Puzzled, she noticed her mother's beatific smile. Was Dorothy smiling at Rayburn? Flirting with him, hoping to make Jim jealous? No, she seemed oblivious to Rayburn and to everyone else in the kitchen. The beaming smile was directed toward the far end of the kitchen. Tammy noticed that Nigel, his brow furrowed, was following Dorothy's rapt eyes too. There was certainly nothing to cause joy about that wall. Fog pressed thickly against the panes of the window, providing a background like cotton wool for the bright curtains and the

230

row of geraniums. A clock, fashioned like a dinner plate with a blue-and-white pattern of windmills and tulips, ticked away above the window. At one side of the curtains was a walnut-framed barometer, the glass front cracked, and a gaudy calendar displaying a buxom blonde in a bikini sitting on a tractor.

The door swung open and Jim, balancing a tray, stepped into the kitchen. He glanced at his wife and Dorothy turned, gave him a radiant smile, but didn't really seem to notice him. Clattering the tray down, he shoved his hands into the pockets of his coat. "We'd better get going, dad. If we don't get some heat into this place by tonight we'll all have to bunk where we can keep a fire going. This is unbearable."

"I agree. Where's Andy?"

"Right here." The doctor stepped into the kitchen. He'd pulled what looked like a golfing hat down over his ears and wore brown fuzzy mittens. Holding out his hands, he grinned. "Saw these in my chest just after we got here. Never dreamed they'd come in handy."

"You're late for breakfast," Rayburn snapped.

"I'll have some when we get the furnace going, Ray."

Philip snorted. "A born optimist."

His grandfather glared at him. "You and I will take the sheds, Philip. Andy, you and Norman search this house. Every corner, mind. Nigel, Jim and you have a look through the boathouse. If you find anything you think would do for a belt, bring it along. Report to me in the sheds. Now, get going." Turning to Dorothy, he said in an entirely different tone, "I would suggest you take your breakfast into the library. Norman has a fire going there. You're only out of sickbed, you shouldn't get chilled." He jerked his head toward the shed.

Andy put a hand on his son's arm as the other men filed out after Rayburn. "Let's start the search, Norm."

Nadine watched the doctor and his son leave and then she started to fill another plate. "That fire sounds like a good idea. Neither Tammy nor I have eaten yet. We'll join you, Dorothy."

In the library a fire was crackling on the hearth and the desk had been moved back so there was room to ring the hearth with the club chairs. Dorothy took the one closest to the fire and started to eat with every evidence of good appetite. Tammy sank down beside her mother. The two older

231

women chattered about the lack of heat, then they moved on to clothes, to the two kittens Dorothy was going to get. Tammy heard only the drone of their voices, not their words. Her own mind was busy, filled with the effort it had taken to come downstairs, to face Rayburn and Jim. She was thankful the dark lenses masked her eyes. Her expression she could control but she knew the look of repulsion in her eyes might have alerted them. She wondered what had happened to her mother, why the woman crushed and forlorn the previous day was now radiating joy? She wondered what Norman had done with poor old Blue—

"Tammy," Nadine's voice broke through her thoughts. "Stop daydreaming and eat. You haven't touched a thing on your plate."

Tammy put her plate on the floor. "I'm not hungry."

Nadine thrust a mug into the girl's hands. "Drink this coffee and no arguments."

Dorothy was gazing into the fire. "And I think I'll do over my bedroom. I've never cared for the color scheme. Blue and white seems so...so cold. Perhaps a combination of lilac and pink and a soft blue. What do you think, Tammy?"

"Sorry, mother, I'm afraid I wasn't listening."

"My room at home, Tammy. I said I was thinking of doing—Oh, Norman. Any luck?"

His bulging eyes swept over them. "Nothing so far. Daddy's looking through the junk in that schoolroom." Striding over to the bookcase, he peered through the glass doors.

Nadine smothered a smile. "I hardly think Jeb would have kept a furnace part in here, Norm."

"Granddaddy said to search," he told her doggedly. He pulled at the top drawer of the French desk. "Locked. Wonder if I should break it open."

"I hardly think Rayburn would like that," Nadine told him.

"Mebbe not. Better ask him first." He pulled a lower drawer open and rummaged through it. "Look." He held up a leather folder. "My grandma." Walking over to the cluster of chairs, he held it out to the three women. It had two leaves and his finger pointed to one of them. "Pretty, isn't she? Just like Ruth."

The photograph she looked at was much like Ruth, Tammy thought, a delicate, porcelain face with large dark eyes and a fall of fine dark hair. There was a difference. Ruth had

232

missed beauty but this woman *was* beautiful. Her expression made the difference, the girl decided, the compassion, the sensitivity, the grace of that face. "She was lovely," Tammy told the boy.

"Her name was Jenny. Granddaddy calls her gentle Jenny." Norman frowned and pointed at the other picture. "He looks like her. Don't know who he is."

"Micah," Nadine said softly, "his name was Micah."

Ruth's twin, Tammy thought, and a twin in most ways. But again in that young face there was no trace of Ruth's expression. Micah had truly been gentle Jenny's son.

Bowing her head, Nadine murmured, "Put it away. They're both dead, they're both gone."

In the shed where the water pump was located it was even colder than it had been in the house. Rayburn and Philip were methodically searching every shelf, every box. Swearing viciously, Rayburn aimed a kick at a carton of odds and ends. "Jeb must have saved every bloody piece of junk he could get his hands on."

Pausing in his own search, Philip glanced apprehensively at the older man. "This is getting to you, isn't it?"

"I *hate* discomfort. And this is so unnecessary. Everything was going smoothly and then this."

"I wonder who did it."

"I damned well know who did it!"

"You do? Who was it?"

"None of your business. But rest assured, the culprit will be punished."

Pulling himself to his feet, Philip toed the door of the cabinet shut and rubbed his hands vigorously together. "My hands are numb." He shoved both hands under his jacket. "Might as well give up, nothing here. We'd better get more wood in the house. We're going to need it. Guess if we light a fire in the drawing room there'd be room enough for all of us to bunk down there tonight. We can push the furniture back and lug some mattresses down—"

"I am not," Rayburn broke in wrathfully, "accustomed to sleeping in a room with eleven other people."

His grandson gave an exasperated sigh. "What do *you* suggest?"

"I suggest you get that furnace going. I suggest you shut

your—" Breaking off, Rayburn turned his rage on the two men entering the shed. "Well, Jim, find anything?"

His son mumbled but Nigel said courteously, "I'm afraid not, sir. Not even a piece of rubber in the boathouse."

"I fell," Jim said morosely. "Nearly broke my ankle. Fog's so thick—"

"—you can't see your hand in front of your face," his father acidly finished for him. "Must you always be so trite? I told you to watch your footing."

Jim flushed an ugly red. "Noticed you didn't try to get down that bloody path. No way, took the easy way, close to the house."

From the direction of the door a low chuckle sounded. "Are the Quillers quarreling? Gentlemen, there's nothing to gain in fighting among ourselves."

Tearing enraged eyes from his son's flushed face, Rayburn beamed them at Andy. "Did you find anything?"

Norman stuck his curly head around his father's arm. "Not a thing, granddaddy, and we searched and searc—"

"Shut up, you moron!" Rayburn bellowed.

"Hey," Nigel intervened. "There's a mound of stuff in here."

Philip grimaced. "You better believe it, and we've been through it."

Nigel nudged a big box with the toe of his gleaming boot. "What's all this?"

"Ropes," Philip told him. "Tons of ropes, mainly worn out. Jeb was a junk hoarder. Bits of metal, old parts, rusted bolts and screws, crooked nails. It's hopeless."

Crouching, Nigel scrabbled through a wooden crate pushed against the wall. "What's this?"

"A radio tube," Rayburn told him. "Think how many years ago that was in service and that drunken fool hung on to it."

Tugging at the heavy crate, Nigel panted, "Did you pull these boxes out? Get them clear of the wall?"

The other men crowded around his small figure, and Andy asked, "What for?"

Hunkering back on his heels, Nigel grinned up at them. "That belt from the furnace looked pretty new. Occurs to me if Jeb kept everything he might have kept the belt he took off. Could have slid down behind one of these boxes."

"Say, it might have," Philip bent and helped his cousin pull out the crate. The other men spread out, pulling out

234

boxes as fast as they could. It was Rayburn who gave the sharp cry that brought the rest to his side. He was tugging a narrow coil of black rubber from behind a cardboard carton. He held it up. "Look!"

"Let's see, granddad." Philip ran a hand along the strip. "A miracle. The old V-belt."

"Take a lesson on what can be done with a little perseverance," Rayburn told them complacently.

"We're not out of the woods yet," Jim said shortly. "Is it of any use, Phil?"

"It's worn in a couple of places but...yeah...I think it'll hold for a while."

Clapping the young man on the shoulder, Rayburn told him, "Don't just stand there, my boy. Into the shed and install it. Then a good strong drink for everyone."

The last two men out of the shed were Andy and Nigel. Pausing to shut the door, the doctor peered down at the little man. "That's Ray all over. Completely forgets a few minutes ago he was in the middle of a temper tantrum and is now again a suave, debonair gentleman. You don't seem amused."

"No," Nigel said grimly. "Nothing about Rayburn Quiller amuses me."

"Wise beyond your years," the doctor mused. "Very wise, indeed."

By late afternoon some semblance of order had returned to Winchfield House. The belt had been installed in the fan by Philip, surrounded by a shivering, admiring audience, and gusts of warm air clanked through the vents, at first sluggishly, and then in a delicious rush.

With the flood of warm air, the house and its inhabitants took on a faintly festive aura. Layers of coats, sweaters, and heavy shirts were peeled off and one by one the Quillers went up the austere staircase to the bathroom and then to their own rooms. The first one to reappear was Rayburn, freshly shaved and modishly dressed, wafting the lingering fragrance of expensive cologne and an attitude of satisfaction.

The only person, with the exception of Thelma, not to appear was Buddy. When questioned on the boy's absence, Rayburn, reverting momentarily to his earlier ill temper, snapped, "Buddy's grounded and must remain in his room for naughtiness."

No one dared asked what direction that naughtiness had

taken. Recovering quickly, Rayburn genially told his relatives that the rest of the afternoon was theirs. Drinks were mixed and Jim and Philip and Nigel, followed by Ruth, disappeared into the game room for a game of pool. Thelma remained in bed and Tammy went to the kitchen to help Nadine with dinner preparations. Dorothy also volunteered to help but after getting in their way for a time, she was persuaded to sit at the table and watch.

Rayburn retreated to the library where he ensconced himself in a chair behind the desk, the leaping fire still sending extra warmth through the room, sipping aged brandy, and reading a book. His son-in-law stuck his balding head around the door. "Got a minute, Ray?"

"Come in, Andy. What can I do for you?"

Andy sank into the depths of the club chair before the desk. He hadn't bothered putting the sling back on his arm but his hand was still bandaged and the dressing on his cheek emphasized the leaden tint of his face. His lips looked cracked and dry and he darted out his tongue to moisten them. "You know what I want."

Pushing up his sleeve, Rayburn glanced at his Rolex. "Little early today. Still a couple of hours to go."

"All this upset, Ray, running up and down in that fog. I need it, I really—"

"One moment." Putting a finger in the book to mark his place, Rayburn gazed past the doctor's shoulder. "Another visitor, I see."

"On your summons, dad." Jim perched on the arm of a chair. "What's so pressing to take me away from the game?"

As the doctor mumbled and made to rise, Rayburn waved him back. "Stay where you are, Andy. This won't take long." Giving his son a quizzical look, he chuckled. "Think it's about time we...ahem, we share the wealth, in a matter of speaking."

"What do you mean, dad?"

"Something you no longer care about. I'll explain precisely."

He did. As he spoke the doctor's face became even grayer. Rayburn's words had the opposite effect on his son. As Jim listened, color inched up under his tan and his eyes glinted with anger. When his father had finished, the suppressed anger roughened his voice as he said, "No way, dad."

236

"Come now, Jim. Have I been delinquent as host? Can you claim that your time hasn't been filled adequately?"

"Of course not. You've been most . . . generous. But not this, dad. You can't spend years with a person and . . . No!"

Flipping the book open, Rayburn bent his head over it. "Very well. That's all. Get back to your game."

Standing up, Jim looked down at that smooth head, his expression puzzled and slightly wary. "Is that all there is to it?"

"Of course. I made a request. You refused it. I don't force anyone. If I covet something, Jim, I want it offered freely. Now, if you don't mind, I wish to speak with Andy."

Jim left the room slowly, closing the door softly behind him. The doctor stared at the man behind the desk. "Trying to drive the last nail in the boy's coffin, Ray?"

Snapping the book shut, Rayburn stretched. "You speak in riddles."

"Possibly in metaphors, not in riddles. What I meant was that you're intent on stripping the last shred of decency from Jim. I've watched you and Ruth working on him ever since he fell into your clutches again, breaking down any instincts of decency he's gained through the years. Using every dirty trick in your filthy book to—"

"Tsk, tsk. How dramatic we are today. And what a way to speak of your wife."

"She isn't my wife, hasn't been for a long time." Andy stared miserably down at his bandaged hand. "Not since Norman was born. Deserted both of us then. Blamed the boy's condition on me. Left the poor kid without a mother, me without a wife. Funny, the other day I was telling Tammy how we met and everything came back for a moment. My joy, my delight, how I loved Ruth then. But the only reason Ruth even looked twice at me was because you ordered her to. Saw a chance to get a good front for your business, a captive doctor who could never open his mouth and denounce you."

"Hindsight, Andy, and completely unfair, although I will admit I did have a hand in your marriage to my daughter. If you couldn't gain her love, that's not my concern." Hooded eyes examined the haggard features of the other man, and then Rayburn continued with relish, "Let's be frank. You weren't then, you certainly aren't now, a very competent doctor. I doubt you'd ever have made a go in practice yourself.

237

We gave you a cushy job, one you could handle. At any time you were free to leave. You certainly weren't a captive."

"Free! First there was Ruth. I loved her, in fact—may the Lord have mercy on me—I still do. All she has to do is crook a finger. Then there was Norman. My son, a poor defective kid. For his sake I *had* to stay and then I had to watch you take him over. Norman might have been helped, Ray, if you'd allowed it, there was a chance."

"Boil and bubble. What a witches' cauldron you're stirring up, my dear doctor. Leave us anytime. You're free to go."

Andy's sound hand rubbed at his sleeve and he moistened his lips again. "I can't, and you know that too."

"I've a feeling you're about to blame me for that too. Your weakness, I mean."

"Put it bluntly. My addiction. I'm a dopehead—"

"A vulgar term."

"That's what I am. Thanks again to you. Sure, you didn't force drugs on me but first you gave me every reason to take them and then you made them temptingly accessible."

Leaning forward, Rayburn said coldly, "Remember who provides them. An expensive habit, Andy, and one you certainly can't afford on your meager talents. Keep another point in mind. We don't need you any longer. You're expendable." Taking a ring of keys from his pocket, Rayburn selected one and unlocked the top drawer of the desk. He pulled out a long flat metal box and unlocked it with a smaller key. He flung the lid up. "There it is. Take all you want. Take an overdose if you wish. Sit there and rub your arm and think about your Hippocratic oath."

The other man's eyes were glued on the tiny plastic packages, but he muttered, "Dangerous advice, Ray. If I thought about ethics for long I might be off to the police."

Rayburn barked a laugh. "Go ahead. You'd be involving your wife, your son, and yourself. You're up to your neck in it, Andy."

"Maybe I don't care any more. Maybe I've reached the limit of what I can condone. You'll break Jim down. I know you will. What then? Who's next?"

"There will still be two left. Both delectable. Tread carefully, Andy. Don't make threats. As I said before, you're expendable." He tapped the box. "I think you need a rest from this. About twenty-four hours without it and I trust you'll be more reasonable—"

238

"No! I couldn't stand it. I'd be out of my mind."

"So you would. You're well on your way just thinking about it. A weak quivering excuse for a man, let alone a doctor. And you dare to threaten *me*." In one smooth movement, Rayburn was on his feet. "Down on your knees. Beg for it."

"Don't make me do that, Ray. Please."

"Down and beg!"

The doctor crumpled to the floor. Sweat poured down his face and he held beseeching hands up. "Please, Ray, I'll do anything."

Picking up one of the tiny packages, Rayburn held it over the other man's head. "Are you going to interfere further with my pleasures?"

"No, Ray, do whatever you want."

Contemptuously, Rayburn threw the package on the floor. He watched Andy scrabbling after it, scooping it up into shaking hands. "Get out of here, *doctor*."

He watched the man leave and then, wearing a beaming smile, he walked across the hall. In the game room, under the light of a beautiful Tiffany lamp, a game of pool was being hotly contested. Nigel had brought a footstool from the drawing room and he was standing on it, carefully lining his shot up. Jim and Philip bent attentively over the table and Ruth lounged in a chair pushed against the wall.

"How goes the game?" Rayburn asked.

Philip raised his head and the light glinted on his shining skull. "Even though he has to push that stool around, Nigel's licking both dad and me."

"It would appear your cousin has many talents, Philip. Don't become too confident, Nigel, I may play you myself later and I'm a worthy contender."

Nigel slanted a smile at him. "I don't doubt that, sir. I'll look forward to picking up some pointers."

"Notice how nicely spoken the boy is, always so polite. Take a lesson, Philip. This modern habit of speaking rudely to one's elders is sometimes an error. Now, I have no wish to interrupt your enjoyment. Ruthie, dear, may I have a moment?"

Leading the way back to the library, Rayburn shoved a chair close to the hearth, and seated his daughter. He leaned against the desk and smiled down at her. "You look most fetching in that outfit, my dear."

She preened, smoothing down the tight black skirt. Her

present choice of clothing was a far cry from her usual flowing garments. The dull black skirt was slit up both sides, exposing flashes of shapely legs, and the matching top was close fitting, sleeveless, with a high mandarin collar. The only color was on the back of the jacket. Instead of the customary dragon coiling its length up the fabric, there was a spray of brightly colored, improbable-looking flowers.

Without warning, Rayburn leaned over and grasped at her arm. His nails bit into the tender flesh. "You've failed dismally, my girl."

She gasped and smothered a cry of pain. "Jim?"

"Precisely." Releasing her arm, he watched her rub at it. "If I can't move him on this, the girl is out of our reach. I'm not pleased with you, Ruthie."

"I don't understand." The smooth skin between her brows wrinkled, bringing a network of fine wrinkles around her eyes into play. "He's been softened up, dad."

"Not enough." He reached out a long finger and lightly ran it over the wrinkles raying out from the corners of her eyes. "Stop scowling, you're showing your age."

She jerked away from him and glared up into his face. "Stop that! That girl, all you think of is her!"

"Don't pretend you won't enjoy it, Ruthie."

The frown disappeared and she smiled. "Oh, how I'll enjoy it! But Jim. I've worked on him about being used, having that spoiled bitch of a woman dominating him. He seemed ready for this step."

Sinking down on a chair, Rayburn thoughtfully stroked his mustache. "He's had too many goodies. Too easily. Now, he's being a dog in a manger. We'll cut his supply off." His hand dropped. "Cool him."

"Nigel?"

"He appears to be *your* weak point. Most eager to experiment, aren't you?"

"I like challenges."

"You might find that boy too much of one. Nigel is still an unknown quantity. Definitely an *X*. I can't get into him and I've a feeling he's eyeing the same target I am. Not Nigel. Try the logical one."

Her smile widened. "Old bull and young bull?"

He nodded. "Hit him where it hurts."

Gracefully, she got to her feet, smoothing black cloth over her hips. "You do have robust appetites, don't you?"

"And such a brief time to enjoy them." He sighed. "None of us grow younger, Ruthie. Food, drink, other things. Must enjoy while we can."

"Maybe," she said wickedly, "that's why your tastes get younger and younger."

He eyed her up and down. "Too bad for you, Ruthie."

She stuck a pink tongue out at him, tossed her head, and tripped lightly across the hall to the game room. Jim glanced up, smiled, and beckoned her to his side but she languidly circled the table and stood beside his son. Philip didn't look up, all his attention was on Nigel's shot. Leaning against the young man, Ruth murmured, "This game is so interesting and I don't even know how to hold a cue, Phil."

"I'll show you how, Aunt Ruth."

He held out his cue and she said, "Don't call me aunt. It makes me feel so old."

"You're not old. Here, you stand in front of me and I'll get you in the right position." Obediently, she slipped into the circle of his arms, resting her back against him. "Now, put your right hand here and—"

"Have you forgotten we're in the middle of a game?" his father interrupted acidly. "If you want to give your aunt a lesson, you'll have to wait. Right, Nigel?"

"Not at all. They're not bothering me."

Completing his shot, Nigel jotted down his new score, and stepped down from the stool to reach for a cube of chalk. As he chalked his pool cue, he covertly watched Ruth and Philip. The boy's face was flushed and he was moistening his full lower lip with his tongue. Nigel could see why. The room, large as it was, was pulsating with heat. Ruth's supple body, clasped in the boy's arms, exuded an emotion that brought to every male in the place the realization of urgent sexual yearnings. Ruth's face appeared broader, her dark eyes languorous, dark hair sensuously brushing her shoulders. Her lips were parted, the surprisingly fleshy upper arms seemed to swell. Dull black tightened over breast, hips, and thighs that seemed engorged with juices, bursting with illicit promises. Nigel's nostrils quivered. He fancied he could smell the woman, not the smells of powder and perfume, but the age-old scent of a female in heat. A hot, decaying odor of overripe fruit—no, not fruit. A meaty smell, a musty, rancid odor. Bitch in heat? No, nothing of a canine about this woman. One of the big cats, perhaps, sending out her readiness to mate to any male in range. Nigel felt the effects himself, felt his loins warming, expanding, and God knows he was only getting the indirect impact. Philip was getting the full load. The boy's body was involuntarily contorting against the woman's buttocks, his hand was pawing at her arm. In a moment, Nigel thought wryly, the poor devil was going to be jerking off.

Tearing his eyes from the pair coupled at the table, Nigel looked at Jim with curiosity. Jim's face was flushed too, his eyes were murderous. "Your turn," he told his son abruptly, and took a step toward Philip.

Ye gods, Nigel thought, there's going to be a fight. Ruth averted it. "I'm in the way," she said and dexterously extricated herself from the boy's embrace.

She glided over to an oval mirror hanging on the wall, turned her back to the men, and ran a finger over one eyebrow. Philip, scarcely glancing at the positioning of the balls, took his shot and, without waiting to see what he scored, eagerly followed the woman.

It was Jim's turn but he made no effort to take it. His face blazing with wrath and lust he watched Ruth. Philip slid an arm around her waist and without glancing away from her mirror image, she told him, "When I was a little girl I used to play a game. I'd stand before a mirror like this and I'd ask, mirror, mirror, on the wall, who is the fairest of them all?"

"No doubt about that," he breathed. "You are."

"How kind you are. Do you play chess, dear?"

"I'd like to learn."

She pressed against him. "Come up to my room, Phil. I'll teach you how. In return, you can show me how to play pool."

Jim gave a harsh laugh. "You're lousy at chess."

Her mirror image smiled languorously. "But I'm a good teacher."

Philip was close to panting. "Let's go now."

Jim threw his cue on the table. "You win," he told the woman. "I'll speak to dad."

"Do that," Ruth told him. Moving away from his son, she watched Jim lunge out of the room.

Philip said eagerly, "Let's go up now, Ruth."

She patted his cheek. "I'm afraid I forgot about Buddy. He's having a nap. I'd better check on him."

"But our game," the boy wailed.

"Later, Phil, don't be impatient."

242

Watching her movements as she left, the slither of brightly colored flowers down the back of her jacket, Nigel heaved a sigh of relief. Close. A few more moments and she'd have had Jim beating hell out of his son. At least, he told himself wryly, he now knew what those odd flowers were. Had to be Venus flytraps. Or, in this case, mantraps.

Philip gazed after her with bemused eyes. "Jes—sus! What a woman! I thought I'd seen them all but I've never met anything like her before." He sighed. "Cleopatra!"

"More of a Mata Hari," Nigel said drily.

"Man, can she turn a guy on!"

"Like swallowing a handful of aphrodisiacs."

Philip tugged frantically at his scalp lock. "Now I know what Thelma's been hinting at. Dad's got something going with her. His own *sister*." He stroked the bulging fly of his jeans. "How beautifully *decadent*!"

Nigel was watching his cousin, his expression cool and remote. "Doesn't repel you?"

"Hell, no. Too bad *I* haven't got a sister. But an aunt's just about as good. What a trip, man! Hey, sorry to bust the game up but I gotta get upstairs. See a man about a dog—maybe I should say bitch."

"You're wasting your time with Ruth."

Philip grinned and winked. "Gonna really waste my time but if you gotta, you gotta."

He flipped a hand at the tiny man and followed his aunt. At the landing of the second floor he paused, cast a longing look at Ruth's door, and opened Thelma's. She was huddled under a mound of blankets, her back to the door. He tiptoed around the bed, pulled a corner of the blanket back and asked, "Hey, baby, how you feeling?"

Her eyes snapped open. "What do you care?"

"Don't be like that, Thelma. I come all the way up to see if I can get you something—"

"Balls. What do you want now, twerp?"

"That's gratitude." Sinking to his haunches, he twisted a lock of her hair around his finger. "Look, if you feel up to it, we could have a little piece of tail."

Her eyes wearily closed. "Go away."

He flipped the blankets back. Through a transparent nightie her body was exposed. Her breasts and stomach were marred with great purple splotches. "Christ!"

"Satisfied?" She pulled the blankets back into place.

"Who did that?"

"Norm, on orders from big daddy. I was naughty and lipped off at him."

"Whew...so that's the penalty for being naughty. Hurt much?"

"Of course not. It was a fun time." A tear trickled from the corner of one eye. "Anyway, it wasn't as bad as the last time. Norm put me in bed for over a week."

Sinking down on the floor, Philip crossed his legs. "Why put up with it? Why don't you take off?"

"With the Quillers you don't take off. You stay around as long as they want you to. I tried it twice." The blankets trembled with her shudder. "Rayburn brought me back and had Norm teach me not to be naughty."

He was watching her closely. "Bet I can guess who little Buddy's father is. It's Rayburn, isn't it?"

Another tear followed the first down her cheek. "Just walked in on my wedding night, no by your leave or anything, climbed into bed. Said he was the surrogate bridegroom. Told me I was going to be a surrogate mother. After Norm was born, Ruth had an operation and couldn't have any more babies. She wanted one. I was just an animal to bear it." Tears were pouring from her eyes. "Both of them in bed with me. Me, just a thing. Hated the bloody brat even before he was born. Andy delivered him with Ruth and Rayburn hanging over us...and the kid was put in Ruth's arms." Sobbing, she scrubbed her fist across streaming eyes.

He stroked her head but his pale blue eyes had a faraway look. "And granddad uses you any time he wants to, doesn't he?"

"Like a public urinal," she said bitterly. "Don't think I don't need it too. Starved for sex. Oh, he'd loan me out to some male patient he wanted to con if the old guy could get it up. Old men, how they smell!"

"Uh-uh, but you got a randy young one here. Dear Aunt Ruth's got me jumping outta my pants. Come across, baby."

"Have a heart," she pleaded, throwing back the blankets again and exposing her bruised body.

He zipped down his fly. "Face it, baby, you're up for grabs. Granddad's put his seal of approval on it and there's cousin Norm to enforce. You're pussy for Quillers and I'm one of the clan."

"You're inhuman!"

244

He squeezed one of her soft breasts and she winced. "Not going to put it to you thataway, Thelma. Raw meat and garbage pails I don't relish. But your mouth still operates. Open wide."

With utter despair she gazed up at him. Her eyes were puffed and her expression hopeless. "You are a *real* Quiller," she whispered.

Then, docilely, she did everything he demanded.

Sixteen

The feeling of festivity extended into the evening hours in Winchfield House. After dinner Tammy and Nadine retired to the kitchen to do the dishes and Dorothy, charming in sapphire wool, sat at the table, not watching them work, but with her eyes fixed on the far wall. Those eyes didn't shift even when Jim came up behind her and dropped a light kiss on her hair.

"Dad's organizing a bridge game," he told her. "Would you like to join us?"

"Who's playing?"

"Ruth and dad. I thought you might be my partner."

Then she did look up at him, and her smile was warm but slightly remote. "Lead on, partner."

"Good." He caressed her shoulder. "Dad wondered what you'd like to drink and I told him I'd whip up a pitcher of martinis, the way we both like them, ice cold and just a whisper of vermouth."

Jim made a great production with the drinks, laughing and talking with his wife as he worked. Then, with Jim balancing the frosty pitcher and Dorothy carrying a tray of glasses and a saucer of olives, they left the kitchen.

Nadine raised her brows in silent question but Tammy shrugged. She had no idea what had changed Jim from a surly indifferent stranger back to the man who doted on her mother. While she finished wiping the dishes and putting them away, she tried to figure out his about-face but she was too tired to even think. When she'd finished she wandered down the hall, glanced into the library and then continued to the drawing room. She slumped down in a chair near the archway.

Near the fireplace a card table had been set up and her mother, her stepfather, Rayburn, and Ruth were playing bridge, sipping drinks, laughing, and talking. At least Dorothy and the two men were laughing and talking. Ruth played quietly, managing to fade into the background. Jim and Rayburn directed their attention and most of their comments at Dorothy, who seemed to be accepting it as her due.

Tammy watched her mother for a few moments, admiring the play of firelight across her vivid face, across the shining masses of her hair. The belle of the ball, the girl thought, and then too tired to really care any further, she allowed her head to sink against the chair. She couldn't remember ever having felt so listless, so drained. Perhaps it was all the work she'd been doing around the house, more likely it was the nights she'd spent, the lack of sleep, the constant tension. The previous night after she'd left Nigel and the warmth of his little heater she'd quietly undressed in darkness, felt for her pyjamas, and crept into bed beside her mother. Dorothy had slept soundly but Tammy had spent hours lying rigidly, trying not to move around, trying not to disturb her mother. She'd been conscious of the cold in the attic room, the frigid fingers of air against her face, the creak of ancient timbers, the faint night sounds. For a time she'd dozed but there was no rest to be found even then. All the events of the day, all the unease of the previous week, had raced through her mind, muddled, out of proportion, at times hideous. In a state not quite dreamlike she'd felt Rayburn's big hand painfully grasping her hair, dragging her along, her body chilled and apparently nude. Again, she saw the cottage as a raging inferno, smelt the odor of burnt flesh, saw the charred remnants of that snug little home. Terror had pursued her through the high, dark rooms of the house, along the shell path leading to its front door. She was calling for Rob Brome, calling for his help. When she awoke she found his name was on her lips—

Tammy's eyes snapped open. They fastened on the group before the hearth but didn't see them. Had her mind, drugged with weariness, been seeking to enter Rob's? She didn't know whether she could send as well as receive. Her father had got an occasional thought from her when he'd been conducting tests, but Marc Syles had been attuned to her, his mind had been open and receptive. On her lap, her hands balled into fists. She must keep the barrier up, she couldn't allow herself to call to Rob. If she managed to reach him she sensed he was the kind of man who would come regardless of the cost. And the cost could be too high. Fog blanketed the island, the sea. Rob was a fine sailor but he could run up on rocks, the *Caravan* could capsize, Rob might drown. Tammy shuddered. For Rob's safety she mustn't try to reach his mind.

A flurry of movement around the card table brought her eyes back to her mother. Jim was missing, he must be dummy. As Dorothy played she laughed at something Rayburn said, and Tammy listened to that laughter, trying to spot a false note, a brittle edge to her mother's gaiety. There was none. It was a normal, pleased, happy sound. For some reason there was nothing reassuring about it. There was something false here, some false note that didn't come from Dorothy. Should she search their minds, enter Rayburn's, Ruth's, perhaps Jim's? No! She couldn't bear it. After that child's mind, she couldn't take a chance. She couldn't control her own reactions well enough. She might alert them.

Jim stepped through the archway and paused beside Tammy's chair. He carried a fresh pitcher of drinks. "You looked bushed, honey," he told the girl.

Swinging around, Dorothy, for the first time that day, looked directly at her daughter. "You look tired, Tammy. All that running up and down yesterday looking after me. Why don't you go to bed and take a couple of those pills Doctor Thule gave you?"

"I'm waiting for you, mother."

"You'll have a long wait, honey." Jim laughed and brandished the pitcher. "Your mother's going to play a while longer, help me win I hope, and we're both going to get a little tiddly. Right, darling?"

Giggling, Dorothy held up her empty glass. "I'm a little tiddly right now."

Her daughter frowned. "You've been sick, mother, don't drink too much."

"The mouths of babes," Jim said and patted Tammy's shoulder. "You get some rest, honey."

Pulling herself to her feet, she moved away from him. "I'll leave the light on for you, mother."

"Don't bother." Rayburn looked up from his cards. "Your mother's going to be where she should be tonight. Much too chill up there for a lovely lady just out of sickbed."

Tammy shrugged and didn't argue. She made her way through the hall to the staircase. Tired as she was she knew she wouldn't rest properly. She would take a couple of the pills Doctor Thule had given her. They were strong and would knock her right out. Tomorrow, she thought wearily, she'd try to figure this latest development out.

Nigel was trotting down the stairs. "Going to bed this early?"

"Sure am. I'm exhausted."

"Where are the rest of the zoo?"

"Spread out." She waved a hand. "Bridge in the drawing room, poker in the library. I think your mother's still in the kitchen. I guess Thelma's in bed. We sent a tray up for her with Norman but she didn't touch anything on it. Maybe I should stop in and see her."

He shook his head. "Leave it to morning. Goodnight, Tammy."

He watched her mount the stairs, her hand trailing along the bannister, her shoulders hunched and sagging. Tammy's face looked thinner, the cheekbones and the clean line of her jaw sharper. Such a frail girl, he thought. He continued down the stairs and stopped to peer into the drawing room. Quite a tableau, he decided, looked almost like a stage setting. The beautiful people—well dressed, handsome, animated. Ruth provided a background of passiveness to complement Dorothy's vivacity. Dorothy taking over the role of queen, complacently accepting the men's homage.

Nigel frowned. He really didn't care much for Tammy's mother. She was a vain woman, self-centered, overly fond of her own comfort. Dorothy obviously had never made any effort with that poor confused kid of hers, had left it all to Marc Syles and then blamed him when he'd tried to do it. Doubtless she blamed the girl too. After Marc's death Dorothy had mended her own life neatly, taking Jim Quiller on as doting husband, and shuffling Tammy off into the hands of that incompetent old doctor. Since Dorothy had arrived on this island and her husband's interest had turned to Ruth, she'd suddenly become aware of Tammy again. But only in what
250

Tammy could do for *her*. Now that Jim was snapping to again she probably had forgotten all about the girl. No, he didn't like Dorothy. Damndest part of it was that even though Tammy saw her mother clearly, her father's last plea would linger. She'd do her best to look after this indulged child, to play the part of mother with a woman who didn't give two hoots in hell about her.

Abruptly, he swung away from the archway and opened the massive front door. Stepping out onto the warped boards of the veranda, he peered into the fog. Thick as ever. He glanced down. Light fell from the hall along the veranda floor and he could see its boards and the first step. Beyond that was a solid white wall. He pictured the fall of land toward the pier, the expanse of water between the island and Amoston. He wondered if Rob Brome watched that fog from the cafe, watched and thought of Tammy. Nigel sensed that Brome was half in love with the girl, or thought he was. What would Rob be like with Tammy? Nigel wondered. Rob's size and coloring would go well with Tammy's slender height and frail blond beauty. Obviously Rob had problems of his own brought on because of that stupid, pointless war. But would Rob be able to use compassion and understanding for the girl's problems? Would he have enough imagination to know what a hell she lived in? Would he be able to set his own problems aside to help her?

Nigel's mouth twisted sardonically. He didn't know what Rob was really like. Let him be sensitive, Nigel pleaded, not knowing who he was directing the plea to, let Rob Brome be a good man.

"Nigel . . . Nigel."

He turned around. His mother was standing in the doorway. "Are you dreaming? I called you and you didn't hear."

"I guess I was, mother, half asleep. Guess I'll go to bed."

Shivering, she closed the door behind them. "It's so cold. You look as tired as Tammy does tonight."

As they started up the stairs she reached out a hand and he took it. His mother had certainly changed in the past few days and for the better. For the first time in his life, Nigel felt she really was his mother, actually viewed him as an individual, not just an extension of her own desire. Even the way she'd held out her hand was different. Before it was always for his sake, an unconscious indication that she didn't consider him a man, merely a child-sized male who never

251

would be an adult. Now her hand sought his for comfort, for support, for a warm human contact. Nigel smiled. One good thing had come from all of this. No...two. He'd met Tammy and found he was capable of love. For that, he told himself, I'm grateful.

In the drawing room Dorothy continued sipping her drinks, playing cards, basking in more than the warmth of the fire. Jim and Rayburn and Ruth watched her. A tiny smile played around the corners of Ruth's lips. Those lips, soft and red and wet, widened into a yawn and she delicately patted her mouth.

Rayburn chuckled. "Looks like we have another one here all ready for bed." He threw his cards down. "It's been a tiring day for all of us."

"I want to play another rubber." Dorothy pouted. "Let's have a drink."

"Don't be naughty," her father-in-law said playfully.

She held her glass out. "More, Jim."

He waggled a finger at her. "Uh-uh. You're cut off." Getting up, he lifted her from her chair, and held her in the circle of his arms. "See, you're wavering around. A touch drunkie." He told his father, "We're off to bed, dad."

"Pleasant dreams." Rayburn watched his son guide an unsteady Dorothy from the room.

"Now?" Ruth asked.

"Patience, Ruthie. We'll give them a little time." He glanced at the window pane blank with fog. "Time we have a great deal of, and haste destroys pleasure."

Stretching full length on her bed, Dorothy watched her husband undressing. She did feel a bit light-headed. One too many martinis. But what a wonderful evening. Her Jim was back, the man she'd loved for years. Lovely, attentive Jim. He'd removed her clothes, his hands sliding deliciously over her body, caressing her breasts, stroking her hips. Tracing the long lines of her legs as he slipped off her panty hose. Lovely Jim who would come into her bed and make lovely love to her.

She rubbed her brow. There was something she must tell Jim. Something he was going to be happy about. What must she tell him? Fuddled old mind, she thought dizzily, wonderful, fuddled mind. Ah, now she remembered. How could she have forgotten?

"Jim," she said gaily, "I've a lovely surprise for you."

"Really?" Stepping out of his shorts, he turned to face her.

He's ready too, Dorothy thought, as anxious as I am. She tried to push herself up against the pillows and nearly fell off the bed. She giggled. "Lovely surprise for a lovely Jimsie."

"Jimsie has a surprise for you too, darling," he told her.

Striding to the door, he flung it open. Dorothy blinked, trying to focus. She must have had *several* drinks too many. Seeing things. Imagining she was seeing Ruth and Rayburn and Buddy stepping in to the room. The door closed behind them. Jim was locking the door.

Dorothy blinked again. Ruth and Rayburn were wearing robes, the little boy had on white pyjamas with small blue sailboats on them. Ruth and Rayburn were peeling off the robes. They were naked, their bodies sleek and bare, Rayburn's massive chest was covered with a thick gray mat of hair. Ruth's tiny figure was deep breasted and lush. The images were all moving closer, standing around the bed. Four faces looking down at her, four pairs of eyes exploring her own naked body.

Hugging a blanket to her breasts, Dorothy jerked up against the pillows. They were real! They were actually there. Rayburn wrenched the blanket from her grasp and he bent over her, his hands avidly exploring her body. Ruth smiled and touched her breasts and then the woman's on the bed. Dorothy's mouth flew open and Jim roughly clamped a big hand over it. He was grinning down at her, his lips pulling away from his teeth like an...like an animal's.

"My surprise," Jim whispered. "I told you you were going to love my family. Now you are, darling."

Seventeen

The saucer slipped from Tammy's hands and splintered into fragments on the worn linoleum of the kitchen floor. Bending to pick the shards up, she ruefully told Nadine, "Right now I wish I hadn't taken sleeping pills last night. I feel as if I've a king-sized hangover."

"No harm done, that was cracked anyway." Nadine pulled the stopper from the sink and wiped her soapy hands on a towel. She glanced at the blue-and-white face of the Dutch clock. "Your mother must have a real hangover but I guess she's earned hers. Half past ten and not out of bed yet."

"Was breakfast taken up for her?"

"Jim made up a tray. He hasn't brought it back yet."

Watching the sharp edges of the broken china, Tammy lifted the lid of the garbage container and threw them into it. "I'm going up for a bath and I'll stop and see how mother is." She frowned. "Jim must have had a full tray. Not many managed to get down for breakfast."

"I threw out half what I cooked. Thelma's up but all she had was coffee and I haven't seen Rayburn or Buddy or Ruth." Nadine shrugged. "If they get hungry they know where the kitchen is."

Tammy spread the damp dish towels on the bar and started up to her room. As she passed the archway leading to the drawing room she saw Thelma, bundled in a shapeless sweater and slacks, huddled on a chair near the hearth, staring down at the cold gray ashes. Tammy hesitated but when the nurse didn't look up she continued on her way. In her attic room she gathered together a change of clothes and her bath kit. She clattered down the steps to the second floor, eyed the closed door to her mother's room, and turned back down the hall toward the bathroom. As Tammy locked the door behind her, she gazed around with distaste. Of all the ugly rooms in this house, this was certainly the ugliest. The huge fixtures were stained where taps had dripped for years, the mirror over the marble basin was cloudy and chipped, the linoleum was cracked and worn through in places exposing boards under it. It was a big room for a bathroom and looked as though once it had been used as a bedroom. The crowning glory was the toilet, perched on a low platform like a throne, the seat broken, and a tarnished chain hanging beside it for flushing. There was no way anyone could make this room look clean. It had a bad smell too, one of mildew and rot and staleness.

Tammy turned on the tap marked hot and watched lukewarm water puddling on the stained bottom of the claw-footed tub. Quickly she stripped, found her soap and shampoo, and bathed and washed her hair. This was no place to linger, the sooner finished the better. The bathroom was almost as cold as her own room. An electric heater sat beside a base plug but she wasn't about to risk plugging it in. She did use her blow dryer and shivered as hot air blew through her hair while the rest of her body was covered with goose bumps. As soon as her hair was dry she laid out the rest of her jars and bottles. All the trappings of civilization, she thought drearily, most of the products heavily advertised on every media. Deodorant to avoid offending, guaranteed to protect for twenty-four hours, talc for the body and feet, toothpaste that would never allow a cavity to mar the perfection of a smile, mouthwash to finish the job. A dab of perfume to provide an odor to a deodorized body. All the containers bright and joyful, mingling scents and sensations, mint and floral and herbal.

Tammy peered at her image in the ancient mirror. Hair sleek and glossy with lots of body, skin glistening with face cream, eyes that looked like burnt holes in a blanket. No quick dab from a jar or bottle could guarantee to do anything about being marooned on a fogbound island with the Quiller family.

She had a headache, a feeling of disorientation, and she suspected where that had come from. Doctor Thule's miracle pills had knocked her out and as a bonus had made her feel depressed and hung over when she awoke. Doctor Thule was somewhat similar to his medicine. His chief stocks in trade were an ingratiating smile, a fatherly manner, and an overwhelming desire to please the wealthy parents of his students. As for the disturbed young people he sheltered in his school, all he could offer was a, "There, there, ignore it and it will disappear." Tammy slammed down her hairbrush. Doctor Thule had had his last expensive tuition from either her or her mother. Her father had divided his estate equally, half for his wife, half for her. When she went back to Florida the first thing she'd do was see if she could buy back the ranch from its present owners. Her father had loved it, she loved it; the ranch was home. Tammy met the eyes of her mirrored image. The ranch had also been her mother's home. She must have known happiness there. Perhaps her mother would join her on the ranch ... which would mean Jim Quiller too. Could she stand to have Jim Quiller around? After what she had seen in Buddy's mind, could she bear the man in the same house? But her mother loved him. Yes, for her mother's sake she would learn to accept Jim.

Shivering, Tammy pulled on fresh underwear, a checkered shirt and jeans, and an outsized mohair sweater. She stuck her feet into leather moccasins and repacked her case. With a feeling of relief she left the depressing room and walked down the hall to her mother's room. She turned the knob but the door was locked. She tapped lightly. After a moment the door swung open a crack and she could see one of Rayburn's eyes, half his face, and part of a gleaming mane of hair in the aperture. Swinging the door wide, he put a thick, cautioning finger to his lips.

"Mother?" she asked.

"She's resting comfortably now, my dear. Do be quiet, we wouldn't want to disturb her."

Tammy tried to look past him but his tall bulky figure blocked her view. "Is she ill again?"

"You were quite right to warn her last night. Partly my fault, I should have told Jim not to allow her to drink so much. Dorothy must have still been weak from her illness."

"I want to see her."

"Of course. Come in, my dear."

Tammy stepped into the room and then stopped abruptly. Not only was Rayburn there but also Jim and Buddy and Ruth. Ruth was sitting in a chair near the windows, knitting a small red-and-gray garment that looked like a child's sweater. On the low table beside her was a gaping knitting bag with balls of wool, books of patterns, and gleaming needles cascading over the glass top. Jim sat in the chair on the other side of the table, Buddy leaning against his knees, both light brown heads bent over a large book. What could that child be so engrossed in, Tammy wondered, perhaps an illustrated copy of de Sade? As she entered the room they all looked up at her. Both Jim and Ruth smiled but Buddy merely lifted his head and stared.

"Why are all of you here?" Tammy whispered.

"Looking after your mother." Rayburn beamed down at her. "We feel somewhat responsible for letting her overdo it."

Circling around him, Tammy went to her mother's side. The cover was drawn up to Dorothy's chin and her face was white and looked wasted, thin, rather ghastly. Her hair was snarled and tangled, looking as though it had been soaked with sweat. Her eyes were closed and her mouth hung open. Dismayed, Tammy stared down at her. "Mother," she said softly.

A hand gripped her elbow. "She's sound asleep," Rayburn told her. "Andy gave us a sedative for her. Jim tells me she didn't close her eyes all night."

"Has Andy examined her?"

"She flatly refused to let him. Insists she'll be fine once she sleeps. Stubborn lady, your mother."

As he spoke, Dorothy moaned and moved. The cover shifted, exposing one bare shoulder and an upper arm. Quickly, Rayburn twitched it into place. "Mustn't let her get chilled."

He'd moved incredibly fast but not fast enough. Tammy had had a glimpse of marks on that shoulder and arm, small, angry-looking marks. She backed away from the bed, away from Rayburn. Her nostrils dilated. The smell in this room—warm, fetid, a hint of tobacco smoke, a darker odor, one that a den of animals might exude. Tammy felt a stab of primitive fear. The Quillers were watching her, their eyes on her face,

258

her body, crawling over her skin like spiders. Rayburn was trailing after her, he was between her and the door.

"If you'd like to sit with Dorothy for a while, my dear, feel free. We'd be glad to have your company."

Don't touch me, she cried silently, don't put your hands on me. Aloud she said, "No, I'll stop in later, when she's awake. I have to...Nadine needs some help in the kitchen."

She had to pass close to Rayburn, feeling his eyes, watching his hands. For an instant she thought he was going to reach for her. He didn't. Fingering his mustache, he chuckled softly. "Be sure to come back later, my dear."

The doorknob was under her hand. She forced herself to open it slowly, to step into the hall without haste. The door closed behind her and she heard the click of the lock. She had to find Nigel. Then she heard a cheerful whistling, a popular thread of a rock tune, whistled off key. Philip. Philip with his shaven head and a tool box dangling from one hand.

"Hi, Tammy," he called. "How's Dorothy?"

"Sleeping. Have you seen Nigel?"

"No, but I was looking for him awhile ago. Was thinking about a game of pool but Nadine says he's meditating." Philip grinned at the girl and tapped the metal box, "Really, I got no time for anything but this bloody house. First the damn hot water heater acted up and then a socket in granddad's room went on the blink. If I owned this place I'd have a crew of electricians in here pulling out the wiring. It's dangerous! Overloaded circuits, frayed wires, some of the ceiling fixtures hanging by a thread."

"Nigel," Tammy said. "Did Nadine say where he is?"

"Nope, isn't downstairs. Maybe up in his room."

Tammy took the steep flight two steps at a time. Nigel's door was open and she peered into his room. The heater was glowing red, the bed was unmade, but no sign of Nigel. She tapped a fingernail against her front teeth. He wouldn't be outside. Only one place left to look. Opening the door of the schoolroom she looked in. Ah, there he was, sitting in the lotus position on the dais, facing toward the two narrow windows at the rear of the room. He was wearing the same outfit he'd worn at dinner a few nights before, brown slacks, white turtleneck, Gucci loafers, a glimmer of gold on his chest where the medallion rested. His eyes were closed and his face furrowed into deep lines. Sweat oozed down his cheeks and every

259

line of the tiny body looked strained. Strange type of meditation.

Tiptoeing in, she softly swung the heavy door shut. The bulb in the ceiling wasn't lit—Nigel couldn't reach the cord, she remembered—and the room was dim. Aimlessly, she wandered around. Andy had unpacked the trunks and cartons in the corner and hadn't bothered repacking them. The contents littered the floor. More of Jeb's hoarded junk—fishing rods, lines, bits of metal, a couple of small motors, fishing knives, small, sharp and deadly looking, a pile of boathooks, a couple of tattered blankets. Bending, Tammy picked up a cardboard folder. Two young men in uniform, one short and chunky with a wide, pleasant face. The other taller and thinner. Both of them smiling into the camera. Tommy and Pat Amos, the picture Holly mentioned, the one Jeb couldn't bear to see. Sighing, she skirted the pile of toys and the two rocking horses, and wandered back toward the dais. A white patch caught her eye and she picked it up. A piece of paper, looking as though it had been torn from a notebook. On it a list of names, one under the other, eight names in block printing. Rayburn Quiller, Ruth Thaler... her eyes flew down the page. All the Quillers and Thalers. Beside each name a mark. Large X's beside all the names except Thelma's and Andy's. Question marks there. Some of the X's lighter and more hesitant than others. Philip's was very light, Rayburn's mark was sure and heavy. Puzzled, she looked from the page to Nigel. His eyes were open and he was regarding her quizzically.

She held the page out to him. "Sorry, didn't mean to pry."

"That's okay, Tammy." He stuck the paper into a pocket of his slacks. "Bad habits writers pick up. Have to see everything in words." Taking out a handkerchief, he mopped his face.

"You're all lathered up and I thought meditation was supposed to be peaceful."

"Not the kind I do. There's a question trembling on your lips."

"That list of names. Not yours or mine or our mothers. If your name had been down there would there have been an X or a question mark after it?"

"Indubitably an X. What's wrong?"

"Does it show?"

"Even through those shades it shows."

She sat down on the floor beside the dais. "I stopped in to see mother—"

"Isn't she up yet?"

"She's in bed in a room full of Quillers. Rayburn, Buddy, Ruth, Jim. She's sleeping, Rayburn said she's sedated. She looks...queer."

On the dais above the girl, Nigel slipped out of the lotus position and pulled his knees up against his chest. His hands knotted around his legs. "Queer in what way?"

Taking off her glasses, she rubbed at her eyes. "Her hair's matted and she usually keeps it so well. Very particular about her appearance. Her face looks ghastly and..."

"And what?"

"I only got a quick look but there're marks all over her shoulder and arm."

"Could it be a rash?"

"No."

"God!" The knuckles clasping his knees whitened. "They've moved faster than I figured they would."

"What do you mean?" She grasped his ankle. "Nigel?"

He patted her hand. "Could you...would you go into one of their minds?"

"I can't." She shuddered. "Nigel, I'm afraid to. After Buddy's...please."

"Only for a moment, Tammy. You must, for your mother's sake."

"Which one?" she whispered.

"Not Rayburn or Jim. Better make it the boy's."

"I might get trapped."

"You won't. I'll see you don't. Only a moment, Tammy."

"I'll try. Nigel, for God's sakes don't let me stay long."

Her head bent, bright hair fell across her face, masking her features. Lifting the barrier, she allowed her mind to become vulnerable. She had an immediate thought, from somewhere close. Anxiety—Nigel. Ignoring it, she wandered down, sliding effortlessly through wood and plaster, searching for the right mind. She brushed other minds and shied away. Then she found her target and entered it.

The small body she was in perched on a chair. It was night, a light somewhere. A lamp beside a twin bed. Behind it the glimmer of a glass-topped table, the bulk of two heavy chairs. The eyes fastened on the bed. Heaving men...women. So many bodies on such a narrow bed. Swarming over some-

261

thing, something that moved, moaned, that writhed. An arm thrown out, slender, tanned, a fall of sunstreaked hair—her *mother*. Pleasure from the mind she was in, dark, sticky delight. God! Bring me back! Get me clear of this—

"*Tammy*. Come back, Tammy, come back to me."

Her eyes flew open. Arms around her, arms holding her tightly against a narrow chest. A sweater soft against her cheek, the cool metallic feel of a chain, a sensation of security she hadn't felt since her father had last held her. She buried her face against the hard, comforting chest. Tears were blinding her, hot tears, scalding her eyes.

Nigel rocked her in his arms, his cheek pressing against her hair. "Tammy, I shouldn't have. I shouldn't have forced you to do it."

"No, it had to be done." She pulled herself away from him, got to her feet. She looked around the room, at the mass of junk spilling out from the trunks and cartons. "Is there a gun in the house? Nigel, do you have a gun?"

He was on his feet. "No. Even if there were one, it wouldn't help you."

"I'm going to kill them," she said evenly. "I'm going to kill all of them."

Running over to the heap of trash, she searched through it. She picked up a fish knife, looked at it and then tossed it back and selected a boathook. With a fingertip she tested its sharpness. Jeb had kept it honed. The point pricked her skin and she watched a ruby drop well from her finger. "This will have to do."

"You wouldn't even get within striking distance. Rayburn and Jim are powerful men. So is Norman. They'd take it away from you and—"

"Say it! And do to me exactly what they did to my mother. Like rats swarming over a piece of meat. Biting, tasting. Filthy, perverted, beastly!" Her voice dropped. "Even Ruth...doing that to another woman. I'm going to kill them."

His voice snapped like a whip. "Put that down! Use your head. You're playing right into their hands. Get over here, Tammy!"

She went. She stood in front of him. Raised by the height of the dais, his eyes were level with hers. She held out her hands. "Help me, Nigel, help my mother."

He gazed at her, masking his compassion, showing her only hardness. Compassion would only weaken her now, she

262

needed to find a reservoir of strength if she were to survive. The tears were drying on her cheeks and her eyes were hard and cold. There *was* strength in her. From Marc Syles, certainly not from Dorothy. He told her, "Sit down."

She sank on the edge of the dais and he knelt at her side. "What's that room like? Size, positioning of windows. Where are the beds?"

Tersely, she told him. He listened, envisioning the room. "A distraction," he said, more to himself than to her. "Get those bastards shook up and keep them that way. They'll be sated now, off guard." He lifted his head. "We'll have to have my mother's help Tammy, this is what you must do—"

"No more minds," she told him stonily.

"No more, I promise." He managed a smile. "And I always keep my promises. Listen closely, Tammy."

He spoke rapidly and she listened.

In Dorothy's room, Rayburn leaned back comfortably and sipped the hot coffee that Jim had brought up from the kitchen. He was sitting in the chair that Jim had occupied earlier with Buddy kneeling at his feet, turning over the glossy pages of the book. Across the low table from him, Ruth continued knitting, red and gray wool sliding over the steel needles. On his bed, Jim sat cross-legged, a mug clasped in his hand. Regarding his wife's unconscious face, Jim asked, "What now, dad?"

"We wait, my boy. Relax and gather strength for the next of our pleasures." Rayburn closed an eye in a wink. "Wasn't as tough as you thought, eh?"

"Once we got going, I liked it. Great idea, making her drink that stuff. What was it—an aphrodisiac?"

"My own little secret. Interesting to watch Dorothy struggle against a mind completely inhibited with a body full of chemically induced desire. Being degraded and hating it and loving it and fighting it and wanting it. We still have a few more tricks for dear Dorothy but we must wait until that sedative wears off. She must be well aware of what's going on."

Ruth dropped a stitch, mumbled a curse, and said, "Better hurt her more this time."

Putting his mug on the glass top, Rayburn smiled at his daughter. "That's the part you like best, isn't it, Ruthie?"

"Everyone has a hangup. That happens to be mine," she

263

said pleasantly. She pointed a needle at the bed. "But I've a feeling we've just about drained her."

"Why don't we get on with it, dad?" Jim asked eagerly. "Get on to the fresh one."

His father bayed with laughter. "How quickly *you* shed your inhibitions, son. In the proper time we'll get on to the next one. The young are always so impatient."

Jim licked at his lips. "Tammy?"

"The most succulent of the lot," Rayburn mused, stroking his mustache. "Still in most ways a child. Definitely a virgin. Probably hasn't even received her first kiss yet. Ah yes, Tammy." His eyes bored into Jim's. "She'll be the last. In a manner of speaking, the *pièce de résistance*."

One of Ruth's fingers tapped his knee. "Is there time, dad?"

Turning, he scanned the window behind him, masked in drifting fog. "As soon as this fog breaks we'll have to put the last part of our plan in operation. To be creditable, that must be done. But there's no sign of it breaking yet and on this coast it may well close in for several more days."

"Why not take Tammy next?" Jim persisted. "Then, time permitting, we can get to Nadine."

"Let me try to explain." Rayburn's eyes, below the dark brows, were introspective. "Have you ever noticed how I relish my food? You probably have but what you may not have noticed is the order of the items I eat. Since I was a child I've always eaten food I don't care much for first. Vegetables I don't particularly like but know I should eat. For instance, carrots and cooked tomatoes. I bolt these down. Baked potatoes dripping sour cream I enjoy, so I eat them next. Or, alternately, mounds of creamy whipped potatoes with rich gravy—"

"Hey, dad," Jim broke in. "What's this got to do with Tammy?"

"Everything. Kindly bear with me. So...I eat the things I like next. But what I crave I always leave for last." He chuckled. "I'll admit I'm a carnivore. Rare roast of beef, thick pink slices of ham, fine browned lamb, pork chops with crisp fat and covered with layers of apple sauce, steak broiled, running with red juices and fresh mushrooms—Ah, I get carried away and only awaken another appetite. What I'm trying to say is that half the pleasure is not attaining an objective but the anticipation of attaining that object."

264

His daughter looked fondly down at Buddy. "Like Christmas."

The child lifted his face. "Rosemary," he said gravely.

Rayburn chuckled again and bent to caress the boy's hair. "A true Quiller, Buddy, you always understand. Yes, exactly like Rosemary. Same innocence, same budding body—"

"Dad," Jim broke in hotly. "I don't see why we should bother with Nadine at all. She's not bad-looking but I vote we get directly on to Tammy."

"You have no vote," his father barked. "Don't incur my displeasure. You've only been introduced to our hobby and already you feel like an expert. Bear in mind, I'll make the decisions."

"I'm sorry, dad. But...why Nadine?"

"A long overdue account with the lady. Very long, Jim. Dorothy—she simply was a diversion. Standing in the way of all that lovely money. But Nadine and Tammy! There's more than one reason for their use and their deaths. Before they die, they'll both know the reason."

"That lovely money," Ruth repeated. "How much actually is it, Jim?"

He shook his head. "More millions than you'd believe possible. But Marc willed only half of it to Dorothy. That I'm sure of because she's made an airtight will in my favor. The other half is held in trust for Tammy." He turned his head toward his father. "How will that work out?"

"Use your head, you're supposed to be the financial expert. Has Tammy any living relatives?"

"Not that I know about. Dorothy certainly hasn't. Marc was an only child and his parents have been dead for years."

Rayburn spread his arms in an expansive gesture. "As her stepfather, you'll inherit. When we're done here and have all the loose ends neatly tied up we'll go abroad. To England first, I think. Then on to the Mediterranean area—Italy, Greece, Spain, possibly North Africa." His eyes sparkled. "In many of these places children are still sold. Young girls, nubile boys. We'll take a house.... No, an estate would be better. Good food, the best wines, cars, a yacht. Everything I've always wanted and never had. Every fleshly appetite catered to." He rubbed his hands together. "All my dreams realized. It's been a long wait, but it will be worth it."

"Servants," Ruth said dreamily. "Clothes and furs from

Paris. Jewelry from the finest—" She broke off. "What are you muttering about, Jim?"

"I said it was *my* money, not yours."

His voice was defiant and so was the expression on his face. Ruth stiffened and cast an apprehensive glance at her father. Instead of looking at his son, Rayburn lifted his brows at Ruth. "I think it's time Jim was brought up to date, Ruthie. We wouldn't want him to get out of hand through ignorance, would we?" He transferred his gaze to Jim. "Keep your mouth shut and listen! The only reason you'll be inheriting those millions you boast about is not through your own efforts but ours. I had my eye on Marc Syles for years—"

"Why?" Jim demanded.

Rayburn leaned forward and his face was cold with menace. Hurriedly, dragging the book with him, Buddy scuttled across the floor to Ruth. "I told you to be quiet, son," Rayburn said softly. "I don't wish to discipline you, but if you persist I will. Now, I watched Syles's affairs from a distance and when the time was ripe I sent you to Florida to become acquainted with him. I even had the foresight to see your education was not only ample but directed toward business administration. An education, I will remind you, that was paid for at great personal sacrifice by your family.

"I never interfered with your personal life. When you graduated you went to California, found a position, married a woman I didn't like, and she had your son. I never complained because of Veronica's treatment of us or the way she kept you apart from us. We weren't even allowed to see Philip. No, I left you strictly alone until I knew Marc Syles was urgently in need of a man with your qualifications. I see you wish to question, Jim, you may proceed."

Rubbing his forehead, Jim asked, rather humbly, "How could you foresee that accident of Marc's and Vinnie's? How did you know Dorothy would fall in love with me and marry me?"

"Dorothy? I'd checked her out carefully. She wasn't happy with Marc Syles. It was my educated guess that with a good-looking, available male like you around an attachment would spring up between you and Dorothy Syles. Particularly, as she needed a man to wait on her hand and foot. A faithful doggy." Rayburn laughed harshly. "Your type, Jim. Never a leader, always a follower."

Jim flushed hotly, but he asked, "But the accident?"

266

Ruth giggled. "You still think that was an accident? How naive you are, darling Jim. Dad planned that carefully. In a letter you mentioned that Marc was going to Pensacola on business and gave the date. Dad was there before he was, found out where he was staying, and phoned your little wife pretending to be Syles. Dad enticed Veronica to Pensacola, told her there was an urgent reason that must be kept secret from everyone. Like a good little dope, Veronica came."

"Yes, she would have," Jim agreed. "Vinnie liked Marc, trusted him. But when she arrived didn't he catch on? He was a pretty sharp guy."

"Extremely sharp," Rayburn echoed. "And with guts too. Of course he suspected something was wrong but he took her out, wined and dined her—"

"Marc always felt sorry for Vinnie," Jim broke in. "Knew I was bored and disgusted with her."

"A perfect gentleman, was Marc Syles, son. When he brought her back to the motel, Norman and I were waiting for them—"

"Norm!"

Reaching for the pot, Rayburn poured coffee into his mug. With a lavish hand he added sugar and canned milk. "Oh, for some cream. I loathe this canned substitute. Yes, Norman. He has his uses, you know. Follows orders and never questions. Also, Norman has developed a taste for this sort of thing. A bit over eager at times but...anyway, from there on it was simple." He brought a big hand down in a chopping motion.

Jim's eyes were wide. "Then...then, Tammy was right. They were murdered."

"Tammy?"

"Yes, Tammy. I don't like this, dad, I don't like it one bit—"

"Compose yourself. Explain to your sister and me what you're babbling about."

"When Marc was killed, I went out to the ranch. Dorothy hadn't told the kid about it. She went into the kid's room and Tammy was catatonic. Just like a piece of wood. In the night Tammy had had her first period and we kind of figured maybe it was the shock that sparked her state. She was always a funny, withdrawn kind of kid." He took a deep breath. "She started to pull out of it, took quite a time and—"

"Will you get to the point," Rayburn ordered.

"The point is that Tammy told her mother and Doctor Thule that Marc and Vinnie had been murdered. Said someone had crushed their skulls in with a club. *How* did you kill them?"

"With a club." Rayburn stroked his chin. "Hmm, it would appear there's more to Tammy than one would suppose."

Ruth pursed her lips and put her knitting on the table. "Could have been a lucky guess."

"Naming the weapon was a lucky guess, Ruthie?"

"What's it matter now?" Getting up, Ruth went to the sleeping woman's side. She pinched Dorothy's cheek. "Come on, sleeping beauty, show some signs of life."

Coming off the other bed, Jim poked at Dorothy. "Nobody believes Tammy, dad. Ruth's right, it doesn't matter." He poked harder. "Wake up, you bitch!"

"Just a minute." Rayburn got up. "I think we better—"

His voice was drowned out by a crash, followed almost immediately by another. Two chunks of rock came crashing through the windows, splintering the panes, spraying glass in all directions. One rock barely missed Rayburn's head. Ruth gave a shrill scream and clasped her wrist, and Jim cursed and clapped a hand to his upper arm. Buddy, in a perfect position for the shower of splinters, started to wail. His face was studded with tiny slivers of glass. Rayburn grunted and felt gingerly at his scalp. Blood was coursing down his brow.

"Out!" Rayburn shouted. "Out of here."

Grabbing Buddy's arm, he hauled the boy with him. Jim and Ruth reached the door before they did. They flung it open and dashed into the hall. Philip came running to meet them.

"What's wrong?" the boy called. "I heard—Jes–sus! Blood all over you."

The hall was a scene of confusion. People were running up the stairs from the main floor, asking questions and screaming. Buddy was howling at the top of his lungs, and Jim and Rayburn were steadily cursing. Tammy came running down the stairs and met Nadine at her mother's door. The two women raced into the room.

"Stop," Rayburn shouted after them.

They didn't stop. Shining shards of glass littered the bottom part of Dorothy's bed, gleaming against the wool blanket, but the upper part, and Dorothy's face, was untouched. Ripping the blankets back, Nadine hauled Dorothy's naked body

268

to a sitting position. Already Tammy had scooped up the velvet robe lined with fur and she pulled it on her mother's limp body. Each woman grasped one of Dorothy's arms and they hauled her to her feet.

"Watch the glass on the floor," Tammy panted. "Her feet are bare."

"Lift her," Nadine urged. "Carry her over it. Ah, that's it."

Somehow they got the unconscious woman into the hall. No attention was paid to them. Ruth was crying and threatening to faint and Rayburn had disappeared. Jim was holding his arm and groaning. Nigel caught Tammy's eye and jerked his red head toward Andy's bulky form.

"Doctor," Tammy called. "Help us. Please help us."

The man's face was dazed. Rubbing his eyes, he made his way to them. He pushed Philip out of the way. "Is she hurt?" he asked.

"Yes," Nadine snapped. "Tammy and I can't handle her. Help us get her upstairs."

He took Dorothy's weight and lifted her into his arms. "Where?"

"My room," Tammy told him.

She led the way up to the third floor. Andy came next, cradling Dorothy in his arms, and Nadine brought up the rear. In the attic room preparations had been made. The heater was glowing, the bed was neatly turned back, and on top of the chest a kettle of hot water, a basin, and a pile of towels were ranged. Andy didn't appear to notice any of these. Carefully, he lowered his burden to the bed, straightened, and rubbed at his arm.

"There she is," he told the two women, and turned to the door.

Nadine grabbed his arm. "Aren't you going to check her over?"

"Later, it looks as though the others are badly cut."

"Now," Nadine said. "Right now. Tammy, go down and get the doctor's bag."

She waited until the girl left and then she swung the door closed. Andy stood beside the bed, his bandaged hand cradled in his other hand. Nadine stripped the velvet robe from Dorothy's body. "Have a look," she told the man coldly.

Dorothy's body was ghastly. A network of scratches and bruises covered her arms and breasts, near the groin three cuts extended from one hip bone to the other, dried blood

269

caked the scratches and cuts, and the hair in her pelvic area was matted with blood.

Andy cleared his throat. "None of them deep. Must have got sprayed with flying glass."

"Come off it. The glass was on the lower part of the bed, on top of a pile of blankets. You know how she was hurt." With horrified eyes, Nadine stared down at the woman's body. "Just as though a pack of wolves had ravaged her."

"Or rats." Andy gestured at the chest. "You seem to have everything there. We'll wash her down first and then I'll dress the cuts."

Tammy swung the door open and Andy turned so his big body blocked the girl's sight from the bed. Nadine took the black bag from her. "You wait in Nigel's room. Andy and I will do this."

"But—"

"Do as I say," Nadine ordered.

Backing away from the door, Tammy retreated to Nigel's room and perched on his bed. She leaned forward and warmed her hands at the coils of the heater. She wished that Nigel was sitting beside her but she knew he planned to stay on the second floor to field any attempts to reclaim her mother. So small, Tammy thought, so heartbreakingly small against the big men down there. But not only did he wear a lion on his medallion, Nigel had the heart of a lion. Her eyes glued to the door of her room, she waited. Time passed. Then the door opened, and Nadine beckoned to her.

She went to her mother's side. The blond hair had been brushed out and now lay against the pillow in shining masses. Dorothy's lashes rested against her pale cheeks. One arm was outside the covers, and Tammy saw they'd put a pair of her own pyjamas on her mother.

"Wake her up," she told Andy.

"She's sedated, Tammy, let her sleep it off. I've got to get down and see what I can do for the others who were hurt."

"To hell with them!" Pulling her glasses off, Tammy lifted cold, hard eyes to the man's. "I said wake her up. Now!"

Sighing, he opened his bag and took out an ampoule. Cracking it, he held it under Dorothy's nose. A sharp smell filled the little room. After a moment, Dorothy's lashes quivered and lifted. For an instant blankness filled her eyes and then they fastened on her daughter's face. "Tammy...it's morning then. What an awful night. Jim being so mean to

270

me and then that terrible fire. I hope you didn't mind me spending the rest of the night with you."

Tammy blinked and looked helplessly at Nadine. Quickly, the other woman gestured. Tammy managed to stammer, "Not at...not at all, mother."

"Poor Jeb and Holly. What an awful way to die!" Dorothy fumbled at the covers. "Where's Blue? I brought him up with me."

"He's...I put him outside for a while, mother. How do you feel?"

Dorothy's eyes wandered past Tammy. "Nadine and Andy." She shifted position. "I'm so stiff and sore. Did I hurt myself?" The skin between her fine brows puckered. "I don't remember falling but that path's so rocky. There was so much confusion too, everyone milling around. Philip trying to bring water in a pail with a hole in it." She moved again and gasped with pain. "Did I fall?"

Tammy looked at Nadine again and the other woman said quickly, "Yes, you did but not down near the cottage."

"On the stairs, mother," Tammy hastily improvised. "You must have got up half asleep and forgot you were on the third floor. Probably on your way to the bathroom."

Nadine nodded. "Someone had foolishly left a tray with glasses and cups on the steps. They crashed down with you and you got some cuts. Nothing serious but you must remain in bed. Right, Andy?"

"That's right." He fished in his bag. "I'll give you something for the pain. Help you rest too." Tammy grabbed at his hand and he paused and looked down at her. "I *am* a doctor," he whispered. "I'm not about to hurt her."

"How clumsy of me," Dorothy was muttering. She watched Andy slip back her sleeve and swab her upper arm. She watched him press up a vein and slide the needle in. "Strange," she told her daughter. "I feel so tired. And there's something I wanted to tell Jim and I've quite forgotten what."

Bending, Tammy tenderly kissed her mother's brow. "It will come back to you. Now rest."

Stepping away from the bed, Tammy jerked her head toward the door. Andy patted Dorothy's hand and then both Nadine and he followed the girl out. Tammy shut the door and leaned against it. "What is it?" she asked abruptly.

He drew his hand wearily across his eyes. "Amnesia."

"You mean she doesn't remember anything since the night of the fire? Not last night or—"

"That's what I mean. She's blanked it out."

"Thank God," Nadine breathed. She slipped an arm around the girl's waist.

Staring up into the doctor's gray face, Tammy asked, "Is it temporary?"

"Who knows? It might only last hours. Then again, she may never remember that lost time. With a terrible shock, the mind sometimes takes protective measures, shields the person from a memory she can't bear. It does happen, Tammy."

"You knew what they were doing to her, didn't you?" When he didn't answer, Tammy asked, "What kind of man are you?"

The bag dropped from his hand. He pulled up the shirt sleeve on his sound arm. He held it out, letting Nadine and Tammy look at the mass of needle scars. "That kind," he said grimly. "Ray controls the heroin and if I'm a naughty boy he punishes by withholding. You've no idea what that means. I'd steal for it, I'd grovel—" Breaking off, he groaned, "I'd even shut my eyes to Ray's pleasures."

"*Pleasures*," Nadine spat. "I'll tell you what I think, Andy Thaler. I think Rayburn picked you damn well!" She swung away from him as though unable to stand the sight of him. "You couldn't have been much of a man to start with."

"Tammy," Andy pleaded. "Try and understand. I'll do what I can for you. I'll tell Ray that Dorothy has lost her memory, that no one knows about it. That may protect you and your mother for a time."

The girl was paying no attention to him. Nigel had just appeared on the landing. He called, "Andy, your services are urgently needed in Ruth's room. Rayburn's bleeding like a stuck pig and so are the other three."

Picking up his bag, the doctor lunged past the smaller man as though escaping. Nadine and Tammy gazed down at Nigel. He jerked his red head at the door. "How is she?"

"Lost her memory," his mother told him. "Can't remember one thing since the night the cottage burned. Thinks it's the morning after."

"Trust Dorothy. But it should make it easier for us."

Nadine's arm tightened protectively around Tammy. "They can come and take her any time they want—"

"No," Tammy said explosively.

272

Nigel patted her arm. "For some time they're going to be too busy thinking about themselves."

"How badly are they hurt?"

"Jim and Buddy and Rayburn have shallow cuts from flying glass. Look worse than they are. Ruth has a piece of glass driven into the back of her left hand."

Tammy's eyes looked even harder. "I wish they'd been killed," she said evenly.

Nigel nodded gravely. "It would be better if they had been. Better for the world at large. Now, let's get into my room and have a powwow."

Eighteen

Ripping a narrow strip of tape loose, Andy snipped it off and deftly wound it around his wife's bandaged hand. She winced and continued to sob. "You can turn the tears off now," her husband told her. "It's all over." He held up a pair of forceps clamping a jagged piece of glass. "Operation successful."

"It's going to leave a scar," Ruth sobbed.

"Probably a tiny one. Never mind, your dad will hire a good plastic surgeon to fix it up."

"You're so unfeeling. It pains horribly."

"You don't seem to care for pain when you're on the receiving end, Ruth. Never mind, that painkiller should be working in moments." Andy picked his bag up and turned to Rayburn. "Sure you don't want one, Ray?"

"Got all I need right here." Holding up his glass, Rayburn squinted through the amber fluid in it. He stretched long legs toward the hearth. "Fire feels good too. What about you, Jim?"

Jim raised his own glass and grinned. "I'll stick with brandy too, dad. Only got scratched anyway. The way it felt at first I figured it was torn half off, my arm, I mean."

Glancing around his wife's room, Andy said, "You were all lucky. Buddy looked pretty bad but it was only a matter of tweezing those tiny splinters out and putting ointment on the cuts. Ray, you may have a headache but your scalp will be healed in no time."

"No thanks to you," Rayburn grunted. "I could have bled to death while you were upstairs."

"I didn't have a choice." Andy snapped his bag shut. "Tammy and Nadine couldn't carry Dorothy upstairs by themselves."

"What about Dorothy?" Jim asked. "I suppose she's conscious and yapping her head off."

"Conscious and talking, but not about you."

Rayburn stared at the doctor. "What do you mean?"

"She's lost any memory of the past few days. When she came to, she thought it was the morning after the Amoses died." Andy added quickly, "Tammy and Nadine don't know anything about last night."

Ruth's sobs trailed off and she too was staring at her husband. "Where do they think the marks on dear Dorothy came from?"

"I convinced them the same place your injuries did—flying glass."

Rayburn gave his rich chuckle. "Well, well, what a development. So the other two lambs are still in ignorance. Not that it matters, but it is amusing. How long do you think Dorothy will be in this...ah, blissful state?"

Shrugging his bulky shoulders, Andy moved toward the door. "With a traumatic shock it's hard to say. Could be hours, might be the rest of her life. My guess is she'll never recapture those lost days."

Setting his glass on the dressing table, Jim laughed. "Mine too. Dear Dorothy, she always manages to escape unpleasantness. Maybe we should get her down here and refresh her memory."

Andy stiffened. "I wouldn't recommend that."

"We aren't asking your advice," his father-in-law said shortly. "Get out of here. If we want you, we'll call."

Andy didn't argue. He jerked open the door as Philip was lifting a hand to knock. "Ah, Philip," Rayburn called. "I was about to send for you. Come right in."

Lounging into the room, Philip sat down on the floor in front of the fire. He held his hands out to the heat and rubbed them together. "I was just checking out Dorothy's room and it's like ice, granddad. I turned the heat vents off. No sense

276

pumping heat into a room with no glass in the windows. Jes—sus, the mess that room's in. Those rocks are huge."

"Don't I know it, my boy." Rayburn fingered his scalp tenderly. "I'm still in shock. I was sitting near one window and if I hadn't got up an instant before that rock came in I'd be dead. It missed my head by inches."

Philip was staring at Buddy. The boy was lying under a blanket in his crib, his face was pocked with red marks. "At first I thought all of you had been ripped to pieces. Blood running all over your face, granddad, and the kid looked like a porcupine with glass sticking out all over his mug." The boy peered at Ruth. She was curled up on her rose bedspread. "How are you doing, Ruth?"

She held up her bandaged hand. "I'm going to be scarred," she whimpered.

"She's okay," Jim said shortly. "What did you want Phil for, dad?"

"You were the first one to get to the room, my boy. Tell me, where were the rest when this happened?"

Tugging at his scalp lock, Philip gazed into the dancing flames. "It all happened so fast...let's see. When I ran down the hall I passed Andy. He was standing in his doorway. I can't remember anything else, granddad."

"Try. Take your time."

"Someone came racing down the stairs from the third floor." Philip frowned. "Tammy, that's who it was. The others were crowding up from downstairs. I think Nadine got there first."

"Very good." Rayburn tipped more brandy in his glass. "So, Nigel, his mother, and Thelma were downstairs—"

"And Norm," Philip pointed out.

"Norman doesn't count. He certainly wasn't tossing rocks through those windows."

The boy's eyes widened. "Hey, you don't think one of them...Come off it, granddad!"

"Watch the way you speak to me!"

"Sorry. But those aren't pebbles, you know, they're boulders. The biggest one must be a foot and a half in diameter. Thelma and Nadine are both strong for women but they couldn't throw them across this room let alone two stories up. As for Nigel—hell, he couldn't lift one."

Pulling at his lower lip, Rayburn looked down at the boy. "What is your explanation, then?"

"Rock slide. That damn cliff hanging over this house. Must have started near the top of it and catapulted down."

"How neatly too," his grandfather said sarcastically. "One boulder through each window of that room. If it was a slide, where are the rest of the rocks?"

Philip was looking longingly at the bottle of brandy but he wasn't invited to have any. Sighing, he said, "Probably more rocks crashed against the side of the house and slid down on the ground. Probably a mass of them out there. As for two rocks coming through two windows in one room, freak things do happen. One thing I can tell you. There's not a person in this house who could stand out there in thick fog and bean those rocks through the windows. Impossible!"

"Sounds as though he's got a point, dad," Jim admitted grudgingly. "I'm forced to agree with him."

"In that case," his father said, "another slide could break loose at any time. I didn't like the way this house was tucked under that cliff the first time I saw it." Swinging around, he stared at the windows in his daughter's room. "Philip, you go outside and see if there are any rocks under those windows. Then you board up the windows in here and in my room."

"What about mine, granddad? Sure, I'm on the other side of the house but a slide could break loose over there too."

"Make it the three rooms then, Philip. Get moving."

The boy hauled himself to his feet. "What'll I use to board them up with? And how can I do it alone, granddad?"

"Can't you think for yourself?" Rayburn touched his scalp and winced. "My head's throbbing like a toothache and all I get are stupid questions. Tear boards off those sheds, off the boathouse. Get Norman to give you a hand."

"Norm! He's useless."

"I agree," Ruth said. "Couldn't even tie his shoelaces until he was twelve."

Rayburn swung a wrathful face toward her. "You be quiet. Hmm, Norman *is* a bit slow. What about Nigel?"

"Right on, granddad. He's a runt, but for his size he's strong and can he move. I'll ask him."

"Not so fast," Jim snapped. "What about my room?"

Philip grinned at his father. "Do it yourself. You're not a cripple."

Rayburn clutched his head. "No bickering. Philip's right, Jim. Either do it yourself or share quarters with your son. Philip, you do my room first, I want to lie down and rest."

"Consider it done." Pausing on the way to the door, Philip put a caressing hand on the swell of Ruth's hip. He gave his father another mocking grin, patted her rump, started to whistle off key, and left.

"One of these days," Jim growled. "I'm going to finish that scalping job."

Closing his eyes, Rayburn muttered, "Do it quietly, and not while we still need a handyman. That boy is useful."

"Dad," Ruth called softly, "let's have fun and games with Dorothy again."

"You're feeling better, Ruthie. No, we're through with Dorothy. As soon as I regain my strength we go on to Nadine." He gave a short laugh. "Her mother's gypsy blood may add an extra fillip. *Gypsy*." Opening his eyes, he gazed at the play of shadows across the ceiling. "Have either of you ever heard of a poltergeist?"

"That's a kind of ghost," Ruth said lazily.

"Not really. The researchers feel the manifestations of a poltergeist may be centered around disturbed adolescents. A kind of unconscious telekinetic, moving objects around, some of them quite heavy."

Jim moved closer to his father. "You're thinking of Tammy. Wondering if she caused those boulders to crash through the windows. But her mother was in there. Tammy would never hurt her mother."

"I said unconscious. Perhaps that girl has powers she isn't aware of. That guess about the club killing her father was too accurate to be a guess. When Tammy was in to see her mother this morning, she was disturbed to find us in the room. I wonder..."

Ruth sat up on the rose satin spread. "It sounds insane, dad."

"It does." Suddenly, he shivered. "For some time I've felt something in this house, something malignant toward me."

His daughter gave him a shadowy smile. "Maybe the ghost of Kat Winchfield."

"Don't be ridiculous, Ruthie! I'm serious."

Jim looked down at the raw gash on his father's head. "This isn't like you, dad. That wound...could you be concussed?"

"Possibly. Andy really isn't much of a doctor."

"Speaking of Andy," his daughter said. "He's only extra baggage now."

Eagerly, Rayburn grasped at the change of subject. "Indeed he is, and expensive baggage too. His habit costs entirely too much."

Jim said, "We don't need Thelma either."

"Norm does. He's attached to her. Still—" breaking off, Rayburn rubbed his hand over his black mustache. "She is rebellious. Maybe I can find another sugar tit for the boy, one who will be easier to control. Now we have an excellent chance to dispose of them. If we wait until we leave here it will be harder, and also, if they become suspicious, more difficult to accomplish. Both Andy and Thelma could be two more victims of our approaching tragedy. Think you could play a grieving widow, Ruthie?"

She waved her sound hand. "Depend on it, dad. A grieving mother-in-law too."

"How sad it will appear. Jim's wife, your husband and daughter-in-law, a poor disturbed young girl, and my son's widow."

"And the widow's only son," Jim reminded the older man.

"Not necessarily. Nigel I'm still watching. He'd be an asset provided he can be brought around. He's our blood, you know, and he's clever and witty and a handsome lad. Ruthie—"

Jim stepped between his father and the woman sprawled across the bed. "Leave her out of this, dad. She's not working on Nigel or Phil, either!"

"Philip I have no concern about," Rayburn said mildly. "He's definitely one of us. As for Nigel, if I tell Ruthie to work on him, she will. Watch yourself, Jim, I've warned you repeatedly."

Despite the mild, almost kindly tone, something in Rayburn's expression alerted the younger man. He wilted and waved a hand vaguely. "I spoke out of turn. It's up to you. Know what? I'm feeling pretty good now. Let's get Nadine and give her a dose of that stuff you used on Dorothy."

"Not for a while, Jim."

Ruth swung her legs over the side of the bed. "Getting soft?" she jeered.

Laughing, he rubbed his stomach. "Getting hungry and Nadine's a fair cook. I intend to have another of her excellent din—" Breaking off, he swung his head toward the door. "Here comes our repairman now. Did you two get my room done?"

Nigel, a tool box swinging from one short arm, followed

280

his cousin into the room. Philip was panting under a load of boards. Smiling at his grandfather, Nigel said cheerfully, "Both windows boarded up, sir. You're safe as churches, now."

"Fine, my boy, but I wish you hadn't used that particular expression. When I asked Jeb Amos about this house that's exactly what he said and look what's happened."

"Yes, indeedy," Nigel said, handing Philip a hammer. "Just look what's happened."

Night had fallen over the island, marked only by a darkening of the fog-shrouded windows. Ruth, wrapped warmly in a robe, stood over her father's bed. Poking his shoulder, she whispered, "Dad, you awake?"

He opened one eye. "I am now."

"Come on, get up. Jim and I are rarin' to go." She giggled. "In this case, the condemned woman cooked a hearty meal."

"Chicken cacciatore. One of my favorites. You and Jim get to bed. Nothing on for tonight."

She giggled again. "You going to excuse yourself because you've a headache, darling?"

"Enough poor jokes, Ruthie. Let an old man get his rest."

"*Old* is right."

"Tell me that tomorrow night."

Excitement flashed across her fine features. "Tomorrow's the day?"

"Correct. Last weather report said the fog would start lifting late tomorrow. So, haste is now imperative."

"Trust sneaky old dad to have a hidden transistor. After warning everyone else, no radios. Too bad it will be over so soon. Guess we'll have to skip Nadine."

"As young Philip would say—no way. One in the morning, the other in the afternoon or evening. I've waited too long for this. I'm going to have it."

"Funny Jim hasn't clued in about Nadine and Marc Syles."

"He was so young when he left us to go to school, Ruthie. Don't mention this to Jim but he closes things out of his memory as easily as his wife does. So, tomorrow we take care of our lambs and then we light—"

"The signal fire! What a sight that will be."

"Glorious, Ruthie, absolutely glorious."

"Nigel?"

"No time, Ruthie, no time at all. Alas, poor Nigel."

Flinging back her head, she laughed. He shoved her away

from his bed and laughing softly himself, went peacefully back to sleep.

Almost directly over Rayburn's bed, Nigel crouched on his suitcase, pushed close to the only chair in the room. A blanket was draped over his shoulders and his mother, seated in the chair, had another hugged around her.

He was holding the crumpled page that Tammy had wondered about that morning. His eyes wandered down the list of names. "You're positive that Andy knew what was happening to Dorothy?"

"He admitted it, Nigel."

Sighing, he picked up his pen and drew two heavy strokes through the question mark after Andy Thaler's name, turning it into an X. His mother spoke in an urgent whisper. "Can't you do something now? God knows what they'll be up to next. That innocent kid in there with Dorothy...Nigel!"

"I know, but it's not simple, mother." He smiled but his face showed exhaustion. "I have to get them all in the same place, and you know why. Then there's this weather. No use getting people out of the Quiller hands only to have them perish from exposure. Have to wait for the fog to break enough for Rob Brome to see the signal fire."

She regarded him anxiously. "Do you think you can do it?"

"I've been practicing but maybe you were right. Maybe I haven't the courage." Sadly, he looked down at the page. "The only one doubtful now is Thelma. I can't come to any decision about her."

Across the hall, in the other attic room, Tammy sat beside the bed. Only the bedlamp was on and it cast a narrow beam across Dorothy's wan face. She stretched and then whimpered. "I'm still so sore. I even hurt inside." She fumbled along the blanket. "Didn't you bring old Blue up, Tammy?"

"No, he seems to have wandered away."

"Did Jim ask how I was?"

Tammy averted her eyes. "I didn't see him, mother. I was up here all afternoon with you and when I picked up our dinner tray they were all in the dining room."

"I don't understand Jim. Last night telling me I was selfish and possessive—" Breaking off, she peered up at the girl's
282

shadowed face. "Are you crying, Tammy? Heaven, I keep forgetting about Holly and Jeb. No wonder you're crying."

Leaning forward, the girl took one of Dorothy's hands in both her own. "I love you."

"Of course you do, dear, I'm your mother."

"No. I mean I love *you*." There was no comprehension in her mother's face. Tammy bit down hard on her lower lip, feeling hot wet drops on her hands. No sense in blaming her mother. She had no idea what those three words, spoken aloud, meant to her daughter. Her mother...Nigel...Rob. I'm breaking out, Tammy thought, breaking through the wall that has enclosed me for years. I feel!

Dorothy held out a tissue. "Dry your tears and come to bed. You must be tired. Running up and down those steps. I've been selfish. Maybe Jim is right. You should be spending your time with someone closer to your own age. Philip or that little Nigel—"

"He isn't *little*," Tammy said fiercely. After a moment she added, "He's seven feet tall and a warrior."

"Come to bed," Norm called. "Come on, Thel, I want to play."

Thelma didn't move. She stood by the window, gazing sightlessly at the dark pane, the bottle clutched in one hand. Despite the chill air, her hand was wet with sweat. "In a minute, Norm."

"I want to play."

"Not tonight. I'm too tender. Tomorrow morning, Norm, you can play all you want then."

"Good. I'll be your little boy and you'll be my mommy. Did I hurt you much, Thel?"

"You hurt me."

"Granddaddy told me to, Thel, told me to teach you not to be bad."

"I know, you're a great teacher."

Rolling over, he pushed himself up on an elbow. "Do you like that Phil better'n me, Thel?"

She touched her lips. "I hate him."

"So do I. One of these days I'm going to punish him. I'm going to give it to Phil good."

"I hope you do," she said softly. "I sure hope you do."

"What's that you got, Thel?"

"A glass of water and some pills, Norm. They'll make me sleep so I'll feel better. Now, go to sleep like a good boy."

"Okay, I'll go to sleep. In the morning—" he yawned, "—in the morning we'll play."

You'll play, she thought grimly, I won't. She spilled pink pills into the palm of her hand. One...two...three. Enough. One advantage of being a nurse, you knew the exact number. Not too few, not too many. The right dosage for the right weight. Funny, when she'd brought these with her she was only toying with the idea. Now, she was going through with it. Enough time spent with the Quiller family. Phil, and then that ghastly business with Dorothy. Now, they'd have a go at that poor kid, Tammy. She'd had all she could take.

Thelma glanced at the bed. Strange, she still didn't hate Norm. She never had. Poor mindless guy, a dupe of big daddy all his life. Viciously, she hoped the time would come when he used those hands on Phil. Break him in two! That one was just like the rest of the Quillers, a proper bastard.

She wondered if she should say goodbye to anyone. The only person she could think of was Andy but he'd probably had a fix and was right out of it. Never mind, all Andy and she had in common was bondage to the same bunch of bastards. Weak guy, Andy. Thelma's lips quirked. She should talk. Something rotten in both Andy and her. Must have been there long before the Quillers latched onto them.

Popping the pills in her mouth, she raised the glass, held it for a moment in a silent toast, and then drained it. Farewell, cruel world, she thought, so long all you greasy guys and your greasy gropes. Thelma gropes no more.

She tiptoed across the cold floor and slid into bed, pulling the covers down between her body and her sleeping husband. Fervently, she wished she had something nice to remember, something to ease these last moments. Nothing good had ever happened to old Thelma. Let's see, there must be something.

Ah yes. Against her closed lids a picture took shape. How old had she been? Pretty young, papa had died before she was five. First time she'd seen the moon. Perched on papa's lap, stretching out her chubby arms toward a window that framed a night scene. A big moon, full and silver, rising. Looking as though it balanced like a bright ball right over the picket fence. "Want it, papa," a tiny Thelma begged. "Get it for Thelma."

She wailed when his deep voice told her papa couldn't get

284

the moon for his baby, and only stopped when he bribed her with an ice cream cone. "Tomorrow," he told her. "Chocolate," she bargained. "Two scoops," he agreed.

"Read a story, papa."

"A fairy story, baby. They always have happy endings."

No longer was Thelma in bed beside Norman in the fog-shrouded house. She was cradled in the loving arms of her papa, listening to his deep voice, drowsily watching a silver dollar moon rising over a picket fence. The deep voice told of a land where all the girls were lovely and virtuous, where the men were handsome and gallant and kind. Happily, on the wings of three tiny pink pills, Thelma rose to meet that silver radiance and then drifted past it into the darkness of oblivion.

Nineteen

As Nigel walked down the hall toward the front door he noticed that even the meager breakfast he'd forced down had been a mistake. It wasn't sitting well, his stomach felt queasy. He also noticed that the fan of colored glass above the door looked lighter, the jewel tones of amber and red and green brighter, more vibrant than they'd been for days.

Swinging the door open, he stepped out onto the warped boards. His guess was right, the fog wasn't as heavy. He could see the rickety steps leading down to the path, the crushed shells on that path, the faint outline of the crookedly hanging gate. Part way to the gate, Tammy was bending over one of the stunted plants. In one hand she cupped a bronze blossom. When she saw him she straightened and walked back to the steps. She was dressed in a thick pink sweater, denim pants, and her suede jacket. She didn't have the huge round glasses on but he could see them protruding from a pocket of her jacket. She sank down on a step and he sat on a higher one so their faces were on a level.

"Getting some air?" he asked, and thought immediately how inane those words were.

"I couldn't stand it in there any longer. Nadine offered to stay with mother for a while." Turning her head, she peered down the path. "The fog is starting to lift."

"There's wind blowing in from the sea and it's hitting here first. Be a while before it hits the mainland."

Her head drooped. "Then there's no sense of lighting the wood on the pier."

"I was thinking of that myself but it couldn't be seen from the mainland yet." He added glumly, "May be night before it lifts enough to try."

"How much more can we stand, Nigel? You, me, your mother? Thelma's dead and I don't seem to even care. When Norman came down to breakfast complaining to his grandfather about Thelma not playing games with him, how stiff and cold she was, I knew. Even before Andy examined her, I knew she was dead. Did they poison her?"

"I doubt it. Thelma must have taken the easy way out."

Throwing back her hair, she cried, "Why don't I care? I worked beside her, I laughed at her jokes, I felt terrible when she was beaten . . . yet, it doesn't seem real. None of this seems real."

"It's real, Tammy, believe me, it's real. Too many shocks, you're suffering from a kind of battle fatigue. That's why you feel numb."

And I hope you continue to feel that way, he said under his breath, the worst is still to come. With the fog breaking up, Rayburn wouldn't dare wait. Any time now he'd make his next move.

Nigel's eyes devoured the girl's face. She had lost most of her tan and her skin was translucently white. He was so close to her he could see tiny pores in that fine skin, larger across the nose, shadowing under the violet eyes that made them look even larger. Hungrily, he studied that lovely face, seeking imperfections and finding them. One of the blond brows a fraction higher than the other, the iris of the right eye marred by a dark blemish near the pupil, a small separation between the front teeth. Imperfections, as beloved by him as the beauty. He thought with mingled grief and sadness never will I know all there is to learn about my love, never will I know all the tiny imperfections of this girl. By Zeus and Hermes and Apollo, by all the ancient gods, to know that never will I have a chance to know her body, her mind, her soul. I know she is fine and valiant with a quality of innocence that has looked upon the evil of this island hell and, although she shudders with repulsion, it has not yet blemished that innocence. What a feast she must appear to the Quillers, what

288

a pure morsel to practice their ageless sexual torments on. I'll kill her first, he promised himself, I'll see her dead and out of their filthy reach, as Thelma is now out of their reach, before I let them torture and sully Tammy.

Leaving her face, his eyes traced the slender lines of her body, without lust, only with a warm rush of regret. Tammy would age. That body slim as a sapling would thicken, the small breasts outlined against pink wool would sag and become pendulous, that silken skin would dry and wrinkle, the deep color of those amazing eyes would fade, but beauty would remain. Those bones, those fine shapely bones, would retain beauty long after the flesh sagged and coarsened. Long after that mane of hair had dried and whitened. Tammy, my love, my love for such a few precious hours. All I have, he thought, all I'll ever have, but it is enough.

Without volition, his hand crept out and brushed the mass of hair away from her cheek. Avidly, he studied the small ear. An ear again perfect, not marred by holes to drop jeweled rings through, but perfect, as a shell is perfect. And yet again, one tiny imperfection. On the lobe a minute mole, black as midnight against the white skin. His hand touched the silkiness of that hair, the finest silk, the skin of her neck alabaster, but warm and with a velvet touch. Fool, Nigel thought, I'm a besotted fool.

"What are you doing?" Tammy whispered.

"Studying the lobe of your ear."

Jerking her head away, she turned her eyes full on his face, eyes wide with disbelief. He forced a laugh. "No, not mad. At least, not that kind of madness. Another kind. Could you love me, Tammy?"

"I do you love you."

"But you're not *in* love with me."

"No," she said hesitantly. "Better than being in love. Falling *in* love is only a prelude to falling *out* of love. But loving...that lasts forever."

"Forever," he echoed. "How wise you are, yet you're supposed to be a child."

Her smile was tender and radiant. "A quote for Nigel, who loves quotes. 'When I was a child, I spake as a child, I understood as a child, I thought as a child: but when I became a man, I put away childish things.'"

"Corinthians," he murmured. "So...Tammy is now a woman. For the woman, I have a quote. 'Thy hyacinth hair,

289

thy classic face,/Thy Naiad airs have brought me home/To the glory that was Greece/And the grandeur that was Rome.'"

"'To Helen,' by Poe." She sighed, touching the splintered step she sat on. "And this is Greece or Rome." She shook her head, as though rousing from a dream. "This is hell, Nigel, we speak of love and tenderness but we're in hell. And the hell is made by the child born to Kat Winchfield. Rayburn Quiller is Kat Winchfield's son."

"Yes."

"That's why you traced the connections between all those families. Rayburn is a remote descendant of Sawley Bean."

"Yes."

"Is he mad?"

"Mad is such an overworked word, Tammy. Legally, I suppose none of them were mad. They understood right from wrong but they chose wrong. They're not immoral, they're amoral. Ordinary rules they consider have no bearing on them. In a way, I suppose they feel they have the *right* to behave any way they wish. How did you guess?"

"You stressed many similarities between the different families but there was another common bond, and this one you didn't stress. They all behaved incestuously." Her voice sank to a whisper. "Like the Quillers."

"And, like Rayburn, they saw nothing horrible, nothing despicable about incest. I think Rayburn even finds something admirable about it, considers it keeps his bloodline pure. The divine right of kings."

Tammy made a muffled sound. "The Pharaohs."

"Exactly." Nigel caressed her arm. "I hate to do this, Tammy, but I think you must know about Rayburn Quiller. I'll make it as brief as I can." He took a deep breath. "When Piety York left Amoston she went to Kansas, ironically, to a town not far from where the infamous Benders once lived. There she raised the boy she pretended was her son. Piety claimed she was a widow and eventually she married a crotchety, elderly farmer named Rayburn Quiller. Quiller didn't live long after the marriage but he adopted the boy and gave him his name. The old man deeded his small farm to Piety, and young Rayburn and Piety lived there until her death in 1930. In 1933 a young man named Quiller turned up in Topeka and found a job as handyman with a retired doctor, a William Langry. With the help of his daughter, Doctor Langry ran a rest home with a few elderly patients—"

"Rayburn was on the track of the survivors from the lynch mob," Tammy broke in. "One of the patients—"

"No. When I traced this, years later, that's what I assumed. But his target actually was two houses down from the Langry house. This house was owned by a maiden lady in her seventies, a Miss Abigail Ware. With her an even older cousin lived, a retired blacksmith."

"Edward Ware."

"Right. Nearly three years passed and in that time Rayburn made no hostile move against the Wares. He fell in love with his gentle Jenny, married her, and the twins were born. After Doctor Langry died, Jenny and her husband continued to run the rest home. All the neighbors, including Miss Abigail and Ed Ware, liked and respected the young Quiller couple. From letters written by a neighbor who lived directly across the street from the Quillers, another old maid named Miss Lavinia Clarke, I was able to reconstruct those years. In 1936, at Christmas time to be exact, the Wares received visitors. Lonny Ware came from Utah and he brought his wife, Belinda, and his thirteen-year-old daughter, Annie, with him. Before this, neither Ed Ware's surviving son nor his daughter, Pearl, had come."

"Rayburn killed them, didn't he?"

"Most of them. He—" Breaking off, Nigel said slowly, "Remember Holly's description of Piety York? The woman was a fanatic. She obviously had an obsessive passion for Kat Winchfield. She was the teacher here so she'd have lists of names and relatives of the local children, addresses, that sort of thing. Piety hated the people of Amoston with a deadly hatred. That's what young Rayburn was raised on—a diet of hate and revenge. His mission in life, taught by Piety, was to wipe out every last soul even remotely connected with his family's murders. Keep that in mind, Tammy.

"That Christmas Eve in 1936, Miss Abigail and young Mrs. Lonny Ware went to a church service. The little girl, Annie, was supposed to go but at the last minute her mother decided that the child was getting a cold and she had to remain at home. Ed and Lonny Ware stayed with her, catching up on family news, and sharing a bottle of whiskey. When the two women got back the house was in flames. Working with the firemen was their good neighbor, that nice boy, Rayburn Quiller—"

"Who had killed all of them before he set the fire," Tammy said tonelessly.

"And probably raped the little girl in the bargain." Nigel grimaced. "Rayburn has a taste for very young girls. Anyway, Miss Abigail and Belinda sheltered with Miss Lavinia Clarke. Miss Abigail, like her cousin Ed, was a big, strongly built woman but she had a weak heart. Shortly after the fire she had a heart attack and Jenny and Rayburn Quiller kindly moved the old woman over to their house. Belinda settled the business affairs and then she returned to Utah. Two months later, Miss Abigail died during the night of another heart seizure."

"Brought on by Rayburn."

"Once he got his hands on Ed Ware's cousin, he probably tormented and frightened her to death. Miss Lavinia, in a letter to Belinda, admitted that Rayburn was pressing everyone about the location of Pearl Ware. But Pearl had become estranged from her family and no one knew where she was. Rayburn made a fatal mistake though. Jenny was pregnant at the time and she must have discovered her husband torturing Miss Abigail. According to Miss Lavinia, who never tumbled, dear sweet Jenny was in such a nervous state that her dear sweet husband had to set aside a room for her to be confined in. In other words, Rayburn had to imprison his wife. Jenny found an escape. After she gave birth to Jim, she slit her wrists and died."

Tammy was staring at the fog bank beyond the gate. "Do you think Rayburn cared?"

"He was desolate. He worshipped Jenny. Rayburn took his three children and left Topeka. Somewhere along the way he picked up a housekeeper, a woman named Gerda Munester. She was a big, harsh woman who sounded the same type as Piety York had been. Just as fanatically loyal too. With her help, Rayburn raised his family. There was rivalry between Gerda and young Ruth, probably about the affection of Rayburn. When Ruth was fourteen she managed to polish off her rival."

Tammy gasped and Nigel gave her a bleak smile. "Yes, Ruth started on the Quiller trail young. The family were preparing for a trip to England and Gerda was going to visit her sister in Iowa during their absence. All the luggage had been removed from the house and they were closing it up. Before they rented this house it had been owned by a woman terrified of burglars and the basement windows had been barred and the doors reinforced. Ruth managed to decoy Gerda down into the basement, locked the woman in, and then she went merrily off with her family. Gerda died from thirst and starvation. No charges were preferred. The police were convinced that lovely young Ruth had unwittingly done it."

Tammy buried her face in her hands. Her voice was muffled. "Did they continue to run rest homes?"

"Absolutely. What better places to corner aging people from Amoston? Also a living. A number of elderly women, doting on charming Rayburn, made wills in his favor. Sometimes a small piece of property, sometimes only a few trinkets. Most of them died rather rapidly."

"Why weren't the Quillers stopped? All those deaths— someone must have got suspicious."

"It was a different world, Tammy. Looser regulations on homes for the aged. Many of the people who died had no relatives, no friends, no one who cared a hang for them. Some were ill, all were old. Rayburn was shrewd. They moved frequently, rented houses and ran homes for short periods of time. He got away with murder after murder. How many I really don't know."

"The people from Amoston?"

He held up a tiny hand and ticked his fingers off one by one. "Nineteen thirty-seven in Seattle, Washington. A woman named Laura Spence and her stepdaugher, Lillian, were waylaid in a vacant lot. They were bludgeoned, raped, horribly mutilated. Rayburn Quiller was renting a house two blocks west of the lot. Luckily the other girl, Peggy, had quarreled with her stepmother and left Seattle. In 1949 Rayburn and his family were holidaying in England. A Mrs. Jeff Ware—"

"He was killed in the first world war, Nigel."

"Yes, but Jeff married an English girl and she bore his son. The widowed son, his two daughters, and his mother lived in a cottage in Dorset. They were bludgeoned to death and the two girls were raped. An effort had been made to fire the cottage but it was built of slate and stone and didn't catch. The British papers described it as 'a crime unsurpassed in sadism and barbarity.'" Nigel paused and mopped his brow. Despite the chill air, he was sweating. "I won't go on. Suffice it to say that every connection of the Amoston lynch party was wiped out. With the exception of two people. Mark Spence's daughter, Peggy, and Pearl, the daughter of Edward Ware."

"Four," Tammy said stonily. "Holly and Jeb Amos."

"The reason for the location of this house party. The last members of the families in the lynch party in the house where the deaths had occurred. Rayburn, with the able help of Norman, killed Jeb and Holly and set fire to the cottage." Nigel's smile was shadowy. "Which leaves you and me and my mother."

"Why?" the girl cried. "Why us? I thought it was mother's money he was after."

"That too," he told her grimly. "The Quillers have always lived hand to mouth. Rayburn loves luxury, money, the power wealth would bring him. But that's only a bonus. Dorothy, he hasn't much personal interest in. You—you're the one he wanted here."

"I don't understand."

"What about your father's parents?"

"My grandfather was Greek, a self-made man. His name was originally Sylitaxapoulus."

"What of your grandmother?"

"I never knew her name. Both of them were dead by the time I was born."

"Her hame was Pearl Angeline Ware. You, little Tammy, are the great granddaughter of Edward Ware."

Tammy sprang to her feet. Her eyes were blazing. "*He* killed my father!"

Sadly, Nigel gazed up at her. "He did. Rayburn tried for Marc Syles for years but Marc was a wealthy man. It was difficult to get at him. So Rayburn sent a Trojan horse—"

"Jim Quiller!"

"Yes."

"How *could* Jim? How could he pretend to be my father's friend, pretend to love my mother? How could he, Nigel?"

"Sit down." Gently he urged her back on the step. "I don't think Jim was in on it. Rayburn's bright and he knew Jim isn't. Jim wasn't capable of sustained acting. No, Jim had no idea about Marc Syles or why his father wanted him to get a job with Marc. Until he reached this island, he lived a decent life. I believe he was your father's friend, he did love Dorothy. But the Quiller blood was in him." Nigel's face darkened. "That blood, no matter how diluted, is always there.

294

All Rayburn did was stir it up, set Ruth with her ungodly sex appeal loose on Jim. And Jim was lost. Now, he's as bad as the rest of them. Phil's well on his way too. Rayburn corrupts, he sullies. He's an expert in that field."

"Which of the Amoston families is your mother descended from?"

"You're fast on your mental feet, Tammy. Mother's gypsy mother was Peggy Spence."

"Not Magda."

"A harmless fantasy. Mother never tumbled to the real reason Rayburn hated her. Of course, she knew nothing about the Winchfields until we got here."

"But *you* did. Why did you let her come?"

He shrugged. "I had no choice. Even if I'd told her what I'd learned through the years about the Quillers, she'd have come. Even more eager for revenge."

Tammy patted his cheek tenderly. "Micah wasn't like the rest of them."

"Micah was gentle Jenny all over again. He was also weak, under his father's thumb. I don't think Rayburn let Micah know about his...hobbies. He'd learned his lesson with Jenny. Then Rayburn made his second mistake, he sent Micah to the restaurant where mother worked, using the boy as bait. Micah wasn't as dull as Jim. He suspected Rayburn meant no good to Nadine. Nadine and Micah fell in love, ran away and married. Why Micah returned to Saint Louis and Rayburn, I can only guess. Perhaps it was because mother and he were so poor. Micah couldn't earn a living. All he was was a poet, an artist. Perhaps he felt that since a baby was on the way his father would be merciful."

"He found out differently."

"Rayburn has no comprehension of mercy. When he found Nadine was pregnant, he wanted her badly, even more than before. Maybe he would even have spared her until her baby was born. Another little Quiller for Rayburn to twist."

"You."

"Me," Nigel said bitterly. "This time Micah wasn't fooled. He understood exactly what would happen to his wife and child if Rayburn could get his hands on them. As I said, Micah was weak, he both loved his father and feared him. He must have realized it was only a matter of time before Rayburn would force him to disclose the address of Nadine. So...he did all he could to protect us. He hanged himself."

Putting a hand over his clenched fist, Tammy squeezed. A hand twice as long as his own, Nigel absently noted. He cleared his throat. "Again the Quillers received a bonus. They lost Micah but they found John Andrew Thaler. He was perfect for their needs. Not only was he a doctor, which they badly needed, but with a small legacy from his mother. Andy was an unattractive young man, not even a skilled doctor. Ruth swept him into almost instant marriage."

"Thelma. I suppose they wanted her because she was a nurse."

"More unpaid labor? Yes, that was part of it. When Norman, working for a time in a hospital, came home raving about this nurse, Rayburn and Ruth looked her over. Ruth and her father wanted a child, their own child—"

"Again the Pharaoh complex."

"Ruth couldn't bear a baby so Thelma was picked to be the substitute mother. In every other way, Buddy *is* Ruth and Rayburn's son. Thelma also came in handy with Norman and his craving for a mother. So they snagged Thelma off and kept her with threats and physical violence. Andy they kept with drugs. Both slaves."

"Do you think—" Tammy's voice was hesitant "—that Thelma and Andy were involved in the murders of the elderly patients?"

Nigel shook his head. In the dim light, seeping through the fog, his hair glowed with rich color. "Not actively, but I think both Andy and Thelma were quite aware of what was going on. But the Quillers enjoy this sort of thing far too much to let anyone else do it."

"There are other things I still don't understand. Holly and Jeb—Rayburn wasted no time in killing them. Why did he bother to make their deaths look accidental? Surely, with all the rest of us helpless on this island, there was no necessity. And why has he kept on acting, trying to appear to be a fatherly image? Why does he care whether we know or not?"

Nigel's eyes fastened on the glossy toecap of his boot. "Remember Mary Bateman? How she enjoyed toying with her victims? That's what Rayburn has been doing with us. Giving us brief glimpses of danger, then allowing us to relax. The cat-and-mouse game. The cat pretending it's harmless and sleeping, then jumping on the escaping mouse, worrying at it, then repeating the whole business again. Rayburn enjoys watching his human prey trying to escape him. As for

Holly and Jeb, he had to make their deaths look accidental. The Quillers have to leave this island scot free. Everyone in the area knows about Jeb and his pipe and his drink. With the condition of the Amoses' bodies no autopsy will be conclusive. It will look like an accident."

"What about our bodies? Thelma's? The Quillers won't be able to explain all those."

He made a sound not quite a laugh. "The extra bodies will be looked after by Rayburn's signal fire."

"No, it won't." She shook her head violently. "He can't burn bodies on that pier—"

"Who said anything about the pier?"

"But, that's where the signal fire is planned for. The wood—" She broke off, one hand flying to cover her mouth. Over the hand, her eyes were wild with terror. Turning, she stared at the house bulking behind them, lifting those terrified eyes to the gingerbread trimming that outlined the roof.

She's coming out of it, Nigel thought with pity, the numbness is wearing off. And there's nothing, absolutely nothing, I can do to allay that bone-chilling fear. He kept his voice even. "A house that is noted for the unstable furnace and faulty wiring. A house tinder dry. A house that a good brisk fire would burn to the foundation. A fire that could easily be seen from many points on the mainland. A signal fire and a crematorium. That's why Rayburn was so infuriated when he found the gas had gone up with Holly's cottage. He didn't want it for the boat, he wanted it for the house. When the rescue crews arrive they'll find a grief-stricken group and a double tragedy. The cottage and this house. And the poor survivors unable to even summon help because of the fog."

Her voice was shrill. "The fog—how could he count on it?"

"Rayburn's a gambler. And on this coast, at this time of year, you can almost count on fog conditions. Rayburn was prepared to wait for them. Ever notice the amount of provisions he laid in? Enough food to keep them going indefinitely. He wasn't worried about a time lag, in fact he welcomed it. Don't underestimate Rayburn Quiller. He's an expert at murders that look like accidents. Ruth and he are accomplished actors and Jim and Phil will go right along with them. Norman and Buddy have been trained to keep their mouths shut. A foolproof plan."

Tammy's voice sank to a hoarse whisper. "You knew all this and you still came."

His eyes were cold and remote. "Knew some of it, guessed at the rest."

"There isn't even a gun on this island, you said that yourself. Nadine...you let her walk into this without even bringing a weapon."

"Oh, she brought a weapon, Tammy."

"Strong enough to work against these...these monsters?"

He shrugged. "Perhaps. Perhaps not. If conditions are optimum, but if they're not..."

"I don't understand anything," she cried. "Even with a weapon, I don't know why you came."

"Tammy, Tammy. Get a grip on yourself. Put yourself in my place. I've spent a number of years tracking down the history of this family. I found they are true descendants of human beasts. The Quillers have actually outdone their predecessors. They've left behind them broken lives, murdered innocents. A bloody trail that makes even the Beans look merciful." He shifted on the hard step. "Consider a scientist who has located a particularly virulent disease, say cancer cells. For the sake of humanity he must destroy them. For the sake of that same humanity I must destroy the Quillers—"

"But *you* are a Quiller—" Breaking off, she looked stricken. "Nigel, I'm sorry."

"Don't be. I'm well aware of that. Which makes me even more determined. If I thought their evil was over, that this was the end of blood and horror...well, I haven't the making of an executioner. I might have stayed away, forced my mother to have left well enough alone. But I knew you would be here. I knew about Holly and Jeb. The Quillers moved so fast with the Amoses that I couldn't save their lives. But you—there's still time, Tammy." His brow furrowed. "All of them must die. Every single one. Rayburn's bad but there's a Quiller coming along who promises to be even worse."

"Buddy."

"Yes."

Wordlessly, she held out her hand and he clasped it in both his own. Her hand was dripping sweat and yet the skin was cold to his touch. He pressed his hands around hers, trying to warm it. They huddled silently together, both deep in their own thoughts.

* * *

High above them, Nadine stood at the window of the attic room, gazing pensively at the white mist. As usual, her son had been accurate. It looked as though the fog was starting to break. With the thought her heart started pounding, and she pressed a hand against her breast. In a way, she wished Nigel hadn't told her about the Quillers. For the first time in her life she admitted she was deathly afraid. Could Nigel handle all those men? She wondered.

She shivered. Despite the red glow of the heating coils, this room was so cold, cold and quiet. The only sounds were the faint ticks of the traveling clock in the green leather case, and the steady breaths of the woman on the bed.

Turning away from the window, Nadine gazed with cynical eyes at Dorothy. Her patient had taken another pill a short time before and she was peacefully sleeping, a faint smile touching the crooked mouth. Nadine had been relieved to see the woman drift off into drugged slumber. Dorothy had steadily whined—about the rotten, sleepless night she'd had sharing the narrow bed with her daughter, Tammy's lack of concern when she'd left her mother for a breath of fresh air, the fact that Tammy hadn't bothered bringing old Blue up when she'd asked.

Was she being unfair to the woman? Nadine wondered. Certainly Dorothy was in pain, but all memory of why had been erased. That poor kid, Tammy, was bearing the full weight of not only that horror but her desperate fears for her mother's safety.

I should talk, Nadine told herself derisively, I've been a wretched mother to my own son. Since Nigel had been a baby...how old had he been? About eight months and sitting in his highchair that morning. He stretched his hand out for the pink plush bunny with the droopy ears he loved, and it was out of reach. She turned just in time to see the toy wavering through the air right into her baby's dimpled hands. In her line of work one knew all the words and, under her breath, she muttered the name for this one. From that moment, Nigel had no chance. Even when she found her son was dwarfed, would never grow to normal size, would never have a normal life, she hadn't cared. If anything, she'd been glad. One more way to bind her to him, one more way to help make him a weapon.

Nadine's hands balled into fists. It wasn't too late. In the last few days she'd discovered how much she loved him. Tears sprang to Nadine's fine dark eyes. Lord, she prayed, forget about me and this petulant woman on the bed. We've had our lives, loved our men, borne our children. Save my son and the girl he loves.

A soft tap on the door made her jump. She clutched at her breast again. Nigel? Tammy? Perhaps both of them. With a sigh of relief she went to the door. Sliding back the stiff bar, she opened it a crack. She couldn't see anyone in the dim hall. How dark this house was. She swung the door wide. No one. Taking a couple of steps across the hall, she looked into Nigel's room. He wasn't there.

"Mother," a voice whispered.

She turned toward the sound. One of the heavy doors to the schoolroom was standing ajar. The light must be on in the room because she could see the shadow of a boy-sized figure silhouetted against it. "Nigel," she called.

"Come here, mother," the shadow whispered.

She walked down the hall. "What are you doing in there? Is Tammy with you?"

As she reached the threshold, she peered down at the little figure. She turned to run but by then it was too late, much too late.

When Tammy forced herself away from her whirling thoughts and actually saw what she'd been staring at, she clutched at her companion's arm. "Nigel, the fog *is* thinning. Look, you can see past the gate now. You can see rocks on the path to the beach."

He nodded. "We'd better get back to Dorothy and mother."

"Wait, just a little longer," she pleaded. "I was thinking about Rayburn. He must have had to wait until Jim changed too. The Jim who came to this island would never have allowed him to touch either mother or me." He nodded, and she continued, "That paper I saw yesterday, the one with names on it. You were trying to decide if...if you could spare any of them, weren't you?"

"Yes. Phil I wasn't certain about for a time. He seemed a bit of a useless ass, but harmless. But the way he accepted Ruth's advances, the way he thought incest was a new trip...I started to wonder. Then, there was Phil's treatment of Thelma. He was contemptuous of her. When he heard she was dead, he didn't turn a hair. It meant no more to him than the cat's death did."

300

Her grip on his arm tightened. "You said if your name was there, there'd be an X beside it."

He pulled away from her. "I'm a Quiller, you said that a while ago."

"I didn't mean it that way. You're not like them."

"In my veins," he said coldly, "runs the same blood. That of the Beans, Mary Bateman, the Benders, the Winchfields." The eyes he turned on Tammy were hard and merciless. "Can you guarantee if I have children one of them wouldn't be a little Rayburn, a Norman, a Buddy!"

She whimpered, like a hurt animal. He put an arm on her shoulder. "Tammy, don't weaken me, please. This is tough enough—what's the matter?"

She was on her feet, her hands pressed to the sides of her head. "*Nadine*. They've got Nadine!"

Twenty

Nigel lunged up the steps. He wrenched at the massive door but it didn't move. "Stand back," he told the girl.

Taking his hand from the knob, he stepped back beside her. "The back door," Tammy said.

"It'll be locked too."

He stared at the door and suddenly, with no warning, it burst open with such force that it was ripped from its hinges. The heavy panel plummeted into the hall and came to rest at the bronze feet of the Atlas.

Andy Thaler came running from the direction of the kitchen and stopped short. Rubbing his eyes, he opened his mouth to speak. Ignoring him, Nigel raced up the stairs with Tammy at his heels. "Where?" he called over his shoulder.

"Third floor. Schoolroom."

Nigel hit the second landing and sprang up the steeper steps to the third floor. Tammy's longer legs gained on him and she passed him in the hall and reached the double doors before he did. They weren't locked. She flung open a door. Then she screamed.

Nadine's tall figure was spread-eagled on the dusty floor near the gray rocking horse. Her hands were pinned to the floor by Jim, Philip was holding her feet, and Rayburn stood over them. Norman, a fish knife dwarfed in his big hand, was cutting the cotton dress from her body. Ruth, one hand on Buddy's head, was watching from the middle of the room.

As Tammy, followed by Nigel, ran toward them, Norman lifted the knife and drove it deep into Nadine's breast.

"You fool," Rayburn raged. "You bloody fool! Why did you do that?"

"Look behind you, Nigel—"

As Norman spoke, one of the boathooks from the pile of trash near the steamer trunks, rose, pivoted through the air, and lanced into his chest. Blood spurted over his shirt, his pale eyes bulged, and his mouth opened in an agonized but silent scream. He toppled backward. His reddish curls brushed the rocker of the rocking horse. He was dead before he hit the floor.

At the same time the two doors, standing ajar, thudded closed. One of them knocked Andy Thaler on his shoulder as he entered the room. The doctor's eyes settled on Nadine and the blood staining her breast. Dazedly, he moved toward her.

Nigel was standing quietly and when he spoke his voice was low but clear. "Keep away from her, all of you. Back off, or you'll get what Norman got."

"But I want to help her," Andy said. "She's hurt."

"Get over there with them. You're the one who tried to lock us out. Don't *touch* my mother."

Silently, the Quillers backed away from Nadine. Andy followed them and went to stand beside his wife. Ruth had one hand pressed to her mouth. Above it her eyes bulged almost as much as Norman's had when the hook tore through his chest. Clinging to her skirt with both hands was Buddy. Ruth turned toward Jim but he paid no attention to her. After a moment, Andy put an arm around his wife's shaking body.

Nigel sank to his knees beside his mother. Gently he lifted her wrist, the other hand touching the base of her throat. With a tiny hand, he closed her eyes. He waved toward the trunks and an old blanket detached itself from the heap and hovered through the air until it touched his hand. Tenderly he tucked it over her body. The Quillers watched with wide, unbelieving eyes.

Nigel called over his shoulder, "Tammy, up on that dais. Keep clear of them."

Obediently, hardly aware of what she was doing, she backed away from the Quillers. When her heels touched the dais, she sank down on it. She was so weak, she nearly fell back against the desk.

Nigel pulled himself to his feet, his movements that of an aged man. Swinging around, he stared at the huddle of people in the middle of the room. "Move one hand," he warned softly, "and you're dead."

He circled them and climbed up on the dais. Tammy's arms went around his leg as she hid her face against it. Through the material of his trousers she could feel the warmth of that leg. He stroked her head, his hand as gentle as it had been on his mother's body. "It will soon be over, Tammy," he told her.

She moaned against his leg, "They were going to...the same as mother."

"They didn't. She called you and we got here in time." His voice broke. "Not in time to save her life. She wanted me to act. I kept making excuses." He said violently, "She was right. I didn't have the guts. But now I have, and the Quillers themselves gave them to me."

"The girl," Rayburn muttered. "All along I knew there was something amiss. I figured it was the girl."

Nigel had himself under control. His face was cold and set, his voice even. "Tammy's a telepathist. I'm telekinetic."

"My door," the girl clutching at his leg said in a muffled voice. "You bolted it twice. Those rocks...you're the weapon Nadine brought."

"You *did* throw that chair at me when I was disciplining Tammy," Rayburn said. The rest of his relatives were still dazed and terrified but the older man, like Nigel, had regained control of himself. "You're the weapon that Nadine boasted about on the beach. I had both your luggages searched but there was no gun there. Not a gun but a man."

Nigel stared into his grandfather's eyes. "All my life I've considered this ability as a curse. My mother forced me to develop it, to control it. Now, it's a blessing. You butchered the Amoses and you savaged Dorothy. You killed my mother. Tammy, you won't get."

Ruth pressed against Andy but she said, "Dad."

"Shut up," her father snapped. "I can hardly imagine Nigel killing us one by one the way he did Norman. Nigel is my grandson. I believe we can strike a bargain."

Nigel's gaze was almost admiring. "Never give up, do you? What bargain can my mother's murderer strike with me?"

"Your mother's murderer is dead. You killed Norman." Rayburn's voice became husky. "I can understand your grief, my boy. My own mother was raped and killed on that very spot." Dramatically, he pointed a thick finger toward the rocking horse. Seeing Norman's crumpled form there, he hastily dropped his hand by his side. "I've spent my life avenging her. Because of my dedication I lost both my dearly loved wife and your father. In the veins of Nadine ran the same blood as the beasts who killed our family in this house. Instead of condemning me, you should be grateful." His hand lifted and he pointed at the girl slumped at Nigel's feet. "There is the descendant of Ed Ware, the fiend who urged the butchers of Winchfields on. Ware was the vilest of the lot. She must be punished. Surely you see that, my boy."

"He's *mad*," the girl whispered.

"Yes," Nigel agreed in a low voice. "Mad with hatred." He raised his voice. "What bargain would you make with me?"

Rayburn looked around at his huddle of relatives. All of them, including the little boy, were gazing hopefully at him. He cleared his throat. "The fog is breaking up. We'll allow you to leave this house. You can light the signal fire and go safely. I'll be generous. That includes both of you. You can take the girl."

The sound that Nigel made, a laugh, but like no laugh heard before, drove the blood from their faces. "Crafty Rayburn Quiller. Making a promise he has no intention of keeping. But clever. Get us off guard, polish me off, and then you have Tammy. You'd never let us go. Even, if by some miracle, we did escape, as long as a Quiller lives, Tammy would never be safe."

Smiling, Rayburn caressed his mustache. "Then it's deadlock, my dear boy. I don't think you've the stomach to finish us off with a shower of knives and hooks."

"I never intended to. But I did need all of you in one place, a place you couldn't escape from. This room is ideal and you picked it yourself." Gazing past the group of people, Nigel looked through one of the tall windows. The fog had cleared enough that he could see the rugged gray of Kat's Rock. "You're an avid reader. Have you ever read 'The Fall of the House of Usher'? Ah, I see by your expression that you have." His voice softened, remote compassion touching his face. "I want you to know one thing. I don't hate you. I'm not seeking
306

revenge. I suppose one couldn't expect more from you. The blood runs true."

Rayburn's mouth twisted. "Then why? Why do you do this? Without hate or revenge, you can't kill six people like this. Not in cold blood."

Ruth was sobbing against her husband's big shoulder. He patted her hair, but Andy's face wore a strange expression of peace and resignation. Philip was whimpering and Buddy clung to Ruth's skirt with tight little fists. Nigel raised his voice. "You'd never understand. For love. Love is stronger than hate." He stroked the girl's bright hair. "Go, Tammy, take your mother and light the fire. There're oil and rags and matches in the boathouse. Rob will come for you. Go, my love."

She clung to his leg. "Not without you."

"Strength. For just a little longer. Have strength enough not to sap mine."

He bent to loosen her grip on his leg. As soon as he took his eyes off the Quillers, Jim and Rayburn lunged at him. A motor near the trunks swooped up and smashed into Jim's head. Rayburn jumped back and his son crumpled and fell, the side of his head a bloody pulp.

Tammy let her hands fall away from Nigel. She staggered to her feet.

He smiled at her, and it was a beautiful smile. "Tell me, Tammy. Is it just?"

For the first time, she looked directly at the Quillers. As she did their figures, their bloodless faces, and their terror-filled eyes, blurred. She saw the Beans, clad in filthy rags, gathering around a body, wrenching flesh from the limbs. She saw Mary Bateman, a cruel smile on her lips, bending over a helpless patient. She saw the Bender family dragging a screaming little girl to bury alive in their orchard. She saw Kat Winchfield avidly watching her male relatives brutalizing Rosemary Fiscall. For an instant, she saw her own father, standing proudly, watching a club arc over his head. She saw Holly's bright blue eyes and kind face. She saw a parade of horrors extending down through the centuries. She blinked, and again she saw the Quillers, Philip on his knees, Ruth sagging in Andy's arms. Rayburn, tears streaming down his face, was babbling for a mercy he didn't even understand.

She said in her clear voice, "It's just."

"I promised you," Nigel told her, "that you would have life. Will you make that life count?"

Taking the dark glasses from her pocket, she threw them to the floor. One boot ground them into shards. Her shoulders straightened, her slight body pulled tall and erect and proud. "I'll make it count. For you."

"Go. Don't look back. Life's waiting, Tammy. Run toward it."

She went. Behind her in the schoolroom, Nigel stood like a young Atlas, his legs widely straddled, his hair glowing like a battle flag. He no longer saw the Quillers, he no longer heard them. His mind, with deadly accuracy, searched down through the mass of rock, found the fault in the seam far below the surface, and, with one tremendous effort, wrenched Kat's Rock into motion.

Debris started to drop on the gabled roof of the old house, slowly at first, sounding like pelting hail. It came thicker and the cliff swayed over the building. Then, with an immense surge of will, and for love, Nigel brought down the House of Winchfield.

Twenty-One

On the television screen a fat man wearing a derby hat, a green velvet coat, and a kilt was trying to break a balloon filled with water that was suspended over his wife's head. As the emcee had chuckled in an aside to the audience it might prove a "wee bit hard" because the fat man's hands were tied behind him and the weapon to break the balloon was a pointed rod, clutched between the contestant's teeth.

Shifting on the couch, Rob Brome reached for a can of beer on the coffee table. He had to be desperate, he thought, to be sitting here watching this tripe. The room around him showed his restlessness. It was neat and tidy. The glass tops of mom's tables had been washed, the desk had been put in some kind of order, and its velvety finish shone with a fresh coat of wax. Out in the cafe, all was in its usual state. He'd washed a sink full of sticky dishes and pans, got down on his knees and scrubbed the tile floor, and had even dusted the tables and stacked chairs.

Anything to get his mind off Winchfield Island, Tammy, and the blasted fog. He hadn't been successful. Granted he hadn't had a nightmare last night but this was even worse. A sense of urgency gripped him, a rising tide of unease, at times downright fear. Banging the beer can down, he reached over and clicked the television off. Damned if he'd wait any longer! He was going to phone the Coast Guard and demand that they check that island. To hell with what they thought about him!

He got to his feet and banged open the door to the cafe. Without even glancing toward the window, he grabbed the phone and started to dial. As he did a bright ball of pain burst above his eyes. Dropping the phone, he grabbed his head. In his mind a shriek resounded, not heard but felt, and felt with agony. He rocked back and forth. His name. *Tammy*.

Weak and sick, he managed to turn and look at the window. After a moment, he realized he wasn't looking at the window, but through it. The fog was breaking up. Running around the counter, he threw the door wide. A spanking breeze lifted the hair away from his aching brow, fingered his face, and riffled the collar of his shirt. For the first time in days he could see the four vehicles waiting for the Quillers' return—the dusty station wagon, the two luxury cars, the crazy quilt pattern on Philip's van. Beyond them he could see the road, the sand on the beach. Past the beach mist was still billowing. Never mind, it was breaking up.

He fumbled under the counter and found his field glasses and on the way to the door he scooped up his pea jacket. Thank God the *Caravan* was fueled and ready to go, shipshape and prepared to challenge the sea. He'd done that the previous evening, working mainly by feel. As he ran past the vehicles he realized he hadn't bothered to close the cafe door. Hell with that too. Tammy was calling.

As he jumped up on the dock and unwound the lines securing the *Caravan*, he felt a steady wind in his face. Good. There was still fog here but he knew as soon as he got out further it would clear. Keep blowing, he told the wind, and clicked on the motor. Good old *Caravan*, she caught immediately and he could feel a steady throb of power through his body. Cautiously, he headed out to sea.

She cut cleanly through the waves, spray flying back over him. Ahead he could see a lessening of the white mist, and then he broke clear of it. Around him the blessed sun shone, gilding the waves with gold. Holding the wheel with one hand, he lifted the glasses to his eyes. With disbelief he traced the lines of the island. There was smoke, a tall wavering column of smoke, from the direction where that stone pier jutted into the water. That's where the fire was. But that wasn't what was making his heart thud, filling him with an

310

impending sense of doom. For untold years Kat's Rock had been a landmark, standing tall and rugged, the highest point on this part of the coast. The pinnacle was gone. Winchfield was now a long, low hunk of an island. Rob cursed wildly. That house, that bloody house, right under Kat's Rock.

Tammy, he thought despairingly. Wait a minute, no sense in panicking. Someone, maybe all of them, could have got out. That fire. Someone had to start it. Perhaps, a gloomy voice in his mind pointed out, the fire was lit before those thousands of tons of rock had crushed the house.

He drove the *Caravan* mercilessly. She plunged like a whipped horse through the waves. Let her be safe, he prayed, let Tammy be safe. If I ever get my hands on that girl I'll never let her out of my sight.

The bulk of the island grew larger. He could distinguish the site of the fire. Near the end of the pier. A big one. Must have taken a lot of wood to get that going and the wood was kept up beside the main house. Rob had seen Jeb splitting it there. They must have carted it down that winding path to the pier. He'd been right all along. They had been in trouble.

Throttling down, he guided his boat cautiously in past the blazing pyre, in as far as he dared go, before he nudged her against the pier. He could feel the heat radiating from the fire. As he tossed lines and leaped after them, his eyes raked the surrounding area. Nothing moved. Despite the sunlight it was still cold. Maybe they'd taken shelter in the boathouse or Jeb's cottage. Better check.

Racing across the pier, he flung open the door of the boathouse. After the radiant sunlight on the water, it was dim and shadowed. He felt his way to the bay and squinted down into Jeb's boat. There was someone down there! Under a couple of tattered blankets he could see a huddled figure, a froth of rich fur. Ruth? No, only Ruth's mink. Thick blond hair tumbled over the mink. Tammy! Joyfully, he got into the boat, and knelt by the figure. He brushed thick hair back and Dorothy Quiller lifted drowsy eyes. "Rob," she said huskily. "I'm so glad to see you. Tammy said you'd be here—"

"Where is she?"

One long hand detached itself from the musty blankets. "Out there somewhere. I begged her to stay here with me but...Rob, you don't know what it's been like. One minute

311

I was sleeping, the next Tammy was yanking me out of bed. An earthquake!" Tears spangled her lashes. "Jim. He's dead, Rob, buried in that house."

He patted her shoulder. "I'll get Tammy, Mrs. Quiller."

"Yes. Take us away from this...this awful place, Rob."

Afterward he retained no memory of leaving the boathouse, no memory of climbing the slope. He did remember turning through the rocky defile and seeing, with no sense of surprise, the remains of the Amoses' cottage, exactly as it had been in his dream. But the vivid image he'd carry for life was the sight of a tall slender figure near the ruins of the building, her back to him, staring at the mounds of rubble where once a path had led up to Winchfield House.

He knew it was Tammy but for an instant, as he'd mistaken Dorothy for her, he thought it had to be her mother. The figure stood tall, the shoulders erect. There was no sign of hunching, of shoulders protectively drawn forward.

"Tammy!" he shouted.

She turned and raced toward him, long hair streaming brightly behind her. His arms were reaching for her long before they met. Clasping her hungrily, he pulled her body roughly against his. He buried his face in those shining masses of hair. "Tammy," he whispered.

"You heard me."

"I heard you."

They stood for moments, aware only of the warmth and comfort of their embrace. Then, almost fearfully, he cupped her chin, lifted her face. Whatever he feared to see in that face was missing. There was exhaustion there, an exhaustion much more than physical. There was sorrow, but it was gentle sorrow. The face cupped in his hand wore an expression of peace, a luminous, tender look of peace.

"Can you tell me?" he asked.

"I don't think you'd believe me."

"Try me."

Softly, at times haltingly, she told him. She didn't try to cover everything but she sketched in the days on Winchfield Island. At times his fists clenched, at times he muttered, at times he simply stared down at her. When her voice faltered into silence, he nodded. "I believe you. A while ago, no, I wouldn't have. Now...yes. How did Nigel bring down that cliff? Are you certain he couldn't have planted a charge, maybe plastic explosives, and set it off by remote control?"

"No. He did it with his mind." Her eyes searched his face. "Can you believe that?"

"If I can accept the way you called me," he muttered. "The way I saw that burnt-out shell of the cottage—yes, I can believe it. But the Coast Guard must be on the way here. They'll have spotted that fire. *They* won't believe it."

"But if you back me up—"

"Me?" He laughed harshly. "With my record? Tammy, my discharge was on mental grounds. And you—straight out of Doctor Thule's school. Babbling about mind reading, telekinesis...they'd have both of us in straight jackets. Hey, wait a minute. What about Dorothy? Is there any chance she might remember?"

"I don't know but I doubt it. Even if her mind should reclaim that lost time I don't think she'd back us up. She doesn't like unpleasantness." Her head sagged to his chest. "Mother was drugged when this last...when this happened. She's still half asleep. Does it really matter if anyone else knows the truth?"

He shook his head. "No, they're all gone. Let me handle the Coast Guard, Tammy. I'll tell them a story they *will* believe."

She fell more heavily against him. "I'm so tired, Rob, so tired."

Scooping her up, he carried her down the path. As he reached the pier they saw a slim, powerful boat making a smart turn into the cove. On its mast fluttered the Stars and Stripes. The marines arriving, he thought, at least the local equivalent of the marines. Welcome aboard, Rob thought.

He carried the girl onto the deck of the *Caravan*, put her down beside the wheel, and pushed a cushion behind her back. She murmured, "Mother?"

"Our brawny reinforcements will bring her aboard, Tammy. You sit here and rest."

Sunlight beamed down on her, warming her, making her more drowsy. She was aware of men coming aboard, two of them carefully carrying a fur-clad figure. Later she heard voices and sleepily realized that Rob was talking to a tall officer in an immaculate uniform. She caught some words.

"—knew Jeb Amos slightly," the officer was saying. She heard "pipe" and then "fire." He lowered his voice and she dozed. Then, in a louder tone, "Always did think whoever built that house under the cliff was insane. That company

313

who owns this island, common knowledge about the condition that house was in. Wonder *it* didn't burn too. What a tragedy. Ten people in it. Lucky these two women got out." A pause. Then, tartly. "If I were them, I'd sue that company."

"I don't think they will," Rob said easily. "Kind of an act of God. That company sure couldn't help an earth tremor. Mrs. Quiller and her daughter are pretty beat up. I'd better get them back to the mainland."

"We'll radio ahead and have a doctor waiting. The older woman was cut with glass from a previous slide, you say. Wonder why they didn't get out of that house then?"

"No place for them to go. Jeb's cottage was burnt and the fog closed in. They had a pile ready to light for a distress signal. The first tremor only sent down a few rocks, broke a couple of windows. Probably figured they were safe enough."

"There will have to be a hearing, Mr. Brome. Will I be able to reach the three of you at the motel?"

"We'll be there."

Tammy dozed and when she awoke, the boat was moving under her. She looked up at a cloudless sky. The sun—she never had thought she'd see it again. Beside her Rob stood, his tall figure outlined against that brilliant expanse. He smiled down at her. "It's okay, Tammy, it's all okay now."

She tried to get up and he reached down and pulled her up beside him. Steering with one hand, he clasped her to his side with the other. She stared ahead at the mainland. After a time, he said, "I still can't believe that tiny guy—"

"Not tiny," she said tenderly. "A giant, Rob. I think of him as Atlas, holding up the world, bringing that world crashing down when he had to. As a Samson, destroying a temple of evil, as a—" She broke off and then she said firmly, "No words for Nigel, not even one of his beloved quotes has the right words. I'll remember not his strength, but his gentleness, not destruction, but creation. He led me through hell, Rob, and he led with gentleness. He said love is stronger than hate, and he proved it. There may be hatred and horror all around us, but love and decency are there too. This I'll remember."

He asked hesitantly, "Will you go back to that school?"

"No."

"To Florida?"

"I thought of the ranch, of buying it back. I know now
314

what I wanted to buy was my childhood, the safey of that. No, I won't return to Florida."

"Your mother?"

"I don't know. I'd like to be with her but...she has her circle of friends, her interests. Perhaps she'll find another man. Somehow I doubt there'll be room for me in mother's life. But then, there never has been."

His arm tightened around her. "I've been thinking. I destroyed a fair amount of myself. Time to do a little of that creating you mentioned. Think I'll try for a job. Maybe build a bridge or something."

"Good."

"Would you...do you think you'd like to come along? Watch an engineer build a bridge?"

She smiled with quiet radiance. "I'd like that, Rob. I'd like it very much."

His eyes were on that radiant face. "Casual, isn't it? Neither of us making a commitment. Well—" he took a deep breath "—I'm making one. I'm talking about marriage. Death-do-us-part sort of stuff. I love you, Tammy."

In a way, Tammy thought, both of us are breaking out of years of fog into sunshine. Her mouth firmed and her voice was steady as she told him, "Death do us part. I love you too."

Epilogue

In the cabin of the *Caravan*, Dorothy Quiller shifted into
a more comfortable position on the narrow bunk. Those two
young men had piled blankets over her until she was swel-
tering. Of course—her hand explored—she was wearing that
mink of Ruth Thaler's. Working one of the blankets loose,
she pushed it to the floor. Through the bunk she could feel
the plunging motion of the boat. God! how she hated boats.

She tried to recall what had happened that day. It was all
so blurred. She could remember Tammy bringing up her
breakfast tray and how ghastly the girl had looked. This so-
called holiday had been a terrible one for both of them. First
that dreadful family of Jim's, then the fire and that fall down
the stairs. She still felt sore and bruised from that fall. After
breakfast, Tammy had callously insisted on leaving her. Nadine had sat beside her bed, Dorothy remembered that. Fine-
looking woman, Nadine; it was hard to believe she was dead,
that all of them were dead. Nadine had brought water to
wash down the pills. She'd had to take them. What a night!
Aching all over and not even able to stretch out because
Tammy was in the narrow bed. But the pills had worked and
she'd been sleeping soundly when Tammy had literally
dragged her out of bed.

Dorothy remembered vaguely arguing with Tammy, the

girl pulling her in her pyjamas—really, only pyjamas and thin slippers—down that stark staircase. Earthquake, Tammy was crying, we've got to get out, mother! She insisted on a coat and Tammy reached into that closet beside the front door...funny, there had been no door there. Just a gaping hole. But Tammy grabbed Ruth's mink and then they raced down the path. Tammy wouldn't even pause so she could catch her breath, just kept pulling her along, the rocks cutting through the soles of her slippers. Heavens, her feet must be cut to ribbons.

Dorothy sighed. Never mind, those nice young men who carried her in here had said a doctor would be waiting for her. Funny, she thought, I don't feel anything about those Quillers at all. Although she'd liked Rayburn at first, he really hadn't been very nice, and that Ruth! Jim hadn't spared a moment for his own wife. Should she feel something for Jim? She'd been fond of him but as soon as he was with that ghastly family of his he'd changed. Ranting and raving at her after all she'd done for him. She'd never said a word about his cars, that boat of his, the new house he had to buy. Never complained about all that money he sent to his family either. If Jim had been going to change like that, she was better off without him. She was still attractive, she didn't have to take that from Jim or anyone else.

Jim. She would miss him. What a wonderful lover he'd been. Dorothy felt tears start to her eyes and she shut them, squeezing a few hot drops of moisture onto her cheeks. Jim was dead. He'd been all hers and he was gone. Her eyes snapped open. She'd remembered, maybe in that boathouse with its rank smell of mildew, she'd remembered what she meant to tell Jim. He'd died without knowing her secret. For some time before they came to the island she'd suspected but she was waiting to tell him when she was certain. Jim would have been so happy. She felt a flood of joy, felt her lips, despite the wetness on her cheeks, curving into a smile of joy.

After five years, they'd both given up hope. Now, every time she looked at a calendar she knew she'd beam like an idiot. A scrap of memory nudged at her. She *had* looked at a calendar. For an instant she saw that calendar, hanging beside a barometer in a cracked glass case, a brightly colored picture of a girl on a tractor. Where could it have been? Fur-clad shoulders moved in a tiny shrug. It didn't matter. All that mattered was that she finally had something of her very
318

own. Maybe it wasn't too sad that Jim was dead. Dorothy thought of Marc, he'd come between Tammy and her. As for Tammy, her lips curled, Tammy was selfish, she'd never stay with her now. Tammy would make her own life. Perhaps with that young Brome. Well, let her go.

Dorothy rubbed her stomach tenderly. It still hurt but she knew, with a deep instinctive knowledge, that the baby was safe. *Her* baby. She also knew it would be a boy. Her son! Really, she should think about a name. Her fingers fumbled along the silken fur until they found and reached into a deep pocket. She'd found this earlier. Pulling it out by the gold chain, she held it up to the light. Funny jewelry for Ruth, with her mink and expensive flowing dresses, to have. A cross, old and it looked like ivory, with a couple of pieces of red glass set in it. As she fingered the cross, a name floated into her mind. John. A good, solid-sounding name. Yes, she'd call her son John. John Quiller. Her lips pouted. Might as well make it a family name. Even if she hadn't liked him very well, Rayburn had been her son's grandfather. John Rayburn Quiller.

She stroked the cross, finding pleasure in the feel, and then, not knowing why she was doing it so secretively, she replaced it in the pocket of the coat. This would be her son's, all he'd have from his father's family.

Dorothy was sleepy again. Contentedly, she curled up, her arms cradling her stomach.

CURRENT CREST BESTSELLERS

☐ **THE MASK OF THE ENCHANTRESS**   24418 $3.25
by Victoria Holt
Suewellyn knew she wanted to possess the Mateland family castle, but having been illegitimate and cloistered as a young woman, only a perilous deception could possibly make her dream come true.

☐ **THE HIDDEN TARGET**   24443 $3.50
by Helen MacInnes
A beautiful young woman on a European tour meets a handsome American army major. All is not simple romance however when she finds that her tour leaders are active terrorists and her young army major is the chief of NATO's antiterrorist section.

☐ **BORN WITH THE CENTURY**   24295 $3.50
by William Kinsolving
A gripping chronicle of a man who creates an empire for his family, and how they engineer its destruction.

☐ **SINS OF THE FATHERS**   24417 $3.95
by Susan Howatch
The tale of a family divided from generation to generation by great wealth and the consequences of a terrible secret.

☐ **THE NINJA**   24367 $3.50
by Eric Van Lustbader
They were merciless assassins, skilled in the ways of love and the deadliest of martial arts. An exotic thriller spanning postwar Japan and present-day New York.

Buy them at your local bookstore or use this handy coupon for ordering.

COLUMBIA BOOK SERVICE, CBS Inc.
32275 Mally Road, P.O. Box FB, Madison Heights, MI 48071

Please send me the books I have checked above. Orders for less than 5 books must include 75¢ for the first book and 25¢ for each additional book to cover postage and handling. Orders for 5 books or more postage is FREE. Send check or money order only. Allow 3-4 weeks for delivery.

Cost $_____ Name_____

Sales tax*_____ Address_____

Postage _____ City_____

Total $_____ State_____ Zip_____

*The government requires us to collect sales tax in all states except AK, DE, MT, NH and OR.

Prices and availability subject to change without notice.

8229